COVER AND INTERIOR ILLUSTRATIONS: ALLEN KOSZOWSKI
INTERIOR PHOTO ART: NATU SHABBEY
EDITOR AND PUBLISHER: TOM ENGLISH

www.DeadLetterPress.com **ISBN-13: 979-8-9927092-3-0**

ALLEN K. '09

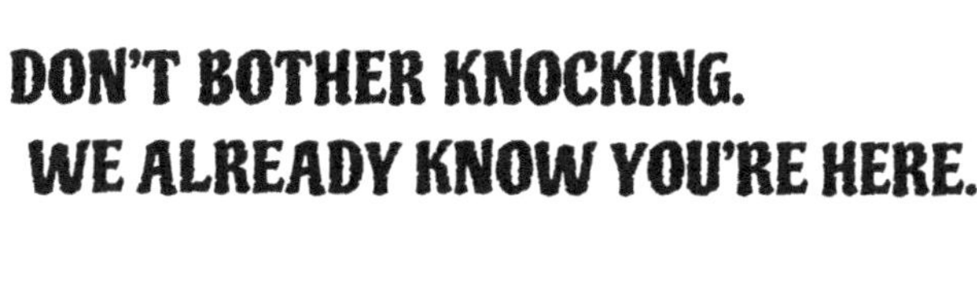

DEAR ABBEY

ENTER, IF YOU DARE. BUT LEAVE THE LEASH AND THAT CAN OF DOG REPELLENT AT THE DOOR. THE ONLY "MACE" WE ALLOW HERE AT THE ABBEY IS THE HEAVY, SPIKED CLUB WE KEEP DOWNSTAIRS IN OUR "RECREATION ROOM"—OCCASIONALLY USED TO KEEP ROWDY GUESTS ~~IN LINE~~ ENTERTAINED. (BY THE WAY, IS ANYONE HERE FEELING FRISKY TODAY? NO? TOO BAD. I WAS HOPING FOR A BIT OF SPORT. PERHAPS LATER.) THOSE OF YOU WHO FREQUENT THE ABBEY MAY BE WONDERING WHY *I'M* WRITING THIS, AND NOT THE EDITOR. TOM IS, SHALL WE SAY, INDISPOSED. I RECENTLY TOOK HIM TO THE VET FOR HIS DISTEMPER BOOSTER SHOT, AND I DECIDED TO HAVE HIS NAILS TRIMMED WHILE WE WERE THERE. I DON'T BELIEVE HE ENJOYED THE EXPERIENCE—HE'S BEEN LICKING HIS TOES EVER SINCE.

With Tom tied up at the moment—to a stake in the backyard—I'm free at last to voice my opinions. (Surely, you've heard that Huskies like to talk!) In fact, I have a few bones to pick. So please excuse me while I vent. (No, no, not from *that* end! I'm sure you'd rather I break the news, not wind! Although, and I'm proud to say it, Huskies are legendary for their flatulence.)

First, our neighbors have been gossiping that Nightmare Abbey is going to the dogs. What a mangy notion! Yes indeed, alongside our bony, hooded caretaker, I do prowl this petrified pile. (And speaking of piles, I do tend to create a few, usually right where our dear Abbey is stepping. Heh, who says life is boring?) Tom, however, clearly sees some artistic value in my "creations"—because he daily collects them. A strange hobby, if you ask me.

And I do love hanging out with my bestest canine buddy, Magnus, who barks with a cool British accent! But the Abbey is *not* going to the dogs! A few hundred starving rats, perhaps...

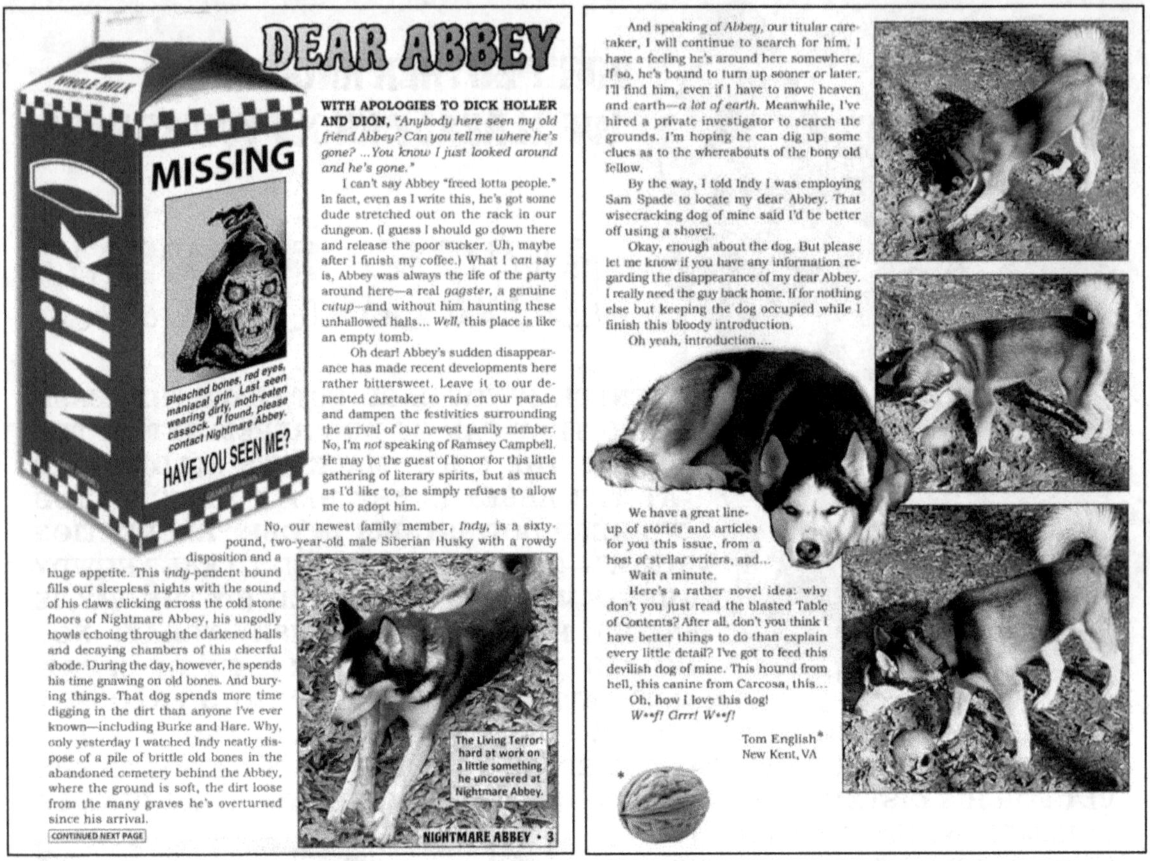

DEAR ABBEY

Milk

WHOLE MILK

MISSING

Bleached bones, red eyes, maniacal grin. Last seen wearing dirty, moth-eaten cassock. If found, please contact Nightmare Abbey.

HAVE YOU SEEN ME?

WITH APOLOGIES TO DICK HOLLER AND DION, *"Anybody here seen my old friend Abbey? Can you tell me where he's gone? ...You know I just looked around and he's gone."*

I can't say Abbey "freed lotta people." In fact, even as I write this, he's got some dude stretched out on the rack in our dungeon. (I guess I should go down there and release the poor sucker. Uh, maybe after I finish my coffee.) What I *can* say is, Abbey was always the life of the party around here—a real *gagster*, a genuine *cutup*—and without him haunting these unhallowed halls... *Well*, this place is like an empty tomb.

Oh dear! Abbey's sudden disappearance has made recent developments here rather bittersweet. Leave it to our demented caretaker to rain on our parade and dampen the festivities surrounding the arrival of our newest family member. No, I'm *not* speaking of Ramsey Campbell. He may be the guest of honor for this little gathering of literary spirits, but as much as I'd like to, he simply refuses to allow me to adopt him.

No, our newest family member, *Indy*, is a sixty-pound, two-year-old male Siberian Husky with a rowdy disposition and a huge appetite. This *indy*-pendent hound fills our sleepless nights with the sound of his claws clicking across the cold stone floors of Nightmare Abbey, his ungodly howls echoing through the darkened halls and decaying chambers of this cheerful abode. During the day, however, he spends his time gnawing on old bones. And burying things. That dog spends more time digging in the dirt than anyone I've ever known—including Burke and Hare. Why, only yesterday I watched Indy neatly dispose of a pile of brittle old bones in the abandoned cemetery behind the Abbey, where the ground is soft, the dirt loose from the many graves he's overturned since his arrival.

CONTINUED NEXT PAGE

The Living Terror: hard at work on a little something he uncovered at Nightmare Abbey.

NIGHTMARE ABBEY • 3

And speaking of *Abbey*, our titular caretaker, I will continue to search for him. I have a feeling he's around here somewhere. If so, he's bound to turn up sooner or later. I'll find him, even if I have to move heaven and earth—*a lot of earth*. Meanwhile, I've hired a private investigator to search the grounds. I'm hoping he can dig up some clues as to the whereabouts of the bony old fellow.

By the way, I told Indy I was employing Sam Spade to locate my dear Abbey. That wisecracking dog of mine said I'd be better off using a shovel.

Okay, enough about the dog. But please let me know if you have any information regarding the disappearance of my dear Abbey. I really need the guy back home. If for nothing else but keeping the dog occupied while I finish this bloody introduction.

Oh yeah, introduction....

We have a great line-up of stories and articles for you this issue, from a host of stellar writers, and...

Wait a minute.

Here's a rather novel idea: why don't you just read the blasted Table of Contents? After all, don't you think I have better things to do than explain every little detail? I've got to feed this devilish dog of mine. This hound from hell, this canine from Carcosa, this...

Oh, how I love this dog!

*W**f! Grrr! W**f!*

Tom English*
New Kent, VA

*

In defense of our excellent breeding, I'm proud to note that in her anthology *The Best Horror of the Year, Volume 17*, editor Ellen Datlow writes that *Nightmare Abbey* is "becoming a strong entry in the horror field" with "notable original fiction [published in 2024, in volumes 5, 6, and 7] by Steve Rasnic Tem, Helen Grant, Ray Cluley, Gary McMahon, Simon Bestwick, Gary Fry, Daniel Braum, Sean Hogan, Ramsey Campbell, Steve Duffy, and Stephen Volk." Hey, there's no fleas on our writers! (Um, no doubt all that scratching is due to dry skin.)

And while I'm at it, I am *not* named after the heroic hound in the creepy horror flick *Good Boy*. That movie was released in early 2025, and I've been prowling these haunted halls since 2023. Check out Tom's intro to *Nightmare Abbey 5*, published in early 2024, and reprinted above.

Tom rescued me from a dog shelter where I'd been incarcerated for destructive and disorderly conduct. (Don't judge me, I'm a Husky, after all!) Some idiot had named me Bullwinkle, probably because I have an obsession with flying squirrels. (Don't get it? Do your research.) Owing to my adventurous nature and propensity to go exploring, Tom renamed me *Indy*, after the movie character "Indiana" Jones, who in turn had taken his nickname from his own beloved dog. Little did Tom know at the time that George Lucas, creator of *Raiders of the Lost Ark*, once had an Alaskan Malamute named Indy. Pretty cool connection—*cool*, as in snow dogs rock!

Uh-oh, gotta run. Tom just got loose again.

Indy English
New Kent, VA

THE CAR IS AN OLD BEATER THAT LEE INHERITED FROM HIS FATHER. IT RATTLES AND SHAKES AS HE NAVIGATES THE PITTED BACK COUNTRY ROADS. Kansas's "Carry On Wayward Son" blasts from the radio. Classic rock. Another thing Lee inherited from his father. He wonders how he got to this banal place in his life.

The air is a strange, hazy yellow-green and thrums with a peculiar energy. The radio squawks with static then cuts out. Reception has always been terrible out here, Lee reflects. Like they are cut off from the world. Often they'd have no television or radio in the cottage, and Lee and his mother would have to endure another of his father's stories. He loved telling stories.

There was one particular story that tormented Lee—*The Grinning Woman.* Lee's father and mother were both in on it. As a child Lee suffered night terrors, waking in the night, moaning and screaming. Trembling. His parents would rush to his room and comfort him til he settled. This went on for weeks, night after night. One night, though, as his father held him, soothed him, patted his head, he whispered "Lee, go back to sleep now. *Shush.* Please. Go to sleep. If you don't, the grinning woman will get you." And he pointed to the corner of the room. In the darkness Lee thought he saw another even darker shape in the corner. It turned, as if awakened. Then a light snapped on under its chin, and a pale grinning face was revealed; a wide, feral toothy rictus that sent Lee whimpering under the covers. It was just his mother. It had to be.

And this went on: the night terrors; the grinning woman; Lee under the covers, petrified, hand over mouth so as not to draw attention from the dark shape looming in the corner, until the morning light breached his blankets and his eyelids and he dared a peek over the covers.

In the day, tired, timid, glancing at his stoic mother, he would ask who she was, the grinning woman? Where was she from?

"She's everyone, Lee," his father had said. "From everywhere. A thing that came from the oceans and lakes. Evolution's progeny. A creature from the trees, stalking the countryside. A mimic." And here he looked to Lee's mother. "Something a lot like us. Maybe from another world that pierced the soft spots in our world. It's anything and everything, Lee." And Lee remembers his father tousling his hair. "That's what stories are. Make-believe. They don't hardly ever come true. They don't come to life."

IT IS NEAR DINNERTIME when Lee arrives at the cottage, and his parents aren't there but someone is.

"I'm Kate," she says. "Nice to meet you."

Of course, Lee thinks, yet another set-up from his parents who are still trying to marry him off. Still hopeful of grandkids.

And before Lee can ask Kate where his parents are, there they are, huffing through the door, dinner in hand.

"Oh," his mother exclaims, bags dropping at her feet, no doubt surprised at Kate's early arrival, "it's—"

"—yes, *Kate*," Lee says, vexed.

And *Oh* his father squeaks, breathless. "Kate, then. How utterly lovely. Let's eat."

Dinner is small talk between his parents and Kate—weather, sports, films, current world affairs—and passes pleasantly but without substance, Kate deflecting personal questions, and his parents peering at him, expectant, waiting for him to take the lead. But he is still too angry to address their complicity, so he says nothing.

Dinner done, dishes put away, the dark pushing at the windows and the wind prying at the door, his father summons him outside. By flashlight they pick their way down to the lake.

Late summer, chilly for the time of year, Lee and his father sitting in the midnight-dark by the lake sharing a six-pack of cheap, cold beer. His mother and Kate are in the cottage. "Too many bugs," they'd said, sensibly, when Lee tried to get them to come along.

It is dark except for the ice-white stars that stud the black canvas of night sky, and the small fire that crackles and spits at their feet. And silent but for that snapping fire and the slow *lap lap lap* of waves like the beat of black wings.

"This place," his father says, looking all around, "exists outside of everything. You can't really find it unless you're looking for it or know where it is. An oddity. The world is full of these thin places."

Lee hands another beer to his father, says "Shouldn't we talk about Kate. Address the elephant in the room."

His father twists off the bottle-cap, takes a swig. "Yes. She seems lovely. But let me tell you a story first."

Christ, Lee thinks. Him and his stories.

"You ever notice, son, how when we come up here that everything starts looking...off?"

"Off?"

His father scrunches up his face, all serious, sharp shadows in the firelight. "Yeah, like the trees are gnarled, and twisted unnaturally. The strange squirrel-like rodents. Even the fish in the lake here," and he gestures toward the water with his beer bottle, "are strange. Big eyes. Bulbous and bug-like. Lots more teeth." He gulped down the dregs of his beer, dropped the bottle. Looked up. "Even the light is different. In daytime it's got that greenish tinge. At night, well, just look. Have you ever seen a dark so dark? And those stars. Shining with some weird intelligence. Don't you think?"

Lee shrugs. His father is having him on or the beers are already getting to him. "Hadn't really noticed, to tell the truth."

"About that story," his father says. "For this one you just need to know that this place where we are is *different*."

Lee waited. Even as a small child, his father was always making up stories. They'd come to the cottage, tromp through the woods on a grand quest like noble knights; sit on the deck under the canopy of night and visit strange worlds; row their boat on the lake as pirates plundering and looting distant shores. His father liked a tall tale.

A half-moon, like a lidded eye winking, hangs in the night sky. Across the lake a loon calls. There's a small *plink* from the water and a rustling from the woods. The night creatures stirring.

"Up a ways," his father says, vaguely gesturing across the lake, "where the waters meet and go out to the vast sea, there's a large bay and a harbour. It's still there. It used to be a fishing town. A busy port, in fact."

Lee opens another beer, drains half in one easy pull.

"This was a long time ago," his father continues. "My father told me this story. And his father told him. And one day you can tell it to your son. Or daughter." He smiles, glances at Lee. "When you and Kate decide the time is right, of course. If nothing else, it whiles away a nice summer evening."

The fire spits sparks and smoke. Lee peers at his father's face, orange and ghoulish in the firelight. *When you and Kate decide the time is right.* The unmitigated gall. Lee had only just met her and hadn't said two words to her. His father was yanking his chain.

His father coughs, waves smoke and ash from his face. "Story goes that one summer day a vicious squall swept over the bay and the town. The harbour master and even the townsfolk could see a ship out in the bay. One they didn't recognize, and one they weren't expecting. But there'd been rumours of this ship and its mysterious cargo. It wasn't a whaling vessel, as such. It purported to deal in more *exotic* fare."

His father exhales sharply. "You have to remember; it was a time of tall tales. The taverns overflowed with beer and gossip. Rumour had it that this black vessel carried creatures the likes of which man had never seen, from the farthest corners of the earth, to be turned into food or pets, or put into zoos and aquariums. Strange and abnormal things from deep down in the ocean. Giant sea snakes with no eyes, just a mouthful of teeth." His father stops, gnashes his teeth together. Grins. "Lots of sharp teeth. Things that should have stayed down there deep in the dark. All thrashing about in their watery holds.

"It's told that many of the ship's crew took ill and started to die. Scurvy laid waste to the men. It was common practice those days to dump the corpses overboard. But the Captain of this vessel fed the bodies to those *things* in his hold. They acquired a taste for human flesh."

Lee shivers, glances up at the baleful stars. Pale light arcs across the sky, a comet or shooting star. The wind briefly gusts like a breath held too long, and the trees sway and smash into each other. Pine prickles his nostrils. Lee turns toward the woods, but all is dark. And in that darkness Lee thinks he sees an even darker wedge of night detach from the trees and amble toward the cottage. But that can't be right. No, that can't be right.

"Ah, but the storm," his father continues. "Torrents of wind and rain slammed the ship. The squall was so intense that the ship bobbed like a cork; then mighty waves crested and dashed the ship against some rocks. Wood and bodies splintered and flew. Some survived; mostly the creatures in the hold. Some swam back out to the sea, to the deep. Others...well, others apparently took a liking to the freshwater lakes, and headed inland. Far inland."

Lee laughs, and his father only smiles. They finish their beers in silence under the black and starry sky and pull the last two icy bottles from the cooler.

A sudden splash startles them both.

"And some clearly didn't stay in the deep," his father says. "Some evolved. Grew appendages, like roots, crawled from the lakes and hid among the shadows and tall trees. Kept evolving, probably. They could be walking among us. This is a thin place, remember."

"It's getting late," Lee says. "We should get back, check in with mom and Kate."

"I'm sure they are getting to know each other," Lee's father says.

"Surely they already do?" Lee says.

"Hmmm, yes, probably. First, let me tell you another story." He holds up his bottle. "Just while we finish the last beers."

Another call rings out, more like an anguished cry.

"Chrissakes, dad—"

"A quick one. I promise. And a true one."

Lee looks back to the cottage. The porch light spills a sickly cone of yellow onto the deck boards, briefly flickers. The only other light is the blue-white static of the television in the living room broadcasting dead air. Lee can just barely make out a shape at the window, vaguely humanoid and unmoving. He has the sense that it is watching. And waiting. And smiling. No, not smiling. Grinning. But that can't be. No, that can't be. His mother playing at that goddamn game again.

"So, these thin places," his father says, "these liminal voids, they allow things—creatures, beings—passage to our world from their world. I've been reading up on it. Most of the evidence is anecdotal, but...

"...well, you know me. I like a good story. All those ones I told you over the years. But they're just made up. Not real. Stories don't come to life. That's what I thought."

Lee kicks at the dirt, impatient.

"We came up early," his father says. "Last night. Didn't want to deal with the Saturday traffic. I came down here alone, had a few beers, just like we're doing. No fire. Just me and the dark. To listen to this quiet blue world. Bliss. To see the moonlight glint on the lake. Your mother was already in bed. The air felt charged somehow. Maybe a storm was coming. I'm looking at the glassy water, probably half dreaming, when I see... *something* just rise up from the water and wade to the shore. I blink, rub my eyes. But it's still there. So I grab the flashlight and head to the water's edge. I'm about twenty feet away, and I call out 'Hey! Hey, are you okay?' My light catches its face, and I see it's a woman, a sort-of woman—its features are a bit too angular—wet and pale as a grub. Naked. And she is smiling. Or sneering, rather, in a menacing way. Then it, she, whatever, turns and darts back into the water."

"Well," Lee says, "you do like your beer."

"It wasn't that," his father says. "See, last year around this time the same thing happened. I was on the porch that time, watching the moths flit and dance when—how can I put this?—above me the sky opened like an eye and something dropped into the woods. Flashlight in hand I waded into the trees. I found a pathway, and I could barely discern a shape moving along the path, coming toward me. 'Hello' I called, and it stopped. I fixed the flashlight on the path. And it was a woman. A normal woman. Dressed casual. Pants. A top. Long hair. Pale face. A normal woman. Except... except for that long shit-eating smirk creasing her face. That time, *I* ran. Back to the cottage, where I sat on the couch in the dark, heart thumping, listening, waiting."

Lee chuckles, but it isn't a happy sound. "Women don't just fall from the night sky."

"I know."

"Why didn't you say anything?"

"I didn't mention it because, well, I'm not certain even I believed what I saw. Now, though, after last night..."

Lee sighs. "How do I know this is not just another of your stories?"

Lee's father shrugs. "I guess you don't."

"Come on," Lee says. "I've had more than enough. Let's put out this fire and go back up. Mom and Kate have probably packed it in."

"About Kate," Lee's father says, "you didn't bring her up here, did you?"

"What? Of course not," Lee says. "I thought—"

They both turn back to the cottage. The porch light has been extinguished, but the dead-static glow illumines the front window and the shape that still watches them. Then there is a small flash of light, and even from the water's edge they can see that face and that mad, mad grin.

Michael Kelly curates The Best Weird Fiction of the Year, *and is former Series Editor for* The Year's Best Weird Fiction. *He's a World Fantasy Award, Shirley Jackson Award, and British Fantasy Award winner. His fiction has appeared in a number of journals and anthologies, including* Best New Horror, Bourbon Penn, The Dark, Black Static, Nightmare Magazine, *and* The Year's Best Dark Fantasy & Horror. *He is the owner and Editor-in-Chief of Undertow Publications, and editor of* Weird Horror *magazine.*

AMY ROBSART (1532-1560) BY WILLIAM FREDERICK YEAMES, c1864

WHAT HAPPENS TO CREATIVE ARTISTS WHEN THEY CAN NO LONGER CREATE? JONAS DELAMERE AND ROSE VERNON WERE TWO SUCH PEOPLE. They had both known considerable artistic success, but in very different fields. I suppose I must take some responsibility for bringing them together at the end of their careers, but not for what followed.

"I'm RP, not RA, you see," Jonas Delamere used to say to me. I think he resented the fact that he had been recognised as a portrait painter—hence a member of the Royal Society of Portrait Painters, or RP—but not as a fully-fledged artist, and so not a Royal Academician. More significantly, in his early seventies Jonas was finding it hard to get good prices for his paintings since he had gone out of fashion as a portraitist.

He thought he deserved better, a common feeling among artists who have fallen from favour.

He lived alone in a flat in Holland Park which he had bought in the days of success, even though he might have been more comfortable had he sold it and moved out of London. I and various friends helped him whenever we could and visited him regularly, but Jonas did not take kindly to accepting charity: what he wanted was paid work.

I was, in any case, not in a position to lend much financial support. I had retired from my post as music critic for the *Sunday Bystander.* Though I had my pension, and some savings, I had little money to spare; then, by chance, I saw an opportunity to help Jonas.

Despite being officially retired, I do still occasionally write pieces for magazines on musical subjects. One such article that I pitched to *Allegro*, the classical music magazine, was an in-depth interview with the great operatic soprano Dame Rose Vernon. The editor was keen on the idea, though he did warn me that "Dame Rose" did not apparently give interviews these days. I thought I knew better.

To say I was a friend of Rose Vernon, would be an exaggeration, but I certainly had known her quite well in her glory days, and had always written admiringly of her work. But that was some time ago now; she had retired in the 2000s. However, I still had her address and telephone number, so I rang her up.

A male voice answered the phone and was very short with me. No, "Madam" was not available to speak to. *Madam? Why not Dame Rose?* No, Madam did not do interviews. No, Madam did not know who I was and did not wish to be disturbed. I rang several times but on each occasion the phone was answered by the same disobliging voice. I wrote letters, but there was no response.

Then, in September last year, I was invited by the Royal College of Music, to give a talk to a select audience of staff, students, and patrons of the institution. The subject was to be "The Role of the Music Critic," not one I would have chosen myself, but just the kind of vaguely portentous topic that satisfies the requirements of academic officialdom. As far as I was concerned, the Music Critic has no Role; it was just a job, that I found myself doing early in my journalistic career, because nobody else suitable could be found, and which then developed almost by accident into the occupation of a lifetime. But I could not possibly have refused the RCM; besides, they were offering a small fee and a reception afterwards "with refreshments." It was an opportunity to burnish my fading reputation.

I think the talk was a modest success. I was self-deprecating, and occasionally almost witty; I told a few mildly amusing anecdotes, and I was just serious enough about the subject to satisfy the authorities. What made the occasion worthwhile as far as I was concerned, was an encounter I had at the reception afterwards.

I had just been officially thanked and offered a glass of reasonably palatable Chardonnay when I saw a woman coming towards me who seemed oddly familiar. She was old, perhaps even in her eighties, and almost skeletally thin, but she held herself well. Her white hair was immaculately coiffured, and she was very expensively dressed. There was something regal in her bearing. I felt I ought to have known who she was, but recognition eluded me. She was not tentative in her approach.

"That was a most amusing little talk, George," she said graciously. "Thank you so much. I think we all enjoyed it."

So, she knew my name! And now I knew hers. It was the voice: so rich and well-modulated, so much younger than the face from which it had emerged. Even after all these years it was unmistakable.

"Dame Rose! How delightful to meet you again!"

"Oh, Rose, please, George! Just Rose!" All the same, she seemed not unhappy to have been addressed by her title. "And why have you not kept in touch with me, you naughty man?"

This gave me the opportunity to tell her about my recent attempts to reach her.

"Oh dear. That must have been Adrian. Don't you remember Adrian?" I did not. "He was my dresser for years, and now he looks after everything for me. He's a darling, and keeps me from being bothered by the usual nuisances, but he can be a wee bit over-zealous at times. So protective!"

I realised that I should not complain too much about Adrian's rudeness. Rose was obviously indulgent towards him, as grand people often are with their loyal underlings. I told her I quite understood and outlined my proposal for an interview.

"Of course! I'd be only too happy. Give me a call in a few days' time and we'll fix something up. Meanwhile, I'll have words with Adrian and tell him not to be such a naughty boy with you on the blower." Only an eighty-three-year-old diva like Rose could still refer to the telephone as a "blower."

And so it was arranged. I was to visit her the following Wednesday at tea time and we would have our first talk. She seemed to take it for granted that it would take several sessions before everything important had been said by her. I communicated this to the editor of *Allegro* and he was delighted.

Rose Vernon's career as a leading soprano began at Glyndebourne in the late sixties when her Fiordiligi in *Cosi Fan Tutte* attracted attention, but it was in 1977 that she made her breakthrough into international operatic stardom. This was when she was cast in the title role of a new opera called *Amy Robsart* at Covent Garden.

The composer was Hubert Van Dyne, an established figure in the musical world of the time, and it was he who had selected Rose to play Amy. She was his inspiration for the piece; there were rumours, of course, that she was his lover, but we will come to that later.

The story of Amy Robsart is a tragic one. In 1550 at the age of only seventeen, she married Robert Dudley, Earl of Leicester. It was at first a love match and the couple endured many trials together before Elizabeth succeeded to the throne in 1558 and Leicester became a court favourite. While Leicester pursued his ambitions and an amorous flirtation with his Queen, Amy was left alone in the country. She died mysteriously from a fall down stairs at their home in Cumnor Place, Oxfordshire. That fall became a subject much beloved by Victorian history painters. Leicester was suspected of arranging her murder, and, though nothing was proved, his reputation was tarnished. It was said that he was haunted by Amy's ghost who appeared to him a few days before he died.

The opera follows these events with considerable dramatic licence, and Amy Robsart from first to last is the central figure in the drama. Her great aria came in the second act. Amy is in the garden at Cumnor Place with her serving maid. She is in despair at Leicester's neglect of her and sings what many still remember as the "Sad Gardens Aria." The words to it were in the style of an Elizabethan love lyric:

Death welcomes me and will unlock the gate
To that obscure and melancholy grove
Where I may mourn my most unhappy fate
And drain the waters of forgotten love

Here in sad gardens, let me be laid
No sound, but one last lover's sigh
Where no birds sing, beneath a cypress shade
Here let me weep, then take my rest, and die.

Many critics compared the aria's tragic melancholy to Dido's great Lament from Purcell's *Dido and Aeneas*. Some cruder spirits among my fraternity even suggested that Van Dyne was plagiarising Purcell, but this was not the case. The mood and the tempo may have been very similar, but the notes were quite different.

In the final act, Leicester and the Queen are walking in the knot garden at Nonsuch Palace, a royal residence. He is telling Her Majesty that the scandal surrounding Amy's death has been forgotten and that she should therefore be free to marry him. Elizabeth is about to be persuaded when Amy's voice is heard singing the Sad Gardens Aria. Leicester starts back in horror. We do not know if Elizabeth hears it or not, but she is sufficiently alarmed by her suitor's behaviour that she leaves the garden at once. Then Amy's ghost appears and she and Leicester embark on a long, impassioned duet. He at last realises that she has always been his true love and stretches out his hands to touch her spectral form. But before this can happen, Amy, in a spectacular *coup de theatre*, vanishes, and Leicester drops to the ground senseless. The curtain falls.

Amy Robsart was rapturously received by both critics and public. Van Dyne's music had been composed in a lush, Mahlerian, late romantic style, rather dated perhaps for 1977, but still very acceptable. However, the greatest success of the piece was undoubtedly Rose Vernon's performance.

It was a revelation: I was there on the opening night, and I can vouch for it. Rose not only had a lovely voice, she had presence, and beauty, and she could act. Her international career was launched. The same could not be said for Van Dyne. *Amy Robsart* was revived once or twice, but it did not thrive without Rose in the title role. Other works of his enjoyed little success thereafter.

For quite some time Rose had lived in The Boltons, an exclusive but rather sombre region of South Kensington. Her house, number 10 Ellington Square, is a grand neoclassical white stuccoed villa, built like others of its kind in the mid-nineteenth century. It has four floors and overlooks a large communal garden, situated in the middle of the square, which is fenced round with iron railings and available only to key-holding occupants of the enclave. I saw it only from the outside, but it did not look very inviting, being well tended but intensely shady and lacking any colour other than green, mostly dark green.

I arrived at her house that Wednesday, precisely as ordered, on the stroke of four. The door was opened immediately after I had rung the bell by a man in a dark suit and black tie, dressed almost like an old-fashioned manservant, but not quite. This, I presumed, correctly as it turned out, was Adrian.

I had somehow expected someone small, wiry, and nimble—dressers often are—but Adrian was a large, florid man in his sixties with thinning curly hair that had been dyed an unconvincing shade of orange. He was, however, for his age and weight, surprisingly light on his feet. I later discovered that he had once been a dancer with the Royal Ballet.

Adrian was formal and polite, but he made no apology for his former behaviour on the phone. Having taken my coat in the hall, he led me upstairs, explaining as he went that "Madam" and he lived on the ground and first floors, the top two being occupied by students from the Royal College of Music to whom Rose let rooms "at a *very* low rent." Adrian was emphatic about this point; giving the impression that, while he respected his lady's magnanimity, he also disapproved of it.

The drawing room on the first floor was a model of faded tastefulness, upholstered and papered in various shades of dove grey. Pictures on the wall celebrated her glittering operatic career. On the immaculate shiny black surface of a grand piano stood silver-framed photographs of Rose shaking hands with the Queen, Princess Diana, and other royal notables, and of her standing in costume beside Pavarotti, Domingo, Carreras, and the occasional conductor. Rose was sitting by the window, in a wing chair, upholstered in grey watered silk.

"George! How nice of you to come so carefully upon your hour. Adrian, you can fetch the tea now."

Rose was at her grandest and most gracious. We exchanged general conversation until Adrian returned with tea on an oval silver tray. Having poured the tea, he seemed disposed to remain.

"Thank you, Adrian," said Rose with a meaningful intonation. He made no move until she had said: "*Thank* you, Adrian," with even greater emphasis. When he had gone, she said: "Now, George, I see you have brought your little recording machine with you. Why don't you switch it on?"

She talked for over two hours. Several times Adrian entered the room to clear the tea things, but she waved him away. She talked so fluently, that I rarely had the chance to ask a question, and, when I did, she usually ignored it. It was interesting enough, if a little unspontaneous. There were a few indiscretions, but even they appeared to be calculated. When she discussed her great operatic roles, she invariably referred to them with the possessive pronoun attached: "*my* Violetta," "*my* Norma," "*my* Butterfly."

"Of course, when I did my Tosca at the Met, I was rather nervous because Callas had made such a big success of it not long before." That was the extent to which she was ready to admit vulnerability.

To my surprise and disappointment, she did not talk directly about *Amy Robsart*. Once or twice, she would say of a particular engagement that "that was before *Amy Robsart*" or, "that was *after* Amy"; but it was never "*my* Amy." When I tried to ask her about that opera in more detail, she would always cut me off, so I gave up and waited for her to allow me the opportunity.

The room, which had not been artificially lit, began to darken in the autumn twilight. Adrian entered and Rose allowed him at last to remove the tea tray and turn on a standard lamp with a pale pink damask shade. I stood up and thanked Rose profusely for her time.

She said: "Well, you must come again. I have so much more to tell you."

I asked if, before I left, I could have a closer look at the pictures on the drawing room walls. She nodded but remained in her chair pointing at items of interest with her ebony stick: "that was my Marschallin... my Lucia... my Gilda..." I thought I saw an opportunity.

"There don't seem to be any of you here as Amy Robsart."

There was silence, and the response when it came was spoken in a distant, glacial voice.

"How very clever of you to notice, George."

I thought it best to leave it at that, so I began to study the framed photos on the grand piano. Among the stars and royalty, I saw, almost obscured in that forest of larger, grander images, a small picture in an oval frame that I had not noticed before. It showed the head and shoulders of a dark-haired man of middle age with heavy, brooding features. His large, dark eyes peered out from under black brows. I recognised the face. It was *Amy Robsart*'s composer, Hubert Van Dyne.

My thoughts were suddenly interrupted by Rose's voice. She spoke in a slightly more emollient tone.

"As a matter of fact, I was wondering..." Another pause. "You wouldn't happen to know of a good portrait painter."

"As it happens, I do. Why do you ask?"

"I want one done of me as Amy Robsart. There *was* one made at the time. It was going to be given to me, but it was... I think it was destroyed... Who is the artist that you have in mind?"

I named Jonas Delamere and was beginning to outline his credentials, when she interrupted me.

"Yes, yes! I know exactly who you mean. He sounds very suitable. I didn't know he was still going. Will you be so kind as to have a word with him on my behalf? I am prepared to pay quite handsomely, but there are certain conditions..."

It was another hour before I was shown out the house by Adrian, who seemed unashamedly relieved to see me go. The street lights were on in Ellington Square, but behind the railings, the communal garden was thickly shaded in darkness, its trees rising up to obscure the violet evening sky. I stared into it and thought I saw something moving in the shadows.

Some distance away a figure, half obscured by a laurel bush, was standing on the serpentine gravel path which led to the garden's gate. It appeared to be a man, but I could not make out his features which were in shadow. I had the impression that he was looking at me, or through me and up at Rose's house. A rather breathy whistling sound was coming from his direction. I tried the gate, thinking that it might be unlocked, but it was not. My feelings were troubled enough. I decided to investigate no further and return home.

The following morning, I rang Jonas. He was initially delighted by the prospect and grateful to me for my recommendation, though when I described the conditions under which he must work, his enthusiasm waned.

Rose wanted a picture of her as Amy Robsart that was to be, as far as possible, in imitation of the Elizabethan style of portraiture, with all the textures and lustres of fabric, jewels, skin, and hair meticulously rendered. She herself would sit for him in the original costume of the 1977 Covent Garden production which she had in her possession, but the features of her face and the complexion of her skin were to be derived from photographs of her younger self. Jonas was to come to her house and paint her there in her own drawing room. He was not to take the canvas away at night. It would remain in the room and all work on the picture must be undertaken at her house.

When he had heard her terms, Jonas said: "Bloody hell! I'll want twenty thousand for this one: ten thousand up front, and ten on completion."

When I conveyed this to Rose by telephone, to my surprise she made no attempt to haggle, but agreed immediately. A cheque for ten thousand pounds was sent to Jonas the very next day. Dame Rose was, naturally, a stranger to internet banking.

I did not hear from Jonas for almost a week, then one evening he rang me.

"How's it going, Jonas?"

"Oh, God! Don't ask!" But I already had asked, and he was only too willing to tell me.

"It's a bit of a bloody nightmare actually. I get there at ten in the morning and set up my easel and stuff in that ghastly grey drawing room. This bloody flunkey of hers, Adrian or whatever his name is, faffing around the whole time. Obviously, he hates the whole portrait business and me. Well, it's bloody well mutual. Then Rose appears and she and matey bugger off to put her Robsart togs on. So, she comes back and sits down in her throne ready for the session, and here's the first real nightmare. The clothes and the jewels and whatnot are still in pretty good nick after nearly fifty years, but she isn't. She's kind of shrunk. You'll remember better than I do what a looker she was. Good figure for a diva: voluptuous you might say, but not fat like these other opera types can be, but now she's gone all withered and bony. I mean, fair play to the old Dame, she is over eighty, but it's not a good look. However, she can still sit up straight which is something. The trouble is, she talks. Now, I don't mind my subjects talking as long as they remain fairly immobile which, to do her justice, she does. I just switch off and go into the zone, as they say nowadays. The trouble is, she expects you to respond, and she gets a bit ratty when you don't. So, look, this is where you come in. Can you come over and keep her company while I paint. I've squared it with her and she was actually keen on the idea. She seems to think there's some unfinished business over an interview or something anyway. Can you make it tomorrow?"

"Yes. I suppose so."

"Good man! Good... Good..." A silence.

"Was there something else?"

"As a matter of fact... Look, do you think there's something funny about that house?"

"Not really, why?"

"Once or twice while I was painting Rose and there was just us in the room, I felt there was someone else there as well. And no, it wasn't that shit Adrian who *was* always barging in and out to see that 'Madam' was okay. Always poking his nose in when he wasn't wanted. Do you know, he once had the gall to tell me I'd got the colour of Rose's gown a bit wrong. No, this was something else. It usually happened when Rose turned on the record player, as she occasionally did. Of course, it was always records of *her* singing, and usually one of that awful tripe *Amy Robsart*. She seemed to think it would give me some sort of inspiration. Not bloody likely. Sorry, I suppose you think it's a ruddy masterpiece, but I'm not into that kind of music. I like a good brass band, and that's about it. Anyway, she plays this stuff, and we hear her singing that dirge about gardens or whatever, and I get this feeling I'm being watched. I look round and there's nobody there. Then I hear something. Quite quiet, but somehow close to my ear, and it's like someone is whistling along to the music. Or more like just breathing along to it, if you know what I mean. Anyway, it freaks me out a bit. I can't exactly tell the Dame to turn off her ghastly music, so I make an excuse about needing the loo and leave the room. When I get back, the record's finished and we're back to her talking again which is a bit better. But I still can't get it out of my head that there's someone or something around."

"Do you think Rose noticed anything?"

"Hard to say. She might have done.

Doesn't give much away, does she? For all her jabber."

"I'll be there for you tomorrow."

"Thanks, George."

When I rang the bell at number 10 the following day the door was, as before, opened almost instantly by Adrian.

"They're up in the drawing room," he said. He pointed upwards but did not escort me.

As I was mounting the stairs to the first floor, I met a young woman carrying a violin case coming down. She must have been one of the Royal College of Music students who rented rooms on the top floors of the house. She can have been no more than twenty and, though not a beauty as Rose had been, there was something of beauty about her. The look on her face was radiant: she was on her way to the Royal College to learn music and to play it. She smiled at me and I smiled back. An unguarded moment was shared and we passed on.

When I reached the top of the stairs, I looked back down to the hallway. Adrian was holding the front door open for the student, a sour expression on his face. She smiled at him, too, and went out into the sunlight.

In the drawing room, Jonas was already at his easel and Rose was sitting in an upright wooden armchair.

"Ah, there you are, George. Do sit down. I was just beginning to tell Jonas here about his picture."

Jonas looked at me, winked and gestured towards a seat not far from him, but out of sight of his canvas. I had noticed that he had made considerable progress with the velvets, silks, and jewellery of her costume but the head and neck were a mere outline. Attached to a board on a separate easel were several photographs of the young Rose as Amy Robsart. She was beautiful, and the expression on her face was meltingly sad.

I looked from her young self to her older one. Yes, she had shrunk, but she had also hardened. The lips had thinned and the eyes had become watchful. I noticed that she had put discreet padding in her dress to compensate for the collapse of her figure. Ropes of pearls about her neck covered some of the signs of age. The gown was of deep plum-coloured velvet, garnished with gold thread and seed pearls, the underskirt was of dark grey brocaded silk. It was a rich but sombre confection.

"Hubert saw me at Glyndebourne, and he just fell in love with me, I think." There was a pause as Rose eyed me searchingly. "George, you're not to put this in your article. Is that clear?" I nodded. "I'm telling you this because... Well, because it is time." Suddenly she turned and frowned at a Louis Quinze armchair about three feet away from me. "Where was I? I was his inspiration for Amy. It's by far and away his best piece, you know. And yes, we became lovers. Hubert was married, of course, but he and his wife were estranged, so there was no... No great fuss about it from anyone. He became rather infatuated with me, and when *Amy* was a big success, he wanted to have this portrait of me done, you know, in the Elizabethan style. He was going to give it to me as a gift at the end of the run. So, I sat for this artist in my get-up. I forget his name, but he did it very well. But then something happened. I was enjoying this huge success you see, and of course Hubert was sharing in it, but he got rather jealous. And he was terribly possessive, like all men really. I was getting these offers to play all sorts of wonderful roles, at the Met, La Scala, Munich, Berlin, Moscow, the lot, and he wanted to manage me, choose what I was to do. Well, I wasn't having that, so we began to drift apart. I think he took it badly. Of course, I was still terribly fond of him, but I couldn't have him control my life. Still, when we came to the end of the run of Amy, I was expecting him to give me the picture, but he didn't. He got rather nasty about it actually. Said if he couldn't have me, he'd keep the portrait. So silly. And we parted, but he did promise he'd leave it to me in his will. I went off to do *Manon* at La Scala and that was it really. I did keep in touch, but I was very much in demand at the time, and what with one thing and another... Poor Hubert, I think he rather went downhill after that. I don't see I was to blame or anything, but he was rather shattered by it all. He took to drink, I'm afraid. Last time I saw him, only a year before he died, poor soul, he was living in this dreadful room above a pub with a rather ghastly woman. I think she was a sort of barmaid or something." She smiled at me mischievously, and made little clawing movements with her hands. "Miaow!"

"Dame Rose, would you mind keeping your hands still, please, for a moment," said Jonas. "I was just beginning to paint them." I think he was as shocked as I was by the sudden self-revelation.

"Oh, so sorry, dear." Then suddenly she turned her head again towards the Louis Quinze armchair. I looked also and thought I saw a slight movement on its cushioned seat. There must have been a draught in the room because there was a creaking sound and something like a sigh, or a faint whistle.

Dame Rose rallied herself. "Well, when poor Hubert died, naturally I went to the funeral. It was rather a dreadful business. Cremation. In Croydon of all places. So of course, when it was all over, I enquired after the picture, but nobody seemed to know anything about it. I even offered to buy it if it was still there. No luck. The barmaid was very rude to me over it. Personally, I think she had it destroyed out of spite, but I'm not making any accusations. I wanted that picture. That's why..."

She fell silent. The room was quiet apart from the faint sound of Jonas handling his brushes and palette, and something else. Someone was whistling, so indistinctly, that I could barely hear it. I looked at Jonas and then Rose, but the noise was not coming from them. I even suspected that I might unconsciously be doing it myself. I held my breath and listened intently. The sound faded, but I was sure I had caught a whisper of the melodic line of "Sad Gardens." Then Rose started talking again.

"*Manon* at La Scala was really my first big international success. I went on to do other Puccini roles: Mimi, Butterfly, Tosca, of course... I was quite the Puccini specialist. The Italians loved me for it. They used to call me *La Superba*. '*Viva la Superba*!' they used to shout. Bless them..." And so she continued to talk of her triumphs while Jonas painted until Adrian came in to announce that her lunch was ready. This was the signal for us to take our leave. Rose only posed in the mornings.

Before she left the room, she stopped in front of Jonas's canvas and studied it briefly.

"Oh, yes!" she said. "Coming along nicely! Are you going to put a highlight on those pearls?"

"Damned condescending old bitch!" Jonas muttered after she had left the room. "Come on, let's get out of here. I need a drink."

We found a nearby pub. Jonas had a pint of Guiness and a whisky chaser.

"George," he said after he had drunk deeply. "I'm afraid it's not going to work. Sorry about this."

"You're giving up the painting? But it's really rather good."

"No, no. Not the painting! You! I thought your being there would help me, but it doesn't. It actually makes it worse. Not that I'm blaming you or anything."

"Well, that's a relief."

"No, no. Don't take it like that. I thought you could stop Rose bothering me, but it doesn't help at all. Quite the reverse. That feeling that someone else is there is even stronger. And another thing... You remember what she said about the highlights on the pearls? Well, I could swear I put those highlights in yesterday, and this morning they were gone. And things like that have happened on previous days. It's like... you know that painting by Waterhouse about the Greek girl who is doing this tapestry by day and then she undoes it at night because if she finishes it, she has to marry one of those blokes who are looking through the window at her?"

"Penelope."

"That's the chappie. Well, it's the same with me, only it's someone else who seems to be undoing some detail of the painting each night so I can never finish it. Either that, or I'm going bonkers. Quite possibly the latter. My round, I think. Same again?" He drained his whisky and got up to get another.

After that we talked of other things. I think. Drinking in the middle of the day no longer agrees with me, which may account for an odd occurrence when I was taking the tube back to my flat in St John's Wood.

The Jubilee Line train was fairly full, but I managed to find a place to sit. Opposite me was another vacant seat which, in spite of the crowd, nobody had taken. They were all just standing up. I started staring at the seat for some reason, and I observed that the cushion was moving slightly. Now, I have noticed that this sometimes happens on the tube, some sort of breeze from the movement of the train blows up the cushion covers from time to time, but this was the opposite. It looked as if the seat cushion was being pushed *down*, like someone was sitting on it. I became rather fixated by this phenomenon, until I noticed that quite a few of my fellow passengers were giving me strange looks. It could have been the drink.

A week later Jonas invited me over to his flat in Holland Park to see the finished portrait. I was surprised that Rose had let it out of her sight.

"I insisted," Jonas told me. "I said I couldn't finish it properly unless I could work on the last stages in my studio. I talked a lot of guff about glazes and varnishes and eventually she gave in. But it was true. I could never finish it in that house. Don't ask me why, I just couldn't."

Jonas had put it on an easel in the middle of his chaotic sitting room and placed a sheet over it. He put me in a chair in front of it, then slowly removed the sheet.

I was impressed. He had captured perfectly the way in which the painters of the period, most of them anonymous, showed in minute detail the nuances of fabric, embroidery and jewels and the softer textures of the skin with the Renaissance technique known as *sfumato*. It was almost as I remembered Rose in the role of Amy Robsart. Her head is tilted a little to the right, and she looks away from the viewer into the distance. The background that surrounds her contained subtle shades of darkness which give the impression of a vast but obscure region of space behind.

It was a masterly piece of work. I had only one reservation which I kept to myself. My memories of her performance and the many press photographs that I had seen of her as Amy over the years all showed a meltingly sad expression in the eyes. There was sorrow and melancholy in them, but also a kind of compassion as if, even in the depths of her grief, she was forgiving her errant lover. In the eyes that Jonas had painted there was only bleakness and desolation. There was a hardness about them, perhaps even anger.

"I take it round tomorrow afternoon to Ellington Square," said Jonas. "Where I hope my next ten thousand pound cheque awaits me."

The following evening Jonas rang me.

"I don't know what to do, George. It's a disaster. I went this afternoon to deliver the picture, and this bloke opened the door. Sort of darkish, heavy bloke. Couldn't see him properly, but it definitely wasn't Adrian. And he just snatched the canvas out of my hands and slammed the door in my face. Well, I knocked and rang for ages, but nobody answered. So then I went home and got on the phone to them, but no reply. What is going on? What am I supposed to do?"

I said: "Jonas. Haven't you seen the news?"

"No. Why? You know me, George. I don't bother with that sort of thing nowadays."

"Rose is dead. It's just been reported. They haven't given many details, but she seems to have had some sort of fall in the Ellington Square gardens. She was found by a neighbour."

A long silence.

"Oh, God! Now I'll never get my bloody money... Sorry. That sounds callous. Look, I know this is a lot to ask, but could you go round there and find out what the hell is going on. I simply can't face it. That bloody man Adrian is just not answering the phone, so it's no use ringing. Obviously not tonight, but tomorrow. Would you?"

On the News that night, there were fulsome tributes to Dame Rose. There were also reports that police were "looking into the circumstances of her death," but nothing further.

The following morning, I went to Ellington Square. I had little hope of gaining admission, but I was fortunate. Before I could ring the bell, the door opened and the student with the violin case whom I had once met on the stairs was coming out. She had been crying. I expressed my condolences and explained that I had to see Adrian. She said he was in the drawing room and let me in.

Adrian was standing at the window looking out onto the square. The room was in disorder. Papers were scattered about; what looked like Jonas's canvas was propped against a chair covered by a white damask tablecloth. He was, as I expected, not pleased to see me, but I could not blame a man in such obvious grief.

"I suppose you've come about that bloody picture. How it got back here, I don't know, but if you think your friend Jonas Delamere is getting any more money, he can whistle for it. I've a good mind to ask for our ten thousand back. It's not finished at all. In fact, it's a bloody mess."

"It most certainly isn't. I saw it myself in Jonas's studio only a couple of days ago. It is an excellent and finished piece of work." I heard myself sounding huffy and pompous, but I couldn't help it.

"Oh, you think so, do you? All right then, look!"

He went over to the canvas, picked it up, stripped off the tablecloth, and, without looking at it himself, held it up to my face.

I stared at the portrait in disbelief. Someone—Could it have been Jonas? Surely not!—someone had altered the painting horribly.

It looked as if acid had been thrown over the face. The features had collapsed into devastated old age; the eyes, staring and bloodshot, had almost come out of their withered sockets; the mouth gaped. Was it a cry of pain, or was she singing? Or both?

It was some time before I could speak. At last, I said: "Believe me, it was nothing like that when I last saw it. And you say that it was like this when you found it?"

Adrian turned the picture round to see for himself. I saw his face turn white. He stared at it, his features rigid with shock and disbelief.

"What the—! It's got worse!" he said.

There was nothing more either of us could say. I left the house, and, almost without thinking, crossed the road to the garden in the square where she had died. The gate was locked but someone had leaned a small bunch of roses against it. I stood still and allowed my heart to stop beating so violently. Around me London was as quiet as it ever could be. I heard a faint whisper, almost like a whistle coming from the trees beyond the iron railings. There it was once more, that melancholy refrain.

Here in sad gardens, let me be laid
No sound, but one last lover's sigh
Where no birds sing, beneath a cypress shade
Here let me weep, then take my rest, and die.

Reggie Oliver is an actor, director, playwright, illustrator, and award-winning author of fiction. His published work includes six plays, four novels, an illustrated children's book, ten volumes of short stories, including Mrs Midnight *(2011 winner of the Children of the Night Award for best supernatural fiction), and the biography of Stella Gibbons,* Out of the Woodshed *(Bloomsbury 1998). His stories have appeared in over one hundred anthologies, and four "selected" editions of his stories have been published:* Dramas from the Depths *(Centipede Press, 2010),* Shadow Plays *(Egaeus, 2012),* The Sea of Blood *(Dark Regions, 2015), and* Stages of Fear *(Black Shuck Books, 2020). Most recently published is his tenth volume of "strange stories,"* This Haunted Heaven *(Tartarus, 2024), and* Wings of the Night, *a novel about a haunted theatre (PS Publications, 2025).*

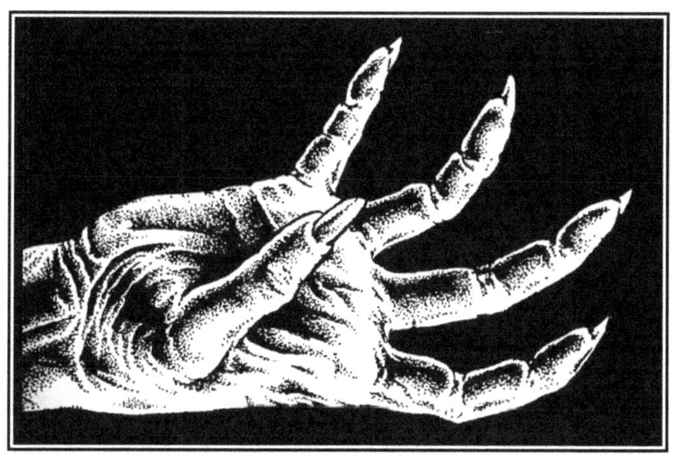

MAM-GU

By **Stephen Volk**

Art by **Allen Koszowski**

YEARS AGO, WHEN DAYS WERE LONG AND LIVES WERE HARD, IN A VALLEY THAT LAY UNDER A DRAPE OF DUST, IN A TOWN WHOSE NAME YOU CAN'T PRONOUNCE, there once lived a family with seven children, who all slept in one bed, *cwtched* up like sausages in a pan, in a tiny stone house next to all the other tiny stone houses, and in the house next door lived Tad-cu and Mam-gu, that is to say, their grandfather and grandmother. And one night when they were drifting off to the land of Nod, their mam creaked open the door and told them in a soft voice, trying to hold back tears, that Mam-gu was dying and the children needed to say goodbye to her.

They'd been dreaming of mermaids and pirates and wanted to sink back into that slumber, but they weren't allowed. Mam combed the boys' hair savagely, like it was a punishment. Off they trooped, ducklings in a row, bleary-eyed in their night shirts, four girls and three boys. They arranged themselves in a line facing the bed, as they were bidden, glad to get in from the cold of the street. They'd seen Mam-gu a week ago and she'd looked peaky. She looked more peaky now.

The old woman's head was a windfall apple sunk in a vast pillow. Her mouth like a hole made by a rock dropped into snow. Her eyes had given up the gleam and were now barely slits. Sensing the children's presence, with huge effort she raised her arm from the blanket, withered and crusted as it was with liver spots and blemishes. It stretched out and hung in the air like the branch of a tree.

One by one the children stepped forward and gently took her hand in theirs. Such was the custom in those days. One by one they observed the tradition, stepping forward into the candle light, then retreating back into the shadows. Presently it was the turn of Clifford, youngest and smallest of them all. No bigger than a bar of soap, his mother used to say as he sat in the tin bath after his Tad had made the water grey.

Clifford asked his mam where Mam-gu was going, that they had to say goodbye to her. She told him in a whisper Mam-gu was going to heaven.

He walked to the bed. Reached out his soft, warm hand. Mam-gu's bony fingers closed around it. He noticed the knuckles bulging with arthritis, turning white. Which was the very moment her hairy chin jutted into the air and the last breath exited her body. They say it is a rattle but it isn't. It's a puncture. Her chest flattened, life evaporating. All sobs in the room were held in abeyance. The children's father upright as a soldier, Dai cap clutched to his chest like a ragged heart.

Mam kissed the top of Clifford's head, thinking he didn't want to let go, poor thing, poor *cariad*, and squeezed the boy's shoulders, pulling him back gently, but the boy didn't move. It wasn't that he *wouldn't* let go, it was that he *couldn't.*

She tugged him back again, a little more forcibly this time. His arm became straight. He didn't let go. Mam-gu's was straight. She didn't let go either. Clifford's mam pulled harder still, but the two arms, young and old, were as firmly connected as the links in an iron chain.

This is daft, this is, said Clifford's father, replacing his wife, rolled-up sleeves criss-crossing the boy's chest and heaving-ho. This man who had hauled a laden billy underground, yet could not move his son from the spot. After four or five increasingly rough attempts he too stepped back, his exertions plain in the pink of his cheeks.

Mam-gu, eyeless, open-mouthed, and dead, did not let go of Clifford's hand.

The aunties muttered prayers, as was their wont.

Next the uncles took over, one wrapping his arms around Clifford's waist, the other hooking a muscled arm throttlingly around the youngster's neck. After a count of one, two, three, they pulled with all their colliery might, which resulted only in Clifford having a coughing fit and rubbing bruised ribs with his one free hand. *Dampo dee*, cursed one uncle while the other wheezed.

Clifford, his mam said, kissing him on both cheeks, tidying his hair, and pleading with him to let go, as if it was Clifford's fault. But it wasn't.

He too applied himself to the task, jerking his shoulder back, panting with the strain as he used his whole body, leaning back at an angle, trying to twist his arm out of the trap of the old woman's grasp. His shoes slid on the rug, bunching it up in waves, but the dead woman held him in a grip as fixed as if they were held together with rivets.

Clifford looked to his father for solace, or an answer.

None was forthcoming.

And so the hour passed, as Clifford writhed and struggled, his arm undulating like a whip, then pumping up and down like a piston, to no avail. And to the consternation and bafflement of all present.

Tad-cu came forward. If anyone could break Mam-gu's spell, surely, it was her husband of two score years and ten. But for all the old man's huffing and puffing, Mam-gu's stubborn paw did not relent. She was stronger than all of them. Even in death.

In desperation, someone balanced the family Bible on the backs of their two hands, and quoted a psalm or several.

Made no difference. Tad-cu snatched up the Good Book and brought it down hard as a hammer on their conjoinment. Clifford let out a shriek like a scalded monkey, and Mam petted his tears with the hem of her nightgown. Still mewling, Clifford made his arm rise and fall, taking Mam-gu's arm with him. Up, down. Up, down. Giving the illusion he and the corpse were playing some kind of horrible skipping game.

The clock struck three.

Mam fetched soap and water in a bucket from the scullery, but it was hard to get soap between the two sets of tightly entwined fingers. When the little chap's hand was starting to redden she stopped rubbing, realising her efforts were useless.

There was nothing else for it. The grown-ups lined up either side, held each wrist and set to it with vigour in semblance of a tug of war, three on the boy's side, three on Mam-gu's. The abject failure of which only gave them a thirst, resulting in the aunts bringing them cups of tea the colour of thick gravy, which went down well, as distraction as well as fortification.

Mam-gu sat with her eyes closed and her mouth open, dry as a ditch. Clifford, wiping tears from his eyes, could see into her drainlike throat.

One uncle hobbled off to rouse the doctor, who listened to Mam-gu's chest and pronounced her well and truly deceased. He put on his glasses and examined the interlocked hands. Rigor mortis, he said with supreme confidence. Unusually early, but scientifically explicable. He snapped closed his black bag. Give it twenty-four hours. The muscles will relax again.

The clock chimed six.

The men went off to work. The women stayed.

Shortly thereafter the children went to school, shuffling next door to fetch their satchels and running to get there in time for assembly, where they sang in spirited voices: *Guide me O thou great Jehovah, Pilgrim in this foreign land, I am weak but thou art mighty, Hold me with thy powerful hand.*

Meanwhile Mam spooned porridge into Clifford's mouth and the lad relished feeling like a baby again, which becalmed his soul and allowed a placid resignation to settle in his heart.

At nine o'clock, Tad-cu answered a knocking at the door. The undertaker, bald as a bat, circled the bed, measuring Mam-gu from head to toe and shoulder to shoulder, noting his calculations in a threadbare little book with his stubby little pencil. Before leaving, the man finished his cup of tea with four sugars, assured Tad-cu a suitable plot had been procured, then patted him on the shoulder. Tad-cu nodded.

At two o'clock the neighbours called to see Mam-gu and Clifford, hats and scarves carefully removed as they stepped over the threshold, letting the sun in with them. Mam told them he was doing all right considering. He was a brave boy. Clifford had a smile on his face. One asked if it hurt. He shook his head. Not really. One gave him a Welsh cake. He licked off the sugar first, like he always did. They kneeled and kissed his other hand, and prayed. They didn't seem to want to leave. They said everyone was talking about the little boy who loves his Mam-gu.

Everyone was bringing gifts. The house was filling with them. By the end of the day, Mam was hoping that Mam-gu's body might soften, but it didn't. And, as dawn crept in behind the closed curtains of the front parlour the next morning, the old lady's grip appeared to be, if anything, firmer. More determined.

Forty-eight hours, the doctor said, when confronted with the fact. I said give it forty-eight. It's scientific. And don't bother me again, I'm a busy man.

The locals knew better than to question a medical expert.

The family brought in chairs from the other rooms, so as not to be inhospitable. Tad-cu poked the fire, which had been losing interest. It crackled and spat at his oaky palms. He slapped his knees and sat, and slapped them again.

By the end of the second day, when Clifford's father returned black-faced from the mine to find the hands of his youngest son and Mam-gu hadn't budged, it was clear to everyone he'd had enough. Telling Clifford to be brave, he fetched a bread knife from the kitchen drawer and wiggled the blade between the fingers, trying to prise them apart. Mam shot to her feet, protesting at the zeal with which he went about this activity, but he barked at her and shoved her aside. For all the good it did, he might as well have tried to break a marble statue with a feather, for he succeeded only in making Clifford weep as blood pearled.

Iesu Grist! Mam snatched the blade off him. No knives! No nothing!

Tad grabbed the knife back and lay it across the dead woman's knuckles, ready to saw.

Sacrilege! cried a figure in a long black gown. The vicar had entered the room. To Clifford's eyes, almost filling it. The abuse of the dead is the gravest of sins! If you commit such an atrocity you will not be allowed through the gates of heaven. And neither will your son.

In the name of God. Clifford's father dropped the bread knife to the floor. What do you advise, father?

In God's name, I advise you to pray. Reviewing the scene before him, the holy man wiped away the blood on the back of Clifford's thumb and rested his palm on the conjoined hands with a sense of awe and benediction. It is a sign.

A sign of what? Clifford's Mam asked.

A sign to stop doing it. To put away foolish things. Like knives. As it says in the Bible.

Tad asked, Where does it say in the Bible about my son?

It says about God's son, and that's all you should worry about.

So saying, the vicar left, assuring all those present he would be seeking the counsel of the highest authority regarding what to do next. Whether that meant God Himself or the bishop, nobody was quite sure.

Hallelujah, said the aunts.

Hallelujah, said the uncles.

Clifford's father knelt down beside Mam-gu's bed and, with his coal-stained fingers, plucked the supple flesh on the back of his son's living hand, then the parchment dry skin on the back of his mother's dead one. Hallelujah. Now it was he who sobbed. Hallelujah in the highest. Did not the son of the Almighty suffer, as does mine?

Good point, said one of the uncles.

Bless him, said Tad-cu, the widower. And bless her. Bless both of them. Give her a shake though. You never know, eh?

They did, but the two hands did not come apart. They were still as fast as if glued. Nothing had changed and nothing would. They had come to that unfortunate conclusion.

On the morning of the third day there was a smell like boiled cabbage in the air. Mam crushed lavender in a pestle. One aunt washed Clifford's cheeks with a flannel, and then washed Mam-gu's forehead as well, brushing the old woman's white hair in a parting and tying a black ribbon around her head to keep her jaw from sagging. Another took out the chamber pot Clifford had been utilizing and swilled his night-water in the gutter.

One of the children reported to Mam that in school they'd started to say bad things about Clifford. They were saying it was the work of the Devil. Mam told them it was just ignorance and stupidity when everyone knew it was the work of God. They don't understand, she said with more than a tinge of pride. Nobody understands. They're just jealous, is what they are.

The vicar returned at long last, having acquired his counsel with whomever, on high or in Llandaff, and the grown-ups quickly knotted into a huddle at his behest. Clifford couldn't make out with any clarity their sibilant whispers. His Mam was singing *Sospan Fach* to him when they beckoned her over. He watched as more whispers ensued. Tad looked pale, his face newly washed. An event in itself. Tad-cu's whiskery chin jutted out with horizontal steadfastness.

Mam? Clifford asked, but his mother didn't answer as she tightened the bow of her shawl.

In her cabbage-ness, Mam-gu lay, her skull sunk deep in the pillow.

Clifford heard the clip-clop of horses' hooves and saw two black plumes glide past the window. He saw the undertaker wearing a top hat covering his shiny head. He heard the sonorous knock on the door.

The boy is purity itself, proclaimed the vicar. For was he not made in the Lord's image? Clifford's brothers and sisters never pictured God looking like Clifford. They never pictured God with knock-knees and sticky-out ears.

And that makes it plain, the vicar said, this time dressed in the grandest of vestments, a white surplice and stole, as befitted the occasion. This is something put here to test our faith. So be sure to pass that test and not fail it, he said to the faithful. What is God's will must be obeyed.

Hallelujah, said the uncles and aunts and neighbours. Hallelujah.

From then on, the townsfolk in the valley no longer attempted to separate Clifford from Mam-gu, which felt odd and worrying. Clifford almost wanted them to, in case this time it worked. Though he knew in his heart it wouldn't.

We must be resolute and trust in God, said Tad-cu. God knows best.

The coffin was brought into the passageway, then carried into the parlour.

It's for the best, said Clifford's father, giving a wan smile that Clifford felt obliged to emulate. It wasn't the easiest thing in the world. The boy looked at his mam and she was smiling too, so that must have meant it was all right because she loved him. He knew that.

There must've been talk of making a bigger coffin, but the coffin was roomy enough. Clifford was only little, and, if anything, on the undernourished side in undernourished times. He will fit inside neatly.

Four pallbearers peeled back the top blanket and lifted up Mam-gu's corpse, holding her above the bed while two others slid the coffin under her. Then they lowered her inside. She was barely the weight of bones. Clifford climbed up with his knees onto the mattress and lay flat on the bed, their hands clasped together, cemented as one, like those of lovers, of newly-weds. One of the cold brass coffin handles was next to his warm young cheek. The undertakers gently lifted him and squeezed him down at her side.

One of his sisters wanted to run over and kiss him, but dared not. So she hugged Tad-cu, who was standing next to her. The menfolk took the shoes from Clifford's feet. The womenfolk took scissors and cut off his nightshirt.

Clifford did not complain. He did not say a thing. What could he say? It was not his place to speak. He was a child and it was wrong for a child to speak once grown-ups had decided something. Let alone God.

They sang *Abide with Me* and *How Great Thou Art*.

Mam-gu was lying on her back. Clifford was lying on his side facing her. Her hand looked pawlike and bloodless with long fingernails that hadn't been trimmed for months, but his chubby little hand was perfect.

A shadow fell across his face as the coffin lid was nailed down. Every man took his turn with the hammer, passing it one to the next as the women prayed silently, their lips moving under their head scarves.

Clifford didn't cry out or say goodbye or say anything. Which made some think he must have been, in some way, at least, content. If not happy. It was an honour, after all.

The family walked behind the hearse to the cemetery. Adults, children, all.

Rooks amassed on branches in a dark choir. The gravediggers brushed out their cigarettes on their knees at the approach of the cortege. The grave was already dug, next to the statue of an angel with a missing head. The coffin carried. Not much weight to it, a little old lady and a child. And no noise from it. Not a dicky bird. What a brave boy was he.

The sister who clung to Tad-cu now gripped her mother's hand. All she could think of was the ugly claw that held her brother's hand so tightly under the dirt that was piling on top of them by the spadeful.

God bless him, an aunt said. Dear Lord look after him. He was a good boy. Too good for this world. That's why He wants him, probably.

The women all nodded as they waddled away from the graveside back to their housework and soap. The whistle blew for the shifts to change and the men went underground to renew their blisters and broken backs, and the vicar to his altar.

And Clifford's sister, the one who had wanted to kiss him, remembered her teacher telling her about Ancient Egypt at the time of the Old Testament. She remembered that when they buried a Pharaoh in a pyramid or tomb, they'd always bury something precious with them to accompany them into the afterlife.

And she thought to herself, that's what Mam-gu had done. It was as simple as that. She'd taken something precious. The most precious thing in all the world.

My brother.

Stephen Volk is best known as the creator of BBC TV's notorious Halloween mockumentary Ghostwatch *and the award-winning paranormal drama series* Afterlife. *His other screenplays include* The Awakening, *the miniseries* Midwinter of the Spirit, *and Ken Russell's cult classic* Gothic *starring Natasha Richardson as Mary Shelley. He is a BAFTA winner, a two-time British Fantasy Award winner, a Shirley Jackson Award and Bram Stoker Award finalist, and the author of four collections of short stories:* Dark Corners, Monsters in the Heart, The Parts We Play, *and* Lies of Tenderness. *His acclaimed Dark Masters trilogy consists of three novellas featuring Peter Cushing ("Whitstable"), Alfred Hitchcock ("Leytonstone") and Dennis Wheatley ("Netherwood")—with a guest appearance in the latter by Aleister Crowley. His most recent books are* Under a Raven's Wing, The Good Unknown and Other Ghost Stories, *and* The Confirmed Bachelors.

Visit www.stephenvolk.net *for more information on Stephen's work.*

JOHN LLEWELLYN PROBERT'S

POE OR LOVECRAFT? ROGER CORMAN'S *THE HAUNTED PALACE*

IN 1963, HORROR CINEMA WAS IN THE MIDST OF A FULL COLOUR RENAISSANCE, ONE WHICH HAD BEEN KICK-STARTED BY THE HUGE WORLDWIDE SUCCESS OF HAMMER'S 1957 *THE CURSE OF FRANKENSTEIN* and *Horror of Dracula* in 1958, and added to, both by further productions from Hammer and by other UK companies like Anglo Amalgamated. At the same time Italy was also in the throes of a colour gothic horror revolution spearheaded by directors Riccardo Freda (1962's *The Horrible Dr Hichcock*) and Mario Bava (1963's *Black Sabbath*). Meanwhile in the US, Samuel Z Arkoff and James H Nicholson's American International Pictures, a company previously known for their ability to make two films for the price of one, had taken a gamble with producer-director Roger Corman's suggestion that for a change they try making one picture for the price of two, and had scored a massive hit with their adaptation of Edgar Allan Poe's *House of Usher* (1960).

Horror icon Vincent Price as Roderick Usher in Corman's *House of Usher* (1960)

American International Pictures/MGM

More than any other production, *House of Usher* was the movie that made a horror star of leading man Vincent Price, and a follow-up was not long in coming. Arkoff and Nicholson once again engaged the services of Corman, Price, and screenwriter Richard Matheson for *The Pit and the Pendulum* (1961). After that, Corman entered into a minor financial dispute with AIP and decided to take his next Poe project elsewhere. Vincent Price was under exclusive contract to Arkoff and Nicholson, so Corman cast Ray Milland in the lead for *The Premature Burial* (1962) which he started off making for Pathé Lab, the company that developed movie prints for AIP and which wanted to move into film production and distribution. After this first Pathé production Corman intended to make a non-Poe film titled "The Haunted Village" starring Ray Milland, Hazel Court (who was also in *Premature Burial*), and Boris Karloff. Both Corman's and Pathé's plans were scuppered, however, by AIP head Sam Arkoff, who threatened to take all AIP lab work away from Pathé unless they

The Pit and The Pendulum (1961) AIP/MGM

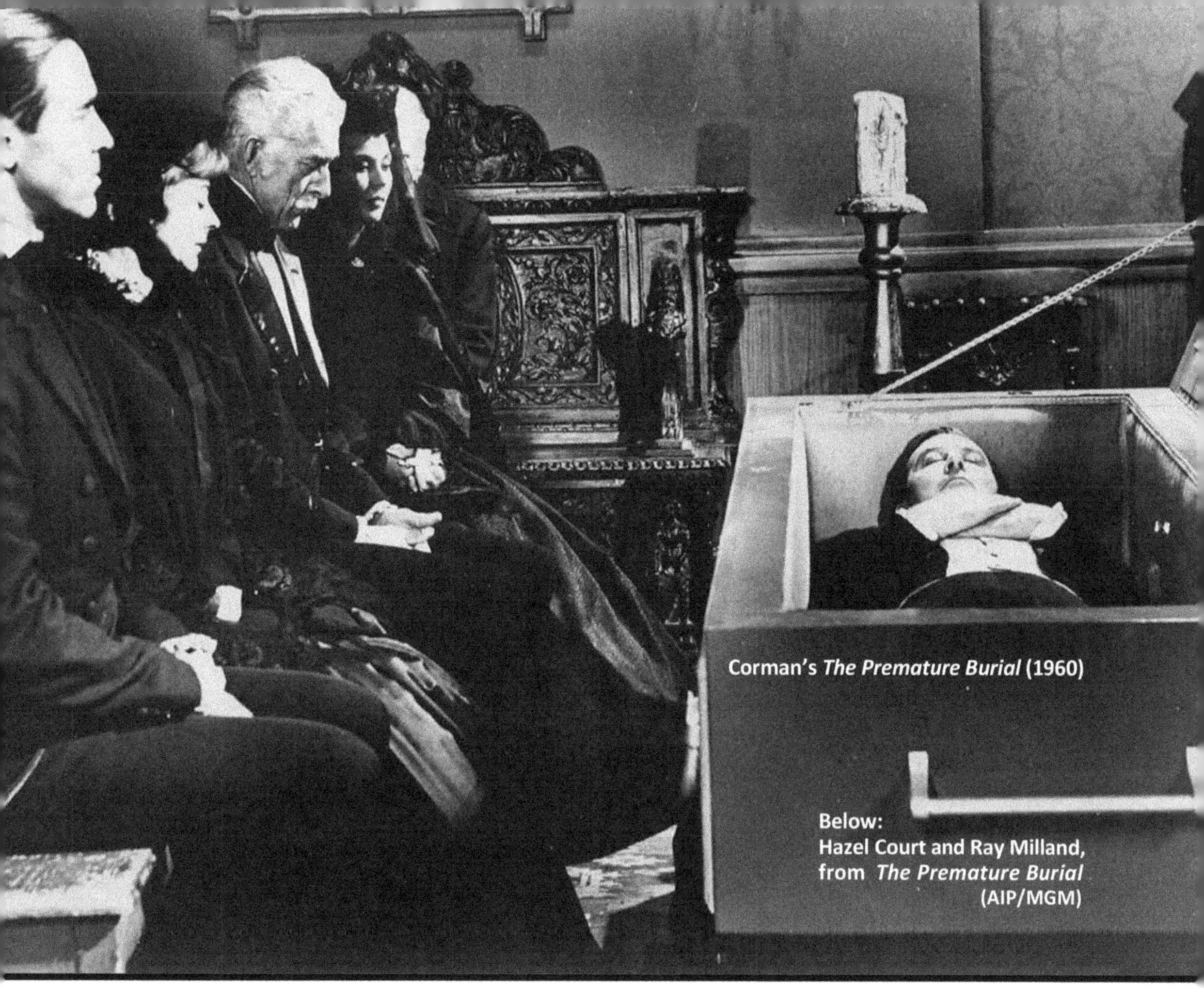

Corman's *The Premature Burial* (1960)

Below:
Hazel Court and Ray Milland, from *The Premature Burial* (AIP/MGM)

relinquished both those projects to American International. Thus, both movies became AIP productions, and by the time it came to shoot The Haunted Village it had been retitled "The Haunted Palace" by an AIP keen to continue capitalising on the success of their previous Edgar Allan Poe pictures. Milland and Court had been replaced by Vincent Price and Debra Paget, with Lon Chaney Jr. standing in for a Karloff who needed to cry off after contracting pneumonia shooting *Black Sabbath* for Mario Bava in Italy.

In issue 179 of his seminal *Video Watchdog* magazine, editor and critic Tim Lucas states that, while it might be not in league with popular opinion, he feels "*The Haunted Palace* may be the most frightening and confidently made of all the Poe films, at least of the American productions." Of course, Tim knows, as many reading this article will, that while AIP insisted on attaching Poe's name to it (and his poem to qualify the title), Roger Corman's *The Haunted Palace* actually boasts as its source a work by H P Lovecraft.

The Case of Charles Dexter Ward was one of the author's longer pieces (it actually clocks in at around 51,500 words) and was written in 1927 but not published until 1941, four years after Lovecraft's death, in the May and July issues of *Weird Tales* of that year. Corman's film was a conscious attempt to move away from Poe while still allowing him to work within the gothic milieu that he had established for himself so successfully. Instead of Richard Matheson, Corman turned to author and screenwriter Charles Beaumont to adapt the property. At the time, Beaumont was at the height of his powers. He was also incredibly busy and reportedly found it impossible to say no to projects. As a result, he frequently became overwhelmed and would turn to writer colleagues to help him out. Sometimes they received credit (the screenplay for *The Premature Burial* was co-written by Ray Russell, while *The Masque of the Red Death* would need the input of R Wright Campbell to fill up the script's running time by incorporating Poe's "Hop-Toad" into the screenplay), but not always. In the latter cases, this was because the contract Beaumont had signed stipulated he receive sole credit. However, authors he collaborated with in this manner have gone on record saying that Beaumont made that situation clear to them beforehand, and that he was always scrupulously honest in them always receiving a 50:50 split of the fee. It looks as if Beaumont had sufficient time to work on *The Haunted Palace* screenplay alone, and turned in a reasonably faithful work of which he was justifiably proud. In one of the introductions to the impressive, limited edition Centipede Press collection of Beaumont's work, *Mass for Mixed Voices*, the late author Dennis Etchison talks about attending the UCLA Advanced Science Fiction Workshop (one of the first of its kind) taught solely by Beaumont himself. In one of the sessions Beaumont took his class to a sneak preview of *The Haunted Palace*, told them all to invite friends, and when they turned up at the World Theater on Hollywood Boulevard, Beaumont bought tickets for everyone. "Needless to say," said Etchison, "we all applauded when his name came on screen."

The Haunted Palace broods over the fog-shrouded village of Arkham. (AIP/MGM)

So where better place than that opening credit sequence to begin our look at one of the most interesting, atmospheric, and artistically successful adaptations of H P Lovecraft's work, even if it's Edgar Allan Poe's name that appears above the title. Except that it doesn't, not quite. After the AIP logo, accompanied by a fanfare written by composer Ronald Stein, the first title card we see misspells Poe's name, so we get "Edgar Allen Poe's The Haunted Palace." As a spider weaves its web to trap a Milkweed butterfly (or Monarch in the US) in Armand Acosta's creepily designed title sequence, when Beaumont's screenwriting credit comes up they spell Poe's name wrong again ("based on a poem by"), but at least H P Lovecraft (spelt correctly) does get name checked for his source story. We'll talk about the principal cast and crew in a bit, but for now let's concentrate on composer Ronald Stein. Recruited because Corman felt regular AIP composer Les Baxter's scores were too anachronistic, *The Haunted Palace*, along with the previous *The Premature Burial*, represent the pinnacle of Stein's recording career. The main theme takes the form and structure of a macabre waltz, and we're going to hear numerous variations of it throughout the film. Stein was pretty much left alone to write the music and was able to experiment successfully with writing the main theme in the bass and having the harmonies playing above the tune. He repeated this technique in his subsequent score to *The Terror* (1963) but it's not something you encounter very often in film music of the period. The entire score was recorded in a single day and was performed by the Munich Symphony Orchestra over in Germany, all for budgetary reasons.

Leo Gordon and Elisha Cook Jr.

As the titles come to an end, we find ourselves in a superbly gloomy Panavision Arkham, and a street that was built by regular Corman art director Daniel Haller using forced perspective, which Corman then shot using wide angle lenses to make it look even bigger. The first two characters we see onscreen are Ezra Weeden (Leo Gordon) and Micah Smith (Elisha Cook Jr.). Both actors were familiar faces in Corman's (and AIP's) repertory company, with Gordon also being responsible for the screenplays for such low-budget fare as *The Wasp Woman* and *Attack of the Giant Leeches* (both 1959). They watch through a tavern window as a young woman (Darlene Lucht, who would go on to appear in *Five Bloody Graves* for Al Adamson in 1969) walks in a trance down the high street. They follow as she passes through a moodily lit (by Corman regular cinematographer Floyd Crosby), gorgeously designed graveyard to arrive at the "Palace" of the title. It's the home of Joseph Curwen (Vincent Price in the first of two roles). While Ezra and Micah go

A gothic ritual ends in terror for Darlene Lucht when she sees what's lurking beneath the grate.

back to town, Curwen and his accomplice Hester (Cathie Merchant, whose only major role this was) lead the girl across an impressive set, through a secret door next to the fireplace, and down into a dungeon the size of a warehouse, all to Ronald Stein's theme rendered appropriately *maestoso.*

Our victim is chained up, and we quickly realise there's something horrible lurking in the pit beneath her. We don't see it, but she does, and it's ghastly enough to break the mesmeric spell she has been placed under. Meanwhile the torch-wielding mob has arrived. Curwen is dragged outside while it transpires Ezra is actually the husband of Hester, whom the devilish Curwen has obviously lured away with his promises of unholy delights. If that's true, then she's certainly looking good on it. In a scene which echoes the opening of Mario Bava's 1960 *Black Sunday* (and a number of other, subsequent Italian gothics) Curwen is burned at the stake, but not before he has cursed his executioners, vowing he will return to take revenge on the descendants of those who caused his death.

This entire opening sequence lasts just over ten minutes and forms an exciting and vibrant prologue to the main story, succinctly setting the scene and establishing the atmosphere for what is to come. We then jump forward 110 years as we hear Vincent Price's voice reciting lines 41–44 of Poe's poem "The Haunted Palace," which can be found in its entirety within Poe's tale "The Fall of the House of Usher": "And travellers, now, within that valley, through the red-litten windows see vast forms, that move fantastically to a discordant melody." The words are spoken over a lovely, gloomy matte painting of Arkham. It seems the weather hasn't changed much over all that time, and it's still pretty foggy, as Charles Dexter Ward (Price again) arrives in the town with his new bride Ann (Debra Paget). Paget had also appeared in the M. Valdemar sequence of *Tales of Terror* for Corman the previous year. *The Haunted Palace* was her final film role, after which she married a Chinese millionaire, retired from acting, and became a born-again evangelical Christian with her own Christian TV show in the 1990s.

Carmody (I. Stanford Jolley) the coachman hangs around just long enough to warn the couple that the town is cursed. It's certainly empty, but that's because everyone

seems to be in the pub. The Wards enjoy an "American Werewolf in London" moment on entering The Burning Man as chatter ceases and everyone stares at them. The landlord is played by Bruno VeSota, another Corman regular, although he's probably best known as Yvette Vickers' cuckolded husband in Bernard L Kowalski's *Attack of the Giant Leeches* (1959). He denies any knowledge of the place the Wards are looking for, while Leo Gordon, playing his own descendant (as do several of the cast) gets to utter Beaumont's delicious line "It isn't a house, it's a madman's palace, as old as sin," apparently brought over from somewhere in Europe and rebuilt "stone by stone." Eventually Dr. Willet (prolific character actor Frank Maxwell who was also in Corman's classic 1961 William Shatner-starring tale of racism *The Intruder*, also written by Charles Beaumont) gives them directions and they make their way there, encountering an eyeless, web-fingered child on the way.

The Wards get their first look at their new home to Ronald Stein's creeping, crawling underscore, and what a gorgeous, expansive Daniel Haller set they wander into, complete with Joseph Curwen portrait hanging over the fireplace. Some of the rooms are festooned with cobwebs, and someone has left a live snake in a desk. Charles seems to have an uncanny knowledge of the layout of the place despite never having been there before. As they wander up a broad stone staircase Stein's main theme gets a reprise, coming to an abrupt halt at the appearance of Lon Chaney Jr. Chaney was past his career peak here by some years, but was certainly still capable of giving performances of note, both in this and after, when he went on to star in Don Sharp's *Witchcraft* (1964) and Jack Hill's *Spider Baby* (1967), Here Chaney is Simon the "caretaker" (actually one of Joseph Curwen's long-living warlock compatriots), and he is currently getting the Wards' rooms ready in the dark because he is "accustomed to it."

Note the blue candles in the Wards' bedroom that contrast with the red ones downstairs. Daniel Haller was keen on using different vividly coloured candles, perhaps most notably in Corman's later *The Masque of the Red Death*. There's also a lot of blue used in the look of this film, from Curwen's blue-themed portrait (and Price's subsequent makeup) to the very lightning itself that we'll be seeing in a bit, sometimes flashing across a castle stock shot from *The Pit and the Pendulum*.

Charles and Ann have decided to spend the night. Meanwhile back in Arkham, Edgar Weeden (Leo Gordon) is having a bit of trouble with the carnivorous, green-clawed thing he's keeping locked in his attic. This scene also provides, and blink and you'll miss it, an appearance from Corman standby Barboura Morris as Edgar's wife. Morris had previously starred in Corman's *A Bucket of Blood* and *The Wasp Woman* (1959) and would go on to appear in Daniel Haller's second attempt at filming Lovecraft, AIP's *The Dunwich Horror* (1970). Back at the palace, Charles Dexter Ward stares a bit too long at that portrait of his ancestor and becomes possessed by him. The process is all conveyed to the audience via a fine piece of acting from Price, while Simon observes the proceeding from afar.

Chaney, Price, and Paget.

The next morning Ann is all packed to leave, but Charles now wants to stay, and we know why, although for the moment his

possession by Curwen is only temporary. Charles and Ann head to Arkham high street where they find everything closed. In a superbly eerie and disorientating sequence that must have been all the more effective back in 1963, they are approached by a group of silent townsfolk with abnormal gaits and boasting strange facial abnormalities including absent eyes, all rendered by makeup artist Ted Coodley, who was no doubt making the most of limited resources. At dinner that night, Dr. Willet explains about these mutated townsfolk as part of a monologue that in part explains to Charles and Ann what we saw in the film's prologue. Apparently, he says, Joseph Curwen was a warlock who had gained possession of the Necronomicon. This was the first time Lovecraft's legendary tome had been mentioned in popular cinema, and the same goes for the concept of the Elder Gods. Frank Maxwell is the lucky actor who gets to wrap his tongue around names like Cthulhu and Yog-Sothoth, and he does a pretty good job. Curwen was trying to mate human women with the Elder Gods to create a new race but ended up with mutated births, the genes of which have apparently persisted in the town for the last hundred years or so.

That night Ward hears the ghostly voices of the mob who burned his ancestor and, at Simon's suggestion, stares at the painting, becoming Curwen once more. Simon has brought the Necronomicon and gets Curwen up to speed with events, after which they are joined by Jabez (Milton Parsons) to re-form the original trio of warlocks described by Dr. Willets at dinner. Parsons was a prolific character actor with close to 200 credits that included *The Twilight Zone* as well as bit parts in 1970s TV horrors like *The Cat Creature* (1973) and *The Dead Don't Die* (1975).

Dr. Willet (Frank Maxwell) tells the Wards (Price and Paget) about Curwen's failed attempts to mate humans with the Elder Gods of Lovecraft's Cthulhu Mythos, which have resulted in the horribly disfigured mutants now roaming the streets of Arkham.

Despite Charles fighting hard for possession of his own body, Curwen is soon digging up Hester while the locals get to have another grumble at the doctor in the tavern. Ann has a very cold exchange with Curwen (nice acting from both) after which Curwen and Ward have a battle of wills (even nicer acting from Price) witnessed by Ann who by now must be thinking her husband is suffering from a case of split personality. The warlocks have carried Hester's coffin into the dungeon where it's ready to be opened. Meanwhile Debra Paget gives "good gothic heroine" as she gets out of bed and creeps downstairs (some lovely lighting effects here from Floyd Crosby) in a lengthy sequence, only for Simon to confront her and carry her back up. Meanwhile Hester is looking a bit rough after all that time in the grave, but Curwen is determined to persist with getting her up and about.

The next morning Charles, now himself again, tries to leave with Ann, but Curwen is getting too strong, and Charles doesn't even get as far as the front door before his face has turned grey and he's denying to Dr. Willet that he's had anything to do with last night's episode of grave-robbing. Happy that Ward is now effectively "dead" Curwen is now free to get on with the serious job of mating women with monsters, but not before he has a little revenge

Jabez (Milton Parsons) and Simon (Chaney) advise Curwen (Price) to forget his campaign of revenge.

Curwen: "I'll not have my fill of revenge until this village is a graveyard."

Below: The grave has not been kind to Curwen's accomplice, ~~Hester~~ (Cathie Merchant)

to take care of first. Ann decides to stay with "Charles" despite his insistence she leave. In a nice low angle shot filmed through a flickering fireplace, Curwen says he might need her after all, and we the audience all know what that means.

Back at the tavern the locals are still convinced Ward was responsible for digging up Hester's grave. We also get a handy brief reminder of who the descendants of the original burning are. Weeden is keen that they get Ward before he gets them, but the rest aren't so sure. That's bad news for Weeden, as we see someone unlock that attic door to release whatever he has been keeping in there. There's a nice gliding camera approach to Weeden's house as we see, though the window, something come downstairs. Then we're inside with Weeden who hears clicks and grunts emanating from the darkness. Weeden burns to death, the victim of his own offspring, as Curwen, who has made a list presumably in case he forgets who he's supposed to be having revenge on next, tears the first name off it. The next day, at Weeden's funeral, Smith (Elisha Cook Jr) gets the look from Curwen and, sure enough, that night he meets with his own conflagration on the splendidly foggy Arkham high street.

"I'll not have my fill of revenge until this village is a graveyard," Curwen tells his warlock colleagues downstairs in the palace. Meanwhile poor old Debra Paget, who seems to end up in bed quite a lot in this film, is back in one yet again, this time about to be threatened by Curwen, who she eventually manages to fight off. Curwen returns to his dungeon and Hester's corpse. Meanwhile Dr. Willet comes calling and wants Ann,

Not exactly the best way to be the toast of the town.

Left: Jabez and Hester prepare Ann for the mating ritual.

now back downstairs, to tell him everything. Curwen interrupts the two of them as Ann is trying to attack his portrait with a poker. Curwen takes the doctor aside and explains how the house is having a strange effect on "his" wife. He asks the doctor to take Ann back to Boston, with the suggestion she be placed in a hospital there. Again, we the audience know what that means. By the way, in the original story Charles Dexter Ward is from Rhode Island, and some have suggested the script uses Boston as his hometown in an attempt to squeeze in another connection to Poe.

Back in the dungeon, the Hester reanimation project has once again been resumed, while in Arkham the body of Gideon Leach (extremely busy character actor Guy Wilkerson whose only Corman picture this was) has been found burned to death. The townsfolk are understandably restless, but before they form a torch-wielding mob the doctor and Ann, who have just arrived there, set off back to the palace to warn "Ward." By now, if not before, we can see that Corman's considerable skills as a director aren't quite sufficient to distract us

from the fact that this film features an awful lot of to-ing and fro-ing, both from upstairs to downstairs in the palace, and from the palace to Arkham and back.

Hester is finally up and about again, which just goes to show that all you need if you're a necromancer is a little persistence. The mob sets off while Ann and the doctor reach the palace. They find the door to the secret passage and are soon in the dungeon. They (and we) get their first real glimpse of the greenish thing that's been living beneath the iron grating all these years, while, as they make their way between the tombstones, the mob is doing an excellent job of looking like they belong in a much earlier Universal horror picture, or even several (it was often the same footage). Curwen and his helpers appear at the top of the stairs in the dungeon (where have they been?) and soon Ann is chained up to become the latest subject of Curwen's attempts at crossbreeding with other-dimensional entities. The grating is raised, and we get a blurry image of a multi-limbed and roaring, if somewhat static, creature. Apparently Corman was so unhappy with the monster that he rang

classic AIP monster maker Paul Blaisdell (who provided the monster suits for 1956's *It Conquered the World* and *The She Creature*, amongst others) to help out. When it became apparent Corman wasn't actually willing to pay Blaisdell any money the special effects artist understandably bowed out.

The mob storms the palace and sets it on fire. As the painting is consumed Curwen leaves Ward's body, enabling him to free Ann who is taken to safety by the doctor. Most of the time the fire we see is unique to this film, but there are a couple of insert shots of Corman's burning barn footage, originally filmed for 1960's *House of Usher* and still being used as late as 1980 for the climax of Joe Dante's *The Howling.*

The doctor retrieves Ward from the conflagration, but it looks as if he might actually have rescued Curwen in the kind of shock ending audiences were probably expecting from these films from *The Pit and the Pendulum* onwards. The film is rounded out with Price quoting lines 45–48 of the final stanza of Poe's poem, "...While, like a ghastly rapid river, through the pale door, a hideous throng rush out forever and laugh— But smile no more." Poe's name is spelt correctly this time. Perhaps his spirit had a word with someone during the course of the running time.

A fifteen-day shoot (par for the course with the Corman Poes) and a final dialogue polish from Francis Ford Coppola (who also

helped with line readings) all contributed to *The Haunted Palace* being ready for its US release, which was staggered in different cities (as was the way then) over August and September 1963. In the UK the film failed to secure a release until February 1966 when it went out as half of a double-bill with production designer-turned director Daniel Haller's *Die Monster Die* (1965). Reviews were, on the whole, typical of the period's disdain for such fare, with the most complimentary coming from Tom Milne of the UK's *Financial Times*, who wrote "Vincent Price gives a superb performance as a New England warlock who is burned alive for his evil practices ... to wreak a picturesque revenge well-seasoned with ground fogs, creaking doors, cobwebs, electric storms and mutant monsters." Corman subsequently said that he had never intended to create a Lovecraft cycle to equal his Poe pictures, but AIP were obviously keen to have a couple more goes, with *Die Monster Die* in 1965 and *The Dunwich Horror* in 1970. Both were hampered by the essential difficulty of rendering some of Lovecraft's more interesting ideas (for example, a colour that has never been seen before) onscreen. It seems the most adaptable Lovecraft was picked first, and at just the right time that Stein, Haller, Crosby, and of course Price and Corman were able to do it the most justice.

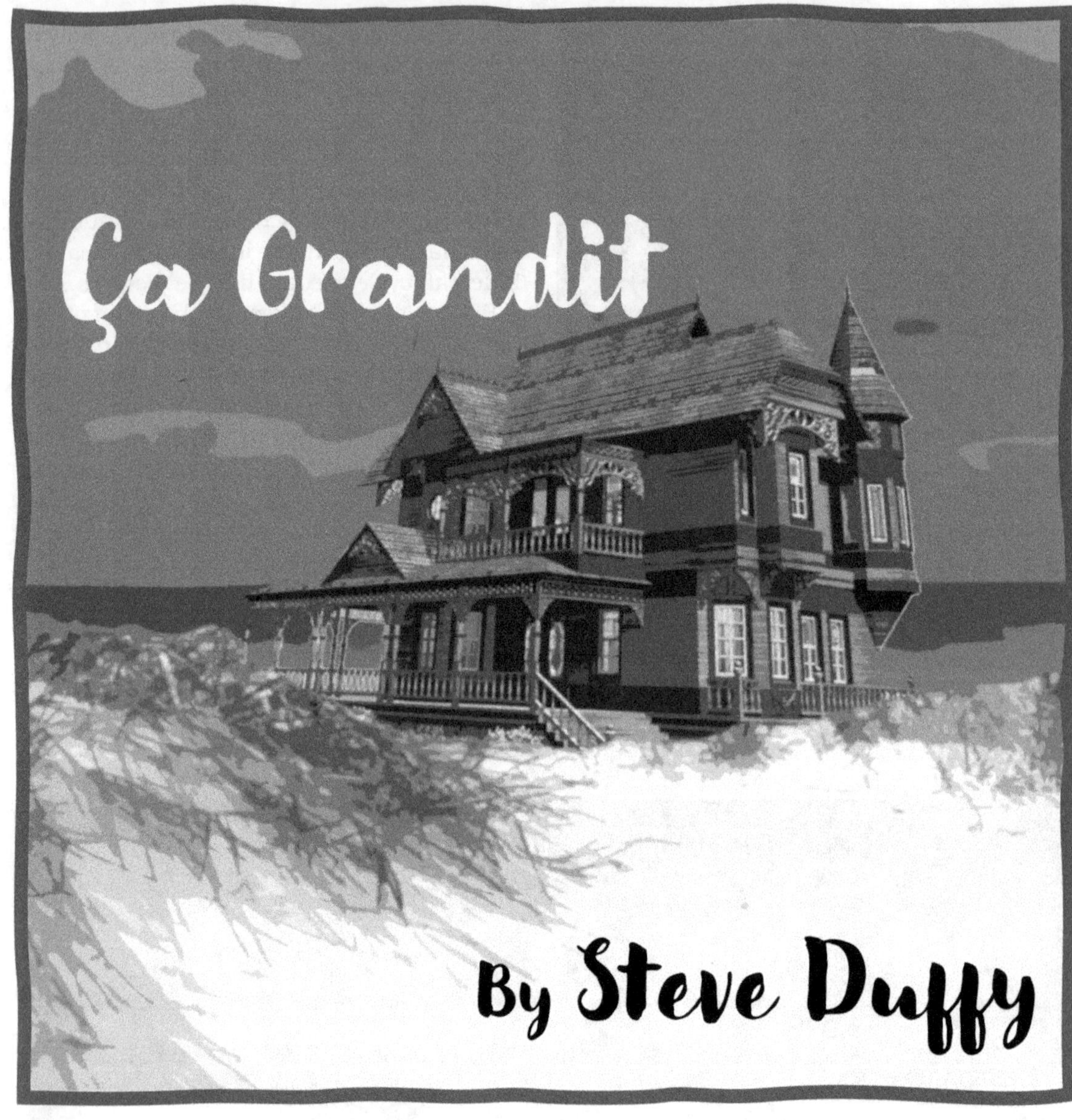

Ça Grandit

By Steve Duffy

"IT WON'T BE LONG NOW," HIS COUSIN SAID FROM THE SEAT OPPOSITE.

"I don't remember any of this," he said, turning away from the window. "Did it always take this long?"

"Time ran differently when we were kids," Christine said mildly. It was very much the sort of thing he remembered her saying, when he thought about her at all, which wasn't often.

"Is there much more of it, do you think?" He got to his feet and tugged at the sliding window in the carriage door. "I've absolutely no idea where we are," he muttered, as it screeched halfway open.

"Can't you smell the salt marshes? We can't be far away."

He'd slumped back into his corner of the carriage, lighting a cigarette as if to block out the seaside smell. A shrug was his only response.

"How long is it since the last time you were here, Nick?"

He considered. "Years. I mean, obviously years, but years and years. I was still at Pinningfold, I think—end of the Lent term? No, summer vac. The summer before I left, now I come to think of it."

"So you'd have been...?"

"Sixteen, just. Remember, I was asked to leave Pinningfold embarrassingly early, at the end of the autumn term. Finished up at St Godric's. About the only place that'd have me—damaged goods." He laughed.

"That'd be 1957, then. Gosh, fourteen years ago."

"I suppose so." He swung his legs up on the cushioned bench seat. "How about you?"

"Oh, I came twice a year, every year for a long time," she said. "It was our regular meet-up, back then, wasn't it, holidays at Aunt Dora's? The last time for me would have been, let's see, seven Christmases ago?" She paused for a moment. "Anyway, that means the last time we were there *together* would have been the summer of '57. All summer long it was you and me, the good old days."

"Don't remember it." And after a pause, "God, that sounds awful—don't take that the wrong way or anything. I'm sure we had a fantastic time. The thing is, you see, I actually remember very little about Aunt Dora's place."

"Really?" She seemed startled.

"Oh yes." He blew smoke out in a long exhalation that merged into a yawn. "Everything's sort of blurred into everything else when it comes to Auntie's. It's all like one long and rather boring day-trip, and when you got there everything was closed."

"I used to look forward to it so much," Christine said. "It was so romantic, Le Grand Maximin, the big house on the coast, like a fairytale. It just seemed a thousand miles away from Haywards Heath."

Nicholas shrugged again. "They couldn't wait to get rid of us, could they? Your father, my mother... do you suppose they wanted us out of the way so they could console each other back home in Blighty? Brother and sister, the dignified widower and the brave military widow? Stranger things have happened."

"That's horrible. No, don't laugh, it's horrible."

"I don't know, I think it's rather charming, myself. If a trifle reminiscent of Greek mythology. See, that expensive public school education was good for something after all." She frowned, and he went on carelessly:

"I mean, the funny part of it is, they didn't even stop to think what sort of an environment they were sending us into. Maybe they thought it was like *Heidi*, with warm fresh goat's milk and soft white rolls. Not a glorified loony bin at the back end of nowhere."

"I don't remember you complaining at the time."

"Pervy Aunt Dora, the debutante occultist of the 1918 season." He grinned.

"You are awful, Nick. Honestly."

"Well, she married money, didn't she, some bloke twice her age and then some, and voila! he had the good grace to pop his clogs before the year was out. But he was rich, wasn't he? Our families were practically paupers by comparison. That was what swung it, don't you think, our being allowed to stay with her in the holidays? The prospect of an inheritance, all in good time."

"I thought you were happy at Aunt Dora's," she said in a small voice. "I used to be."

"Was I, though? Do you know, it's hard to say. It was the sort of place people went, the South of France, it had that going for it. It was a glamorous sounding location, if you'd never actually seen Auntie's place, that is. Gave me something to boast about to the other boys. I think I might have spiced it up a bit in the retelling, actually." He paused, as if some long-buried memory was coming back to him. "Do you know, I *did*. I told the boys at Pinningfold that I'd met a girl there, and we'd had a torrid seaside romance in the long vac."

"Nicholas, you didn't!"

"I did, though. It might have accelerated the process of my departure, when word got out." He grinned. "I said she looked like Brigitte Bardot. Naturally."

"You're hopeless. Did she have a name, this fantasy girl?"

"Can't remember," he said, after a little while. "They all fell for it, anyway."

She scoffed. "Boys. Aunt Dora said that was all they ever thought about."

"Oh, Aunt Dora! She was a fine one to talk. She had a positively filthy mind on the Q.T., did old Dora Sarony. No need to look outraged, Chrissie. Five minutes' browsing through her library would have told you as much. Jammed full of the kinkiest occult rubbish. She may have looked like Miss Marple, but she was a proper degenerate when you got right down to it. The stuff she used to talk about! The books she gave me—I don't suppose dear Mama would have been half so keen on my coming here, if she'd only known."

"Your mum wouldn't have minded you reading. Reading's different from..." She let the thought lapse.

"From 'doing it'?" He laughed. "Yes, well, that was one reason I lost interest in holidays with Auntie." He flicked ash on the floor of the compartment. "Not that I was asked back after that last summer, come to think of it." He yawned, stretched out his legs across the length of the train seat. "*You* were still welcome, obviously. I mean, you were modesty incarnate back then. Probably still are, come to that," he added carelessly. There was no wedding ring on her finger—he'd made a point of checking when he'd met her at the station in Arles.

Christine blushed. "Funny, isn't it, that we haven't met up since August 1957," she said. It felt to Nicholas very much as if she was changing the subject. "After spending all those summers together before that."

"Not really that funny, when you think about it. My dear mama pegged out in the spring of, let's see, 1960, I was off furthering my education, you were... what were you doing?"

"I got a job," she said. "As a nanny, in Belgravia."

"After finishing school, was this?" She didn't answer. "Well, there you are. We might have bumped into each other on the escalators at Sloane Square tube, I suppose, round about 1965 or whenever. I'd have been heading for the King's Road, I hasten to add, not Eaton Square."

"Well, we're together again now. Oh, Nick, it'll feel very strange without her." They'd both received letters from Aunt Dora's solicitor, a Maître Lacombe, advising them that their aunt had died—how exactly, he didn't say—and summoning them to the Camargue to hear the reading of her will.

"Are we her only relatives? We must be. I wonder who gets what?" For the first time he seemed animated.

"There's the housekeeper, of course, Madame Duveen."

"Eh? Housekeeper, you say? Did Auntie have a housekeeper when we were there?" Nicholas screwed his face up in recollection. "She must have, I suppose: can't see her cooking and cleaning, now I come to think of it. Not to worry, it'll be a token bequest at most to the domestic staff, a few hundred quid or something."

"Nicholas, of course she had a housekeeper! You must remember Lélie! Madame Duveen?"

He spread his hands wide, palms up. "She must have been fascinating."

"You really don't remember any of it, do you? That's so strange."

"What can I say? I've had a lot on my mind."

"Perhaps it'll come back to you when we're there," she said, eyes on his sulky adolescent face that had changed remarkably little down the years. The cares of adulthood, she thought, barely registered on it.

"If we ever do get there," he yawned.

Christine turned her attention to the scenery. "It looks like a maze, doesn't it?" she said, half to herself.

Nicholas lit a fresh cigarette from the butt of the previous one. "What does?"

"These bushes—the way they break up the grassland. Like Hampton Court on the grand scale."

"Mazes are regular," he said. "Symmetrical. That's how you find your way around them. If they looked like this you'd never get out."

"If you saw it from the air," she said, "it'd probably look like the surface of the brain."

"A brain? How on earth do you work that out?"

"Surely you know what a brain looks like, Nick. The folds, the, what d'you call them, the convolutions. The shapes they make on the surface of the cortex. They're rounded, natural, like these bushes. From the air." She gave up. "It doesn't matter."

"So we're travelling across a massive brain. By train, across the brain." He saw the corners of her mouth turned down, tried to make an overture. "It's a surrealist masterpiece. Wish we'd get where we're going, though. It's been hours."

"Do you like the surrealists?"

Nicholas shrugged. "Take them or leave them, really."

"I think they're fascinating. There's no element of time in those paintings, you know?"

"How do you mean?"

"You've seen those Dalis, Magrittes, de Chiricos? They all look static, inert, as if time had been drained out of them. As if the clocks had failed, and everything had come to a halt... I don't know. They almost frighten me, sometimes. Some of them." Which took Nicholas by surprise, a little. This depth of aesthetic insight didn't fit with the Christine of his memory, such as it was, the Christine of fourteen summers ago, a prim and sunny schoolgirl all eager smiles and sudden seriousness, polite beyond her years, eyes the colour of violets.

"Hang on." Nicholas hauled himself upright. The progress of of the train, already glacial, was becoming slower still. "I think we might be here."

"Are we?" Christine joined him at the window. The train was rasping to a halt alongside a bare stretch of platform—no ticket office, not even a shelter from the elements, just twenty yards of mossy concrete. "Oh yes! This is it. I remember it as if it were yesterday."

"Really?" He eased down their cases from the luggage rack. "Didn't there used to be, I don't know, more of it?"

"No, you idiot," Christine said. "I think you're growing senile in your old age."

"Eight months older than you, that's all," he muttered, opening the carriage door as the train took one last jerk into inertia. "Then again, I've had a hard life."

NOBODY ELSE ALIGHTED; nobody was waiting to get on. Neither driver nor conductor was in evidence, and there was no porter waiting to carry their luggage as they stepped down on to the platform. A dusty footpath crossed the farther end of the track, where unpainted wooden buffers marked the terminus of the branch line. Away off in the distance a bicyclist was heading down the path towards them; nothing else was stirring in all that wide and patient desolation.

Hacking up a cough of steam, the train began to reverse back down the track. "It's going a damn sight faster backwards than it did forwards," Nicholas said resentfully. As it slid away into the long light of the advancing afternoon, he felt an unexpected throb of unease, for no reason he could understand. In his head it was still the Seventies; and yet here at this countryside halt he felt stranded in some version of the past in which he had no agency, over which he could exert no influence. Modernity, where he'd planted his flag, seemed to have no relevance in these surroundings. Even the man on the bicycle might have been arriving in a tranquil afternoon some year before the war; before the first war, quite plausibly.

Christine was waving the cyclist to a stop as he drew level with the platform. Nicholas marvelled at his suit of heavy dark material, topped with an old-fashioned bowler hat. He must have been sweating like a pig, for all that the day's warmth was more than half expended. As he pulled up, Christine began to speak, then stopped. She was looking at the stranger with curiosity, as if he sparked some memory that lay just below the threshold of retrieval.

It was left to Nicholas to ask the question. *"Excusez-moi, monsieur, c'est par là pour Le Grand Maximin?"* He pointed left and right, up and down the path. And when the man didn't answer straight away, *"La maison de Sarony?"* The man stared at him, then at Christine, before mutely indicating the direction from which he'd been pedalling. He remained in place, propped on one dusty foot, while the two visitors set off, suitcases in hand. Only when Nicholas looked back, some dozen paces along the path, did he push off and resume his slow weaving way towards wherever.

"Les habitants du pays sont très sympathiques," he commented, in the crisply stressed measures of the old French primer from boarding school.

"He's not a *paysan*, he's a schoolteacher."

"How on earth do you know that? Or is it an inspired guess?"

"I remember him from my visits. He's from the village."

"Don't see what a schoolteacher would have been doing at Aunt Dora's."

"Probably paying his respects," she said. "People were very respectful of her, hereabouts, the community. The village is only a few miles that way," pointing behind them.

"I don't remember her having much to do with the locals. I mean, admittedly I can't even remember Madame What'sername the hired help, so that's not necessarily an endorsement of my powers of recall, but I can't remember anyone else, ever. Just us."

"We wouldn't have paid much attention to them," she said. "We were mostly bound up in each other."

"H'mm. Well, I shouldn't think the God-fearing provincial folk were falling over themselves to make the acquaintance of some mad old Englishwoman half-cracked on decadent literature."

"Oh Nick, stop it. She wasn't mad, whatever she was. You don't know what her life was like."

"I know it'd have driven me bloody crazy. Out here at the back end of nowhere."

"She read a lot," Christine said, half to herself it seemed. "That library."

"That library indeed. There's no smut like *fin-de-siècle* French smut, that's what I say."

"Stop being so prurient, Nicholas. It wasn't all smut."

"No, there was all the other junk as well. *Démonologie*—it sounds fancier in French, doesn't it?"

"It's the last thing you'd expect," Christine conceded.

"Or it's the first thing. It's actually just what you'd expect to happen when a repressed old biddy who's locked herself away from the world lets her mind run on the sins of the flesh and goes bonkers. I mean, de Plancy and the *Cultes des Goules*, at her age? Really!"

Christine didn't answer. Nicholas wasn't used to being ignored.

"Can you imagine Auntie D staying up at nights in that draughty old pile, bedsheets pulled up to her chin—her *chins*, I should say—reading Huysmans and Crowley and *Les Litanies de Satan*? Textbook repression." A theatrical shudder. "Old maid looking for cheap thrills. All that sex impulse backed up and curdled. Don't you agree?"

He was saying it mostly to get a rise out of her, but still she didn't react. After a few more yards he switched his suitcase from right hand to left and resumed, more sincerely: "No, but it's a sad thing when you think about it. What a way to spend your life."

This time she rose to the bait. "So you think, what, she should have fulfilled her biological destiny after all? Found someone else to impregnate her? Procreated, multiplied? She left England to get away from all that."

"And much good it did her."

"At least she didn't marry some chinless wonder and become some... I don't know, some Home Counties *breeder*."

"Gosh, you put it so romantically, Chrissie."

"Well, you exasperate me sometimes."

She strode off, taking no notice of the penitent face he was making. He called her name again, then when she didn't wait for him hurried to catch up with her. She turned round, mouth open to say something, then her eyes caught something behind him and widened in surprise. "Don't look now," she said, "but we've got company."

IT WAS THE CYCLIST from before, pedalling back towards them. The path had begun to undulate, up and down, at the foot of a line of sand dunes, and by the time he caught up with them he was red-faced and panting beneath his thick felt bowler. Nicholas was reminded of Christine's comment about the surrealists: this man seemed to have bicycled straight out of a Magritte painting.

It took him a moment or two to catch his breath. Speaking, eventually, to Christine: "You are the family of the late Madame Sarony?"

"Yes," she said. "I'm Christine, and this is my cousin Nicholas. I've been thinking since we saw you just now—I know you, don't I?" She frowned. "Sorry, your name won't come."

"Prevel," he said, raising his hat. "I am the schoolmaster of the village."

"Astounding, Holmes," Nicholas muttered to Christine. He waved away the quizzical look turned on him by M Prevel. "Sorry, don't mind us. Private joke."

"You are going to the house? Of course you are." His English was surprisingly good, not idiomatic exactly but with the formal precision of book-learning; he aspirated each H with precision. "You are expected. I have just left Madame Duveen, and she assures me that all is in order." He hesitated for a second, hat in hand, twisting the brim this way and that, then went on, "I believe some years have passed since you last visited Le Grand Maximin."

"Yes," Christine admitted. "It's been a while. Nicholas went to work at an auctioneer's straight from university, and, you see, I had my job in London." She was blushing; Nicholas was sure M Prevel had noticed it as well.

"She spoke of you often. You are her only relatives in England, yes?"

"She'd cut herself off from everyone else, you see," Nicholas explained. "My late mama hadn't clapped eyes on her since her marriage. Same with Christine's pater. Father, you know," unsure whether M Prevel would be familiar with the word.

"But you came often." M Prevel was addressing himself to Christine.

"You have a good memory, monsieur," she said. "It was a very long time ago."

"The circumstances were not usual," he said. Christine blushed, but did not look away.

"Actually, it's me who's struggling to remember much," Nicholas put in. They both ignored him, regarding one another gravely, as old chess adversaries will sometimes study each other instead of the board.

"Is Mâitre Lacombe the lawyer at the house, do you know, M Prevel?"

"Indeed he is," the schoolteacher said. "He gave me to understand that all the necessary papers are assembled."

"Good," Nicholas said, and again neither of them so much as looked at him.

"It's such a long time since I was at Aunt Dora's," Christine said. "Seven years."

"I think you will find it remarkably unchanged."

"Good," she said, "good. That is, I suppose so." Nicholas wondered why she'd added the qualification.

"It is an…an arresting house, is that the word in English? It makes a certain impression. Almost a Gothic aspect." The schoolteacher seemed to feel that exactitude was important in all matters. "Perhaps not the sort of place in which I should want to raise a child."

"We were very happy here," Christine said, ignoring Nicholas's surreptitious nudge. "Very happy."

"I do not think the place has changed. Perhaps you have. Yes, I think you are changed."

Nicholas wanted to warn M Prevel away from encroaching on their private lives, but before he could find the words Christine was speaking again.

"Of course I am," she said, showing no sign of being offended. "It's been seven years—fourteen for my cousin. But some things stay the same."

"All of us have no doubt changed since the first time we set foot on Madame Sarony's estate. Even your aunt: I am sure you would have noticed a difference by the end."

"That seems impossible," she said seriously. "I've got this very fixed picture in my mind."

"She grew more and more fatigued in her latter years," M Prevel said, and he hesitated again, searching for words, or perhaps reviewing them before giving them voice. "Drained. The burden of looking after…"

"The estate?" Nicholas would not be excluded any longer. "I'm sure she made an excellent job of it."

"He doesn't mean the estate, Nick," Christine said, and stopped, though Nicholas was sure she'd been about to say more. What else could he mean, though?

To Christine, M Prevel said, "*Toutes ses obligations.*" And in an undertone, so that Nicholas had to strain to hear, "*Surtout, le babaloum.*"

"The what?" The man could speak perfectly good English, so why had he lapsed back into French? He'd hardly caught that last word, and what he'd thought he'd heard didn't register with him. "What did you say?"

Christine, under her breath: "For God's sake, Nicholas, he said 'all her obligations.' You know French well enough."

"And he knows English," in the same undertone.

"You're not in England now."

"No," M Prevel said, "no, this is not England. There is much that is different." And looking directly at Nicholas, for the first time: "She said you would not remember. She guaranteed it."

Nicholas let his suitcase fall to the sandy ground. Throwing down his half-smoked Dunhill, he ground it under his sole. It was a petty gesture, but it was that or engage in a stand-up argument with the schoolteacher—not that he cared about M Prevel's feelings, but it would only lead to more conflict with Christine. Turning aside, he cupped the flame of his Ronson as he lit a fresh cigarette.

The other two hadn't even noticed. Their conversation continued as before, with Christine asking under her breath: *"Et qu'en est-il de la... de le babaloum?"* That word again, and still he had no idea what on earth they were talking about.

"Ça grandit," the schoolteacher said in the same half-whisper. For a moment, nobody spoke. Three silent statues on the sandy coastal path, Christine and M Prevel *tête-à-tête*, Nicholas standing pointedly to one side; characters from an absurdist play waiting for prompts from an absent stage manager.

Nicholas broke the silence: "We'd better be going. Come on, Chrissie." As if this were the cue for which they'd all been waiting, M Prevel swung his leg back over the crossbar of his bicycle.

"I am sure M Lacombe will answer all your questions, mademoiselle. Lélie also. To the best of their ability." His face was set unreadably. "They have been faithful in the execution of their duties. I shall continue in my own role, or not, as you wish."

"Excuse me, monsieur—I don't quite understand how any of this concerns you?" Nicholas challenged him.

"I too have my duties, monsieur," he said, steadying himself on the toe of one boot, on which all his attention seemed to be fixed.

"Duties?" Nicholas was tired of being talked past. "What duties could you possibly have at Aunt Dora's?"

"La pédagogie," he said shortly. "What else?" He pushed down on the pedals and wobbled away from them. Before he passed out of earshot, they heard his last words, thrown back over his shoulder: "Perhaps you will be more successful than I."

"WHAT THE HELL did he mean, *'la pédagogie'*? Arrogant little bastard."

Christine didn't answer. Nicholas took it as a judgement on his own behaviour, and the assumption did nothing for his temper. "I'm going to tell the caretaker woman he's not to be allowed anywhere near the place. I won't have you spoken to like that."

"I wasn't the one picking a fight with him, Nick." She began to walk away.

"Well, you've never stood up for yourself, have you?" Nicholas said, falling into step with her. "Someone has to. And who the hell's Lélie?"

"I told you—Madame Duveen," she said, as if answering a question put by some not very bright child. "The housekeeper." She laughed, with no detectable gaiety. "You actually don't remember anything. It's incredible. Hey, let's test you. Let's see..." She chuckled. "What did you tell the other boys was the name of your imaginary girlfriend in the South of France?"

"Not Lélie, anyway," he said shortly. But in his thoughts, drifting back from fourteen years ago, faint as the sound of the sea from the far side of the dunes: *Christine.* Rhythmic like the rippling waves: *Christine, Christine, Christine...*

He shook his head, as if it was possible to manually dislodge the impression that way.

"What's up, Nick?" Christine asked mischievously. "Are you dreaming about her now?"

"I just remembered something, that's all." He'd actually remembered it earlier, when they'd been talking about the library at Le Grand Maximin; it had come as an unwelcome shock. He was using it now as a distraction from other half formed memories, some of them less pleasant. "If we're going to talk about sex, you know. Do you remember that huge repro engraving she had hanging in the library? 'Babalon the Great, Mother of Harlots and Abominations of the Earth'."

"Oh yes," Christine said. "Yes, I remember that very well."

"Everything hanging out the front, and octopus tentacles waving round in the background. Imagine your dad seeing that. He'd have had you out of there before your feet could touch the floor."

"He probably would have," she agreed.

"Or if he'd seen that book Aunt D gave me to read, that last summer. *Moonchild*, it was called. Aleister Crowley, the fat old fraud."

"Oh, I read that one too," Christine said.

"*You* did?" Nicholas was lost for words, a thing he would normally have denied was possible. "Bloody hell, Chrissie, that was a bit racy for you!"

"Oh, I see. Alright for you, too racy for me."

"I mean," Nicholas was actually blushing, another first in their relationship, "Christ almighty, it's pure filth—I take that back, it isn't the slightest bit pure. Even my druggie friends in Chelsea couldn't be doing with it. Said it turned their stomachs."

"There's a girl," Christine said, her tone determinedly neutral, "do you remember? She falls in with a gang of occultists, and they keep her prisoner."

"More than kept prisoner. They're—"

"They want to breed her," Christine said. "They want to impregnate her with the soul of a supernatural being."

Nicholas exhaled. "Totally degenerate. A bit of slap and tickle in the Lady Chatterley vein wasn't enough for old Auntie."

"They keep the girl doped up, don't they? She spends all her confinement lying in bed, and I remember she gets very fat, very... gravid, is that the word? It sounds like the word. That seemed to be the most horrible part of it, for me; I can't say why."

"Well, Crowley was a thoroughgoing pervert, you know. He probably liked them on the chubby side."

"Because I wasn't at all fat when I read that," she went on, ignoring him. "Somehow that detail seemed to me to be as bad as... as all the other stuff, you know. I wasn't as skinny then as I am now, I still had a bit of puppy fat in those days, but still, it seemed so utterly apart from anything I'd ever experienced. The thought of being a prisoner of your own human flesh and blood."

She *was* thin, almost painfully so: it had been the first thing he'd noticed back at Arles. Much thinner than he'd remembered.

"Did you—god, you didn't think it was *sexy*, though, did you?"

She didn't answer. Conversation with this new Christine, thought Nicholas, was like trying to play a record so scratched that the stylus wouldn't settle in the groove. Everything was false starts and unexplained hiatus. They were a score of yards further along the path when she said slowly, "I don't know."

Now it was Nicholas's turn to start to speak, and then trail off.

"Ever since puberty I'd been super-aware of all the different ways a girl's body can turn against her," she said. "Embodiment is quite mind-blowing when you come to think of it, Nick, the sheer physical reality of inhabiting this...envelope. This meat suit we wear over our bones. Does that make sense?"

"I suppose so," he said, not knowing if it did or if he was just being polite.

"It's different for girls, you know," she said. "We're forced into a different relationship with our biology. And it happens so much earlier." And when he started to issue a sort of general disclaimer: "You particularly, Nick. You were so at ease in your body at that age, all your newfound masculinity, so peacock proud. Thighs and biceps, hair where there hadn't been any, all the rest. I remember that very clearly. I remember it coming to the fore in that last summer."

Christine; that whisper again, gentle waves on an empty beach. Again he tried to shake it loose. "Oh, come on now."

"How's your love life been, Nick? Since we last met, I mean. Have you—what's the phrase—have you been *putting it about*?" He was too taken aback to speak, and she went on. “I’m sure you swung along with the Swinging Sixties. Don’t be shy about admitting it: it’s absolutely what you were made for.” She laughed, as if to show there wasn’t an edge to her words, that it was just grown-up banter between cousins.

“I don’t know, I... I haven’t been a monk, Chrissie. The Pill freed everybody up. What do you want me to say?”

“Say what you feel,” she said. “Who was your first, Nick? What was your first time? Can you remember?” And when he didn’t answer: “Come on. Everyone remembers.”

He couldn’t. What was wrong with him? *Everyone remembers*: till that very second, he’d have assumed it to be true. Now, though, looking back down the years, there was only a vacancy at the end of it, a void, an obscurity. *She said you would not remember.* “It was a long time ago,” he temporised.

“Not *that* long, surely.” She was mocking him, he was sure of it now. Or was it the fact she’d touched a nerve, one he hadn’t even known existed? “I bet if I said ‘1965,’ or ‘1968,’ or ‘a week last Tuesday,’ you’d have no trouble remembering who you were with.”

Which was absolutely true. Readily, greedily even, his memory pulled up images to go with every single date. But still there was nothing for that first time, the one entry that couldn’t be retrieved from his libertine diary. All he had was a silly bedtime story he’d once told a bunch of schoolboys in a dormitory; a tall tale, a masturbatory aid for cooped-up adolescents. A story about a girl in the South of France called...

“No,” he said, as much to the thoughts in his head as to his cousin.

“Don’t feel bad, Nicko,” she said, using, maybe unconsciously, the name she’d called him in childhood. “I’m not getting at you, really I’m not. Shall I tell you a secret? My first time is a bit of a blur as well. And since then...well, perhaps it put me off the whole thing.” She spread her hands, without slackening her pace. “And here I am, as you find me.”

Christine’s first time? He found himself unaccountably scandalized at the notion. Somehow it had been easier to think of her as still a virgin, than to imagine one single encounter so calamitous as to send one’s entire future sex life off the rails. He tried not to sound as shocked as he felt.

“You’ve had a first time, then? My god, still waters. Do tell.”

“It was here, actually,” she said; “right here, on this very seashore.” She pointed. “Just over those dunes.”

“*Here*? Who... bloody hell, Chrissie, you’re a dark horse and no mistake.”

“You’re not the only one with a past, Nicko,” she said.

Nicholas tried to square this revelation with everything he’d thought he knew about his cousin. He laid a hand on her arm. “But Aunt Dora? What did she say? Did she know about this—did she know the boy?”

“She knew him very well. In fact, she chose him.”

“She *what*?”

“She thought it was time.”

“When was this?”

“1957,” she said, trying to sound nonchalant.

“What? You were fourteen!”

“Nearly fifteen,” she said, just above a whisper.

“Chrissie!” He couldn’t believe what he was hearing. “Did she...did she set you up, is that what you’re saying? Was it all her idea?”

“Not entirely,” she said, after a short while.

“But how could I not have known about it? I’d have remembered!”

“I’d have thought so.”

He opened his mouth to answer; closed it again. They walked on in silence for a while. Vaguely, imperfectly as yet, he was becoming aware of something huge and irreversible gathering above them, something it would be impossible to evade or to explain away. He wanted very much to turn back, but they’d gone too far for that.

The path was still meandering alongside the dunes; they’d passed no farm or cottage, seen nobody except the schoolmaster. Eventually, the stillness was more than Nicholas could bear. “Are we going the right way?”

“Patience,” Christine said. “It won’t be long now.” He paused to light another cigarette, but his cousin didn’t stop for him, just walked on along the path. He wondered if there would always be this newfound distance between them now.

"What did that bloke mean, the doctor, when he said I wouldn't remember?"

"Well, you don't, do you?"

"But how would he know that?"

"He said Auntie told him," Christine reminded him. Nicholas opened his mouth to speak, shut it again, and ended up saying:

"Why did he have to make a mystery about everything? God, I hope the lawyer's not like him."

She didn't answer. Instead, not looking back, she said: "Would you like me to help you remember, Nicko?"

The thought had been gnawing at him: *why* couldn't he remember? His recall was usually sharp and reliable, rich in detail and sensory textures. Here, in the course of a couple of hours, Christine had poked two gaping holes in it. The loss of his virginity was the strangest, and instinctively he veered away from that, but the other lacuna was scarcely more comforting. Why couldn't he remember as much as Christine obviously could about that last summer holiday at Aunt Dora's?

Come to that, why couldn't he remember *anything* about it? Because he really couldn't. Whenever he tried, he found himself backfilling, drafting in memories of earlier holidays, childhood games they'd played, any number of evasions. What had really happened that year when they were both on the cusp of adulthood, that last summer at Le Grand Maximin?

Aloud, he said, "That was the summer I discovered Calvados: maybe that was to blame. There were bottles left lying all over the place, I could get pissed whenever I felt like it."

"Did you think we didn't notice?" Christine's amusement was maddening. "You were a very charming young drunk, Nicko, I'll give you that. Charming, and ever so slightly lecherous. Still, that oughtn't to have wiped out the whole of your memory, you know."

"It was very hot..." He was struggling to bring it back, grabbing at jetsam like a shipwrecked man. The afterimage of the sun on the retinas of closed eyes, the impression of baking heat on white sand. "Inside the house was cool." And surprising himself: "It smelled funny, though. Incense, like in a church."

"That was the library," Christine said. "She often burned incense in there."

"It stank. The whole house stank of it." He thought some more. "We'd have gone swimming, I suppose. We always went swimming at Auntie's."

"We did," she said, from up ahead on the path, and a vivid impression came to him: bare limbs thrashing in the warm salty water, hands gripping after slippery wrists and ankles, diving down beneath the surface, rising under Christine's body—

Christine's naked body. His involuntary gasp made her glance round, wait till he caught up. "What's up? Have you remembered something?"

"Sort of," he said. His tongue felt thick and clumsy in his mouth.

She linked his arm. "Afterwards we'd play hide-and-seek in the dunes." Flashes, scattered shards: wet skin with a biscuity coating of sand, the cries of the seabirds overhead, Christine's violet eyes darkening in the noonday glare, the little hairs on her arms and legs standing on end. "All those secret places." His breath wouldn't come.

"We stayed out very late one evening," she went on. "You had a bottle, we both got hopelessly tipsy. Do you remember, there were lighted torches set along the path to guide us home?"

"There were *what*?" he said doubtfully; only now the fragments that came to him were all lit up in torchlight reds and yellows, long looming shadows cast across the dunes, rising, falling, merging into one another...

She smiled, as if to show him there were no hard feelings. "I wondered if it'd come back, the nearer we got to the house," she said. "Keep it up."

"It's weird," he said, trying to regain his composure, "I never thought there was anything to that business about acid flashbacks, or drugs wrecking your memory. I thought it was just druggie paranoia and tabloid panic-mongers. Can that be the reason? I only tried it a few times."

"She said you would forget," Christine said. Which was of course the same thing M Prevel had said, and he still didn't know what it meant. "She guaranteed it."

"I'll tell you what I *have* remembered, just this second," he said, regretting it as soon as the words had left his mouth. "I remember one night, I was in the bedroom getting ready for bed, and I looked up and there was Auntie, watching me through the half-closed door."

"Oh yes? And why was that so memorable?"

"Because I had—" He stopped, unable to say it. "Because I was—" It wouldn't come; he couldn't tell her. *Because I was touching myself.*

"You were quite a sight for sore eyes," Christine said, squeezing his arm. Guiltily, he wondered if she'd known about it as well—if she knew who he'd been thinking of as he grew hard. She went on:

"All that summer, Auntie told me to prepare for something very special. So special I couldn't begin to imagine it. I thought she was exaggerating, but that was because I didn't know what it was she meant. You probably don't remember, but Auntie would drag me off for hours on end and make me sit and listen to her reading from books in the library. Sometimes after you'd gone up to bed, I'd be sitting downstairs with her, yawning my head off while she told me stories about the old ones, about the planes of existence and the gateways of this and that. The outside, hungry for the inside, that's what she called it."

"God, I bet you wish *you* could forget all this as well," he said.

"I do," she said. "I really do. I wish it could have been like all the summers before, those happy times I loved so much. 1957 was the end of those summers: afterwards, things were different. Look, I'm not saying—" she broke off for a second. "I loved Auntie dearly, and I loved you, Nicko, and I loved Le Grand Maximin, but that summer... things changed," emphasising the last word. "They changed so much."

Everything seemed strange now to Nicholas, even the smell of the salt air and the sound of the seabirds. Strange, but not unfamiliar. "But you still haven't said—where was I during all this?"

"With me," she said. "You were with me, all summer long."

He started to say something, then stopped, as if the implications of what she'd said were finally breaking through.

"All summer long," she repeated.

"If you say so." Guilt was tugging at him like a rip tide, the sense of a terrible realisation stopping his tongue.

"That was how Auntie planned it, you know."

"Planned what?"

"You and me. Getting us together, in that particular way. You don't think she left that Calvados around by chance, do you?" She laughed. "A lot of that summer you were absolutely blind drunk. It lowered your inhibitions, just as Auntie thought it would. No wonder you don't remember everything. But it's coming back, isn't it? Bit by bit."

"I don't know," he said. How much of it was memory, and how much was fantasy? There were images, sensations, things best forgotten coming to light. "Chrissie..." he began, and was cut short by the sudden remembrance of her all those years ago: the sea at her back, a swimming costume left discarded on the sand, the sun sparkling off the waves; her lips, chafed by the adolescent stubble on his face; the taste of salt on skin. How could he ever have forgotten? How dared he remember it now?

At the point where the path finally turned and crested the ridge of the dunes in a series of wooden steps, he came to a halt. Dropping his suitcase at his feet, he sat on it, fumbled for a cigarette. "Chrissie, stop," he called. "Please stop. Come back here."

She stood at the top of the ridge, looking back at him. "What's the matter, Nicko? We're nearly there." When he didn't answer, she stepped back down to where he sat, dumped her suitcase next his and perched on it, facing him. "Talk to me. It'll help you remember."

He couldn't find the words. Memories *were* flowing back, the closer they came to their destination, and they were terrifying. In an attempt to ward off the biggest and most dreadful of them all, Nicholas tried to concentrate on the edges of the jigsaw, the stray pieces of background rather than the central image.

As much to change the subject as anything, he asked, "Hey, Chrissie, what *did* you do before starting your job as a nanny? You didn't say just now."

"I left school," she said. "Like you, in that same autumn of 1957."

The jigsaw image in his mind broke into little pieces. "*You?*"

"I couldn't stay," she said, as if it was all unremarkable. "It wasn't possible."

"What, did your father run out of money, couldn't pay the fees? I mean, don't say you were chucked out? I don't believe it. What on earth happened?"

"Well," she said slowly, "I stayed at Auntie's for rather a long time." Another long pause: "I wasn't well."

"This was when, the Christmas holidays?"

"Around then," she said slowly. "And on through the next year, until it was summer again."

"Jesus, Chrissie, I had no idea. What was the matter with you?"

She didn't answer, and he had to ask her again, and again, till she told him, so quietly that the gentle rush of the sea beyond the dunes almost masked it. He shook his head no, and she had to repeat it, "I was pregnant."

It fell on him like a physical blow to the stomach.

"Now you know," she said.

"Oh God. Oh, Chrissie." Stumbling over the words, "I really and truly hadn't the slightest idea. How... what happened?"

"The usual thing," she said, and he couldn't tell if she meant it ironically, or was just stating the obvious. "I missed my period, went to see the school nurse, and everything followed on from there. That's why I was taken out of school early, you see. There was an enormous row with my father, it went on for days and days, weeks on end, and I finally went to stay with Aunt Dora because," her voice wavered, just a little, "because I had nowhere else to go."

"How?" Meaning, who?

"How do you think?" Her voice rose in impatience. "I was here with you, and then I went home, and then I missed my bloody period, and then I had a—" She clapped a hand to her mouth, breathed deeply behind it.

"I can't believe it."

"I didn't, at first." Her hand was still over her mouth, but she'd regained a measure of control. "I told you, everything changed that year. It blew my life to pieces, and I wasn't ready for it." She let her hand fall to her lap, where it sought its twin and wrung at it.

"But what happened to it—to the baby, I mean?" He tried to remember if there had been anything different about her in the weeks before they parted for the last time, any sign. No swollen belly, of course, it would have been far too soon, but anything in her demeanour, the way she'd behaved around him. And all the time, underpinning everything, that sense of imminent catastrophe, rushing towards them off the waves and up the long-deserted beach.

Christine shook her head. "I was sleepwalking," she said. "Or as good as. They gave me quite heavy medication, you see. A little group of people came over from the town—M Prevel was one of them, that's where I remembered him from—and they prayed over me in a language I couldn't understand. I was the chosen vessel, they told me, and I was carrying a special child—the *babaloum*, they called it."

"But you must know who...?" He couldn't say the words. The thought of it made him feel sickly, somehow, as if it was he who'd been violated.

"I don't even know *how*," she said. "Nicko, don't you understand? There was only you."

"Oh my God." It was all he could say. Nicholas and Christine, cousins, then something more. Sick with shame, Nicholas flashed on that autumn at school, after lights out in the dorm, the lurid fairytale he'd told to entertain the other boys. The girl—he'd given her Christine's features, of course, along with her name; her coltish long legs, her fringe of golden hair, her summer dress of cornflower blue that fell in a puddle at her feet... oh god, he thought desperately, was I really telling the truth all along? *Had* they, she and him? Had that really happened?

"Anyway, I really don't remember much about the actual pregnancy," she said.

"But you must!" he blurted out.

"Why must I?" she snapped back. "You've forgotten the conception!" She breathed heavily for a moment or so, then continued: "Here's what I remember. I was confined to bed for weeks on end, drugged up, as I said, and Auntie would tell me the story of how Zeus birthed Athena—did they teach you that one in boarding school, Nicko?"

"From his forehead," he said, shocked into letting the non sequitur pass unremarked.

"He had a headache," she said, "and they split his forehead open with a wedge. And nobody was more surprised than Zeus at what happened next."

He didn't understand. Was she trying to distract herself, rowing back from this nightmare in her past? That notion was dispelled by her very next words: "In my case, of course, it wasn't the forehead."

Nicholas ran his hands through his hair, pulled at the long fair strands. "My God, Chrissie..."

"We'll be at the house before long," she said. "I think that'll be a big help." She pointed where the path led, up over the dunes. "It was just around here, you know, that we'd been bathing that evening. We were ...messing around in the sand, and we both got very drunk on apple brandy. Then we came back to the house through a long lane of lighted torches—the bride's path, Auntie called it—and the coven were waiting for us. Ah, you're remembering, don't stop."

How did she know he remembered? His face betrayed him, probably. When she said a thing, it appeared in his mind's eye, half-formed yet frighteningly vivid. When she'd said "don't stop" just now, he'd heard her fourteen-year-old voice sighing the same words in his ear, while all around the bed cowled figures shifted from foot to foot, humming a melody that felt older than the *shaduf* chant of ancient Egypt, the song that was heard before the sphinx was lifted up. His aunt's voice, chanting in cut-glass English: *Babalon the Great, Mother of Harlots and Abominations of the Earth...*

It hadn't been his fault, he told himself. Echoing Christine's words: *not entirely.* He'd been too drunk to know better, that was all he could think, and when they'd led him to the old-fashioned four-poster bed, guided him towards his cousin, he'd been conscious of nothing but the overwhelming desire he'd tried and failed to hold back, all that slow intoxicated summer. If he'd spent fourteen years repressing that memory, or if his memories had been tampered with, shut off artificially somehow, well, it was all coming back now.

"You mustn't feel too bad, Nicko," Christine said. "I wanted it too, I think—it's so hard to say. All that summer Aunt Dora was wearing away at us, taking one or the other of us off in private and suggesting...stuff. How it was nothing to be ashamed of, how there was no such thing as right or wrong, there was only what is real and what is right in the moment. No such thing as sin. How were we to know any better?

"But *why*? Why on earth would she do such a thing?"

"I thought it was because she loved us," Christine said, her voice shaking, "because she wanted us to be together. I thought she was silly and romantic, probably because I was silly and romantic as well. I only found out afterwards what the real reason was.

"When I fell pregnant and came back here, Auntie talked very calmly to me about her motives. I was too drugged up to feel much about it, either way, but I've thought about those talks lots of times since. She said that we—our union, I mean, the product of our union—would provide her, would provide the coven, with the *corpus vile.* I didn't know what that meant, at first. You'd probably have known, you did Latin."

"The worthless body," Nicholas said, still not looking at her. "A subject for experiment."

"That's almost it," she said. "Auntie explained that in order for the coven to achieve their working, they needed a pregnancy—anybody's pregnancy, I think they'd tried already with one of the coven members, but she'd miscarried, or something went wrong after the birth." She thought for a while. "The latter, I think. So I was to be the vessel."

"The vessel? Jesus Christ."

"Not him, no." Christine's voice was steadier now. "Not him at all, Nicko."

"Those bastards, they..." Words wouldn't come. "Those *bastards*."

"Anyway, for months they prepared me for the birth, kept me drugged up, fattened me, chanted over me, examined me. There was a doctor, a huge fat man with fingers like sausages. Madame Duveen would hold my hands above my head while he—" She gulped. "Nicko, it was horrible."

Nicholas swore inadvertently: it came out almost as a bark. The rage he was feeling almost, but not entirely, crushed out his own monstrous sense of shame.

"We'd provided them with the moonchild in embryo, she said. What would happen between conception and birth would be that the soul of the baby—of our baby—would be expelled, that was the word she used. The baby's soul would be expelled, and in its place they'd put... oh Nicko, I can't go on. If you'd only seen it, when it was born!"

The revulsion in her voice was horrifying. "Oh, Chrissie. Was it...was there something wrong with it? Was it stillborn?"

"It lived," she said. "Whatever it was." She got to her feet. "Come on," she said. "You need to see."

"See what?" Of course, he knew what.

"Come on," she repeated. "No, leave the bags there, we can send Lélie for them. You have to do it, Nicko darling, you have to take the bride's path with me again."

Trying to blank out everything that was in his mind, Nicholas took her hand. Together they climbed the few steps to the crest of the dunes.

THERE WAS THE SEA, the blue Mediterranean, lapping at the farther end of the broad vacant beach. Along the curve of the strand, a wooden boardwalk half-hidden in windblown sand led toward a great house maybe half a mile away, on a promontory above the beach.

"Le Grand Maximin," Christine said. "Now do you remember?"

Nicholas was mute. As if in a stupor, he allowed himself to be led along the boardwalk.

"It lived," she was saying, "although I don't see how. When I first caught sight of it, amidst all the blood, I thought—Nicko, it looked hardly formed. You could see its brain through these gaping fontanelles, a horrible grey-green, and the whole of the head seemed twice as big as it should have been."

"Don't," he said, barely above a whisper. Christine carried on as if she hadn't heard him.

"I thought it was dead, and for a second I felt terribly guilty and yet terribly happy, all at once. And then it began to scream, and then I was screaming as well, and then I think they put me to sleep with something."

The house was coming into clearer view now. Bare weathered wooden clapboarding on the walls, the roof an impractical profusion of spires and high gables, it looked like a magic château from a child's storybook. All around the property a low stone wall topped with iron railings hid the gardens from sight. Every detail of it was familiar to Nicholas.

"They brought it to me at intervals," Christine continued, her hand tightly clasping his. "To feed. I couldn't look. I think I just wanted both of us to be dead at that point. Auntie would try to explain its importance, tell me that for a little while longer I'd have to be a mother to it. But I got very ill—I lost all the pregnancy pounds, became very thin, emaciated really. I wouldn't talk to anybody, I turned my face to the wall. I think that it had to do with the feeding, as much as with my state of mind. It took so much out of me; more than I had.

"So in the end Auntie sent me back to Haywards Heath, where it wasn't quite as bad as it had been. Auntie had written to Dad, telling him the baby had been stillborn, so the practicalities of the matter were all worked out, so far as he was concerned. All that was left was the shame, and he made sure I never, ever forgot that.

"He worked out that it had probably been you, which was why he forbade me to ever see you again. He didn't tell your mother; couldn't handle that conversation, obviously. He just cut us off from everybody. There was talk of sending me to another, stricter, finishing school, but I was still poorly—I relapsed, physically and mentally. Imagine—that summer he sent me back to Auntie's for the sea air, to recuperate!

"It was still growing. I asked Auntie how they'd managed to keep it fed, and she said they'd weaned it. She started to tell me how, but I stopped her. And then she said to me, very kindly if you didn't know what it was she was talking about, 'Would you like to be mother one more time, Christine? For old times' sake?'

"I came back at Christmas and summers, just as I always had. Can you possibly understand it, Nicko? It was horrible, but do you know what? It was the only place I didn't feel guilty, or like some sort of freak. It went on, year on year, until I was packing to leave one January and Auntie said: 'There's no need to come back anymore, dear. He's strong enough now.' I didn't ask how they were going to manage, or beg to be allowed back to Le Grand Maximin. I walked out that day along this path, all the way to the train station, and I never looked back. It hollowed me out, all of it: that Christine you used to know is long gone. I look nearer fifty than thirty, I know that, you don't have to be polite." She waited a moment. "Oh, you weren't going to be. Never mind.

"Anyway, here we are, Nicko, almost there. Just think, you'll be meeting your offspring for the first time. I say your offspring, but really there's very little of either of us in him. Nothing you'd recognise. But we made him, with Auntie's help, and now I suppose we're responsible for him, to some degree at least. I don't know for sure: by the calendar, he's still a child, but physically...well, you'll see very soon. M Lacombe was placed high in the coven under Auntie, he'll be able to tell us what we need to do. We may have to move in for a while, or maybe—"

Nicholas was pulling back, trying to break her grip on his hand and retreat down the boardwalk. She overcame his feeble efforts quite easily, and after a second or two he gave up. "Nicko," she said gently, "it's too late for that. We have to find out what's in Auntie's will, what it is she's left us, what are our responsibilities."

"I can't do this," he said, and yet he let himself be led again.

They were quite close to the house now, close enough to see through the railings to a garden, once formally laid out with gravel walks and topiaried trees, now grown over and barely recognisable, with huge hanks of ivy smothering every shape. In amongst those masses of ivy, something was moving, something similarly misshapen. It stood the height of a man, or something taller, broad across the shoulders, tapering away below the waist; by any measure, its head was disproportionately massive. Its movements were indescribable, a lurching hunchbacked roll, as if uprightness was not its usual condition.

"Look," Christine said, indicating a woman dressed in black waiting at the gates to the garden. The figure was alongside her now, dwarfing her. "They're waiting for us. And oh! Nicko, there's the *babaloum*. Do you see it?"

He would not look.

"You have to look, Nicko," she said, pulling him towards the gates. "You have to. You own it now."

Steve Duffy lives and works in North Wales. His most recent collection of weird stories, These And Other Mysteries, *was published by Sarob Press in 2024; he's currently in the process of putting together his next. Steve was the winner of the International Horror Guild's award for Best Short Story 2000, and in 2015 he received the Shirley Jackson Award for Best Novelette.*

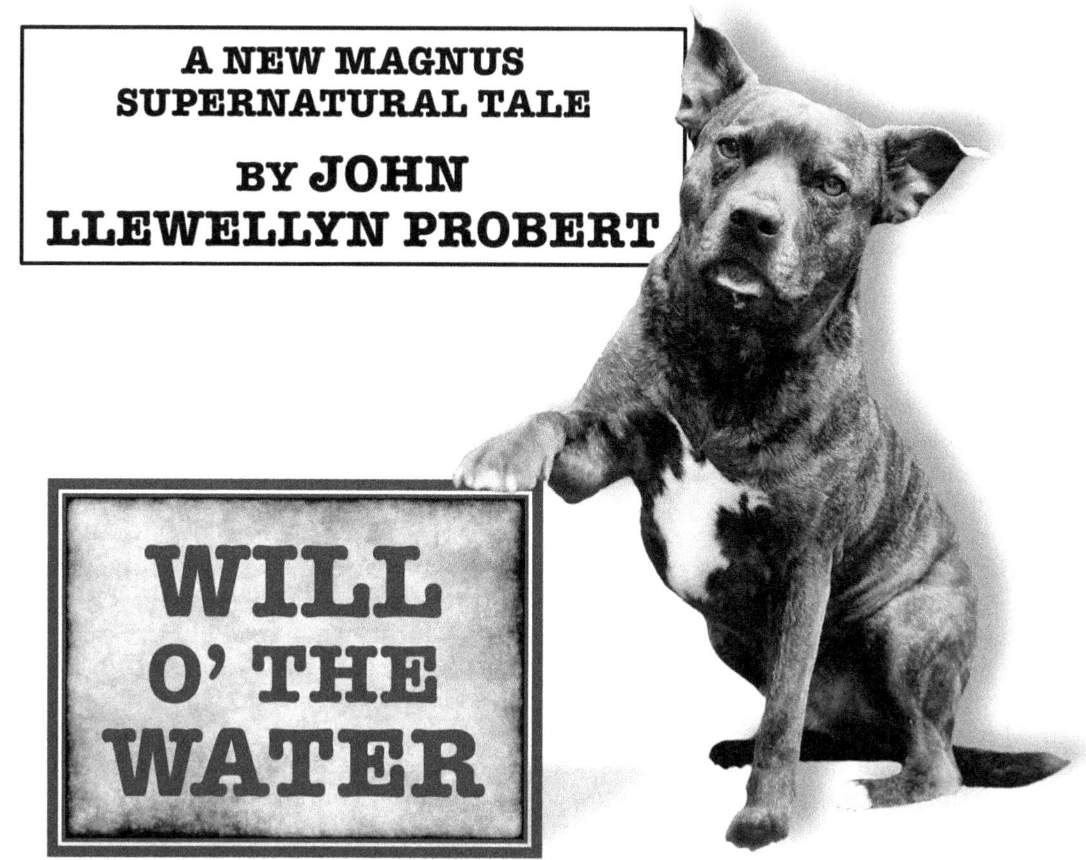

SINCE WE DISCOVERED IT JUST OVER A YEAR AGO, AXBRIDGE RESERVOIR IN SOMERSET HAS BECOME ONE OF OUR FAVOURITE PLACES TO VISIT. By "we" I mean me and Magnus, my faithful Staffordshire Bull Terrier, who has been my constant companion since we first became acquainted.

According to the information boards erected at regular intervals around its circumference, the reservoir is capable of storing up to six billion litres of water (or 1350 million gallons if you are more imperial-minded), much of which is derived from subterranean sources that drain from the limestone of the surrounding Mendip Hills into the Cheddar Yeo, one of the largest underground river systems in England. The reservoir is enjoyed by many kinds of wildfowl, including mallard, duck, and coot, as well as rarer species with such wonderfully creative names as Temminck's stint, ortolan bunting, and red-necked phalarope. Because it is so close to the Bristol Channel, storm-blown seabirds may also sometimes be spotted.

The main appeal to myself and my brindle friend, however, is the alternating gravel and hard-set path which circles the reservoir's entire two-and-a-half-mile circumference, providing us with a most enjoyable walk when we are in the mood for something a little less taxing than some of our more steeply-inclined pursuits. And although some of our other destinations have on occasion resulted in brushes with the supernatural,* up until recently we had encountered nothing strange at Axbridge Reservoir.

Whether it was the date (a crisply bright but nevertheless chill December 21st), or the time (the sun was at the point of setting) I cannot say. I could claim it was Magnus's proclivity to act as a magnet for such strange phenomena, but to blame my canine

* As recounted in *Nightmare Abbey* volumes 6, 8, and 9.

companion would be both unfair and possibly even incorrect. I have come to believe that perhaps I have as much of a nose for this sort of thing as Magnus does, albeit one that is neither as cold nor as wet. Whatever the reason, something very strange was waiting for us that evening.

As soon as Magnus was out of the car, he exhibited his usual proclivity for finding the vegetation right next to where we had parked fascinating, despite my repeated assurances that the real attraction lay up ahead. He claimed our patch of the parking area by his usual doggy method, after which we made our way through a swing gate and up a paved path to behold our destination.

The reservoir is bounded on its north and east sides by the Mendip Hills. To the southwest stretch fields on which sheep and cattle may often be seen grazing. As I have already mentioned, the sun was beginning to set as we arrived, rendering the hills, and in particular the quarried aspects of the steeper slopes, a vibrant brick red. I knew this glorious appearance would likely last just long enough for us to make our circuit, after which darkness would come on quickly.

As usual we went widdershins, Magnus trotting ahead and stopping every now and then to inspect items of interest to him. We encountered other dog walkers, the occasional cyclist and, just past the first of the two hexagonal grey stone water towers, some workmen who were packing tools into their van. There was a general feeling of everyone heading homewards, whereas Magnus and I were setting off to do just the opposite.

By the time we had completed a quarter of our journey it had already become noticeably darker. The sun was little more than a golden thumbnail on the horizon, its dying rays bathing the western pastures in copper. Despite this, visibility was still reasonable and we were hardly likely to lose our way.

We were halfway round, with the sun but a scarlet memory, when Magnus stopped to sniff at the low wall bordering the reservoir. He raised his head and his ears pricked up, following which he placed two front paws on the top of the concrete barrier, which allowed him to look over it. He appeared to be studying the water intently.

"What is it, old chap?"

Despite there being little breeze to speak of, the surface of the water was becoming choppy, with the numerous moorhens on its surface currently being subjected to the equivalent of a mild rollercoaster ride. A solitary pair of swans took flight and did not return. I tried to pull Magnus away, but he was determined to continue watching, fascinated by what was now happening at the water's surface. I couldn't blame him. My attention had also become captured by the odd shapes that were beginning to form.

The undulating waves were beginning to break up, and in their place were what I can best describe as indentations in the water. These increased in size until I could see, by the deteriorating light, that they resembled tiny whirlpools, spread all across the surface of the reservoir. There must have been hundreds of them.

As my canine friend and I stood spellbound, each whirlpool began to rise, forming a spinning column of water about a foot high, crowned by a point that tapered to a spectral mist, that much resembled the marsh phantom Will-o'-the-Wisps of folklore.

I had no idea if anyone else was witnessing this bizarre phenomenon, but if they were it was never reported on the local news later, and a subsequent internet search yielded nothing, making me wonder if ours were the only eyes to see it. We watched as the mist was dispelled by the breeze, as the water columns sank back down, and as the tiny whirlpools vanished. Then Magnus did something he has never done before, and it caused my heart to leap into my mouth.

He has always demonstrated a distinct aversion to water, even going out of his way to avoid puddles of any and all sizes, which made his behaviour at that moment all the more shocking. How his lead had become detached I had no idea but before I had a chance to even draw breath my friend had leapt the barrier. He cannoned at top staffy speed across the exposed slanting brickwork of the reservoir's base, and plunged into the water.

What could I do? It was getting dark, I'm not a terribly good swimmer, and Magnus was already quite far out, the silhouette of his boxy bull terrier head bobbing up and down the only sign that he was still safe.

Then his head disappeared.

I called to him of course, but once my friend has become obsessed with something, no amount of shouting or plying with treats will distract him. All I could do was hope he was all right and that I wasn't going to have to telephone for help.

It seemed like an age (but was likely less than a minute) when I saw the outline of his familiar skull appear once more and start making its way back to shore. As soon as he was out, Magnus shook off as much of the water as he could, clambered back over the barrier, and dropped something close to my feet before emitting the loudest, wettest Magnus sneeze I had ever heard. He sneezed again as I mopped off water, turning my handkerchief into a sopping rag in the process, before looking at what he had brought me.

At first I thought it was a tiny seashell before quickly realising that the irregular encrustations were exactly that. They quickly fell away with a little encouragement, and by the light of my mobile phone I saw that, from somewhere in the depths of the reservoir, Magnus had retrieved a gold ring.

Apart from being a bit damp, Magnus seemed fine. However, I did insist we complete our walk with significantly more haste than my friend is used to, and there was still the faintest trace of light in the sky as we drove back on the A38 with the car's heater on full. By the time we got home Magnus was as dry as a bone. I think he rather liked being blasted by the air conditioning, and I hoped that the pleasure he gained from it would not encourage future deliberate immersions.

I HAD POPPED the ring into my pocket and from there transferred it to my desk drawer, intending to examine it in more detail at a later date. Instead, I forgot all about it until a few days after Christmas. Magnus and I were warmly ensconced in my study, a roaring fire keeping out the chill from the fog that wreathed the garden, its tendrils having crept some way up the windows. Close to the fire is a wingback armchair upholstered in oxblood leather that used to be my favourite place to read until my canine friend claimed it. Now he lay there, squeezed comfortably between its arms, his eyes half open, every now and then a contented doggy groan escaping his lips.

I, meanwhile, having been denied the most comfortable seat in the room (and of course I did not have the heart to move him), was seated at my desk. To my right, the curtains to the mullioned windows had been drawn back, despite the cold and the gloom. When he is not snoozing, Magnus very much likes to be able to see out. I suspect it is part of his protective instinct. That night there was little visible but the fog, the closest wisps of mist rendered a silver blue by the blushed glow of the street lamps.

I was busy working on an article when my attention was distracted by a tapping.

It was not, in case anyone is wondering, coming from my chamber door. Neither was anyone at the window. No, the tapping was distinctly coming from somewhere inside the room. Magnus's ears had pricked up as soon as the sound had commenced, and he quickly became sufficiently concerned that he levered himself down from his chair and commenced sniffing around my desk. Even when that cold wet nose decided the top right-hand drawer was the source of the sound, it never occurred to me that that was where I had deposited his discovery from the reservoir.

When I opened the drawer, of course, it all came flooding back. The ring was right there, nestled in between one of my many fountain pens, a bottle of Waterman's black ink, and a sharp knife with a retractible blade that I use for opening book parcels. However, it was not the ring itself that caused me to draw breath and Magnus to cower.

It was the mummified finger that the ring was now adorning, the moving mummified finger whose cracked brown nail was making the sound as it tapped against the cherry wood of the drawer's base.

More fascinated than repelled (and that attitude in itself helped Magnus to calm down a little) I plucked a pencil from that very same drawer and, very carefully, gave the finger a prod, on the knuckle, just below the fingernail. It responded as a caterpillar might by rapidly moving away before commencing its tapping once more.

Magnus, meanwhile, had retreated to my study door. When I turned to see where he had got to, he gave me a worried look, then glanced at the window, then looked at me with even greater concern. It was only when I looked myself, I realised the finger had not been tapping to attract my attention, but the attention of that which was now standing right outside the house.

I guessed the glass must have been acting as a barrier, because what else was there from preventing it coming straight in. With that in mind I reassured Magnus, patted his head, and then crossed the room to get a closer look at our visitor.

It seemed to be composed of the fog itself, with that silvery blue light lending it a truly spectral appearance. As I watched, the moisture coalesced further until I found myself face to face with the image of a young woman. She was a little shorter than me, and wore clothes suggesting she likely lived in a time several centuries before our current one. I raised my right hand and she mirrored the motion. As I expected, her left ring finger was missing. It crossed my mind to take what was still tapping from my desk drawer, open the window and return the missing digit to her, but Magnus, as always almost supernaturally aware of my intentions, moved in front of the drawer and gave a little "ruff" that I guessed meant "I don't think that's a good idea."

"Well don't look at me," I said to him. "I'm not the one who fished the ring out of that lake."

Which begged the question, why exactly did Magnus, who hates water, plunge into the icy depths of the reservoir to retrieve it in the first place?

There could only be one answer. I turned back to face the ghostly presence at the window. It didn't look at all happy now. I guessed it understood that Magnus and I had no intention of reuniting it with its lost digit, and the jewelry that adorned it.

"You made him do it, didn't you?" I said to the thing through the glass. "You tried with the birds, and when that didn't work you used your powers to force my dog to get it instead."

The spectre's expression changed to a look of anguished hate and, as I watched, its "flesh" of fog fell away to reveal a grinning skull beneath, a few wisps of mist clinging to its scalp suggestive of stray lengths of hair. Now it was a lich that was at my window, a thing of rot and the grave, a malevolent entity that was still intent on seeking entry and was now deliberating how best to do so. It began inspecting the seals on the windows, then it looked up, and appeared to spend some time examining the area that lay just above them.

As the entire apparition rose into the air Magnus began barking, and I quickly realised, to my horror, what it was he was so distressed about.

The air vents above the windows were open.

There are two, each one crowning one of the main windows. I had been informed by those who installed them that it was best to leave them open to avoid damp build up, and so they always were. I managed to shut one in time but when I moved to the second I could see tiny fronds, like threads of silver spiderweb, already emerging from the opening, curling around the ventilation slits, almost as if they were trying to gain purchase to enable something larger to pull itself through.

Magnus had already climbed onto the table that lies beneath the windows, but his barks were making little difference. I looked around the room for anything that could put a stop to this malevolent spectral intrusion. The scissors and the letter opener were no good. Slicing through that mist would be like trying to halt the wind with upraised hands.

But the desk fan might work.

I grabbed it and prayed the cord would reach to the window vent, through which a large, slug-shaped glob of silvery moisture was now crawling. I managed to get the fan within two feet of it before the cord became taught.

I switched it on.

The blast of air caused the ectoplasm (I presume that was what it was) to proceed no further. I think it even retreated a little, but not sufficiently to return it to the outside. I glanced around the room. All the other power sockets were further away, which made moving the fan impossible. However, I could not possibly stay there all night in the hope that the light of day would diminish the apparition, nor could I hope for the elements to provide a brisk dissipating breeze. I looked down at my doggy friend.

"Looks like we're going to need to blow it away ourselves," I said, more to keep our spirits up than because the suggestion offered any practical solution.

Or did it?

Cold air from the fan had caused the thing to dissipate a little. Could warm breath cause it to retreat completely?

It would depend how much breath was needed, I realised. If I spent too long exhaling too quickly there was every chance I might pass out and then the thing would be free to enter and cause whatever mischief it wanted to both myself and Magnus.

Magnus.

My brindle friend and loyal protector was now barking fit to burst, and exhaling a lot of hot air in the process. He wouldn't be able to keep that up for long, I thought, but then neither would I once I started. However, perhaps the two of us together...

I put down the fan. The floating, rotting, spectre, its hollow eye sockets now level with the top of the other side of the window, almost seemed to nod with pleasure as I did so. Then I climbed onto the table. Magnus was already there, still barking at the now rapidly enlarging shape that was the creature's right arm, squeezing through the vent.

Magnus is at the larger end of the Staffordshire Bull Terrier breed, and as a result he weights close to 30kg (around 66lbs for the imperial minded). It's mostly muscle, but even so, the vet has said he should probably go on a short diet. I rather wished we had already done what they suggested, as I hoisted my heavy friend into my arms, ensuring his head was level with my own, and turned him so he faced away from me and towards the ever-thickening, ever-lengthening ectoplasm.

Then I let him bark away.

I helped, too, exhaling as long and as hard as I could against this increasingly substantial intruder to our home. Almost as soon as we began our concerted effort I was delighted to see the creature's ectoplasmic projection retreating rapidly. My arms were tiring quickly, though, and at one point Magnus slipped down a little. Despite my own best efforts my breath alone was not enough to defeat the creature. With a herculean effort I ignored the pains in both shoulders and hoisted him up again. Together we breathed as long and as hard and as noisily (on Magnus's part) as we could, until the entirety of the thing had retreated to the outside. Then I let Magnus slide back down onto the table while I slammed the air vent shut. When I looked back outside the creature had gone. In my desk drawer the finger had gone also, although the ring remained.

"I think we probably need to get rid of that," I said to my now silent chum.

THE NEXT DAY dawned sunny and bright, which gave me confidence that we would likely be safe from our sinister visitor. I pocketed the ring, now thankfully bereft of its mummified digit, and we set out to dispose of it at an appropriate location. We do not have a convenient volcano near our Somerset home and so I had to resort to something a little less Tolkienesque in the form of some building works that were taking place a little way out of town. Magnus provided an excellent distraction while I dropped the ring into the fresh cement that had just been poured into a foundation trench. Then we took our leave, with no one else any the wiser as to what we had done.

As to the nature of the spectre, my further reading caused me to discover some of the facts I have outlined in the introduction to this account. It led me to wonder whether the individual in question had perhaps slipped and fallen, or even been pushed, from somewhere high up in the Mendips. The ring they must have been wearing, and which was perhaps even the source of their power, eventually found its way into the reservoir over the course of centuries.

Back home I turned on the tap and fresh,

safe, magic-free water began to fill the kettle in preparation for making a cup of tea.

"I believe we've had a narrow escape there, my friend," I said to my companion who, as usual, had followed me into the kitchen in the hope of being offered some tidbit. "I think we'll keep you away from water in the future."

I knew Magnus wasn't listening. As always, his eyes were on the delights that resided on the counter in what we have termed "Treat Corner." I remembered what an effort it had been to lift him. "And perhaps we should start thinking about what the vet said after all."

I couldn't tell if the look Magnus gave me was one of acceptance or just relief that we had once again escaped something very supernatural and likely extremely nasty. But then he raised his right front paw, a little trick he's learned that he knows always earns him a treat. It did this time, too. After all, we had both been through quite enough for one day.

The diet could start tomorrow.

John Llewellyn Probert's latest books are the short story collection Chasing Spirits *(Black Shuck Books), the portmanteau novel* How Grim Was My Valley *(NewCon Press) and on the non-fiction front,* The Frightfest Guide to Mad Doctor Movies *(FAB Press). Coming up next will be a couple of novels, another short story collection and more film books, as well as articles for both US and UK film and literary magazines. He tries to fit in some sleep where he can.*

Magnus is an eight-year-old Brindle Staffordshire Bull Terrier rescue who has been part of the Probert household for three years. He is walked at least twice a day, and his favourite routes include the local beach where he loves to chase any crumpled linen that may flap across his path, the golf course after he was shown the 1945 Ealing classic Dead of Night, *and of course Brent Knoll, the subject of his first story, in* Nightmare Abbey 6. *After all that exercise his favourite way to relax is on the sofa where he loves to fall asleep in front of 1970s European horror films. He is very happy that his humans did not name him Zoltan.*

Lucky Lucifer

By Tom Johnstone

"JAMAIS TUÉ QUELQU'UN, RICHIE?"

Was that what the old man just said?

She didn't imagine it. She's sure she didn't.

Her French is getting better, little by little, from listening to the pair of them muttering away together. *Tuer* is *to kill*, right? *Jamais* is *never.*

Never killed anyone, Richie?

Or could it be, *Ever killed anyone, Richie?*

Because the implications don't bear thinking about, and she's almost numb to such thoughts by now, she puts it from her mind. The view from the balcony lets her do that for a while. Gazing out over the valley, she sees the fig tree behind the parking bay below. Maritime pines stretch into the mountainous distance, where salmon-coloured rocks jut out of the evergreen lushness here and there. The wine helps too, golden wine bought from one of the local vineyards lined with ranks of grapevines they visited last week.

She remembers how the silver leaves of an olive grove gilded the edge of the car park as she reversed the hire car into it. The wheels stirred dust-clouds as she struggled to right an error. She'd driven in the wrong way. Richard tutted. Her ability to drive on French roads was proving as poor as her command of the language.

"If you hadn't got all those penalty points, you might have been able to drive," she snapped.

Already cracks were appearing in the surface of us then, she thinks, *faultlines spreading in the desert of our marriage, making way for the chasm in human form that's opened up between us.*

She takes another sip.

She could go into the kitchen, but although the door is open to the balcony, as it always is in this oppressive heat, there's nevertheless a barrier between her and the two of them, the young man and the old man. Their lowered voices, speaking an unfamiliar tongue, shut her out.

She should have shut *him* out.

When he first appeared in front of the car, in pursuit of an errant dog, forcing her to brake hard, she should have floored the accelerator instead.

"A FINE-LOOKING ANIMAL," said Richard of the black retriever.

He took to the elderly stranger straight away. He always was a sucker for that sort of thing: the air of distressed nobility. "Breeding," he called it. He could spot it a mile off, he said, from the way the old man handled his dog. Never mind that he dressed like a tramp and had allowed the animal to stray in front of the car.

Keeping him at arm's length became harder after the Lucy Incident.

Richard thought it would be a wonderful idea to go for a walk in the forest that surrounded the village. Pick figs and blackberries, enjoy the shade of the oaks and pines, that sort of thing. Better that than endure more of Sarah's driving round the hair-pin bends of the mountain roads down to the local tourist hell-hole beach resort. That was how Richard put it anyway. Sarah didn't mind it, but she had to admit they *had* spent most mornings there. They'd even seen the Roman amphitheatre after they got sick of getting sand in their socks, so that was the educational angle covered.

Neither Sarah nor Richard had anticipated how easy it was for a child to get lost in that jungle. Lucy hadn't either. She'd suddenly decided at the age of fourteen that now was the time to cut the apron-strings, running off ahead in pursuit of dragonflies. At home she rarely left her room, but here in the dense woods of Southern France, where Richard didn't know the language as well as he thought he did and Sarah knew it even less than that, Lucy had suddenly discovered her independence, cantering off into the distance. The first few times she'd done this, her parents had eventually found her leaning against a tree, munching on a handful of blackberries, her fingers stained dark purple.

About the fifth time she did this, they lost her.

A shrill, brittle squeak called out Lucy's name. Sarah realised it was her own voice, swallowed up in the vast, sound-smothering maw of the dense foliage surrounding them. She imagined her wandering around lost in it. Beth, their younger daughter, already seemed frightened, so Sarah tried to keep the desperation out her voice.

"It's only been a couple of minutes," muttered Richard, failing to keep the irritation out of his.

He rushed towards a couple of men wearing oddly lumpy, grey-brown cloaks, sullenly indifferent to his enquiries in halting French.

"Est-ce que vous avez vu une jeune fille de quatorze ans?"

One of them said something to Richard neither he nor Sarah could understand. Eventually, the man gave up and began gesticulating at Richard, miming firing a gun. The gestures became impatient shooing-away ones aimed at the foolish English family. As Sarah drew closer to Richard, Beth clutching her hand tightly, she saw that the "cloaks" were in fact bunches of dead animals—

rabbits, pigeons, and other game—along with the firearms that had dispatched them. They'd obviously had a good day's hunting.

"What was all that about?" she asked.

"We shouldn't even be here," was all he would say.

Hours later, they returned to the apartment, footsore, exhausted, sticky with sweat, recriminations flying, phone reception non-existent. As Sarah steeled herself to use the apartment phone to call the *gendarmerie*, who should they see waiting outside the building but Lucy, fussing over the black retriever, as its elderly English owner looked on indulgently.

"Really?" she said, in answer to something he was saying about winning a fortune in Monte Carlo.

"They used to say I was born lucky," he said, then added that he promptly lost it all the same night.

That would explain the aura of a gentleman in reduced circumstances. *Of course, that would obviously appeal to Richard*, Sarah thought savagely. He was a romantic with delusions of literary greatness. After the inevitable scene with Lucy, Sarah sat on the balcony, too over-tired and angry to go to bed, watching the last rays of the sun stain those ancient Provençal rocks on the horizon a deeper pink than they already were, listening to the crickets beginning to whir out their nocturnal rhythm.

As she sipped her wine, she thought back to what they'd escaped with this impromptu holiday, only possible thanks to an old university friend's willingness to loan them this apartment for a peppercorn rent. How different the implacable calm of this heatwave to the English Summer forever blowing hot and cold, wet and dry. The weather's intemperance seemed to add to the fractiousness between her and Richard, usually over his "career break" to write the novel he insisted he had in him. Now he'd completed it, he needed to sell it, and quickly, or get another job. Either way he had to pull his weight. That was *her* view.

"You sound just like my father," he'd grumbled. "'Why don't you get a proper job?'"

"Wouldn't be a bad idea..."

"It's obvious you hate it."

She should never have agreed to give him feedback. She found it impossible to be both objective and kind about the work of someone so close to her. She'd opted for the former course.

"It's not that I don't like it, Richard..."

"It's just that you hate it," he finished for her. "So how am I supposed to motivate myself to put it out there, eh, Sarah?"

She was tired of his petulance, his insistence that she midwife his genius. It made her cruel, sarcastically suggesting he find a patron, like some Tudor court poet.

It was almost dark by the time Richard joined her on the balcony, breaking into these bitter memories, his presence unwelcome. She was just beginning to unwind, enjoy the solitude. For a few moments she barely registered what he said to her.

"We should invite him round."

She stared blankly.

"Nicholas."

That was the first time she'd heard his name. She'd been too busy hustling the children inside for introductions, briefly overhearing the exchange of greetings between the two men. "Richard, eh?" the old man had said, when her husband introduced himself. "I knew a Richard once. In a manner of speaking."

"For dinner perhaps," Richard now went on. "He seems a bit lonely."

"I'm sure there are plenty of other English ex-pats around here for him to bore," she said.

He looked at her as if she was a stranger, as if he'd seen her anew for the first time and didn't like what he saw.

"He seems like someone who needs a friend, Sarah." Richard did sanctimonious reproachfulness so well. "He was telling me how lucky I was to have children... Almost as if he'd lost his own or something. And don't we owe him a meal at least?"

She struggled to come up with a credible objection beyond her own vague misgivings. Furtive noises broke the steady monotone of the crickets. Something moved behind the screen of bamboo under the balcony. It sounded so deliberate it could be the movements of human beings, perhaps young lovers looking for a quiet, intimate place.

She dreaded the contrast between their carefree dalliance and the bickering between her and Richard. But there was no stifled laughter or whispering sighs.

"Richard," she hissed. "Do you hear that?"

"What? The crickets?"

"No. That rustling. Do you get wolves here?"

"Wolves? Don't be ridiculous, Sarah. This is Provence, not Siberia."

"But you can hear it though?"

The noises had ceased. He looked dubious. His sceptical expression made her doubt her own senses. But she *had* heard it. He opened his mouth to speak, but she raised a hand to silence him. There it was again, this time accompanied by a snuffling, a snorting. He slowly nodded his head, but it just seemed to suggest confirmation of something in his own mind rather than an acknowledgement of their shared perception of the sounds.

"ARE THERE ANY ZOOS around these parts?" Richard asked over dinner.

The old man blinked. Or rather his eyelid twitched: an old age thing perhaps. His eyebrows, or rather brow, for they were knitted in the middle, were as silver as his scant hair. A smell of cigar smoke hung about him, an invisible ashen shroud.

"There is one in the nearest town," he replied slowly, sipping his Pastis as steadily as his shaking hand allowed. "Why? Do you want to take the children there?"

Beth jumped up and down in her seat at this possibility, but Lucy looked sullen.

"We were just wondering if something might have escaped from it."

Richard glanced at Sarah as he said this.

"Were you indeed?" Nicholas replied. The fluttering of the eyelid had subsided. Something vital and predatory peered at her from behind the mask of infirmity. It was as if some secret understanding had passed between the two men.

"So you like the zoo, eh?" he said to Beth, who nodded with a grin.

"I once knew a man who had his own private zoo," he said. "Threatened to feed me to one of his pet tigers if I didn't behave..."

Beth's eyes widened in theatrical terror. Nicholas winked at her. After a pause, he chuckled dismissively at his own tall tale.

"I'm sure he wouldn't really have done that!" he laughed. "He had some pretty rare breeds though."

"How old are you?" Beth asked suddenly, beaming her cheekiest grin at the old man.

"Beth!" Richard reproved her.

Nicholas smiled indulgently.

"It doesn't matter," he reassured her father. His eyelid was going nine to the dozen again, Sarah noticed. "In any case, when you get to my age, you can't remember what it is."

She'd have put him at about eighty-one, though spry for his age.

As it turned out, she was only a couple of years out.

SHE GOES INSIDE to refill her glass. The two men stop their muttering. It doesn't matter. She's already caught the tail-end of their discussion.

"Y a t'il besoin de ces mesures tellement drastiques?" the younger one just asked.

"Je crois que non," the older one replied. *"Je connais un médecin très obligeant."*

Why are they bothering to speak French? She wonders numbly. She may not know all the words, but she gets the gist. *Médecin* is a doctor, presumably of the mind rather than the body. And there was something else about *drastic measures*. She puts this together with the younger one's remarks to her about "the strain you've been under lately, Sarah." He means the anti-depressants of course, the ones that don't work and never have done. Not really.

Then there's what she knows about the old one.

She asks the young one how the children are. He glances at the old one, who nods as if granting permission or prompting a prearranged response.

"They're in bed," the young one says, his eyes narrow.

She steps forward.

He moves his chair, blocking her way.

"They're asleep, Sarah. Don't disturb them."

The old one looks away.

Something in her breaks. Messily, she refills her glass with shaking hands, then retreats onto the balcony, the only place left to her.

IT WAS AFTER Sarah tried to tell Richard what she'd found out about his new best friend that he started banging on about her mental health. He hadn't taken much interest in it before. It was about then that those two began to become thick as thieves.

She first had her suspicions when they went to the lake. *He* took them of course. He'd appointed himself their tour guide, as a thank you for the meal and "for your friendship." Well, Richard's anyway. It was already obvious he didn't much care for *her*, and the feeling was mutual, although he stood up for her over the animal noises.

"Actually, Richard, there *are* wolves in Provence. Don't worry though, children: they are much further north. Came over the Alps in the nineties. Mind you, their numbers are growing. A couple of years ago, a lad not much older than Lucy here had a brush with a pack."

Sarah shivered.

"Set your mind at rest, Mrs. Harrison. The animal you heard was probably a wild boar. *Their* numbers are growing too, and forest fires are driving them into more populated areas."

They were walking downhill along a steep path, lined with oak saplings, plain trees, berberis bristling with thorns and velvet-blue berries, mountain ash with bright red ones and of course those ever-present evergreens: cypress and maritime pine. Nicholas distributed titbits of local knowledge about the flora and fauna of Provence as they walked, teaching the Harrisons all the names of the plants—some of the folklore about them too. With his silver beard and shrewd bird-like eyes and weather-beaten skin like pine bark, he was well-suited to the role of guide, forester, wise old man of the woods, the story-book gardener in a felt hat chewing a clay pipe as he hands out nuggets of cottage wisdom. He told them how a pair of cypresses outside a dwelling promises a weary traveller a quenched thirst and a full belly; a third one guarantees them a bed for the night too; a single one means, *Forget it.*

"I've heard it's good luck to have them outside your house," Sarah offered.

He regarded her for a moment, as he seemed to do whenever she said anything, as if affronted that she'd opened her mouth at all. Suddenly those avian eyes took on a glint of humour. His laughter was avuncular, yet from the looks that passed between him and her husband, she sensed that it was for Richard's benefit and at her expense.

"Oh no, Mrs. Harrison! That's an invention of the *agents immobiliers.* The estate agents, my dear," he translated for her when she looked blank. She bristled internally at the belittling endearment, but he carried on unaware. "Traditionally, the cypress is a symbol of death. Hence the phrase, 'dormir sous les pines.'"

Sarah gazed at the imposing, stately conifers. The laughter of Lucy and Beth as they ran on ahead echoed her humiliation. She tried to remember if there were cypresses outside the holiday apartment. The coded offers of hospitality seemed rather menacing now.

"To sleep under the pines," he went on, an odd smile on his thin lips. "When wealthy French people began buying second homes in Provence in the eighties, that notion rather put them off their stroke. So the *agents immobiliers* came up with the idea of the cypress as an overgrown good luck charm."

It should have been idyllic.

The shallows of the lake lapped against a shore girded by oaks whose leaves were already starting to brown, either from the heat or a premature false Autumn; crowned by a higher canopy of the ubiquitous maritime pines. Nicholas had ensured the outing fell on a day of the week when hunting was forbidden, so the party didn't end up unwittingly dodging buckshot again. Sarah had been grudgingly happy for him to organise the trip, but she was growing weary of his assumption of grandfatherly authority. She was growing more than a little uneasy at the way he took it upon himself to discipline the children, with Richard's tacit approval. Lucy's hackles were rising at his reproofs.

"You've got a lot to learn about surviving in the wilderness, young lady," he once said in response to some petty infraction against the natural laws of the place of which he claimed guardianship. As Lucy sulked under his displeasure, Sarah frowned meaningfully at Richard, who simply shrugged.

She couldn't help wondering about this stranger who had come unbidden into their lives—where and how he lived, how he came to be here. With his unkempt hair and beard, his shabby second-hand clothes, he didn't seem like your average English ex-pat. On the other hand, she was grateful to him for sharing his local knowledge with the hapless English tourists they were, and Richard seemed to trust him, so she swallowed her qualms.

He'd got them here, hadn't he? she told herself when her misgivings nagged at her. To this lakeside paradise, where dragonflies dallied around the cool waters while they picnicked in the dappled shade of the maritime pines. She found herself deferring to his wisdom. She wanted to go for a swim but was unsure whether it was safe, only taking the plunge after he'd allowed his beloved black retriever to bound unchecked into the water, then shaking itself dry on exit with canine abandon. The droplets hit her parched skin, and on an impulse, she stripped to her underwear and bounded in too. She swam over to the other side, where the summer heat had exposed part of a tree's massive, knotted roots. She reached out to grasp it.

Something red-raw stared up at her, a collapsed face rendered featureless by its injuries.

Hurriedly she swam back, scattering water boatmen in her wake, shattering their precarious foothold on the skin of the lake. She towelled herself dry savagely, as if scrubbing vileness from her skin, literally itching to get back to the apartment for a shower in sterile mains water.

"Training for the Olympics?" Richard joked.

"I saw something," Sarah gasped, ignoring his facetiousness. Her breathing wasn't just ragged from the swim.

"Really?" Richard's voice dropped as he spoke. *Like you heard something in the bamboo,* he didn't need to say. The open scorn in his voice was enough to plant doubt in her own mind. The water was deep, swirling with clouds of dirt from the bottom of the lake, disturbed by her strokes, obscuring any clear view under the surface. The ruined skull could just have been submerged gnarled roots seen through a filter of red clay particles.

But she stood her ground.

"Yes, really. A face. A broken face."

The look on Nicholas's face when she said it was worth the sneer in Richard's voice. All his folksy composure gone. An eyelid shivering, the one free wing of a desperate moth caught in a spider's web. Convulsively he petted and stroked his precious dog. She felt sure she heard him mutter something about women not shutting up no matter what you did. She couldn't be sure. No one else seemed to react to his words. Yet if she was the spider, she didn't yet know the nature of the skein she was spinning around him.

"You saw a face," said Richard. Again that flat, sceptical voice.

She nodded, despite the doubts crawling like water boatmen over her still-wet skin.

"Like you thought you heard wolves in the shrubbery."

She had to stop herself from laughing at the obviousness of his spoken thoughts. Given their trajectory, it would have seemed a madwoman's laughter to him. Anger helped to stem the tide of mirth. A cold rage welled up within her at his contempt for her, in contrast with his deference to this decrepit, cigar-stinking stranger who had invaded their lives. What did Richard want from him? Was this the patron she'd mockingly suggested he find? Or was his adoption of the old man a kind of obscure, delayed revenge for her scorn at his literary endeavours?

As they glared at each other, working themselves up into a row of insurmountable bitterness, another conflict was developing by the shore. Lucy was shouting at her self-appointed surrogate grandfather to stop striking something Sarah couldn't quite see with a rock, the black retriever barking and bounding around in excitement.

"It wouldn't have lived long," he gasped, out of breath from his exertions. "Its wing was damaged beyond repair."

"That makes no sense!" Lucy said, her wide eyes pleading with her parents to take her side. Her father looked downwards, while her mother searched Nicholas's face for an explanation. He nodded down at the butterfly half-hidden by the rock. Like his eyelid, it was no longer fluttering.

"It landed in the water," he explained. "Lucy admirably tried to save it, but it could never have survived with that injured wing."

He didn't even blink.

"Would she rather have watched it die slowly?" he asked softly.

Sarah looked over to where she sat against a tree, head lowered, arms cradling her knees.

"Why don't you ask her yourself?" Sarah said.

Richard's eyes shot a warning at his wife. She walked away from them both to stand by the water's lapping edge, letting its coolness envelope her toes.

She felt Nicholas's warm cigar breath on the back of her neck as he voiced a warning of his own, his voice lowered.

"Perhaps it's best to stay out of the water now, Mrs. Harrison."

He came forward to stand beside her, staring at a ladder lying half-submerged on the shore, lowering his voice even more, so that it was all but inaudible to the others.

"You don't know what people dump in there."

SARAH DIDN'T HAVE anything to give substance to her unease until Beth started imitating frogs.

The lake seemed to have lost its charm for her after everything that had happened, and they were making their way back to the car up a steep dirt track rutted with the marks of long dried-out rivulets that must have fed the lake at one time. As they made their laborious ascent, she wondered about what the old man had said. A threat? Or just a well-intentioned warning about fly-tipped underwater debris? If it was that, he certainly had a point, because her feet had glanced off a submerged pallet at one point during her swim, possibly inches away from a rusty nail. *Yes*, she tried to convince herself, *he did mean just that—surely he wasn't suggesting that someone really* was *asleep under the pines.*

The sound of Richard entertaining Beth with the legendary omnivorousness of the French broke into her thoughts. It was a timely reminder of the qualities Sarah had always loved in him.

"They don't really eat frogs' legs, do they, Daddy?" Beth asked him, with exaggerated disgust.

He nodded.

"I've heard this is one of their prime hunting grounds. In fact, if you listen out clearly, you might be able to hear them..."

The only sound was the chirring hum of the crickets.

Richard crouched down to her height. "Can't you hear anything going *rivet rivet rivet...?*"

Suddenly everything seemed terribly quiet on the woodland path—except for Beth absently intoning "*Rivet rivet rivet*" as she wandered up the path, hand in hand with her father.

Rivet rivet rivet.

Nicholas had stopped.

Despite his deep tan, his face had turned a colour closer to that of his hair and beard, but more ashen than silver. His black retriever strained and whined on the leash.

He was unmoving. Riveted to the spot. *Quite funny really if you think about it*, she thought. But she was also wondering where she'd heard the word, or rather name, "Rivett" before.

IT TOOK HER a while to remember it.

Because whenever she heard people talk about the case, they'd always forget about *her*, or mention her in passing, a bludgeoned footnote in history.

They often talked about the car with the blood-stained length of lead-piping in the boot dumped in Newhaven, the rumours of *his* suicidal leap from the cross-Channel ferry, the silly-season stories of holiday-makers spotting him somewhere exotic, the glamour and the gambling debts, the bitter child custody battle, the spectacular fall from grace.

And of course, she remembered seeing it on the news: the grainy monochrome mugshot of him with moustache and wolfish mono-brow, sleek and brylcreemed.

Yes, people always remembered him. But they forgot her—poor Sandra Rivett, just a nanny who just happened to be in the wrong place at the wrong time, who died of blunt impact trauma. She borrowed one of Lady Lucan's frocks for the night and so resembled her employer in poor light, so the story went.

THE BLACK RETRIEVER wandered the tables, begging for titbits or just picking up discarded scraps. No one seemed to mind this; nor did the management object to Nicholas's scruffy clothes. They seemed to know him, even to treat him as a valued customer, though it was Richard paying, not him. So much for his patronage. Maybe it just consisted of him leafing through the Manuscript and making encouraging noises—more encouraging than the ones Sarah made anyway.

"*As-tu commencé récemment à travailler ici?*" he asked the waitress, a twinkle in his eye.

"*Oui,*" she nodded coyly.

"*Quel age as-tu?*" he added.

"*Dix-sept ans,*" she replied.

Was it the heat, or did she blush and return his gratified smile?

Nausea surged through Sarah. It was too hot to eat. She'd heard this heatwave was so severe, the French newspapers called it "Lucifer."

She had been about to tell Richard what she'd figured out, about half an hour before they were due to leave for the restaurant.

The words had stalled in her mouth as she imagined his reply.

Do you know how crazy this sounds, Sarah? Listen to yourself! If he was still alive—and that's a big if—he'd have fled to Africa, Australia even, not stayed in France and risked extradition.

Ah, so you've got it all worked out, she might have said back.

"What is it, Sarah?" he'd said.

But as she opened her mouth to speak, she tasted stale, sulphurous cigar smoke.

Nicholas had arrived early, so she'd have to wait to talk to Richard alone, but she didn't think she could bear the weight of this knowledge any longer.

Richard knew something was up from the moment they sat down, shooting her wary glances in between pleasantries to Nicholas in French over the restaurant table. Eventually he muttered an enquiry about her menu choices at her. She swatted a fly away from her arm. The mere thought of food made her feel sick. She felt like she had a migraine coming on.

"Mum, are you OK?" Lucy asked.

Her sincere concern almost brought tears to Sarah's eyes, but there was no way she would cry in front of him. In front of them.

She nodded back at Lucy with the most cheerful expression she could muster, stared at the menu. Words like "escargots" and "moules marinières" swam before her eyes. She was vaguely aware of their meaning, enough to fill her with visions of slimy, legless, boneless creatures, squirming around her tongue. Maybe she could have this one instead. What sounded like a salad of pulped tomato. Yes, she'd settle for that, if that was what it was. Everyone else had closed their menus, ready to order. As the waitress stood there expectantly, she asked her what "poulpe" meant.

As she translated "oct-o-pus," miming tentacles to Beth's mock-horrified amusement, Sarah snapped her menu shut, gazing hopelessly at Richard. Another fly circled before her. Her eyes followed its lazy progress towards her hand. Eventually, he smiled at the waitress, saying, "*Ma femme n'a pas faim,*" before ordering for everyone else. When he'd finished, he leaned forward and spoke to her in a lowered voice that required her to bend her head close to his, a strand of her hair almost brushing his lips. Sarah couldn't have made out what he said, even if it weren't in French, but the girl giggled and winked at him before waddling off back into the restaurant to deliver the order.

Dix-sept ans. She may not be fluent in French, but Sarah knew enough to understand that meant seventeen years old. Three years older than his daughter.

She sat there swatting flies away, watching the others gorging themselves, with the exception of Lucy, who picked at the solitary vegetarian option on the menu. Sarah couldn't understand why the insects were so interested in her when she was the only one not eating. Maybe there was a nest of them right under her chair. They didn't seem to be bothering anyone else. Her hand slapped down on a fly. Or rather on her shoulder. She had missed, of course. It made a loud, meaty noise. Like a gun going off.

Or a length of lead pipe striking the thin layer of flesh and hair covering a woman's fragile skull.

Richard gave her an alarmed look. More of a glare actually. She smiled back apologetically. Her head was starting to throb. The stares from other tables seemed to mirror Richard's.

She felt as if she was slowly becoming enveloped in a cloud of flies, with the rest of them eating on, unawares outside it. Earlier on in the holiday, they'd visited a bookshop. Richard liked to show off by reading exclusively in the native tongue when in France. Browsing, he'd taken out a copy of something by Jean Genet—*Notre Dame des Fleurs*. "Our Lady of the Flowers," he'd translated for her as she'd read the title over his broad shoulder, her chin resting there with easy familiarity. How close they'd still been then, a matter of days ago, and how strong she'd thought him. It was only now she saw how weak he really was, flattered by the confidence of a man of "breeding."

She swatted another one.

This time, when Richard glared at her, Sarah's smile back threatened to turn into hysterical laughter. There was something so ridiculous about that stupidly affronted look on his face. He turned to Nicholas. They exchanged a few words in lowered voices. French or English? She couldn't tell anymore.

"Sorry, Richard," she said in what she sensed was an overloud voice of exaggerated contrition that silenced the murmuring hubbub from other tables, drawing other eyes towards them. "It's just the flies. They keep..." (SLAP!) "...Bugging me." she laughed. She couldn't help letting out just a little laugh. It sounded stupidly high-pitched to her, but she let it out just the same. "Notre Dame des..." (SLAP!) "...Flies."

"Mum!" said Lucy, her eyes filling with tears.

"Come on, Sarah," said Richard, rising to his feet and handing his wallet to Nicholas. "I'm taking her back to the apartment," he said.

Nicholas looked up from his steak, cooked rare. Lucy paused over the vegetarian bake she'd barely touched. Beth by contrast was tucking into her chicken goujons with gusto.

"Perhaps it's best," Nicholas said softly, his yellow teeth bloody, flecks staining his white beard too, his steak knife plunging in to release more red onto the plate. Sarah thought of Sandra Rivett's blood spilling onto the marble floor of an upmarket residence in Belgravia.

"No!" she cried, looking back at Beth and Lucy sitting uncomfortably on either side of the white-haired, pink-teethed old man, who had finished mauling his steak and was now lighting one of his evil-smelling cigars. "You can't leave them with him!" she hissed at Richard.

"Sarah, come on," he snarled, glancing at the people now openly staring at them from the other tables on the terrace. "You two, stay here with Nicholas."

His grip was strong and firm on her arm. She looked back, as the restaurant terrace receded into the distance. The old man was feeding scraps of gristle to the retriever. Lucy looked away, rolling her eyes, every inch the embarrassed teenager. Beth covered her mouth, with dismay or amusement, Sarah wasn't sure which. She was beyond thinking now. Her head was pounding as if someone was trying to crack it open with a lead pipe, and nothing seemed clear anymore.

WHEN SHE AWOKE however, everything *was* clear.

The sun was streaming in through the French windows. She must have slept all through the night and for most of the next day. Maybe the following day as well.

She leapt out of bed, strode onto the balcony. The afternoon heat on the tiles burned her feet. She had instinctively reached for her mobile phone when she awoke and began thumbing in the number of the *gendarmerie*. It came up automatically from her attempts to raise them when Lucy had gone missing.

But where were the others?

She rushed back into the apartment by the French window that led into the living room-kitchen area. She called out, "Richard?"

No answer.

Good. She lifted the phone again, smiling triumphantly. He should have taken it away when he had the chance, confiscated it when he brought her back and put her to bed without any supper.

Obviously not as clever as he thinks he is!

She stared at the number, steeled herself to press the "call" button. She had to do this, didn't she? It was her duty after all. If she was right, he was a wanted man, a fugitive. They would want to know, wouldn't they?

But she could imagine the conversation.

And what...evidence have you, madame?

A few cryptic comments? An aversion to the word "rivet"? They must get hundreds of calls like this.

From cranks.

But what if she *was* right? The face she saw... Thought she saw in the water might have upset him because it reminded him of Sandra. Or maybe she didn't just *think* she saw it. Maybe he had to do some late-night fly-tipping of his own. Maybe there really was a lady in the lake, perhaps more than one.

As she wondered if *she* ever resembled Lady Veronica in poor light, her finger hovered over the call button.

A key in the lock. The acrid smell of tobacco and brown paper.

The bubble of children's laughter and lively adult conversation that rounds off a day of enjoyably frantic activity.

Without her.

"Mum!" said Lucy. "How are you feeling?"

She at least seemed pleased to see her mother.

"We went to the Roman Arena again!" Beth squealed. "And the beach! And the zoo!"

Without her.

"Wow!" Sarah murmured, her phone still held up before her, the *gendarmerie* number staring mockingly, reproachfully back at her.

"Uncle Nick said it wasn't as good as his friend John Asp— As-pi— Asp-pin—"

Uncle Nick.

Rather than help her complete the name she was having trouble pronouncing, "Uncle Nick" sailed in with "And how are you, Mrs. Harrison? I hope you're feeling rested and recovered. You had quite a nasty turn."

"Yes, how are you, darling?" Richard said. It seemed like years since he'd called her that, but God! How like an echo chamber he sounded.

MAYBE THE YOUNG MAN'S right and she does need to see someone about her mind, though not in the way he thinks.

Whom the gods destroy they first make mad after all. The same goes for devils—perhaps more so. That's what the old man did to Veronica all those years ago. Bouts of calculated emotional cruelty interspersed with the adoring father routine. And then of course, there's nothing like enforced separation from your children to break a woman's spirit. By the time he got the family doctors involved, got her sectioned, it must have become a self-fulfilling prophecy. This was someone whose idea of foreplay was thrashing his wife before intercourse. By the time they came to take her to the funny farm, she was probably a genuine candidate for it.

But it didn't work, so more *drastic measures* became necessary.

That was how he operated—Richard John Bingham, Seventh Earl of Lucan, a man who moved in charmed circles, a man whose gambling chums were plotting coups to stop Britain going to the dogs and falling to the reds. So why bother to flee to the other side of the world? Why not hide in plain sight in the Riviera for a little while, wait for the goon squads to seize the levers of power—pay a few bribes to the authorities to get them to turn a blind eye, have a flutter in Monte Carlo to while away the time, just until Aspinall and the others had things under control...

But "a little while" turned out to be

rather longer than expected, so he became "Nicholas." He's had so many names, so many faces. And what of the other Richard, Sarah's poor, stupid husband, who shares his real name. Now Richard Harrison, the failed writer, has become a character in someone else's narrative. She's beginning to wonder if he's becoming his namesake, or they're merging into one another somehow, the two Richards, one going under the alias of Nicholas, both sitting plotting together. He's even started smoking those awful cigars. To her, they don't have names anymore—they're just "the young man" and "the old man," muttering away together in French in a fog of sulphurous tobacco.

It's getting dark out here on the balcony, but she doesn't want to go inside. It's still very warm, as though the sun's heat has soaked into the very ground and all the buildings on it. The sky is a fiery vermilion. Hell is a beautiful land like Heaven on Earth, and the Devil's an English aristocrat gone to ground. She can hear the snufflings and rootings of the wild boars in the shrubs.

And there is another sound too.

A siren.

A man in a black uniform strides onto the tarmac of the parking bay under the balcony, speaking into a radio, a pistol in his holster. His features seem to twitch and shift in the flashing blue light from his car. She's always found it disconcerting the way all police officers carry guns here. She offers him her most disarming smile, but it must seem a little forced. It doesn't disarm him. His pistol remains in his holster.

She hears voices from inside, as the young man and the old man greet the policeman. She can't make out the words, except for, *Elle est sur le balcon.* But she notices how the old man and the policeman chat like friends, while the young man tells the children sharply to go back to their room.

Suddenly the black-clad policeman appears on the balcony, cutting off the door back inside.

She's a bit bewildered that he's here at all, because she never phoned the *gendarmerie* in the end. Or maybe she did after all, and she forgot. It wouldn't be surprising if it slipped her mind, with everything that's been going on. As Richard never tires of reminding her, she's been under a great deal of strain. She keeps smiling, but he doesn't smile back. *Come to take me to the funny farm?* she almost says. But apart from the fact the policeman is obviously in no mood for jokes, when she sees him reach not for his handcuffs but for the pistol in his holster, she realises too late this isn't the case.

She hears the click of the safety catch's removal.

Her last thought is to wonder what they will say to explain the police operation and the shots fired in a sleepy village in Provence.

An accident with a hunting rifle?

A madwoman shot while resisting arrest?

Richard will think of something—either one of him.

Tom Johnstone writes horror and mows lawns, but no blades of grass were harmed in the creation of this story. He is the author of a trilogy of novellas and two collections. His short fiction has appeared in various venues, including, Chthonic Matter Quarterly, Supernatural Tales, Creepypod, Body Shots *(Subtle Body Press),* Medusa *(Flame Tree Press),* Ethereal Nightmares: The Second Sleep *(Dark Holme Publishing),* Infernal Mysteries, or a Compendium of Gothic Reveries and Dolorous Tales *(Egaeus Press), and most recently,* Hiding Under the Leaves *(The Slab Press) and Ellen Datlow's* The Best Horror of the Year, Vol. 17 *(Night Shade Books). More information at tomjohnstone.wordpress.com*

THERE'S A PECULIAR PHENOMENON WHICH LIKES TO REGULARLY INSIST ITSELF UPON RANDOM GROUPS OF FRIENDS OR ACQUAINTANCES ONCE THEY FIND THEMSELVES RELAXING AROUND A CAMPFIRE AT NIGHT, or perhaps a dinner table full of pleasantly emptied plates in the waning hours of twilight. That is when, for reasons unknown, conversations edge into the territory of specters and the macabre. I believe it's a natural part of the human condition to delight in one's ability to send chills down the spines of another. Over the next few installments of this column, I'd like to put together a list of stories which I believe best elicit such feelings from various points in our history, but we'll first need to establish a demarcation point for this initial assembly.

World War I—it was called *The War to End All Wars* because we had never before seen nations aligning to square off against one another on such a global scale. Sadly, there would be more wars to come, but World War I certainly denoted a turning point in the history of our planet. The industrialization of the military brought advances such as rapid-fire guns, the ability to drop bombs from above or launch torpedoes from below. Soldiers now had the capacity to kill large swaths of their fellow humans at an unprecedented rate. Attempts to shield infantrymen against a hail of artillery fire led to the development of trench warfare. This involved digging deep, zig-zagging trenches which soldiers could move through without presenting an open target to their enemy. The conditions in them were truly deplorable, however. Trapped within the narrow earthen walls of the trenches, soldiers were forced to contend with squalor, disease, and rodent infestations. Death was an ever-present cohabitant for those moving about these grim labyrinths, but their sacrifices eventually brought the war to an end. These trenches of WWI will serve as the boundary for the stories we will look at today.

Before we embark upon our list, let's have a look at some of the earliest horror tales ever published.

Head of Medusa
by Godfried Maes, 1680

Polyphemus, by Steele Savage (Edith Hamilton's *Mythology*, 1942)

Depending on the lens used to look at it, an argument could be made that one of the oldest recovered pieces of recorded literature, *The Epic of Gilgamesh*, is semi-horror, or at least has elements of horror to it. Written in cuneiform on clay tablets dating back to 2100–1200 BCE in Mesopotamia, this epic poem pits the titular hero and his friend Enkidu in a fight to the death against a savage, monstrous giant known as Humbaba. Humbaba is a terrifying presence—a force that men who dared enter the Cedar Forest had to fear. He is, in essence, one of the earliest monsters in literature.

Of course, Greek and Roman mythologies were saturated in the streaming torrents of blood let by their menagerie of fearsome creatures. *The Odyssey,* written by Homer in 725–675 BCE, introduced us to a host of frightful beasts: Polyphemus—an enormous Cyclops; Scylla—the six-headed hydra who ravaged ships that drew too near it in avoidance of Charybdis—a beast in the form of a vast semi-sentient whirlpool; and of course, there was the beautiful yet diabolical Sirens who used their allure to coax ships to crash into nearby rocks. My entire column could be filled by just looking at the rogue's gallery of horrifying beasts mythology ushered forth. Medusa, The Minotaur, Typhoon, and countless more are prime examples of things dreamt up to haunt the nightmares of ancient man.

Taking a giant step forward in time to 1816, we have the historic ghost story competition proposed by prominent author Lord

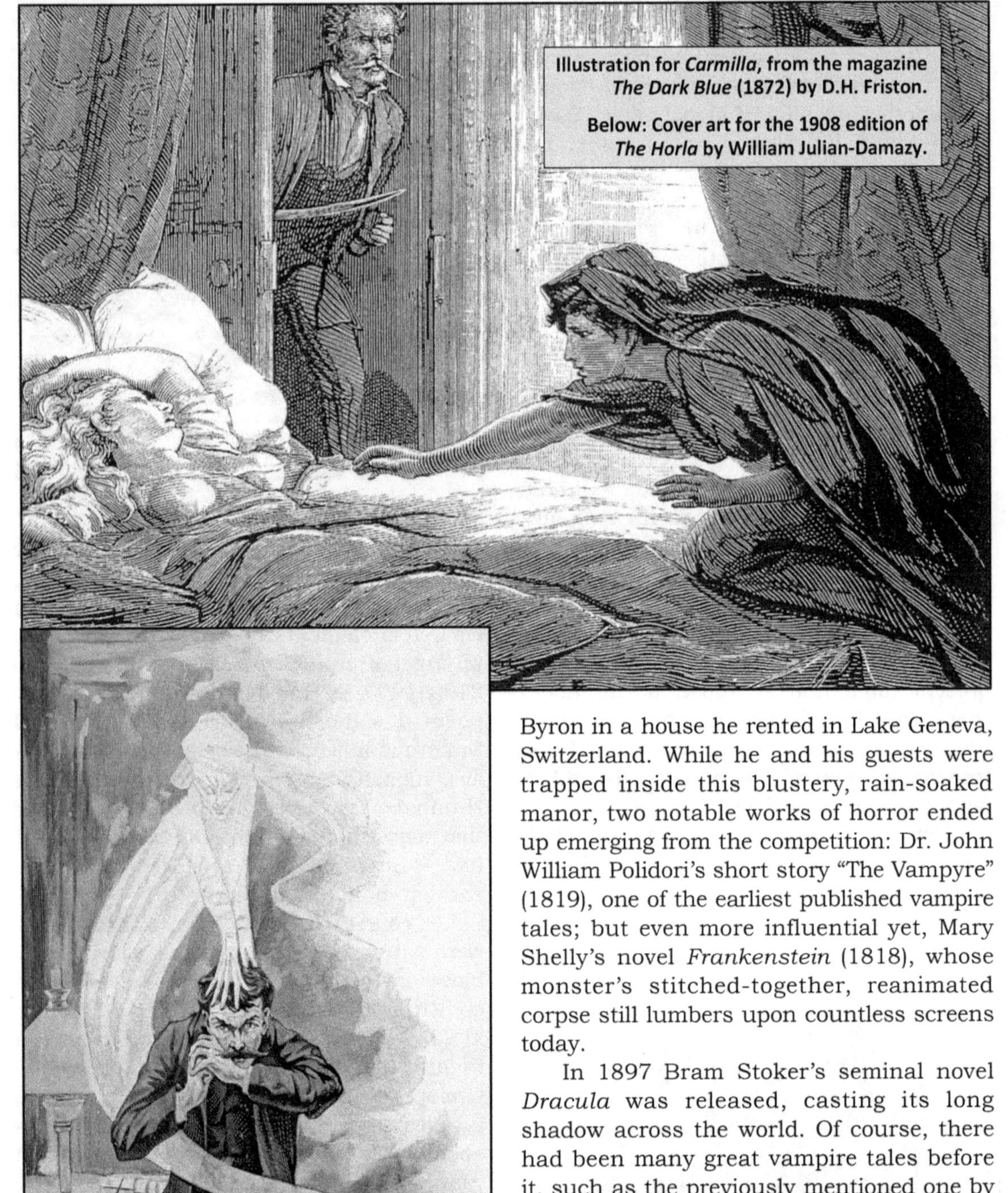

Illustration for *Carmilla*, from the magazine *The Dark Blue* (1872) by D.H. Friston.

Below: Cover art for the 1908 edition of *The Horla* by William Julian-Damazy.

Byron in a house he rented in Lake Geneva, Switzerland. While he and his guests were trapped inside this blustery, rain-soaked manor, two notable works of horror ended up emerging from the competition: Dr. John William Polidori's short story "The Vampyre" (1819), one of the earliest published vampire tales; but even more influential yet, Mary Shelly's novel *Frankenstein* (1818), whose monster's stitched-together, reanimated corpse still lumbers upon countless screens today.

In 1897 Bram Stoker's seminal novel *Dracula* was released, casting its long shadow across the world. Of course, there had been many great vampire tales before it, such as the previously mentioned one by Polidori, J Sheridan Le Fanu's female version in his Gothic novella *Carmilla* (1872) and the psychic-leacher in Guy de Maupassant's short story, "The Horla" (1887). *Dracula* has far outshone all others however, successfully managing to become the definitive vampire for the ages.

Back to the classic ghost story, they don't get much better than the Henry James novella "The Turn of the Screw" (1898) which tells of a young governess who takes the job

The Innocents (1961, 20th Century Fox)

of overseeing a brother and sister at a remote family estate only to find the place is haunted by specters intent on corrupting the children. 20th Century Fox did an excellent job making a film adapting this story, as *The Innocents* (1961).

We add several more great additions to the literary horror scene in the years that follow before the onset of WWI, including the Gaston Leroux novel *The Phantom of the Opera* (1910). Bram Stoker returns with a novel about a massive, shapeshifting snake-entity in *The Lair of the White Worm* (1911). Even the inventor of Sherlock Holmes, Sir Arthur Conan Doyle, got in on the fun with his strange short story "The Horror of the Heights" (1913) where a man encounters some bizarre monstrous life-forms in the upper regions of Earth's atmosphere.

There are countless more, of course, but I think it's high time we moved on to my list of favorite pre-WWI horror stories. In each of the stories I've chosen, the supernatural force, in whatever form it chooses to take, has the capacity to cause physical death or madness to the living who encounter it, making them well-worthy of fear and dread.

THE STORIES (Chronological by publication date):

1. **"The Fall of the House of Usher"**
   Edgar Allan Poe (1839)

   Any list such as this one has to include Poe. He's arguably the most influential horror writer of all-time, and this story is my personal favorite by him. In it, a man travels to visit his childhood friend Roderick Usher in a moldering, old manor house at his urgent request. Roderick is in poor health and appears on the verge of a mental break. His twin sister Madeline, who also resides in the house, suffers from fits of death-like catalepsy. Despite the visitor's attempts to cheer his friend up, Roderick laments how he believes the decrepit house is alive and

Illustration by Julian Portch (engraving by George Pike Nicholls) for "The Fall of the House of Usher" from *Tales of Mystery, Imagination, and Humour*, 1853.

sentient. He later informs his friend that his sister had just died and that he plans to keep her body in the family tomb for two weeks before burying her. Later, they start hearing sounds echoing up from the deepest recesses of the house as a mighty storm rages against the tottering place. This is a quintessential classic of the gothic horror story!

2. **"The Phantom Coach"**
Amelia B. Edwards (1864)

British-born author Amelia B. Edwards was well-traveled and even became an Egyptologist. She wrote novels and travelogues amongst other things. This tale became what she is best remembered for today. It takes place a few days before Christmas when a headstrong soldier gets lost while hunting. With a snowstorm hitting, he lucks upon a man traveling nearby who takes him to his master's house. There he and the lord of the place engage in a conversation regarding theology and the supernatural. The soldier is intent on returning home to his wife that night but knows he can't walk the twenty miles in such bad conditions. The homeowner advises him to take the old coach road to a crossroads where he can catch a ride with the night mail delivery driver. As he embarks on making his way to that location, he encounters an old, rotting stagecoach and enters the carriage to find three silently staring passengers within. His ride will not be a pleasant one.

3. **"The Upper Berth"**
F. Marion Crawford (1885)

I first came across "The Upper Berth" in the anthology *Alfred Hitchcock's Ghostly Gallery* which I routinely checked out of my school library. This creepy tale centers on a man crossing the Atlantic aboard a steam ship called Kamchatka. The previous three occupants of the cabin he's now staying in had cast themselves overboard soon after lodging there. During his stay he finds something unnatural in the berth above him (the upper level of his bunk bed). His description of the entity is evocative and horrifying. This is a top-notch tale of aquatic horror!

4. **"Man-Size in Marble"**
Edith Nesbit (1887)

Publishing primarily under the name E. Nesbit, Edith was a successful writer of children's books, poetry, and many magnificent horror stories. "Man-Size in Marble" is about a newlywed couple who find the perfect house in which to start their life together. Trouble arises when the maid they hire says she must leave before All Saints Eve. When pressed as to why, she claims that a pair of life-sized marble statues inside the nearby church animate and go to the very house where the couple now live on that night. This is another foundational tale of the genre.

5. ***The Great God Pan***
Arthur Machen (1894)

Machen wrote several great horror stories, with "The White People" (1904) likely being his most popular. This one

The thing from "The Upper Berth" by Allen K.

Illustration for "The Monkey's Paw" by Maurice Greiffenhagen (from *The Lady of the Barge*, 1902)

happens to be my personal favorite, however. In this novella, a man witnesses his doctor friend perform brain surgery on a girl in attempts to unlock her ability to see into another realm, an act he terms as "Seeing the Great God Pan." Unfortunately, the process drives her insane. In later years, they learn of an evil, beautiful woman named Helen Vaughan who possesses secret knowledge she imparts to men that drives them to madness upon hearing it. This classic horror tale steadily builds its ever-increasing dread.

6. **"The Yellow Sign"**
   Robert W. Chambers (1895)

The stories of Robert Chambers helped inspire H. P. Lovecraft in creating the unique brand of cosmic horror he's remembered for today. This story, in particular, hits that tone perfectly. Creepiness exudes from this tale which revolves around a painter who's falling in love with his young model Tessie. While painting her, he notices an odd watchman patrolling the churchyard near his house. When the watchman looks up and meets his gaze, the artist is repelled, describing the man as a "coffin worm." When he tries to return to his work, he finds he's somehow ruined the painting of Tessie. Her image's arm taking on an unhealthy look that spreads to the rest of her the more he tries to fix it. When the model returns for another session, she tells him of a dream she had where she saw a man driving by with a coffin, and she's certain the artist was in it and the hideous watchman served as the driver. Later, Tessie finds a copy of the play, *The King in Yellow* and reads it despite the artist's attempts to prevent it. Things become far worse for the couple after that.

7. **"The Monkey's Paw"**
W. W. Jacobs (1902)

I first read this story as a school assignment for literature class in the sixth grade, believe it or not. Of course I loved it, and its power has stayed with me ever since. The story begins when a friend, who spent time in India with the British army, gives a family a withered, severed monkey's paw said to have the magical ability to grant three wishes to its bearers. As a lark, they decide to give it a try. Much to their misfortune, these claims prove far too true and exact a terrible price.

8. **"Oh, Whistle, and I'll Come to You, My Lad"** by M. R. James (1904)

James is one of the original grandmasters of the supernatural horror story. At one point I'd have specified them as "ghost stories," but when you really dig into his oeuvre, few of his nasties would be considered traditional ghosts. However you categorize them, be it ghosts, elementals, demons, or whatnot, they are always malevolent and always absolutely terrifying. In "Oh Whistle..." we find a young Cambridge professor named Parkins, who scoffs at the idea of the supernatural, as he's taking a golf vacation in the town of Burnstow. A colleague of his asks him to check out the nearby ruins of an old Knights Templar monastery during his visit. When he does so, he stumbles upon an ancient, bronze whistle with some Latin etched into it—part of which translates "Who is this who is coming?" After Parkins blows the whistle, a powerful windstorm assails the area, followed by a spectral entity which begins to relentlessly stalk him.

9. **"The Willows"**
Algernon Blackwood (1907)

Blackwood's stories are atmospheric masterpieces filled with both wonder and dread. An avid outdoorsman himself, Blackwood's tales set in the wild are iconic. These includes stories such as "The Wendigo" (1910), "The Valley of the Beasts" (1921) and "Ancient Lights" (1914) to name a few, but I believe "The Willows" is his best. Here we have a pair of friends who take an ill-advised canoe trip down a section of the Danube River during flood season. Bad weather forces them to dock on a small island which is filled with willows. While trapped there, the thrill-seekers bear witness to bizarre events that seem brought about by a powerful unearthly presence. This is a tour de force of horror fiction due to how subtly it moves from obscure hints that something is wrong, to the fearful, awe-inspiring things that happen near the end.

10. **"Thurnley Abbey"**
Perceval Landon (1907)

There was no way I could make this list without including "Thurnley Abbey" on it. Despite having been published well over a century ago, "Thurnley Abbey" has lost none of its power and remains one of the quintessential haunted house stories. When Alastair Colvin asks a stranger if he can share a compartment with him on the ship upon which they are about to embark, he decides he must explain why. He then relates the tale of how he went to stay at a friend's house called Thurnley Abbey. That friend said he had a task he would like him to perform without elaborating as to what it might be. That evening, Alastair ends up encountering an abhorrently hideous specter in his room. This is a chilling haunted house story which has been often anthologized over the years. The description of the ghost and the mind-rending effect it has on Colvin and the owners of the house is palpable. (Reprinted in *Nightmare Abbey 3.*)

11. "Afterward"
Edith Wharton (1910)

Edith Wharton went from someone who couldn't even sleep in a room that contained a book of ghost stories in it, to someone who wrote a number of brilliant ghost stories herself. One of those being "Afterward," a tale perfectly summed up by its title, as reflecting back upon earlier parts of the story is key to its ending. It begins with an American couple who come into money after the husband pulls off a big business deal. They move to England and find an old, secluded house. They are told the house is haunted but in a way that you wouldn't realize until long afterward. Things proceed leisurely until the wife learns of a lawsuit being brought against her husband involving the business transaction that brought them their newfound wealth. Soon afterwards, a man comes to see her husband. After the meeting, she learns her husband unexpectedly, and without explanation, left with the mysterious man. The rest of the story revolves around the search for her husband, the mysteries surrounding his business, and what involvement the previously mentioned ghost has to play in everything.

12. "The Whistling Room"
William Hope Hodgson (1910)

This is the story that originally made me a fan of Hodgson's work. It led me to search out a lot more by him, and I wasn't disappointed. His high seas horror stories, which I wrote about in *Nightmare Abbey 6*, are top-notch! This strictly land-based tale brings famed occult detective Carnacki to investigate a room in an Irish castle from which a whistling sound has been emanating. The room is haunted by an extremely powerful, supernatural entity which pushes Carnacki to his limits. I love the imaginative form this thing takes, as well as the spooky reason behind the haunting. Hodgson, who also wrote a masterful novel of cosmic horror in *The House on the Borderlands* (1908), was killed on the battlefield in Ypres, Belgium, during WWI.

13. "How Fear Departed from the Long Gallery" by E. F. Benson (1911)

E. F. Benson wrote a ton of great horror stories, and I was originally going to put "Caterpillars" in this spot, but since I covered that in *Nightmare Abbey 3*, I decided this was a worthy replacement. Church-Peveril is a large manor house so full of spectral emanations the family and staff have become acustomed to them. There is one manifestation they must take steps to avoid, however. Long ago, an evil man strangled two young twins who were the rightful successors to the estate and cast them into a vast fireplace in the gallery hall. Since then, anyone remaining in the hall after sunset encounters the pitiable twins before suffering a horrible death soon afterward. Benson masterfully relates the terror of being caught after sunset in the dreaded gallery, and the scene where a woman experiences a nightmare on a green couch is so weird and unsettling, it will stay with me always. This is a fantastic ghost story!

So, there you have it, my choices for the scariest Pre-WWI horror stories. The next list will begin where this one left off and go forth to the Second World War.

"POSER," SAID FLORA UNDER HER BREATH.

Jamie was standing on the stone stairs outside the hotel, one foot higher than the other to show off the folds of the kilt and a shapely knee. He was gazing at the distant hills, rather than where he should have been, which was at the group of tourists disembarking from the coach.

Flora went over to greet them. "Fáilte," she said, and then "Welcome," because sometimes using a language other than English confused visitors. She shook back her brilliant auburn hair and smiled winningly. "I'm Flora Bane. I hope you had a good journey?"

Then she turned her head and said, "Jamie," with just enough of an edge in her voice that he stopped posturing and came down the steps to help with the bags. Most of the party were middle-aged, but not so old that they didn't follow the swagger and swing of the kilt with their eyes.

It took some time to transfer everyone and all their bags to the hotel's reception area. Flora flitted about, going up and down the steps and in and out the arched stone doorways, sometimes laying a gentle hand on an arm, or peeping enquiringly into a face. Her slim figure looked charming in her tartan dress; it was a hunting tartan in shades of green and blue and set off her hair nicely.

She heard one of the guests say, "I sure hope this hotel does a decent cup of coffee," and someone else said, "Don came in '19 and he says all the showers are the same. It's like they don't have plumbers here."

Flora's smile did not waver. Her gaze danced briefly over to Jamie. He was leaning over the reception desk, saying something to the receptionist, so she could only see the back of his head; she noticed that he had tied back his long hair with a black velvet ribbon, as if he were Bonnie Prince Charlie himself. In her opinion it was over the top, but the tourists lapped that stuff up.

THEY LET THE GUESTS settle in, and then there was a welcome dinner. The hotel had entered into the spirit of the tour; the dining room was festooned with swathes of black drapery, and the dinner was served by flickering candlelight. Flora had donned black lace glovelettes and jet earrings for a properly Gothic effect. She watched, smiling, as Jamie made a toast: "To the Mystic Scotland Tour!"

The pair of them had debated the name for ages. Flora would have liked something more traditional, with the name of a genuine Scottish apparition worked in, but she had to admit that the target audience probably wouldn't have heard of kelpies or the Cailleach. Jamie had suggested the Loch Ness Monster Tour, but she had vetoed that because it was such a hideous cliché. *Mystic*, they had eventually decided, would bring in the crystal collectors and astrologers as well as the folklore fiends.

She saw Jamie leaning back to speak to the waiter, and hoped that he wasn't ordering more of the single malt; if he drank a lot of it he was inclined to become indiscreet. All the same, it was tempting to cushion oneself against the inevitable moment when someone said—

"I'm Scottish too, you know."

Flora turned her head. The speaker was to her right, a pudgy-looking man with a complacent face.

"Goodness," said Flora. "Really?"

"Oh yeah," said the man. "My great great grandmother was a Campbell."

"Just as well we're not stopping in Glencoe," said Flora, unable to resist. Then she saw his expression of bewilderment and admonished herself silently; these people were their meat and drink, after all. "Have some wine," she said, and devoted herself to being nice for the rest of the meal.

THE NEXT DAY they took the coach to Glamis Castle. Flora looked out of the window at the distant hills while Jamie commandeered the microphone, and related a highly embroidered tale about the monstrous heir of Glamis, legendarily secreted in a hidden chamber within the castle. The way Jamie told the story, you would have thought he had personally seen it. When he began to describe the hideous howling that was heard up and down the ornate halls, Flora had to bite her lip to stop herself laughing.

At the castle they had a well-earned break while the official guides showed the group around. The coach driver went off to chain smoke behind a hedge. Flora put her head on Jamie's shoulder, pressing herself close.

"Well?" she said.

"Well what?" said Jamie, squinting down at her.

She prodded him in the ribs. "You know what I mean."

He snorted. "At least three. The tall woman with the red scarf. The bald guy with the stick. And the one whose great grand-mother was a Campbell."

"Great great grandmother," Flora corrected him. She wrinkled her nose. "You ought to know their names by now."

Jamie shrugged. "Who cares? They're just kyne."

"Jamie!" She gave him a little shove.

"Well? It's true."

"Yes, but you have to make them feel special. That's how it works. You *know* that."

"Aye," said Jamie at last. He looked down at her, and brushed a strand of flaming hair back from her face. "There are better things to do, you know," he said.

Flora looked at him sternly. "That's all very well, but we have to eat."

AFTER GLAMIS they went to Dunnottar Castle—"the most haunted castle in Scotland," Flora informed the tour. It supposedly had, amongst other spectres, a Green Lady, eternally searching for her lost children, and Flora occasionally wondered whether she ought to wear a green dress when they visited—just to set the scene.

There was rather a steep flight of steps down to the area below the castle, and another set leading up into the fortifications, so she stayed on the cliffs with those who couldn't manage it; she led them about to all the best spots to take photographs, while Jamie accompanied the others to the castle. Flora watched his progress. She saw him offer a hand to the woman in the red scarf, as gracefully as if they had been going to dance a minuet, and the corner of her mouth twitched.

After Dunnottar they had lunch and then pressed on towards Inverness, where the group were staying the night. Just before Inverness they made a stop to visit Clava Cairns, a Bronze Age burial complex undramatically sited by a single track road amongst fields. Flora felt that any tour of the eldritch sites of Scotland ought to include at least *one* stone circle or standing stone or the like, and this was the obvious choice. All the same, she felt the need to talk it up, because she was well aware that the site was rather quiet-looking if, say, your last trip had been to Vegas.

She hopped up onto a handy block of stone and turned to the group, waiting for their attention. When every face was looking up at her, she clasped her hands and said:

"Human sacrifice."

She let the words sink in for a moment before she went on.

"It is a terrible thought, isn't it? And when you look at these ancient stones, so long undisturbed in this silent, lonely place, it is hard to imagine that once they ran red with blood."

That bit always made Flora want to cross her fingers surreptitiously. She was pretty sure the cairns were just burial mounds, and they weren't particularly undisturbed either, since the Victorians had poked about in them. But that didn't sell tours, and besides, if she started spouting names and dates, would any of the group really remember them?

"Yes, blood," she continued. "And these structures would have echoed with the last desperate screams of the innocent..."

Flora wondered whether it would be worth putting in something at this point about the blood sacrifices being necessary to guarantee the harvest, like in *The Wicker Man*. Or was that too much of a cliché? She'd have to think about it. Meanwhile, she kept going with a good deal of blood and thunder and not a lot of substance, and all the time her gaze was wandering through the crowd. She gave Jamie a sidelong glance and saw that he was doing the same thing.

The tall woman with the red scarf had a pinched look on her face, which could have been disapproval or outright disgust. Or perhaps the Lorne sausage at breakfast had disagreed with her. Flora suspected the expression was disapproving. She recalled the woman talking rather a lot about "the fae" over lunch, and thought that her expectations of "Mystic Scotland" probably ran to Sithichean and selkies rather than ritual murder.

The bald man with the stick was following everything she said with rapt attention, but she remembered him at Dunnottar; he had looked longingly at the steep stairs leading down towards the castle, and then he had elected to stay on the cliffs with Flora.

What about the descendant of the Campbells? She couldn't see him just now. She threw in some extra stuff about the Ballachulish goddess and the mysterious meaning of petrospheres, and then she climbed down from the stone, dusting her hands together.

While the tourists were strolling about taking photographs, she went over to Jamie.

"Anything?"

He grinned. "Mike. The guy who says he's the last of the Campbells or whatever. Came right up to me and asked if I could recommend anywhere else he could go after the tour. He has four more days in Glasgow, he says."

"What a stroke of luck!" Flora clapped her hands. Then she looked more serious. "He's not meeting anyone, or anything?"

Jamie shook his head. "Don't think so. He doesn't know a soul here, so far as I can tell. He's travelling alone because his missis left him two weeks ago. Went off with the pool boy, he said."

"He told you *that*?"

"Aye."

"They always overshare," said Flora. She became brisk. "Well, that's settled then. Now we just have to get through Loch Ness."

"And the rest of it."

"Loch Ness is the worst," said Flora. "They're always so cross when they don't see the monster."

"We ought to pay someone to dress up," suggested Jamie.

"That's a thought," said Flora, laughing. She was still smiling when the group climbed back onto the coach.

TWO DAYS LATER, the tourists climbed out of the coach again for the last time. It was parked up in front of a large modern hotel with a doorman dressed in tartan trews. The doorman nodded to Jamie.

"Hello again, Mr. Bane."

"Mr. Bane?" said Jamie, grinning. "Why so formal, Archie?"

"He's so handsome, isn't he?" said a voice at Flora's elbow. She looked around to see one of the tourists, a plump, white-haired lady who was probably in her seventies.

"What, Archie?"

The woman tittered. "No—your husband! Though I probably shouldn't say that to *you*."

Flora laughed politely. It was on the tip of her tongue to say, he's not my *husband*, but she didn't.

They had collected a fairly decent amount of tips this time. The only person who hadn't been generous was the woman with the red scarf. Flora suspected she had been correct in her assessment of the woman's interests.

Miserable old cat, she thought. It wasn't as though she and Jamie hadn't worked hard for their crust. She watched the woman's back as she went off into the hotel, and thought that it was almost a pity...

But then she shook her head. She and Jamie had work to do.

THEY TOOK MIKE to a snug in a quiet backstreet to discuss the proposition. Flora sat close to him, looking alternatively charming and encouraging, while Jamie went to the bar to order drinks. He ordered halves for himself and Mike, since it was inadvisable to get him so drunk that he'd have forgotten all about the plan by the next morning. Flora took a small sherry.

Mike was enchanted by the entire place. He admired the oak furniture, scuffed and ring-marked from long usage; the soft lights on wall brackets; the vast selection of single malts behind the bar; the old-fashioned engravings of Girvan Cove and Bennane Head. "Wow," he said, a lot of times, and "Oh my God," and once, "Jeez."

After a while, a stout man in a dark coat and with the remains of reddish hair came in and stopped to speak to Jamie.

Flora leaned close to Mike. "That's Angus Bane. He owns this place."

"That's your name too, right? Is he a relation?" Mike looked agog.

"Yes," said Flora. "Sort of a distant cousin."

"Wow."

To Flora's amazement, Mike stood up and insisted on shaking Angus Bane's hand. "This is a great place you have here, Mr. Bane."

Angus looked at him for a moment. "Aye," he grunted. Then he nodded at Jamie and Flora, and strolled off.

Flora saw Mike open his mouth and she was terribly afraid he was going to effuse about how taciturn Angus was.

She cut in with, "Should we talk about tomorrow?"

"Oh yeah," said Mike, practically rubbing his hands.

Jamie leaned forward, putting a confidential elbow on the table. "Have you heard of Sawney Bean?"

Mike's face fell. "No."

"Well, he's not on most tours. Too grisly for the regular tourists, you see." Jamie shook his head. "People come on the Mystic Scotland tour for the folklore and the fairies. But they don't see the real Scotland. Real Scottish folklore is grim and bloody."

"I'll bet."

"Sawney Bean, he was the bloodiest of them all," Jamie continued. "Sawney is short for Alexander, though he hardly merited such a fine name. They say he was born in the late 1400s, and was a tanner by trade; well used to butchering and skinning. He set up home with a woman called Agnes, in a cave by the seashore in the parish of Colmonell. It was a good hiding place; you cannot get into the cave at all at high tide.

"Sawney and his wife used to go up to the roads that ran through the district, and ambush unwary travellers. Then they would drag the bodies back to the cave, strip them of their valuables, and hack them into pieces. And then—"

Jamie paused for dramatic effect.

"They would eat them, and drink their blood."

"For real?"

Jamie nodded. "So they say. In time the pair of them had bairns, and they fed those wee ones on the same meat and drink. And the bairns grew up and had wee ones of their own, until there was an army of them, preying on those who passed."

"How did they have kids of their own if they were in hiding?" asked Mike, his brows furrowed.

"Since you force me to say it—with each other," said Jamie grimly.

"Oh my *God.*"

"This went on for a long time. They would throw the body parts they didn't eat into the sea, and sometimes they would wash up further down the coast, to the horror of the local people. But nobody had any idea what was really going on.

"Then at last one night Sawney and his family attacked two travellers on their way home from a fair—a husband and wife, riding on one horse together. The husband put up a brave defence but his wife fell from the horse and was instantly set upon by the cannibals, who tore her apart in front of him. He barely escaped with his life, but escape he did. Then the king's men went to search for the evil doers with bloodhounds, and at last they came to the cave where the Bean family lived.

"Boldly they went inside, and what a sight met their eyes! Like an abbatoir, it was. Body parts hung from the walls, and plunder taken from the unlucky travellers lay heaped all around.

"The king's men took Sawney and the menfolk of his family, and quartered them at Leith—you know what that means?"

Mike shook his head. He was round-eyed.

"They cut off their arms and legs and let them bleed to death. And then they burned the women at the stake."

Flora dabbed at her eyes. "I'm sorry," she said faintly. "It's such a terrible story."

"Aye, it is," said Jamie soberly. "And some folk can't stomach it, which is why it's not part of the main tour. But if you think you're up to it, Mike, we can take you on a private trip to see the place where it happened. Sawney Bean's cave."

If you think you're up to it, Mike. Jamie knew that would do it. He waited out the seconds before Mike burst out with an enthusiastic "Hell yeah!"

After that, they had another round of drinks and discussed the money. Jamie didn't push too hard, not wanting to derail the whole thing, but neither did he go too low; if it was a giveaway, Mike might wonder why. Eventually they ordered food, and Jamie became amusing, full of extraordinary, colourful tales, and Flora put her slender fingers on Mike's chunky hand and squeezed it, and by then it was far too late for Mike to meet up with the rest of his tour party again. They tumbled out of the snug into darkness, and laughed their way up the narrow street.

They arranged to pick him up very early in the morning, before the others would be down for breakfast; a necessity, because of the tides. They saw Mike into his hotel, and then Jamie and Flora wandered off hand in hand, back to their own, much cheaper hotel.

IN THE GREY LIGHT of dawn Jamie and Flora pulled up outside Mike's hotel in a hired car. This was the moment which always gave Flora a slight feeling of unease; supposing Mike had changed his mind during the night? That had only happened once or twice, but you never knew. However, there he was on the steps, his shoulders hunched, pulling his jacket close around him.

Jamie got out of the car and opened the passenger door for Mike. Flora was in the back, and she good-naturedly refused Mike's offer to swap places.

"I've seen the M77 loads of times," she said.

As the car pulled away she produced film-wrapped sandwiches and insulated cups of hot coffee.

Mike was blowing on his fingers.

"It won't be this cold all day," said Flora. "Put the heating up, Jamie."

They passed the outskirts of the city, and for some time they travelled through the countryside. It always surprised Flora how quickly the transition from urban to rural went; in Scotland you were never far from the land.

The motorway became a dual carriageway, and later still a single carriageway. After Turnberry it followed the coastline, and the sea was always to their right, vast and grey, with the ominous bulk of Ailsa Craig in the distance. Flora pointed it out and Mike wanted to know if anyone lived there; she said they didn't—it was a lonely rock in the middle of the sea, its lighthouse now automated. She kept talking for a while, about the history of the rock and the other interesting sights along the coast; she could see that Jamie was jittery, drumming his fingers on the wheel.

At last they came to the parking place, and saw with relief that it was empty. That was the last difficulty overcome, though Flora supposed she needn't have been concerned; they were up far earlier than anyone else, and the roads after Turnberry had been almost deserted. They parked up, and set off down the path that led to the beach.

Mike went rather slowly, unused to walking any distance over rough terrain. Jamie went ahead, striding across the grass, but Flora stayed with Mike, and offered him her hand in places where the slope was very steep. She noticed that he held on to it longer than he need have. She smiled at him.

"You'll have such a tale to tell, Mike."

When they got down to sea level there was a strip of grey sand, and then rocks. Mike was breathing hard now, and they had to wait for him. Jamie glanced almost casually up at the cliffs, but there was nobody else in sight; they were quite alone with the rattle and hiss of the sea.

When Mike had caught his breath, they started to climb over the stones, towards the entrance of the cave. It was a long vertical crack in the cliffs, not particularly obvious until you were close up, and very dark inside.

Jamie leaned close to Flora and spoke in a low voice. "You or me?"

Flora didn't turn her head. "You, I think. He keeps smiling at me; I'd feel a bit of a heel."

"Sentimental," remarked Jamie drily. "I ought to make you do it."

"Don't be horrible," said Flora feelingly.

There was a pause. "Oh, alright," said Jamie. He patted his jacket, gave Flora a brisk nod and headed off towards Mike, who was standing at the entrance to the cave, gazing in.

"It's pitch black," Mike said. "I can't see a thing."

Jamie felt in his pocket and produced a small flashlight. "Here you go."

"Thanks. Hey, are you sure you don't wanna go first?"

Jamie shook his head. "You'll not see anything with me in the way. I'll be right behind you—don't worry."

"Well…okay then." Mike sounded a little dubious, but he took the flashlight, switched it on, and stepped into the cave.

Flora leaned against a rock close by the entrance. At last the cloud cover parted and brilliant beams of sunshine lanced down. She felt the cold stone at her back, held her breath and listened.

She heard the crunch of Mike's footsteps as he went further in; they sounded uneven, a little hesitant. His voice was echoing off the rock and she couldn't quite make out what he was saying, although the tone was enthusiastic. *Wow*, probably, and *Oh my God.*

Then she heard Jamie's footsteps as he followed. Jamie trod more heavily, and with confidence. His voice was a bass murmur as he responded to Mike's exclamations.

The sounds became more distant and more resonant as they penetrated further into the cave. After the narrow entrance it opened out into a bigger area and Flora judged they must have reached that. There was more space there, more room to manoeuvre—to swing your arm, for example.

Mike gave a sudden yelp. That first cry did not sound frightened. It sounded startled, perhaps incredulous.

Flora let out a long breath.

A moment later, Mike began to scream. Within the confines of the cave, the cold stone walls, the screams echoed tinnily, as though more than one Mike were shrieking his head off. They seemed to last for a very long time, although afterwards Flora thought it had perhaps only been a minute. Then they stopped, very abruptly. There was silence.

A little while later, Jamie came crunching out of the cave. He was breathing heavily. Flora stared at him.

"What a mess," she said.

"Put up more of a fight than you'd think," said Jamie. "Just as well it was me." He cocked his head. "Come on. I'm not doing *everything* myself."

Flora pushed herself away from the rock and followed him back into the cave.

AFTERWARDS, they went into the chilly sea in all their clothes. Jamie even had red in the roots of his hair; he ducked his head under the water and moved it about, rinsing. Flora stood waist-deep, trying to decide whether she thought the sea was envigorating or just freezing cold. They staggered out of the water, clean but pale and covered in gooseflesh, their clothes sticking to them. Then Jamie ran up the cliff path to the car to fetch dry things and a waterproof holdall.

Flora never liked to eat too much before she went into the water; she was afraid of cramp. While they were putting the little packages wrapped in greaseproof paper into the holdall, she popped one or two choice morsels into her mouth. Then she licked her fingers clean.

What didn't need to go with them, they threw into the sea, for the fish to nibble, or the currents to carry wherever they would. Flora kept the telephone, meaning to drop it into a drain somewhere in the city; the Platinum card was probably useful for a few payments before a PIN was required.

They sat in the hire car for a while before they drove off, running the engine to warm themselves up. Jamie opened the glove box and took out a hip flask full of single malt, which he offered to Flora.

She accepted it daintily, and was about to take a swig when she hesitated.

"We should drink to something. It's been a good day."

Jamie grinned. "To our illustrious forebear?"

"Alright then," said Flora, and flourished the flask. "To Alexander Bane."

"Ach, Flora," said Jamie. "You're always putting on airs and graces." He shook his head. "Just drink to Sawney Bean."

Helen Grant writes Gothic novels, the latest of which is Jump Cut (2023), and short supernatural fiction. Her new short story collection Atmospheric Disturbances was published late in 2024 by Dublin's Swan River Press. Joyce Carol Oates has described her as "a brilliant chronicler of the uncanny as only those who dwell in places of dripping, graylit beauty can be."

Title graphic: an enraving of Scottish cannibal Alexander "Sawney" Bean by Isaac Basire (after J. Nicholls in the 1741 book *A Compleat History of the Lives and Extraordinary Adventures of the Most Famous Pyrates, Highwaymen, Murderers, Street-Robbers &c.*, by Capt. Charles Johnson, a pseudonym for a group of writers that may have included Daniel Defoe).

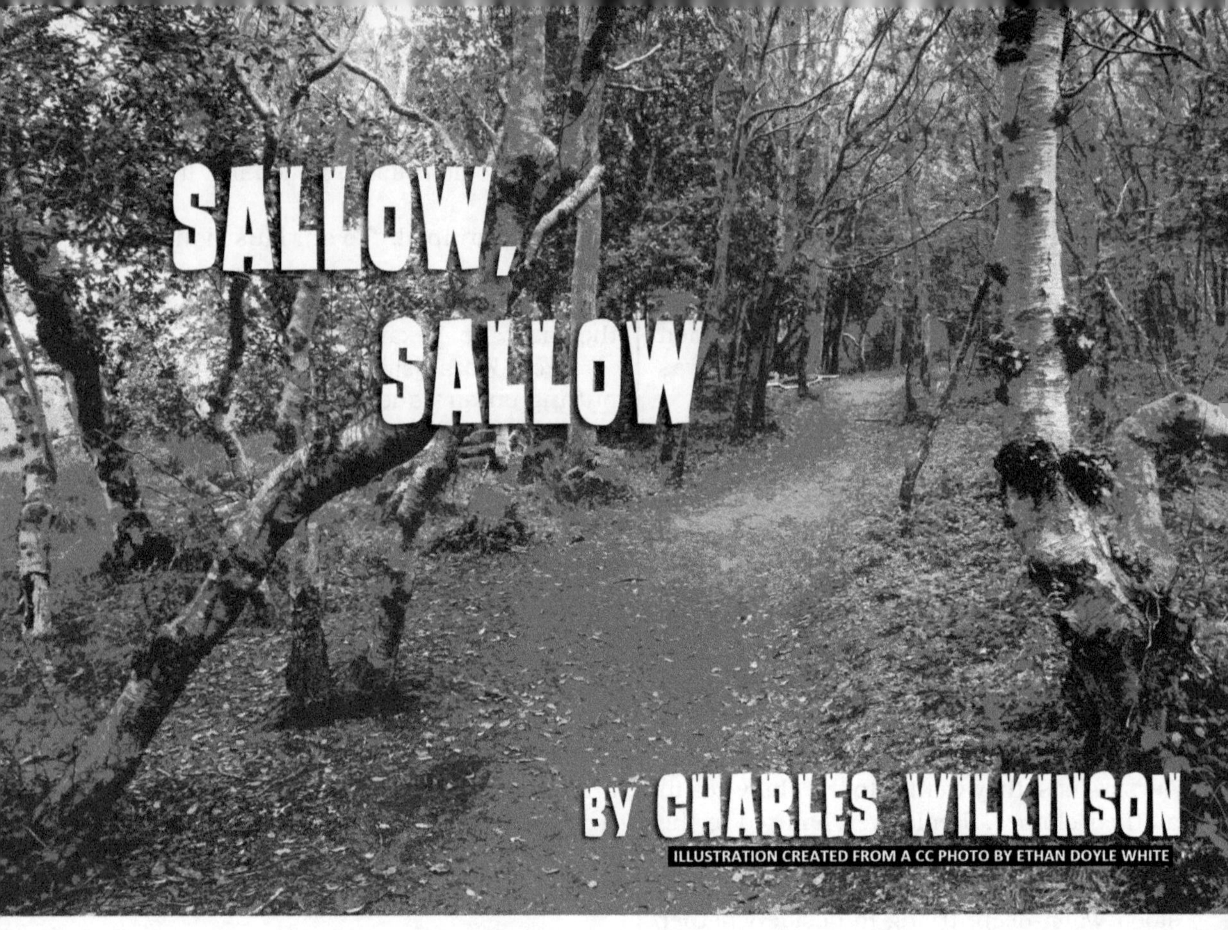

ONCE IT WAS CLEAR TO HER SHE'D NEVER MARRY OR HAVE CHILDREN, SYLVIA ENDED THE RELATIONSHIP AND MOVED TO WALES. The rain matched her mood, its fall through silver-grey light suited to the single life to which she was now condemned. She rented a flat near the centre of the town. She observed the people of that place as they went about their business against the backcloth of cloud, stucco-clad shop frontages and red-brick buildings, which only on rare sunny days held a hint of warmth. It was a month before she spoke to anyone for more than the minute required to order groceries or a meal in the sole café tolerable to her taste and means.

She met Irwin Teague at the opening of an exhibition of Welsh textiles held at the community centre. The woollen blankets, cushions, throws, and comedic sheep did not divert her for long. Now she was standing in the middle of the hall and holding a plastic cup containing a white wine, its tannins the taste of nail polish.

"They must put considerable care into selecting a vintage as awful as that," he said, indicating her hand, held at a safe distance from her stomach. "Are you afraid it's combustible?"

"How do you know what it's like? You're drinking the red."

"I tried the white first. I think it laid a claim to being a chardonnay. Even if it had been properly chilled, one sip would have been enough. The red's not much of an improvement. It's merely a question of whether they want to give you severe or mild indigestion."

It had been a long time since she'd laughed, and she still couldn't manage it. Instead, she issued an involuntary smile. He was slim, perhaps a few years younger than she was. His dishevelled, curly black hair and open shirt under a soft tweed jacket, worn and three sizes too large, as well as his frayed, loose trousers, leant him the look of an artistic outsider flaunting his father's wardrobe. She checked him for flecks of flake white.

"Perhaps they serve it so that everyone will give up after the first glass. To save on the cost."

"You're probably right," he said, taking a swig of wine and then wincing. "Do you want to go on somewhere else? I've seen sufficient cushions for one night."

She hesitated. His eyes were mild and grey; not piercing like those of a potential predator.

"Don't worry," he continued, his smile guileless, even sunny. "I'm harmless. I've had the full frontal lobotomy. I've got the piece of paper with the discharge from the psychiatric unit if you want to see it."

And now she laughed at last. "All right. But I'm not sure that there's anywhere that appeals or is both good and affordable."

"Come back to my place if you like. I've got coffee and a bottle of Gaviscon that I can crack open."

"Sounds good. But I prefer Rennies."

Outside, the light was starting to fade, the shop interiors in darkness, sometimes a solitary light burning above the entrance. A quarter moon was just visible, a pale scratch on the blue-black sky. Although it was not late, the sound of singing, the voices rasping and out of tune, was audible when the door of the nearest inn opened to let the arrivals into the golden warmth.

"You're a newcomer, aren't you?"

"Yes, I've been here for three months. And you?"

"Just over a year. I can't say I like it that much, but it's cheap. And there's a great view of the ovine majority within walking distance."

Irwin's flat was up an alley just off the High Street. A slight smell of damp when he opened the door; then a surprisingly large sitting-room; it would have appeared more spacious if it hadn't been for the unpacked crates and cardboard boxes.

"Are you moving out or still moving in?"

"A good question. I'm still not sure. If I buy bookshelves and get this lot off the floor, it would be a statement of intent. I'm having difficulty in committing to this town."

Irwin made the coffee. They swapped tales of previous lives in London. Her motives for moving were almost identical to his: affordable accommodation and lower prices in the shops. Their laptops gave them the freedom to live anywhere. His tone was light, engaging. And there was still no hint of a hunter's glint in his eyes. It was only when the topic turned to the town and its inhabitants that he became serious.

"Alas, I've little in common with the locals, but I wouldn't want to say anything against them. They're amiable enough, although they keep you at a distance; just not interested in anyone who's new to the area. Your pedigree has to go back a couple of generations or more before you're truly accepted. But I can rub along with them well enough. It's the Private People who cast a pall over the place.

THEY WERE WELL SUITED, Irwin thought: Sylvia had smiled at his sense of the absurd; their backgrounds alike; both strangers to small town life on the Borders. He liked her heart-shaped face and auburn hair. But in his present predicament was it worth pursuing a relationship—or even right? He went into the kitchen and switched the kettle on. As it chuckled to the boil, he remembered what had brought him to the town.

His parents had retired to a large village in the West Midlands. About three quarters of a mile away lay an area of mixed woodland with a stream winding through it. He'd been told that a group of men from a nearby market town had appointed themselves as guardians of this place. In some respects, they'd done good work, taking on many of the tasks formerly the responsibility of the hard-pressed local council: they'd cleared pathways, picked litter, and created primitive but not ineffective flood defences. Yet it was thought they'd become overly proprietorial. There was a rumour they were members of a Christian cult, although this was never substantiated.

The deaths started after the woods were the subject of a compulsory purchase order. Trees were felled and a slip road for the nearest motorway constructed. The road accidents, many fatal, took place where the centre of the wood had been or near the bridge later built over the stream. Road safety experts were at a loss to explain the high mortality rate at a location that, according to their assessment, shouldn't have proved unduly dangerous. On a dark night, when they were coming home from the cinema, both of Irwin's parents were killed in a crash just after they'd driven over the bridge.

Six months afterwards, the cult, known as the Private People, left the area. The deaths diminished and then dwindled to a figure in line with the laws of probability. To his friends, Irwin made a connection between the departure of the cult and the decrease in mortality: a view that gained no credence. Indeed, when he repeated his beliefs, and mentioned that he intended to contact the authorities, some countered with the argument that the public were more aware of the dangers now and took greater care; others looked at him askance, and then changed the subject.

A year later, a friend described how whilst on holiday he had chanced upon the Private People when visiting a small town in Wales. It was his duty, Irwin told himself, to bring them to account or at least to prevent the pattern from repeating. So far there'd been no deaths that he could lay at their door. Were they only dangerous when a wood was damaged or defiled? But after what he'd witnessed late one afternoon in the Withy Beds, he understood something of their nature. And they were no Christians.

Sylvia had left a message on his answer phone; he hadn't replied. Looking back on his last meeting with her, he marvelled at his ability to appear outwardly relaxed, but beneath the geniality and humour he was worried. Did protecting her from risk mean that he'd have to cut off all contact? He wouldn't have thought so if it hadn't been for the incident in the High Street.

He'd been on his way to the convenience store when the man approached him: an ordinary person at first sight—a gardener or forester perhaps. His tan, of a depth not easy to acquire in Wales, suggested a life lived out of doors. He was thin, his forearms well wired with thick veins, his hands gnarled.

"My friends have seen you," he said, not looking Irwin in the eye.

"Really. Well, I lay no claim to invisibility. And who might these famous friends of yours be?"

"Up and down the same street. Resting yourself on a certain bench...and worse!"

"Thank you for your clear answer to my question. But to what does 'and worse' refer to?"

"Not local, are you? Now there's no sin in that. But best to be careful when you've uprooted yourself." The man stepped closer to Irwin, so close he could scent his earthy breath. "Or you'll find out what 'uprooting' really means...sallow, sallow!"

Irwin sipped his tea. It was true that the man was not dressed as a Private Person, but it had been clear enough that he was connected with them; at least before he began to speak in riddles about "uprooting." As to his final two words, Irwin was far from sure he'd heard them correctly.

SYLVIA DISCOVERED the Withy Beds by accident. There was a small nature reserve on the edge of the town, a home for wildlife and the willows that had once supported a local trade in basket weaving, box-making, and brooms. But it had been many years since osiers had been coppiced; now it was a patch of mixed woodland, although the stumps of long felled willows and the low fringes of those still growing that swept the ground were easily discernible. She liked to walk there on the few fine afternoons when the green radiance in the trees was an alloy of leaf-light and gold; the interplay of sun and shadow at its most alluring. A flight of wooden steps and a bridge led down to a timbered walkway through the semi-sodden undergrowth. Muddy paths snaked their way to the river.

Sometimes she bumped into dog walkers who allowed their pets a dip on the occasional hot days, but today it was quiet. She wished she knew the names of the birds that called and sang above her. Perhaps she'd ask Irwin to come on one of her walks. She enjoyed her visit to his flat and felt safe with him, although his change of mood when he spoke about the Private People had proved perturbing. For such a gentle person, his evident anger, and, even more alarming, fear, was out of character.

"Whenever I bring this up," he'd said, "the locals look at me as if I've lost my mind. As the cult don't mix with them or engage in any way with the community, the Private People are simply of no interest."

But when she'd asked him what the present danger was his answers appeared closer to fiction than reality. For a start, he said, they were a cult. Yes, it was difficult to be specific as to their beliefs, but it was not simply a case of holding mildly heterodox views, of that he was certain. These people were harking back to something far older than Christianity: arcane practices, almost certainly ritualistic, even embedded in a sense of nature that entailed dark sacrifice.

"What are you saying then," she asked him, aware of her smile creasing with imminent laughter. "Are they what... Druids?"

He fell silent for a moment, registering her scepticism. "There are Druids in Wales."

"But that's all from the Victorian playbook. An invention to give a sense of continuity. Fancy dress to be wheeled out for the Eisteddfods."

"There's an element of truth in that, but there's far more to it. There's hidden knowledge that has been passed down the generations for millennia. But no, strictly speaking, I don't think the Private People are Druids, although like them they are tapping into an ancient cultural inheritance. One that would be far better forgotten."

"But how do you know this?"

It was then she'd seen terror in his eyes, a glint like the tip of an iceberg, a memory rising of a force cold enough to be fatal. "I'm sorry," he said. "I shouldn't have mentioned this. I'll have to deal with it on my own."

And so he opened a bottle of wine, a far finer vintage than that served at the community hall.

A faint sibilance in the treetops, its timbre unfamiliar, as if it were about to unveil the secrets of dusk. She was approaching the end of the walkway, which opened out onto the spot where the meadow sloped down to the river. As she was leaving the leaf-varnished light behind and about to step into the afternoon sunshine, she glanced to her right. One of the paths, which twisted between gnarled tree roots and ferns and towards the water, seemed darker than she recalled, its mud closer to black than brown; the arch of the trees somehow inimical, as though something nameless and lithe might leap down from the branches, ready to entwine anyone passing through.

Irwin had lied to her. He knew there was no chance he could leave, at least not for now. Trapped in the town, that's what he was. He glanced out of the window. Although the day outside seemed bright, experience had taught him not to be caught without his jacket. In Wales, you were never safe from a turn in the wind direction, a cold-bladed front blasting in from the east.

The High Street was quiet, just a few old ladies with heavily laden bags coming in and out of the convenience store; a huddle of men with flat caps and the rough, raw faces of retired farmers standing on a corner, three furiously pedalling, lycra-clad men speeding through. As he turned down the street leading to the church, he spotted the Rector, a spindly figure but well over six foot, striding towards him. They were on nodding terms, although nothing more than a few pleasantries had ever passed between them. Why had Irwin never asked him about the Private People? Surely he could hardly relish them polluting his parish.

"Good morning, Rector. What's the rush? Not another outbreak of the Pelagian heresy on the top estate."

The Rector stopped, his expression uncertain as he peered down at Irwin through half-moon spectacles. Was he being sent up? An uncertain smile flickered across his face, as if to say "best to treat this as banter." "No Pelegian heresy on my patch; at least not on the top estate. They're Muggletonians up there, every last man of them."

"But you'll root this out?"

"Absolutely! They believe God is five foot six tall and lives sixteen miles above earth. What nonsense!" This time the smile was genuine. He'd evidently enjoyed the chance to showcase his erudition. "In fact, the last

Muggletonian died at some point in the late 1970s, as I'm sure you're aware."

"But now we have the Private People. I'm not sure what kind of Christian sect they are."

The Rector stared at the pavement and then raised the back of his hand to his mouth, as if about to cough. When he next looked at Irwin, the smile was swabbed out. "I haven't had anything to do with them. The group who owned the property before them were... Christians, although their churchmanship was not mine. I believe they did do some good by providing a refuge for women. As for the new lot, they keep themselves very much to themselves—as their name implies."

"But you don't think they're doing any harm?"

After a pause, a sense of weighing up various ways of responding, the Rector, his tone somewhat irritable, replied, "I know nothing about them... except that they are presumably not of the Anglican persuasion. But we must be tolerant. There are many paths to God. And now, if you'll excuse me, I have a..." he waved a hand, leaving an unsaid word stillborn in the air.

As Irwin watched the Rector's rapidly receding back, he couldn't help rebuking himself for failing to be more explicit. At the very least, he should have stated that the Private People presented a threat to the town. Yet as he walked on, he once again found himself, without consciously processing his decision, making his way to the converted chapel where the cult had its headquarters. After his encounter with them, it might have been commonsensical to avoid the areas where they congregated. And so why did he find himself drawn, at least twice a day, to the bench just opposite to the entrance to their citadel, where he would sit sometimes for as much as an hour, or as little as five minutes, hoping to gain a definitive clue as to the cult's practices? But so far there'd been an evidential dearth: the dark grey glass of the windows deadpan, no visitors of significance arriving and departing, the postman seldom stopping and never delivering strangely shaped parcels or packages. Was his continued vigil, in spite of the warning, a way of showing them he was not to be intimidated?

When he was about a minute away from Chapel Street, he saw four men walking towards him on the far side of the road. As always, they were dressed in green and brown: woodland colours, nothing unnaturally bright. There was, as far as he'd observed, no standard uniform, merely a cleaving to certain hues, a suggestion of bark and leafage, earth and grass. More than once, he'd followed a group back into town. Their expeditions had appeared innocent trips to the grocery, the bakery, and the convenience store. They'd appeared unaware of his presence. But today, as he drew level with them, one turned towards him with a sullen stare, and then whispered something to his companion. Irwin hurried on, but after ten yards swung round. All four of them were standing still, their eyes on him. Although they were just a little too far away for him to be sure of their expressions, something about the set of their shoulders, their posture, held an implicit malevolence, a hankering to unlock the gates of horror. He hurried away.

How much of summer was left? she wondered as she walked towards the Withy Beds. Every day night inched further into afternoon. It was important to get as much sun and exercise as she could before the Welsh winter, the winds and rain-heavy skies sweeping in from the west, day upon sodden day, turned the meadow closer to marshland and the Withy Beds into a leaf-strewn, slippery trap.

Earlier that afternoon, she'd heard tentative rain tapping on the skylight for a minute or two, but a deluge had not developed. The path to the Withy Bed led to a flight of rickety, timbered steps, with trees on either side arching inwards. At the bottom was a bridge over a sluggish brook, usually no more than slow moving mud and water, except in the wettest months. That afternoon the leaves were once again gently luminescent, as if water-gilded. And yet, unaccountably, she sensed an occupant waiting in the foliage, covert, yet aspiring to visibility. The walkway beyond the bridge curved into a densely planted part of the woods. Why was she so sure there was a presence on the far side of the corner? She stopped and listened; no slap of footsteps coming either towards or away from her; no pattering dogs or the cries of their owners; no children swishing through on bicycles. It was hard to understand why it was so singularly still and silent; even the birdsong was absent. She'd never had great trust in her intuition, she reminded herself, as she made her way down the steps and onto the walkway. Of course, there was nothing around the corner. Yet she found herself assailed by the conviction that something had only just withdrawn, moved into the willows, the stumps, the bracken, the twisted beech trunks, to conceal itself seconds before her arrival.

There was a bench at a half-way point round the circuit, a spot with a view through the woods that gave a glimpse of the stream. Deciding to defy her demons, Sylvia sat down. In a minute, a dog walker with a Labrador, slick from a dip in the stream, would come by, bringing the return of normality with them.

That morning she'd had a chance meeting with Irwin Teague. They were in a quiet street not far from the town centre. At first, she was not sure who it was. There was a figure, similarly dressed to him, approaching from a distance. Whoever it was moved swiftly and in a manner unlike Irwin. Fifteen yards behind him, there was a group of men dressed in green and brown, also proceeding with a sense of purpose. Less than a minute later, the first man hailed her and hurried over the road. He was indeed Irwin.

"Don't look over there now. I'm being followed," he panted.

But she'd already seen that the men had made no move to cross the road and were still progressing at the same pace and with no apparent interest in either of them.

"I don't think so. They're walking on by."

"But you saw them. They were pursuing me. Surely you can't have any doubts about that?"

"They were behind you and walking in your direction. But I saw nothing to suggest you were being tailed."

He glanced over her shoulder; then started to relax. "I can assure you they were...but at least they've given up for the moment."

"Who are they?"

"The Private People...but I can see you don't understand. Let's not discuss it any further now."

And then they'd made their way to a café in the town.

Now Sylvia stood up. If only there had been the sound of the stream, even the faint ripple of water moving softly over stone, it would have comforted her.

Was she uneasy because of her encounter with Irwin? She continued along the walkway. Then a slithering disturbance, a faint, sporadic rattling, engendered a vision of a gigantic plant: its soil and pebbles being shaken from its roots as it was dragged along the wooden planks. When she reached the spot where the noise was coming from there was nothing—only silence; a strong scent of freshly dug earth. The sun must have gone in, for the light was now silvery, tarnished. She quickened her pace. Just as she was about to leave the Withy Beds she heard the sound again, this time from behind her. She broke into a run, cursing her irrationality yet submitting to it all the same. Was what she'd heard men at work in the woods? This happened, especially when storms broke branches and the walkway became impassable. Yet she'd seen no such obstacle herself.

It was a relief to be on the meadow. The light had started to fail; the day was closer to dusk than she realized. Instead of returning through the woods, she'd take the long route home. A man was leaning on the fence by the stile leading onto the parkland: there were no tools or a wheelbarrow near him; he had the look of an estate worker. He stared at her, his smile indefinable.

"You're out of there just in time—that's what I'm thinking."

"The Withy Beds?"

He nodded. "Another minute or two down there, and things could have turned very nasty for you."

"In what way?"

"They don't like anyone down there once it's dark. Not when they're moving."

"And who are 'they'?"

"That's all I'm saying, girl. They're not that partial to being spoken of, either."

The man turned his back on her and ambled away in the direction of the pavilion, leaving a smell of earth not unlike that in the woods.

Sylvia took the path to the main road. Hardly anyone was in the park now, apart from a few dog walkers up by the perimeter fence. She resented being addressed as "girl," but the warning…was it well meant? Perhaps her panic had been justified; it would be prudent to avoid the place, especially when it was nearly night.

IRWIN READ THROUGH her note again. *I've greatly enjoyed our meetings; but as I implied, when I told you of my recent experience in the Withy Beds, a place that was once a great solace to me, I've begun to find the town and its surroundings oppressive. I should have taken at least some of your fears more seriously. For the time being, I'm returning to London. You will be the first to know if I decide to come back.* He turned the note over: no forwarding address.

For a second, he was assailed by sadness, but this was speedily followed by relief. If anything had happened to her, he would have judged himself culpable. And didn't her departure give him more freedom of action? Now there was no need to worry about her, he could concentrate all his energies on combating them. The principal difficulty, as he saw it, was that if he reported what he'd witnessed in the Withy Beds, not a whit of what he said afterwards would be believed.

A clear evening, he recalled: star glitter inconceivable in the capital; strings of countless galaxies beaded on the blackness. Trapped in the flat, he was overwhelmed by a desire to hear the stream's evening song. He was in the middle of the woods when he saw them: ten men grouped in a rough semi-circle around a tree, which shone with a diffuse light denied to all around it. Moonlight had somehow found a mode of penetrating the thick foliage, shimmering the silver leaves to luminous silver. Their hands raised and hieratic, the men were singing, their tone soft, supplicatory. Then a sound: something struggling to wrench itself from the soil. As he watched, the tree began to uproot itself slowly from its bed of water-mud and earth, its roots spidering, dangling gobbets of dirt. He fled. But before he reached the bridge, he heard a muttering from above, a disembodied voice, moving

as if monkey-like from tree to tree. When he reached the top of the steps, he swung round. To the naked eye, there was nothing to be seen. Yet something heavy was coming down the walkway, muttering and brushing the ferns and foliage as it went. He did not stop running until he reached his flat.

Now he squinted at his watch. The light was poor. A problem with the power supply? Still, the pubs were open for another hour. There was a quiet place he knew, tucked down an alley. He went into the kitchen to get a torch.

The man he'd seen in the street was sitting at the table. This time he was dressed in brown and green.

"How did you get in here?"

"Sallow, sallow," he said, his voice menacing, sibilant. "I'm in here all the time, me; in your wattle, I am, next to your daub."

"Get out."

The man seemed sickly, his skin a silvery green. His hands were moving, clenching downwards, roots seeking water.

"Now my friend, Mr. Oh Zee-ah. He's in the basement, but he'll be up soon. This could take two of us, that's what he told me earlier"

Ozier...a willow. And sallow, now that he came to think of it, wasn't that...the lights went out.

He could just see the shape of the visitor, a darker black on a background of dark. Now the man was growing, changing, rising, sprouting limbs—and jellyfish stalks. Stink of soil and sour water. Then a root, slime-smooth but gripping, tightening its tentacle of sap and bark on his knee. He struggled and thrashed. But already he could hear something climbing up the stairs from the basement: its wriggle-root on stone, the skitter and grate of leaves and branches against the wall. And he knew whatever was in front of him was in no hurry for a kill—as it waited for its companion to join the feast.

NOTE:

"Ellum do grieve
Oak he do hate
Willow to walk
If yew travels late"

Traditional—Katherine Briggs, *The Fairies in Tradition and Literature* (Psychology Press).

Charles Wilkinson's publications include The Pain Tree and Other Stories *(London Magazine Editions, 2000). His stories have appeared in* Best Short Stories 1990 *(Heinemann),* Best English Short Stories 2 *(W.W. Norton, USA),* Best British Short Stories 2015 *(Salt),* Confingo, London Magazine *and in genre magazines and anthologies such as* Black Static, Interzone, The Dark Lane Anthology, Supernatural Tales, Theaker's Quarterly Fiction, Phantom Drift, Bourbon Penn, Shadows & Tall Trees, Nightscript, *and* Best Weird Fiction 2015 *(Undertow Books, Canada). His collections of strange tales and weird fiction,* A Twist in the Eye *(2016),* Splendid in Ash *(2018),* Mills of Silence *(2021),* The Harmony of the Stares *(2022), and* The Water Bells *(2025) appeared from Egaeus Press. Eibonvale Press published his chapbook of weird stories,* The January Estate, *in 2022. His most recent publication is his short novel* Every Place Unlike Home *(Zagava, 2026). He lives in Wales.*

I REMEMBER THE DAY WE STOPPED PLAYING TIG. The day we no longer *dared* to play Tig. The day I grew up too quickly, going from young girl to scarred girl.

Once upon a time—isn't that what people say? How these stories generally start? It implies a ubiquity, implies it could happen anywhere or anywhen. A fable, a life lesson to be obeyed, as it were.

But this is not one such story. I can all too precisely remember when it happened. And it didn't happen in a land of fairyfolk, where the Brothers Grimm design the characters and manipulate the strings and bind the storylines; it happened in the playground of a school you're best of forgetting. The caretaker's trial scoured it from the more delicate history books anyway. It was 2021, during the aftermath of both the COVID-19 pandemic and Dad's bout of car crashes—three in seven months! Life was stuck in those foggy realms between order and chaos and, with the rigmarole of online teaching over, we were back in the classroom and trying to find some semblance of normality. Dad and I would joke when he dropped me off at school by waving me off and saying, "Have a good limbo, Varada!"—but it was accurate. The biggest difference was the segmented playgrounds and staggered lunches; every year group was in one specific section of the school grounds and half the classes took their lunch breaks at noon while the remainder took theirs at one o'clock.

It has to be said, online learning suited me far better. I had friends, but to that young girl they were always undiscovered countries. How could I expect them to see me for me when even I hadn't figured how to?

No class at school goes without its transient and unpredictable fascinations. One term it was fidget spinners, the next it was tournaments of hopscotch, the next it was football cards, and as they gripped us, they all held an allure which was distinct like no other. Football cards especially were good at creeping out of the woodwork and vanishing again more hastily than an

ADHD child's series of hyperfixations.

A cycle doomed to repeat—ad infinitum.

At the time, my class's obsession was Tig. It had a habit of consuming us. A tendrilled beast. A creature salivating over every kid in the class and casting aside those it rejected. In a weird way, we *wanted* it to drench us with its wet, tarnishing maws.

Tig was another of our games that never quite went away, emerging whenever it smelled tears it might gobble up. It thrust a kind of savagery unaffected by gender, race, or creed onto us, and crying was one of its unwritten tenets since, if there weren't tears at being excluded, there were tears after the rough and tumble of being involved.

Our obsession for the previous month had been relentless games of skimming stones in the school duck pond, but after we had caused three head wounds Miss Anwar broke free of her jovial shroud and banned the activity. We needed a new game. We certainly didn't want to see her skin metamorphose into that puce which never failed to scare us witless.

It was perhaps nigh on fate then that we brought Tig back during *that* lunchtime. What else would be there when tears and exclusion were on the horizon?

The rules of the game were simple, as they so often are when a force you can't foresee is placing you in the firing line: someone is It, everyone else must run away from you like a primitive tribe attacked by a foreign evil; whoever is It must then tig someone else and proclaim that person is It, and so it becomes endless—at least until the end of lunch.

Kids find weak spots; they probe them open like vultures do with carrion. They see little Varada, the girl who can't run very fast and doesn't really care about the game, and they make you their private hunt. It came as no surprise then that more often than not myself and Eden, one of the boys in the class, were It, although he still suffered the brunt of Tig's evil. Since I wanted to avoid Tig ending with me feeling how heartless the floor was, I had soon mastered the trick of pretending to fit in; the same was not true of him. Unlike me, he hadn't learned to ready himself against the throng of classmates as they embraced the unceremonious side of their behaviour and shoved one another to the rough floor.

Tig's gnashing jaw was far from his only problem, however. By Christ, he was infuriating. Mooing cows seemingly lined his mouth; they turned his voice into a pitiful foghorn calling the bullies to arms. And I don't just say that with the cadences of a grumpy spinster. Children don't think of each other as children generally, more as chronologically-challenged adults until proven otherwise. But he possessed whining auras in abundance, permeating everything he did, and then demanded we think of him as a child. When he opened his mouth and moaned, it made even the most immature of us look heart-attack serious.

I don't know what he does these days, but I do know he'll be whining.

Eden began Tig from beside the sundial on the grass. Everyone scattered immediately, lines of sweat and alertness creasing their faces.

A cluster of bushes unable to grow leaves even in glorious weather surrounded the sundial and their open spikes prodded me as I flung myself away.

Eden was still It a few minutes later. None of us were supposed to be on the grassy field until the summer and as the seconds passed we knew his shrill cries grew nearer to bubbling over and summoning the teachers on duty. While we obviously wanted to avoid being the dreaded It, someone of a sturdier calibre taking on the mantle rapidly became a necessity. I don't know whether Ashley decided it himself or one of us pushed him into harm's way, but when he slowed and received the title a wave of relief washed over us.

Ashley quickly bestowed the title upon Mamoon; Mamoon bestowed it upon Vinay; the title then persevered on its crusade, each of us becoming It as Tig elongated its claws.

It was inevitable that someone eventually would bestow the cursed title upon me. I could feel it strike me before the cry of "Tig, Varada, you're It!" went up and the alienating world of being It instantly came cascading down around me.

The first trick for being It was always to turn tail and tig the person who just tigged you. In my case, it never worked. Arms too short and fingers not dextrous enough to pull off such a manoeuvre, the parade of figures darted around me and Tig's jaw opened wide to gobble up their glee. I remember changing tack on this day, almost lunging sideways in the hope of catching someone off guard. The bushes' spiked tufts were my sole reward, hastily bookended by the thought of Mum killing me for gouging new holes in my cardigan.

The game continued to progress stodgily. Having an opponent you could outrun or jump free of was one thing, but everyone's faces told me there was little joy in escaping my shambolic chase as they whirled around me like rats bursting from a warren. I was easy prey, not easy competition. Although I gave chase, even I felt my gait worsening and the knot in my chest blooming.

Which is when I settled on my plan. On Millie.

Nicknames are a good way to judge someone, I find, even if it's nothing more than chopping off a syllable so you can call their name more easily when they're misbehaving. Mine was Ol' Smiler, although, like the various games in the playground, it was cyclical and only cropped up a handful of times in a year. A misnomer possibly, because my smile was a rare sight at school—it was because of my effect on teachers. Almost universally there's an age at which, wherever you go, you can make an adult grin simply by being there. Most importantly though, atrocious behaviour won't waver it. This effect seemingly followed me at school, and it became a joke of sorts that I had to be there when a teacher's storm needed weathering.

Millie had no nickname. Not Mils, nor Mil, nor M., nor any other distinction between her and the other Millie in the class. In a class of twenty-five brown and black kids, myself included, there were only two white kids, both of whom were girls, both called Millie. Yet everyone knew, if you spoke that name in all its six-lettered simplicity, you always meant the other one: the chipper, ever-clad-in-a-daisy-chain-necklace one with hair the scent of strawberries. *This* Millie, the one I chose in the moment, needed no nickname—why would she? She was always sad and therefore nobody talked to her. Naturally, the teachers did, but they seemed affected by the stigma too, calling her Pet or Chuck or Kiddo, a go-to nicety rather than a meaningful nickname.

I of course remember Millie's name these days, we all do. The memory of someone stronger than the person. Whereas numerous moments in my childhood are a series of blurs pockmarked by sunspots of clarity, this is a red-hot lesion on my soul.

The decision I made isn't one I'm proud of. I'm still not. Especially as I realise the decline and fall about to be set in motion. Like others used to choose Eden and myself as the weakest links, I chose Millie.

I shouted the vindicative cry almost preemptively that she was It, tigged her, propelled myself backwards before *she* could try the age-old first trick, and bathed in the joy of my achievement. It devoured me so much that a slab of dirt came free beneath my feet and threatened to trip me up; it was by a narrow margin I tossed myself right, keeping myself upright whilst hiding among my classmates also desperate not to be It. Was she on my tail? How near was she to catching us? We sprawled around the sundial and over the field as Tig slavered over the concrete part of the playground as well as the field. Weaving among my classmates, the other players—and even those yet to be It—had wild eyes poisoned by adrenaline. A dive here. A dodge there. We all started throwing in swerves just at the idea of the accursed It breaking open the frenzy and finding its way to us.

A knot having tightened in my chest, I eventually stopped in the furthest corner of the playground and gulped down oxygen to combat it. As all wounded animals do, I then surveyed the hunting ground for Millie. But my eyes couldn't find my victim, the meek girl to whom I had passed the dreaded It. She stayed invisible among the throng of manic creatures and the echo of my cruel, cheap decision creeped ever closer to me.

My eyes never found their target.

As though an act of prophecy, a voice wavered out of the tangled droves of children: "Hang on, who's It?" I imagine it was Caleel, the largest kid in the class and the one whose knack for art made the rest of us envious, saying the question, but possibly this is my brain trying to soothe itself.

The fact is that no one responded.

After the question floated up for a second time, the answer was just the same. Time turned to ice around us, its lethargy bringing every Tig player to a standstill. By the time the question arose for a third time, we realised there was no It anymore. If my classmates were anything like me in that moment, our links to reality were akin to ivy on a fence. Nominal. Nothing more than a connection of physical proximity. Our entire beings immediately an unitchable scratch at the back of the throat.

No one moved.

Were all eyes on me? It felt like it. Are they still on me?

"Varada," piped up Caleel (and it was definitely him this time), "you tigged Millie, didn't you? You were It and then you tigged..." He trailed off.

The bell rang two minutes later, but we remained statuesque. Even when Miss Anwar emerged and called us inside, we didn't do anything other than look around and unite in our perplexity. I'm not sure that we fully apologised to the woman before she died. Would that have been the right thing to do, or would it have simply added salt to the wound? How do you apologise for creating a media storm she couldn't shake, for being the young girl who ruined a woman's career.

For bringing a family more tears than any past Tig game.

We didn't discuss it properly afterwards—the closer we approached the topic, the more we refused to talk about it. Our teachers and then our parents and then the police all asked us, but we never asked one another what we reckoned had happened to Millie. They apparently still turn up to the school reunions though—not me. School reunion ten years later, only two missing: myself and Millie. School reunion twenty years later, only two missing. School reunion thirty years later—you get the gist.

Because I can't.

I sometimes find my thoughts going astray and wondering what the explanation was. Whenever the question has cropped up in my head, it's done so like air being reintroduced to a hermetically-sealed tomb. Letting the decaying begin and letting the rancid, sickly smell out.

I can hear her, you know. Maybe everyone in my class can, though I know it'll be most deafening in my mind even when the voice isn't shouting at me. Somedays she tells me I ought to be ashamed; and at times her voice is a trickle, a gentle stream in my ear which assuages that young girl's guilt by telling me I oughtn't worry as she's in a better place.

I'm alone now, close to my deathbed; hers is the only voice I hear anymore. Do I want to die, to put a stop to the screaming, or do I want to live, to soothe my agony?

That's why we never dared play Tig from that day forwards.

Never.

Because his obsessive love of Doctor Who *and horror films wasn't nerdy enough, Benjamin Kurt Unsworth (Ben) is currently embarking on a degree in Latin, Ancient Greek, and Ancient Classical History. When he isn't doing that, he enjoys confusing all and sundry, writing short stories and reviews for various outlets, drinking copious cups of tea, knitting, and buying far too many waistcoats, bow ties, and velvet jackets. His TBR pile threatens to topple over and crush him any day now. His solo collection,* Into Wrack and Ruin, *is available from Phantasmagoria Magazine, and the collection he co-authored with his father Simon Kurt Unsworth,* Uneasy Beginnings, *from Black Shuck Books.*

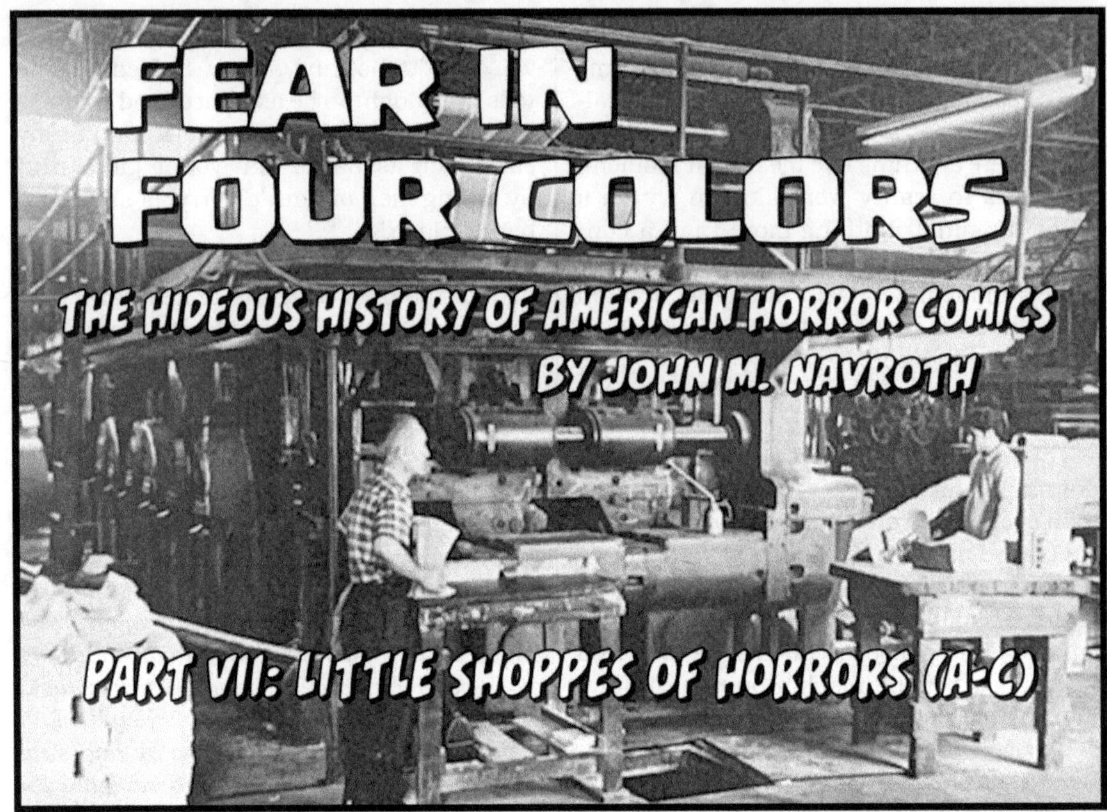

"Goodman never had any significant interest in what he published... so long as it sold."
—John Hilgart, *The Comics Journal*

THUS FAR IN THIS SERIES, WE'VE LEARNED ABOUT THE ORIGINS OF THE AMERICAN HORROR COMIC BOOK AND THE WRITERS AND ARTISTS WHO WORKED BEHIND THE SCENES CREATING THEM. We've also learned how they were relentlessly criticized and maligned throughout their short history by parents, teachers, and religious organizations until most of them buckled and collapsed under the weight of the onerous restrictions brought about as a result of public outcry.

But, what about the people who were actually involved in printing these vile, salacious, and foul things, as they were often referred to by their detractors? Many of these individuals got their start publishing pulps, then superhero, Western, humor, crime, and romance comics, turning to horror only when it became obvious after watching EC Comics' now-legendary titles fly off the spinner racks that they were the new four-color cash cow. At their peak, horror comics were an exercise in which every month publishers sought to outdo each other to produce the most grisly, gory, and blood-soaked books they could come up with in their unbridled imaginations. And readers loved it.

Publishers were well known to form multiple corporations and tiered companies, with any number of brands and imprints for any number of reasons, including legal protection, taxes, and other fees, all with the purpose of maintaining any kind of advantage they could over their rivals.

As a consequence, comic book publishing was an intensely competitive business. For example, the pulp paper that comics were printed on was a coveted commodity and not always easy to acquire, especially during wartime when there were strict allocations. In addition, distribution could be problematic, and the lack of it could make

A. A. Wyn, Harold Hersey, and Warren A. Angel. Below: *Baffling Mysteries* #23 and *Web of Mystery* #22.

or break a fledgling enterprise. As a result, distributors had the upper hand and often made demands that were viewed as underhanded and predatory.

While most publishers were normal, law-abiding citizens, there were a number of cunning thieves, pornographers, cutthroats, and ex-cons who would extort, leverage, and resort to other shady methods to get a leg up on their competitors.

Beginning with this installment of *Fear in Four Colors* we'll take a closer look at the entrepreneurs who published horror comics during the pre-Code years, a handful that are still around today. Some flourished and some floundered, but at the very least, when the presses were rolling, they provided a steady paycheck to business owners, printers, writers, artists and others during a time when it wasn't always so easy to make a buck.

ACE MAGAZINES

Born Aaron Abraham Weinstein in New York City, Aaron A. Wyn adopted his "less-Jewish" name after graduating high school in 1916. In 1919, he was thought to be employed in the printing business as a proofreader. In February 1926, Wyn married Rose Schiffman and they shared the rent on a Greenwich Village apartment with an advertising salesman.

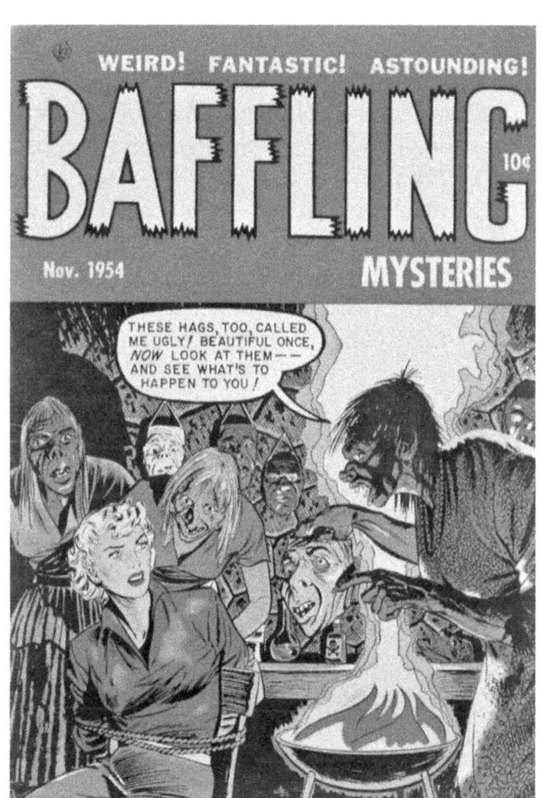

Three panels from Ace's *Challenge of the Unknown* #6

In 1930, Wyn became the associate editor of Magazine Publishers, Inc. who printed and distributed a number of pulps under the editorship of Harold Hersey. When Hersey left the company after a dispute, Wyn stepped in as editor, where in 1932 he was listed as the publisher of the magazines, even though Warren A. Angel is known to have been the owner of the company. One source reports that Wyn "took over" the company after Hersey departed, which might explain his publisher's credit. During the transition, the blue swastika logo used on the Hersey magazine covers (once widely accepted as the Hindu/Buddhist symbol for prosperity and good fortune until Hitler hijacked it for the Nazi Party in 1920) was removed and changed to the ace of spades.

Wyn officially launched Ace Publications on October 19, 1938 by articles of incorporation. Two years later he began publishing comics, starting with the super-hero title, *Sure-Fire Comics* with a cover date of June 1940.

Business expanded and an article in the March 31, 1946 issue of *The New York Times* reported that "A. A. Wyn's Periodical House bought the seven-story building and the two-story taxpaper [taxpayer] at 23 and 25 West 47th Street. He publishes sixteen magazines." His wife, Rose, was also busy as the editor for Ace's line of romance magazines and comics.

As it became more apparent that there was increasing reader interest in horror comics, Ace published its first, the one-shot *Challenge of the Unknown* #6 (September 1950), rising from the ashes of the cancelled romance title, *Love Experiences.* Despite the gruesome cover by Warren Kremer depicting a various assortment of disembodied heads that was sure to attract readers' attention, it was hastily shelved and replaced with the marginally more "horrific" title *The Beyond*, the first of Ace's regularly published horror comics.

Three more followed: *Web of Mystery* (February 1951), *Baffling Mysteries* (November 1951) and *The Hand of Fate* (December 1951), published under the Humor Publications, Inc. imprint(!).

Among the artists who worked at Ace were Reed Crandall, Harvey Kurtzman, Gil Kane, L.B. Cole, Bob Fujitani, and Rudy Palais.

In 1952, Wyn turned his attention to the developing paperback industry and founded Ace Books (now a division of Penguin Publishing Group), which has since become the oldest continuously operating publisher of science fiction and fantasy in the United States. The business thrived, allowing Wyn to cease publishing his failing pulp titles in 1953.

The advent of the Comics Code Authority (CCA) in October 1954 (see *Nightmare Abbey* #8 and #9) forced Wyn to discontinue his

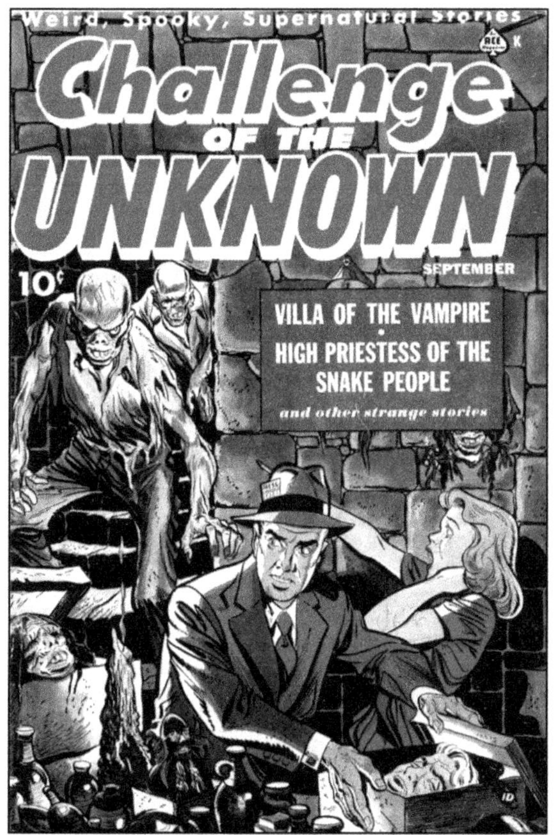

Challenge of the Unknown #6 and *The Beyond* #30

horror comics, which had attracted the scrutiny of anti-comics crusader, Dr. Fredric Wertham for their "unwholesome" subject matter. For example, *Challenge of the Unknown* contained a number of violent images, including strangulation, impalement and hanging. Wyn threw in the bloody towel with Ace's last pre-Code horror comic, *The Beyond* #30 (January 1955) and ceased publishing comics altogether in 1956.

One of the many unfortunate casualties as a result of the impact of the CCA's restrictions was Rose Wyn. After the collapse of Ace's comic books, an embittered Rose left the industry and never returned.

AMERICAN COMICS GROUP (ACG)

One of the most improbable stories in the history of American horror comics—and comic books in general—is that the American Comics Group was founded by a criminal who was sentenced behind bars not once, but twice!

Ironically, Russian-born Benjamin W. Sangor was first an attorney before he was a convict. He received his degree from Marquette University Law School in June 1913 and passed the bar two months later, after which he was hired as a Deputy Clerk at the Milwaukee City Court House.

Sangor eventually became a real estate lawyer, opening the offices of B.W. Sangor and Company in New York City and New Jersey. In 1917 he was convicted and sent to jail for his role in an illegal real estate bankruptcy case. It is not known how long of a sentence he served.

When he was released, he remained in the real estate business and at one time was reported as being "one of the largest real estate operators in the country."

In 1931, Sangor once again got himself in hot water when he was indicted for embezzlement in another real estate deal for which both he and his partner, Anthony Then, were convicted. After stalling their sentencing for years with numerous appeals, this article appeared in the February 1, 1938 article of *The New York Times*:

> TOMS RIVER, N. J., Jan. 31. — Bondsmen for Benjamin W. Sangor

and Anthony M. Then, former Toms River bankers, surrendered them to Sheriff Walter H. Applegate today as a result of last week's decision by the New Jersey Court of Errors and Appeals upholding their conviction two years ago on charges of embezzling $68,000 [the amount varies in different accounts] worth of securities from the estate of James D. Halton and substituting worthless stock in Sangor's hotel enterprise. They will be taken to the State prison at Trenton on Wednesday to start serving terms of two to three years. They also were fined $1,000 each.

Sangor and his partner were released on bail after serving eighteen months. During this time, S.W. Sangor and Co.'s articles of incorporation were voided.

Still dabbling in real estate, Sangor tried his hand at the publishing business. In 1928, he founded Preferred Publications with an office in New York City. He specialized in "French romance novels," code for pornography in those days. He also published a mail-order book on eugenics, which happened to be under copyright by another owner. Preferred Publications went bankrupt in November 1938.

Sangor was determined to make it in publishing, and in particular, comic book publishing, which was suddenly becoming a booming enterprise. Together with his son-in-law Ned Pines (who had recently started his own company, Standard Comics) and a third partner, Paul Sampliner, they formed Cinema Comics, Inc. on September 15, 1939, located at 45 West 45th Street in Midtown Manhattan. Cinema Comics printed promotional theater giveaways as late as 1943 for films such as *Mr. Bug Goes to Town*, *Arabian Nights*, and *Crash Dive*. Records suggest they published only one newsstand title, *TNT*, a digest-sized humor magazine which ran for five issues from March through November 1941.

In the meantime, Sangor opened Sangor Studios–Art Services (aka the Sangor Shop, Syndicated Features Corporation, Editorial Art Syndicate) as a "comic packager," creating comic books for other companies at the familiar location of 45 West 45th Street. Registered at the same address in March 1941 was a partnership between Sangor and Sampliner called Manhattan Fiction Publications which published pulp magazines such as *Movie Detective Magazine* and *Movie Love Stories*.

Still looking for some way to get both feet in the door of what was a competitive industry, Sangor partnered again with Sampliner to form Creston Publications, Inc. on August 1, 1942. Creston published *Giggle Comics* and

Paul Sampliner, Ned Pines, and Richard E. Hughes

ACG's *Out of the Night* #5, *Skeleton Hand* #3, and the one-shot *The Clutching Hand*.

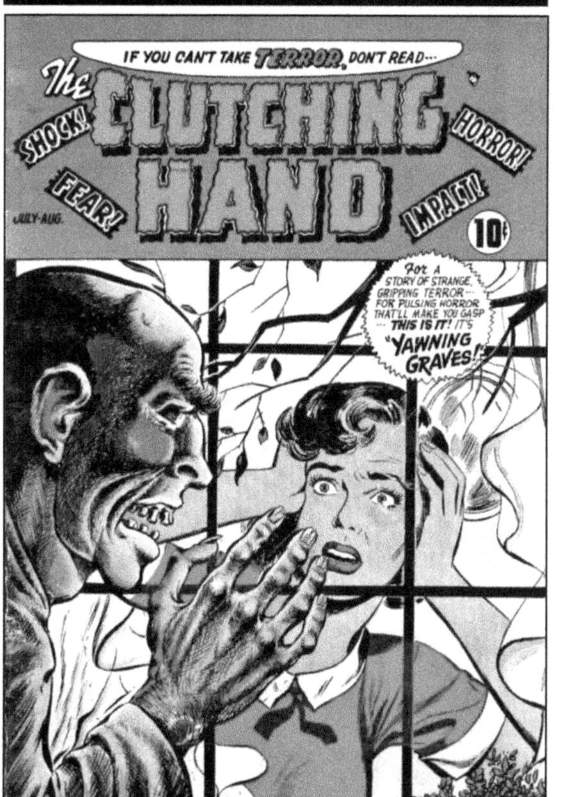

Ha Ha Comics, both with October 1943 cover dates, and which are considered to be the earliest titles associated with the American Comics Group.

Meanwhile, the Sangor Shop was providing Ned Pines with funny animal titles for his own comic line. The artwork was provided by—of all places—the Fleischer cartoon studios (home to Betty Boop), recently relocated to Florida from Queens. Possibly connected by the *Mr. Bug Goes to Town* theater giveaway, animators Jay Morton and Jim Davis were funneling their extra side-work Sangor's way with the help of several other animators, including Joe Oriolo, creator of Felix the Cat and co-creator of Casper the Friendly Ghost.

This long and circuitous sequence of events finally led to the "official" birth of the American Comics Group (ACG) by Sangor in 1943 with financial help from his friend, Harry Donenfeld, co-owner of Detective Comics at the time. Donenfeld also assisted with distribution through his own Independent News Co.

Five years later, in the fall of 1948, ACG published *Adventures into the Unknown* #1, now recognized as the first continuing all-

Artist Paul Gattuso's infamous panel from *Dynamic Comics* #17.
Below: Two panels from *The Clutching Hand* (Edmund Good).

horror comic with all original horror stories (ACG's distinctive American shield logo wouldn't start appearing on covers until issue #5 of *Adventures into the Unknown*, June-July 1949).

Other horror titles followed, including *Forbidden Worlds* (February 1951), *Out of the Night* (February 1952), *Skeleton Hand in Secrets of the Supernatural* (September 1952) and the one-shot, *The Clutching Hand* (July-August 1954), the only ACG title that served up carnage-heavy stories that were comparatively shocking and violent.

Artists that worked on ACG's horror comics included Al Williamson, Frank Frazetta, King Ward, Frank Moritz, Paul Reinman, Henry Kiefer and Sheldon Moldoff.

Another one of their artists, Paul Gattuso, contributed to over a dozen issues of *Adventures into the Unknown*, but he is most noteworthy for the story he illustrated for Harry "A" Chesler's *Dynamic Comics* #17 (January 1946). Under the otherwise unassuming, humorous cover is a story featuring the hero The Echo, with a splash page that has become one of the most infamous panels in the checkered history of pre-Code comics: it depicts a crook with a hot poker threatening a woman bound to a chair. The woman's pose was suggestive enough for Dr. Wertham to include a cropped version of the panel in his notorious screed against comics, *Seduction of the Innocent* (SOTI), using it as an example of the type of salacious images that he was convinced bolstered his argument against the sex, violence and horror he claimed were pervasive in "kid's comics." The caption he used under the panel was: "Children told me what he was going to do with the red-hot poker."

ACG's titles were edited by Richard E. Hughes who had already been in the business for a number of years and eventually became an associate of Ben Sangor. Hughes brought a tempered approach to ACG's horror line and avoided the brutal violence, bloodshed and dismemberment that were creeping into other horror comics from competing publishers. Whether unintentional or by design, this approach kept ACG out of the sights of Dr. Wertham and off the list of publishers in the bibliography of SOTI. *The Clutching Hand* (edited as a one-off by assistant editor Norman Fruman) would have been a surefire candidate to be skewered by Wertham, but fortuitously it appeared after his book was published.

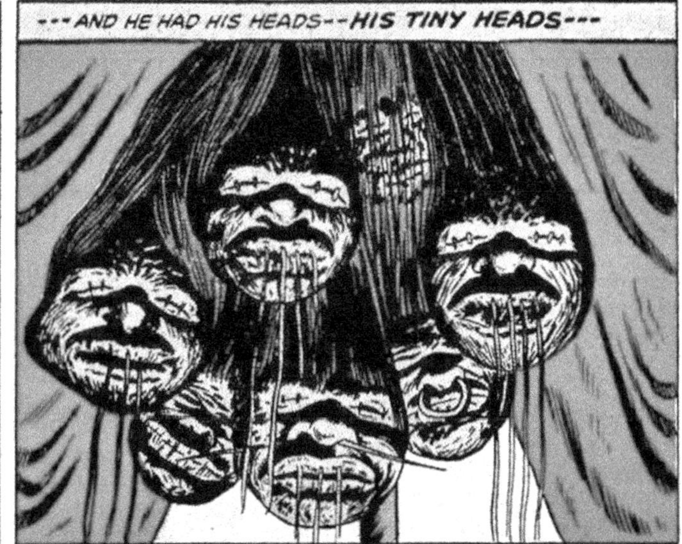

A page from the ACG one-shot horror comic *The Clutching Hand* (July-August 1954) with art by Sheldon Moldoff.

ACG weathered the fallout from the CCA, but opted to discontinue all their pre-Code horror titles with the exception of *Adventures into the Unknown* (174 issues) and *Forbidden Worlds* (145 issues), which Hughes continued to write and edit until ACG shuttered its doors for good in 1967.

ATLAS

Headed by publisher Martin Goodman, Atlas Comics (later renamed Marvel Comics) published the most titles (19) and total number of issues (399) during the pre-Code horror years. Atlas literally flooded the market with titles such as *Adventures into Terror*, *Journey*

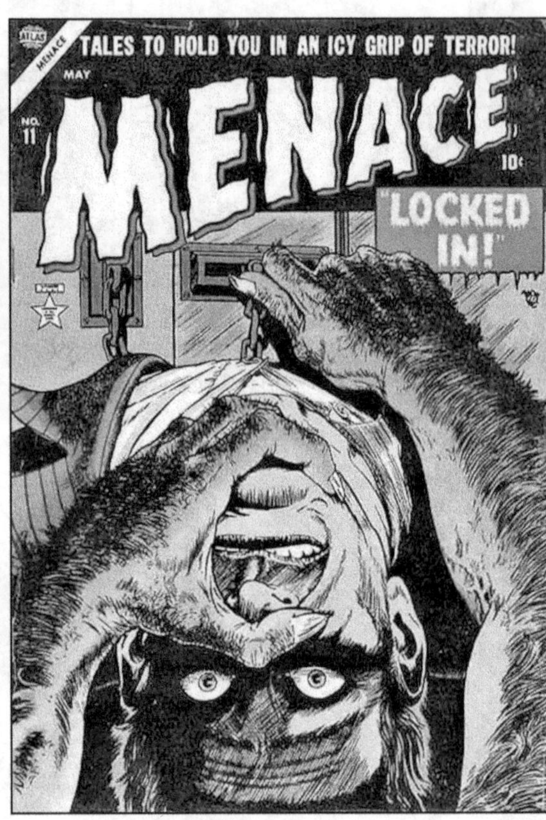

Splash pages from *Adventure into Terror* #43 (art by Russ Heath) and *Menace* #11 (art by Sy Moskowitz), publisher Martin Goodman. Below: *Spellbound* #1 (art by Sol Brodsky). Opposite: *Adventure into Terror* #43 (art by Russ Heath); *Menace* #11 (art by Harry Anderson); *Journey into Mystery* #1 (Russ Heath); and a splash page from *Journey into Mystery* #1 (art by Cal Massey).

into Mystery, *Journey into Unknown Worlds*, *Menace*, and *Strange Tales*. Goodman's strategy to keep "placeholders" for his comics on the stands was if a certain title didn't sell well, he'd immediately replace it with a new one. Atlas had a distinctive "house-style" with stories and art bordering on the sensational, and populated with monsters and madness, thus making them relatively distinctive among the massive assortment of comics that were crammed into the racks.

In his article, "The Secret History of Marvel Comics" from *The Comics Journal* online, John Hilgart described Martin Goodman's publishing practices:

> "How many periodicals could he print and distribute and sell? That was all that mattered. If there was a trend (sadism, science fiction, sex advice, superhero comics, paperback fiction) he copied whatever was selling with multiple imitations. From the 1930s to the 1960s, he threw innumerable pulps, magazines, digests, comic books, and even paperbacks at the wall to see what stuck well enough to justify sourcing content for another issue."

Stan Lee was the editor-in-chief lording over the Atlas Empire, and wrote many of

the stories himself. He maintained a staff of talented artists that included Russ Heath, Joe Maneely, George Tuska, Gene Colan, Bill Everett, John Romita Sr., and Joe Sinnott.

When the CCA was enacted, many Atlas titles were dropped, but some remained to eventually feature the new wave of early 1960s superheroes, such as *Journey into Mystery* (Thor) and *Strange Tales* (The Human Torch).

A splash page from *Spellbound* #1 (Atlas) with art by Al Hartley; The Avon one-shots *City of the Living Dead* and *Night of Mystery*, both featuring cover art by A.C. Hollingsworth.

AVON

Avon Comics, Inc. was a division of Avon Books, founded in 1941 by the American News Company and run by the brother and sister team of Joseph Meyers and Edna Meyers Williams. The first Avon horror comic was the one-shot *Eerie Comics* (Jan. 1947), which has the historical distinction of being the first all-horror comic book. Retitled simply *Eerie*, it continued as a regularly-published title with the May-June 1951 issue.

Avon had only one other horror comic with a regular publishing schedule: *Witchcraft* (March-April 1952); the remaining were a string of one-shots that included *City of the Living Dead* (1952), *The Dead Who Walk* (1952), *Diary of Horror* (December 1952), *The Phantom Witch Doctor* (1952), *Night of Mystery* (1953) and *Secret Diary of Eerie Adventures* (1953), a now-scarce 100-page compilation of remaindered Avon horror comics bound with a new cover.

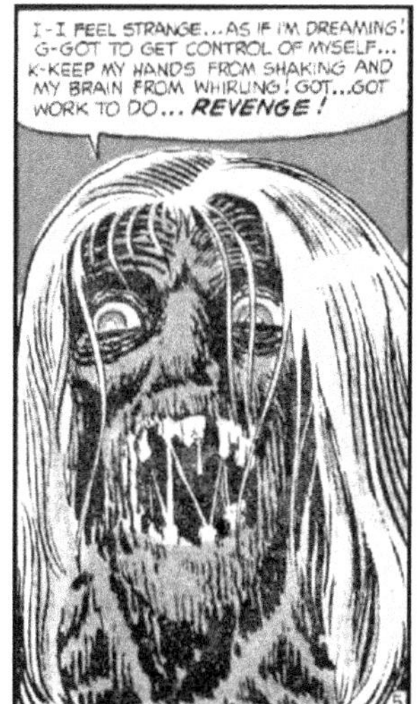

Avon's rare giant collection *Secret Diary of Eerie*; and two panels from Charlton Comics' *The Thing* #14, both featuring art by Steve Ditko.

Sol Cohen was the general manager and editor of Avon's comics division from 1947–1956. He was coincidentally EC Comics' circulation director from 1947–1949.

Artists who worked on Avon's horror comics included one of the first African Americans to work in the industry, Alvin "A.C." Hollingsworth, Joe Kubert, Everett Raymond Kinstler (who later had portraits hanging in the White House), Norman Nodel, and Vince Alascia.

Avon was one of the many horror comic publishers that were called out in SOTI and listed in the book's bibliography.

The last Avon pre-Code horror comic was *Eerie* #17 with a cover date of Aug-Sept 1954, and the company discontinued the rest of their comic line in late 1956.

CHARLTON

Comic artist and creator John Byrne called it "the little comic book company that couldn't quite..." when describing the remarkable story of Charlton comics and its valiant efforts to make its mark amidst the industry giants. Charlton was unique in the comic book industry as it was one of the few comic book publishers who operated outside of New York City and the only publisher who produced their comics and magazines all under one roof: from writing, to art, to editing, color separations and even printing them. At its peak, the 100,000 square foot facility located in Derby, Connecticut housed seven high-speed printing presses, typesetting, and binding equipment, an early IBM computer, and a fleet of delivery trucks.

Founded by ex-construction worker John Santangelo, the enterprise that would become Charlton Publications began its existence in 1931 publishing popular song lyric books. They were popular, but there was one problem: Santangelo was unknowingly using the copyrighted lyrics without permission. After being sued by the American Society of Composers and Publishers (ASCAP), he was eventually arrested for copyright violations and sentenced to a year-and-a-day in Connecticut's New Haven County Jail.

After his release, Santangelo went legit, and with the assistance of Ed Levy, a disbarred attorney he had befriended in jail began publishing the magazines *Hit Parade* and *Song Hits*, this time with permission.

After the long-standing practice of sending their print jobs to New York, Santangelo and Levy decided it would be considerably

Panels from Charlton's *Yellowjacket* #8 and #9 reveal a be-*witching* truth. (Art by Alan Mandel).

more cost-effective to do their own in-house production. As a result, they set up a printing plant in Derby, Connecticut.

In September 1944, they published their first comic book, *Yellowjacket Comics*, under the name Frank Comunale Publications. It included an early comic book horror story, an adaptation of Edgar Allen Poe's "The Black Cat" for the feature "Famous Tales of Terror" with art by Bill Allison. It was followed by "The Fall of the House of Usher" in issue #4 (December 1944), with art by Gus Schrotter and—after skipping an issue—"The Tell-Tale Heart" in issue #6 (Dec. 1945) illustrated by Rudy Palais and Arnold Hicks. The Poe adaptations were discontinued and replaced in issue #7 (January 1946) with an original

Yellowjacket #9

"Famous Tales of Terror" story illustrated by Alan Mandel and hosted by a familiar-looking old woman named "The Ancient Witch."

On a historically significant note, she is named in subsequent stories "The Old Witch," and signs off her tales chuckling "He! Heh!" or "He! He! He!" The Old Witch can certainly be considered a prototype for another "Old Witch," one of EC's trio of "Ghoulunatics" who hosted *The Haunt of Fear*. It's not difficult to miss the striking similarities between the two in both their overall appearance and how they are used for framing a story. EC's The Old Witch first appears in *The Haunt of Fear*'s second issue (#16, July-August 1950). However, Charlton's Old Witch predates EC's character by over four years. The Old Witch appeared until the last issue of *Yellowjacket Comics* (#10, June 1946) with the script and art by brothers George and Alan Mandel respectively.

Initially, Santangelo used comic packager Al Fago to produce the content of his comic books. He later adopted the same economic strategy as he did with his printing operation by hiring Fago as general manager of his comic line in 1951, assembling a staff

Charlton's *The Thing* #11 and #9, and panels from *The Thing* #16 (art by Dick Ayers and Ernie Bache), #9 (art by Bob Forgione), and #11 (art by Lou Morales).

of writers and in-house artists, as well as freelancers. The prolific Joe Gill was the primary scriptwriter and artists included Dick Giordano (who would later become the next general manager), Sam Glanzman, Vince Alascia, Charles Nicholas, Rocco "Rocke" Mastroserio and most notably, future Spider-Man co-creator, Steve Ditko.

Charlton's first all-horror comic was the now-notorious *The Thing* (titled on the cover as *The Thing!*), published under their music magazine imprint, Song Hits, Inc. (future issues would be published by Outstanding Comics, Inc., Capital Stories, Inc., and Charlton Comics Group). *The Thing!* ran for 17 issues, from February 1952 until November 1954.

Charlton published two more pre-Code horror titles, both acquired from Fawcett Publications, which was in the process of shutting down and liquidating their comic book inventory. Charlton took over *Strange*

Horrific #1 (art by the Iger Shop) and #4 (art by Don Heck). Opposite: *Weird Terror* #3 (art by Don Heck).

Suspense Stories with issue #16 (January-Feb. 1954) and *This Magazine is Haunted* with issue #15 (Feb. 1954) using Fawcett's unpublished material.

Charlton's last pre-Code horror comic was *This is Suspense* #23 (February 1955), reprinting Wallace Wood's adaptation of "Dr. Jekyll and Mr. Hyde" and "The Repulsive Dwarf," from Fox's *A Star Presentation* #3 (May 1950).

Charlton ceased publishing in 1986, and in 1999, the building on the property that housed "the little comic book company that couldn't quite" was demolished.

COMIC MEDIA

"Allen Hardy Associates, Inc., 500 Fifth Ave., New York 36, N. Y. Has horror, romance, action, Western and teen-age magazines. Needs the unusual, artists and writers who don't have hackneyed approach to comics. Art Director Jerry Feldman says, "If you got it—you get it." Payment, $8 a page. Synopses go to Allen Hardy."

So read the advertisement in the August 1953 issue of *Writer's Digest*, and as far as Allen Hardy was concerned, he got what he asked for in the talents of Don Heck, Pete Morisi, Rudy Palais, Don Perlin and more.

Comic Media was founded in 1952 by Hardy, the ex-circulation manager of Harvey Comics and was headquartered in New York City. He came late to the game and published only two horror titles, but they have since become recognized for the quality of their stories and art, especially Don Heck's startling covers, which have made them highly collectible.

The first issues of *Horrific* and *Weird Terror* were both published with a cover date of September 1952. Each title ran for 13 issues until September 1954.

Horrific was re-named *Terrific* and held on for one more issue until it folded with its December 1954 cover date, after which Comic Media discontinued publishing due to the CCA, as well as internal problems with the company.

In an interview years later, Don Heck recalled:

> "Allen was an alcoholic. He was a member of AA but he went off the wagon. While he was in this way, I could not leave him. I stayed until I cleaned up the stuff for [him] who, by that time, couldn't do anything. He had to go back for treatment. Not too long after that he died. I heard the story he was smoking a cigarette and it dropped and he burned himself to death. I liked him! He was a good guy as far as I was concerned."

NEXT: Little Shoppes of Horrors continues with Fawcett, Farrell, Harvey, and more!

John Navroth is a five-time Rondo Award-nominated writer who contributes regularly to Dead Letter Press, Castle of Frankenstein, *and* Prehistoric Times. *He also writes for* Black Infinity, Cryptology, *and others. For readers interested in learning more about the history of horror comics and the Comics Code Authority, visit John's site at:* fearinfourcolors.blogspot.com

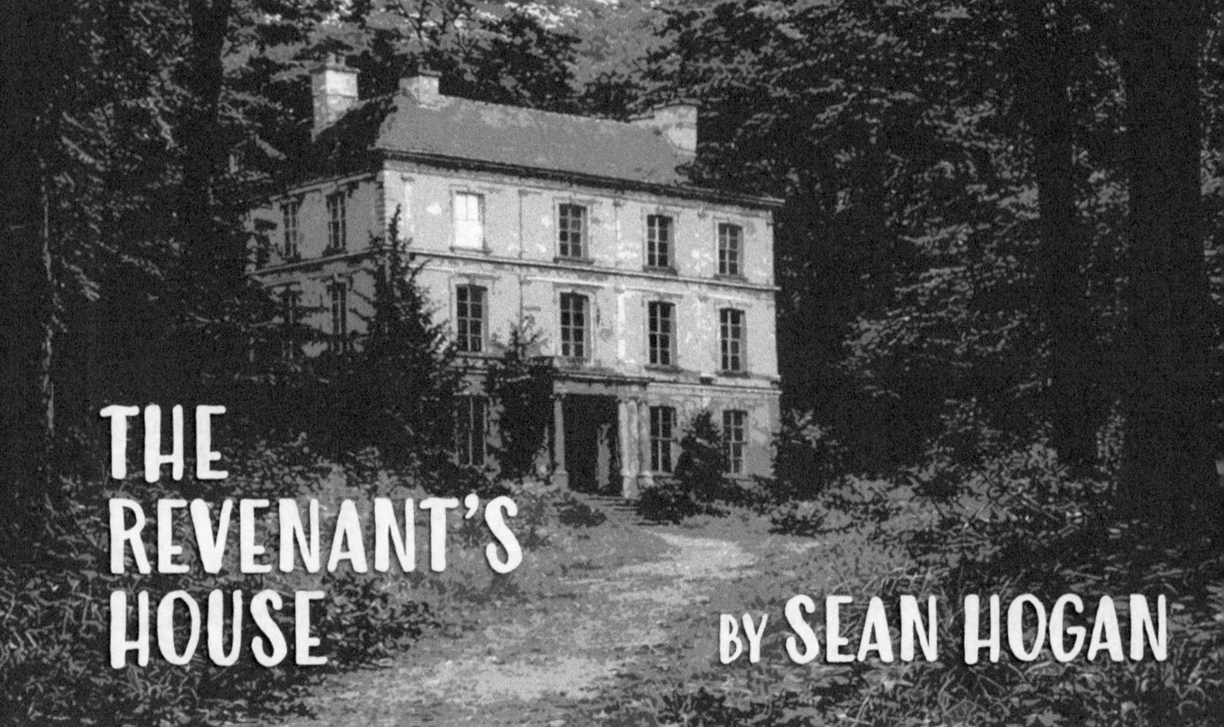

THE REAL PROBLEM WITH GROWNUPS, ANTHONY DECIDED, WAS NOT SIMPLY THAT THEY LIED JUST AS FREQUENTLY AS CHILDREN DO, BUT THAT THEY ALSO LIKED TO PRETEND IT WAS FOR YOUR OWN GOOD. Whenever kids lied, it was because they knew they'd done something wrong and don't want to get into trouble. Or maybe they did it with the aim of getting someone *else* into trouble. Sometimes, they might just fib to make themselves look cooler or cleverer than they really were. But Anthony didn't know a single kid at school who would ever try and claim that they'd lied to spare someone's feelings. That, as far as he was concerned, was something only adults did.

That was, after all, exactly what his parents had done when they'd insisted that they weren't getting a divorce, but simply having a little rest from each other. One lie swiftly led to another, and then another still. The "little rest" soon became a full-blown separation, after which Anthony's dad had moved in with his new girlfriend. And suddenly, divorce was the only thing anyone could talk about. The rest of them were left with no choice but to leave the family home and relocate to a boring little country village, miles and miles away from where Anthony grew up. *It'll be an adventure,* his mum had insisted, with a smile that was slightly too wide to be properly convincing. *We'll have so much fun, the three of us together.*

Another lie. They'd ended up moving into a poky old cottage that only had two bedrooms. This meant that Anthony didn't have his own room anymore and was forced to share with his little brother Calum. Calum, who never, ever stopped talking. Sometimes, his brother's mouth reminded Anthony of a broken tap that can't be turned off, and all you can do is stand there and watch helplessly as the entire room floods with water. When Anthony tried complaining to his mum, she'd frowned and said that it was only until they got back on their feet, and so couldn't he be a good boy and try to make the best of it?

Well, that had been six months ago, and they were all still trapped in the cottage. He missed his old friends and hated his new school, which was full of rugby lads who bullied him and pretty girls who laughed at him. Whenever Anthony spoke to his father on the phone, his dad always promised that he and Calum could come and visit just as soon as he moved somewhere with enough room for them both to stay. But that hadn't happened yet, and Anthony was starting to doubt whether it ever would. To cap it all off, money was always tight, even though his mum had gone back to nursing and got herself a job at the local hospital. She worked all the time now, which meant that he was inevitably stuck looking after Calum once school finished for the day.

So where, Anthony wondered, was the *best* in any of that?

Even at night, he rarely got any peace. Although Calum's bedtime was an hour earlier than Anthony's, his little brother was normally still awake whenever he came up to bed. Just as soon as Anthony undressed and climbed underneath the covers, Calum would start talking again. Very often, the only way Anthony could make him stop was by punching him hard on the arm. That normally did the trick.

On that particular evening, Anthony hadn't even finished undressing when Calum sat up and said, "Anthony, are vampires real?"

"God, you're stupid," Anthony said, scowling. "Course they're not."

Calum's eyes were very wide and bright in the darkness of the bedroom. "Stuart at school says they are," he whispered. "He told me one used to live near here."

Anthony yanked his socks off. "That's the stupidest thing I ever heard," he said. Climbing into bed, he turned his back on Calum. He lay there in silence, unable to decide who he was more irritated at: his brother or himself.

Finally, he surrendered to the inevitable. "Where?"

"There's an old house at the end of this road, right at the top of the hill," Calum said, not needing to be asked twice. "No one lives there now, but years ago, it was a *vampire's* house. Stuart told me everyone in the village is still too scared to go up there."

"Well, Stuart's an idiot, and so are you. Vampires are only in books and films. They don't really exist."

"Stuart says—"

Anthony reared up and threw a pillow at his brother. "I don't care what your stupid friend says! Shut up!"

He was about to leap out of bed and hit Calum when he heard their mum shouting for them both to go to sleep. Calum hurriedly lobbed the pillow back at Anthony, then burrowed safely down underneath his duvet, dodging any further attempts at retribution.

Giving up, Anthony slumped back down onto the mattress. He lay there gazing at the gap in the bedroom curtains, his thoughts floating out through the open window. On and on they drifted, dancing through the night air like dandelion spores, all the way to the top of the hill.

If there really *was* an abandoned old house up there, it must only be about five minutes' walk from their cottage's front door.

Heavily muffled by the weight of his bedclothes, he heard Calum's voice whisper, "It's *true*, Anthony."

Anthony didn't bother replying. He wasn't a stupid little kid anymore. He knew there was no such thing as vampires.

But he found he couldn't stop thinking about the story, all the same.

It took him a very long time to fall asleep that night.

THE NEXT AFTERNOON, Anthony was granted an unexpected reprieve. Calum had been invited round his friend's house after school, meaning his older sibling was now free to do as he pleased. Although he would never have admitted it to Calum, Anthony hadn't been able to get his brother's story out of his head all day. So this seemed like the perfect opportunity to walk up the hill and inspect this so-called vampire's house for himself.

After stopping in at home to change out of his school uniform and wolf down a snack, Anthony grabbed an old rucksack and slipped a torch and a claw hammer inside. Just in case.

Now fully prepared, he set off on his quest. It was a dazzling June day, the sky as blue and clear as a tropical ocean, and the effort of climbing the hill soon left him sweaty and out of breath. Still, it felt good to glance upwards and see the sun blazing away so brightly. The sight of it only served to make Calum's story seem ever more unreal. Because even if vampires really existed—which they most certainly *didn't*—well, they'd never be able to come out on a day like this, would they?

As Anthony drew closer to the top, he started to notice a dramatic reduction in the number of houses. Back down at the bottom of the hill where he lived, all of the homes were jammed right up against each other, so much so that you were forced to keep the curtains closed if you wanted any privacy. But up here, the gaps between the buildings gradually grew wider and wider, until there were hardly any to be seen at all. As though they were keeping a wary distance from something.

Before very much longer, Anthony reached the brow of the hill. The road snaked all the way to the summit, before coming to a dead end outside a walled-off private residence. The flagstone wall surrounding the property looked to be about ten feet high, and Anthony could see jagged shards of broken glass embedded in the top. Behind it, row after row of emaciated beech trees twisted up from the earth like overgrown fingernails. If there *was* a house back there somewhere, it was impossible to see it from out here on the street.

Following the wall along, he soon arrived at an old iron gate. The bars of the gate were corroded and flaking with rust, and there was no sign of a chain or padlock either. Despite the intimations of privacy, it seemed as though anyone with a mind to, could easily wander inside.

Perhaps the house beyond the wall really was abandoned. Derelict and empty, a rotting carcass of wood and stone.

Haunted.

Anthony nervously glanced around to check whether he was being watched. But there was not another living soul in sight. He realised that he couldn't even hear any birds singing; never mind the numerous trees on the other side of the wall.

Growing ever more unnerved, he briefly considered turning tail and running home. But the moment he did so, an image of Calum's smirking face flashed abruptly into his mind. If his brother ever discovered he'd come all the way up here but was too scared to go inside, Anthony would never live it down.

His hand reached out to lift the latch. Anthony steeled himself for the screech of rusty hinges, but the gate eased open without so much as a squeak. After once more checking over his shoulder, he edged through the open entrance. His heart thudding inside his chest, he began to follow the gravel pathway that twisted away through the trees, wincing at his every noisy footstep. Surely somebody would leap out and angrily chase him off at any moment.

But while Anthony continued to flinch at every darting shadow, every fleeting flicker of sunlight, he encountered no one.

It was shady underneath the trees, and much cooler than it had been out on the street. Suddenly missing the feel of sunlight on his skin, Anthony's gaze moved up towards the heavens. But all he could see overhead were densely clustered branches. They hung over him like hungry fingers, poised to reach down and seize the next tasty morsel that took their fancy.

Anthony shivered, then instantly grew annoyed with himself. Somewhere on the other side of these trees, there was a house. All he needed to do was find it. Then he could go home and lord it over Calum, and maybe *that* would make his brother think twice about ever bothering him with another one of his stupid stories.

He pressed on for another minute or two, and eventually noticed the temperature growing warmer again. The trees started to thin out, and Anthony soon emerged to find himself standing in front of an imposing-looking manor house. The building was entirely constructed from white stone, and felt less like a place where people might actually live than some kind of grandiose monument. The lawn stretching away in front of it had degenerated into an unruly mass of weeds and overgrown grass, which made him think that no one had set foot there in a very long time.

But the house itself didn't appear derelict. The windows were all dark and empty and shut tight against the world, but none of them seemed to be cracked or broken. There were no missing tiles on the roof, and no signs of vandalism that Anthony could see. The place looked neglected, but not *abandoned.* Gazing up at the silent building, he couldn't quite shake the impression that it was merely waiting for its rightful owner to return home.

There was something else, though. Anthony struggled to identify exactly what it was, but something felt wrong, weirdly off-kilter. He continued to stare doggedly over at the house, willing himself to understand.

Glancing down, Anthony noticed his shadow stretching up thc front path, impatient to creep closer to the house for a closer look. Nothing strange about that.

And then he looked back up at the house, and realised what exactly was wrong.

The building was, in turn, casting its own shadow in his direction. But that was impossible. The sun was behind *him,* not the house.

Anthony felt a wave of dizziness sweeping over him. Closing his eyes, he took several deep breaths. He reminded himself that he'd accomplished what he'd set out to do. So why not turn around and go back home right now?

But he just couldn't bring himself to do it. There *was* something deeply odd about the old house, that much was inarguable. Nevertheless, the very fact of its oddness was pulling him inexorably towards it, just as a brightly coloured flower might attract a hungry bee.

Anthony opened his eyes. He had to see more. That was the only way his curiosity would ever be satisfied. And yet, he couldn't quite summon the nerve to approach the building directly. The more he looked at the house, the more he felt as though it was staring right back at him. Watching him.

He would have to sneak up on it.

Bearing left, Anthony cut across the front lawn, fighting his way through the waist-high jungle of grass and weeds that blocked his path. He tripped over more than once and ended up with a rash of nettle stings on both arms, but struggled on regardless.

When he at last arrived outside the house, Anthony sidled over to the nearest window. The persistent worry that someone might arrive home at any moment continued to niggle at him. So, even as he raised himself up on tiptoe to peer inquisitively over the windowsill, he was tensed to turn and run at the first sign of anything being amiss.

The room beyond the window was shrouded in gloom, but there was just enough sunlight seeping in over his shoulder for Anthony to see that it looked like some kind of study. He could make out an antique writing desk placed against the far wall, and several shelves crammed with old books. Surely that suggested whoever owned the house hadn't moved out for good. Wherever it was they'd vanished to, they must be planning on coming back. Even if the original homeowner had died, wouldn't someone have come in to clear the house? The book collection looked like it might be valuable. So why would everything have just been left here to gather dust?

Spitting on his fingertip, Anthony rubbed at the grime encrusted on the windowpane. Once he'd managed to create a small peephole, he pressed his face up against the glass for a better look. Even in the dim light, he could make out framed paintings hanging on the walls, an elaborately woven rug laid out on the floor, and all manner of curios and objets d'art dotted around the room. Anthony had no idea what any of it was worth, but it seemed like it might be a lot. Easily more money than he'd ever seen. A small fortune, perhaps.

His gaze drifted back towards the far wall. The sunlight brightened for an instant, and sitting atop the desk, he glimpsed a sudden flash of gold.

Anthony held his breath. He didn't much like the thoughts that were now racing through his head, but try as he might, couldn't make himself stop thinking them. It was quite obvious that whoever owned the house hadn't visited it in a long time. That suggested they didn't care about it very much at all. Or anything inside it.

Meanwhile, his family were desperately short of money. They'd been forced to leave their home and live cooped up in a crappy little cottage. None of it was right, none of it was fair.

But if they came into some money,

they could all move to a bigger house. Maybe even back to their old hometown. Anthony could have his own bedroom again. Be reunited with all his old friends.

And yes, he understood that stealing was bad. But would this even really count as stealing? The stuff inside the house was just sitting there. It wasn't doing anyone any good. And rich people having money and valuables they didn't need or want was just as bad as stealing, wasn't it?

The stupid thing was, Anthony couldn't imagine trying to physically break inside the house. That felt like a step too far. It would make him a burglar, an actual criminal. And he wasn't that at all. He was just a kid who wanted to help his family.

He felt a gnawing, febrile excitement in the pit of his belly, urging him on. Suddenly, all thoughts of escape seemed very distant.

So Anthony told himself that he would take a quick look around, and if he happened to find a window that was already broken or had been left open a crack...well, maybe then he'd consider taking the next step. If not, he would go straight home and do his best to forget about the house altogether.

But moments later, when he discovered the front door had been left ajar, as if in anticipation of his visit, Anthony almost fled in panic right there and then. Because that meant that somebody had to be living here, didn't it? No matter what it looked like from the outside.

Either that, or the house really *was* sentient. Not only that, but it could also tell what he was thinking.

Anthony knew that such thoughts were undoubtedly crazy. But the longer he stood here, the less crazy they sounded. After all, were they really any crazier than a building that cast its shadow in the wrong direction?

Reaching out with one trembling hand, he lifted the door knocker and rapped three times. Waited a few seconds. And then, when no response was forthcoming, poked his head through the gap in the doorway and hesitantly called out, "Is a-anybody home? You left your front d-door open!"

No one answered. Anthony listened to his voice ringing out down the deserted hallway and realised the house even *sounded* empty. He might have been shouting into a bottomless cavern. Nudging the door open a little wider, he leaned inside to take a proper look.

The first thing he noticed was that the hallway floor had been overlaid with a beautifully intricate arrangement of parquet tiles. And in the chink of daylight spilling through the doorway, he could clearly see just how dusty the wooden tiles were. It was obvious that no one had swept or polished the hallway floor for quite some time. Not only that, but if anyone *had* entered the house recently, they would have left a trail of footprints behind them.

The layer of dust was undisturbed.

Once Anthony realised that, he burst into immediate motion, his eager legs ushering him through the open doorway before his brain had even finished instructing them to. The study entrance was located just a few feet over to his left. Hurrying towards it, Anthony seized the door handle, which was large and white and put him in mind of a jutting knob of bone. However, when he tried to turn the handle, he could barely budge it. In the end, he had to use both hands, and even then, it was something of a struggle. As the recalcitrant spindle twisted in its socket, it made a loud clicking noise. Echoing along the empty hallway, it sounded like the brittle snap of somebody's arm breaking.

Easing the door open, Anthony stepped cautiously into the study. Immediately, he sensed a peculiar hush settling over him, as though he'd wandered inside a candlelit church. He felt his anxious heartbeat starting to slow down, his jangled nerves calming.

As he'd already seen, most of the study was given over to books, most of which didn't even have titles written on the spines. The ones that did all seemed to be foreign: French, German, a handful in Latin. An oxblood leather armchair was tucked snugly away in the corner, a reading lamp poised in readiness at one side. Other than that, the only place to sit was at the writing desk. Anthony's gaze moved to a framed oil painting of a mountain forest hanging on the wall above the desk. In the background of the picture, you could see the sun retreating below the horizon, staining the evening sky crimson. The trees in the painting were dense and dark and so vividly green that they almost seemed real, as though you could just hurl yourself through the frame and instantly be transported to that faraway forest.

Like everything else in the room, the picture looked old, probably valuable, but it wasn't what Anthony had come for. His eyes dropped to the desk itself; seeking out the promise of gold he'd glimpsed through the window, hoping he hadn't ventured inside on a fool's errand.

But no, there it was. A small golden statuette of a coiled snake, rearing up and hissing at him. Leaning in to take a closer look, Anthony could see two scarlet jewels embedded in the snake's eye sockets. Were they rubies? How much might something like this be worth? Of course, he had absolutely no idea how to go about actually selling it, but he could worry about that later.

Anthony gingerly picked up the idol, finding it surprisingly heavy. It *had* to be real gold. Angling it towards the daylight, he gently ran his fingers over the snake's glittering scales, scarcely able to breathe.

Take it, it's yours, a soft voice said.

Anthony let out a strangled cry. All at once, the world seemed to be deep, deep underwater, his lungs filling with freezing cold brine. His fingers numb, he dropped the statuette to the rug and whirled around.

There was no one else in the room.

Anthony was positive he hadn't imagined the voice. He stood rooted to the spot, his eyes darting around the four walls of the study. But the only sign of life he could see was his own shadow. It hovered above the desk, just as helplessly frozen in place as he was. Anthony desperately willed it to turn and run, in the vain hope that this might compel him to flee too. But in stubborn defiance of his wishes, the shadow refused to do so.

Just then, another silhouette loomed abruptly into view, mere inches from his own. It was impossible. There was no one else physically present in the room: not to cast the second shadow, nor to whisper furtively into his ear.

Anthony dimly felt his bladder letting go, and his legs buckling underneath him. The colour seemed to drain out of his surroundings, the room rapidly growing fuzzy and indistinct. He took one faltering step towards the study exit, but it seemed to be getting further and further away by the second.

Go and sit yourself down in the corner, the voice instructed. *You've had quite a shock.*

It seemed like his only option, no matter that he was frightened out of his wits. Anthony stumbled over to the leather armchair and collapsed down upon the seat. He gazed dumbly over at the shadow, feeling certain that it was staring right back at him. Never mind that it lacked any eyes to see him with.

Welcome to my home, the shadow said. *It's been a long time since I last had a visitor. A very long time indeed.*

Anthony didn't know how he should respond. What *do* you say to a talking shadow?

You don't need to be afraid of me, it added. *Even if I meant you any harm, what could I possibly do? I'm just a shadow on a wall.*

Anthony finally found his voice. "I don't understand," he croaked. "What are you, a ghost?"

My body was destroyed many years ago, the shadow replied. *This is all that remains of me.*

"And you've been here alone all this time?"

For an instant, the shadow seemed to flicker, to shrink slightly. *This is my home,* it said. *Where else would I go?*

His mind reeling, Anthony thought back to Calum's story. "People say a v-vampire used to live here."

The shadow made a contemptuous sound. *A pathetic superstition. I existed long before such terms became common parlance amongst the ignorant.*

"So what are you, then?"

Now, I am nothing, the shadow said. *Centuries ago, they called us revenants. It seems as good a word as any.*

"I don't know what that means," Anthony admitted. "But it still sounds like some kind of ghost or monster."

The shadow drew itself up on the wall, one long arm sliding malevolently along the brickwork towards Anthony. *Monsters!* it hissed. *Your kind have always insulted us in this manner.*

Anthony cowered. "I'm sorry, I didn't mean it!" he cried. "I'm just trying to understand, honest."

The shadow paused, then retreated back to its original position. *Very well,* it replied, its tone softening slightly. *Then understand this. I cannot enter anywhere I have not first been invited. Do you know what that means, boy? It means I only go where I am truly wanted. Now, does that sound monstrous to you?*

"I...I g-guess not." Anthony's eyes darted over towards the study doorway. He'd made the shadow angry, even if only for a moment, and he couldn't help but be afraid of it.

He heard it chuckle. *After all, you entered my house without being invited, did you not?* it said in an amused voice. *One might just as easily call* you *a monster, eh?*

"I'm really sorry," Anthony said. "It didn't look like anyone lived here anymore."

No matter. I am glad to have your company. All I really have left to me is conversation, and there has been precious little of that in recent times. The shadow grew silent. Anthony couldn't help but feel that it was studying him very closely. *Forgive me if I'm wrong,* it said finally, *but I sense that you might share that very same lack.*

Anthony's face reddened. "Yeah," he muttered, suddenly self-conscious. "We only moved here recently, and I had to leave all my mates behind."

He saw the shadow bring its hands together in a soundless clap. *Then we have both found a new friend today,* it said in a satisfied voice. *I look forward to us getting to know each other a little better. What do you say?*

Anthony hesitated for a moment. "My name's Anthony," he said. "Pleased to meet you."

HE SOON LOST track of how long they sat there talking. The shadow wanted to hear everything about Anthony's life in the village, even though nothing interesting ever happened there. Assuring him that the statuette he coveted was indeed carved from solid gold, it told him he could take it as a gift. All the shadow wanted in return was to hear stories of the everyday world beyond the walls of the house, no matter how boring and trivial Anthony might consider them to be.

So he told it all about his parents and Calum and the other kids at school, hoping that his new friend would respond in kind. For starters, Anthony desperately wanted to understand how it had come to be a shadow in the first place.

But much to his disappointment, it insisted that they would have plenty of time for such stories later. *When you've existed for as long as I have,* the shadow chided, *you soon come to learn the value of patience.*

Eventually, Anthony realised the sky had grown dark outside. By now, his mum would have arrived home to discover that he'd left Calum alone.

He leapt to his feet. "I'm sorry, I've really got to go."

So soon? The shadow sounded disappointed.

"I'm late, I'll get in trouble."

We certainly wouldn't want that. But I do hope you'll come back soon, Anthony.

"I will, I promise." Grabbing his rucksack, Anthony picked up the statuette and carefully placed it inside. It was so heavy he could feel the bag straining at the seams.

Promise me you won't tell anyone where you got that, the shadow said, before slyly adding: *We don't want anyone coming here that hasn't been invited, after all.*

"I promise." Bidding his new friend goodbye, Anthony hurried out through the darkened house and into the garden. He made sure to close the front door politely behind him. He knew it would be open again whenever he next returned.

Once he arrived home, Anthony's mum angrily sent him straight up to bed without any dinner and said that he was grounded for the foreseeable future. He didn't try and argue the point, just shrugged and mutely accepted his punishment. As he slouched upstairs, he glanced back over his shoulder to see Calum sticking his tongue out at him.

Anthony didn't care. He had a secret now; one that his stupid brother and all the stupid kids at school and this whole stupid boring village would never know or properly understand. The shadow had made him realise just how precious hidden knowledge could be; far more valuable than mere gold or rubies. And now that they were friends, it had promised to teach him all manner of secrets. Secrets that would ensure Anthony got everything he'd ever wanted.

Secrets that would help him escape this rotten place forever.

Hiding his rucksack safely underneath his bed, Anthony undressed and climbed between the sheets. He pretended to be asleep when Calum came upstairs later that evening, but that didn't stop his brother from talking. Anthony listened as Calum got into bed and fidgeted about for a few seconds, then heard him whisper loudly: "Where were you this afternoon?"

Anthony thought about ignoring the question, only for the words to come spilling out without him really intending them to. "I walked up to that old house," he said. "The one your mate told you about."

There was a disbelieving pause as Calum absorbed this. "You're a liar!" he hissed.

Anthony rolled over and locked eyes with his brother. "I'm not. I went through the gate and walked all the way up to the front door."

Calum's face was a mask of outrage. "You're *such* a liar."

"And that's not all," Anthony said, quietly enjoying himself. "I even went inside." He paused, wondering whether to commit to the lie that sat poised on his lips. "It's an empty old house, and that's all it is. No one lives there. Your stupid mate's just making up stories. And *you're* even more stupid for believing them."

"Prove it! *Prove* you went inside!"

Anthony turned his back on Calum and snuggled down into the bedclothes. He knew his brother was still glaring across at him, waiting for an answer.

Well, let him wait.

Closing his eyes, Anthony fell asleep almost immediately, and that night, his dreams were filled with shadows.

• • •

THE FOLLOWING DAY, Anthony made sure to come straight home from school to look after Calum. He even played with his brother for a bit, just to keep the peace. And after his mum had finished her shift at the hospital, he helped her prepare their evening meal.

Anthony knew that she probably thought he was sucking up to her to try and get out of being grounded, but that wasn't it at all. He just needed to make sure she wouldn't start poking her nose into his private business. Later, once Anthony got them out of the cottage and back home where they all belonged, his mum would have no choice but to apologise to him. The shadow had told him so. It said that the best way to win any argument was with money, because no matter how stubborn or prideful your opponent was, agreement always had an asking price, just like any other commodity.

And very soon, Anthony would have enough money to pay any price necessary.

After dinner, they all sat and watched TV together for a little while. When Calum's bedtime arrived, Anthony yawned loudly and said that he was going up to bed too. His mother shot him a funny look—Anthony being permitted to stay up an hour later than his younger brother was a treasured mark of his seniority—but she refrained from saying anything. After coming upstairs to wish them both goodnight, she turned off the light and exited the bedroom.

Calum waited for the sound of her footsteps to retreat downstairs before saying anything. "You think you're so clever," he whispered.

"I *am* clever, "Anthony said smugly. "Cleverer than you."

"I told Stuart that you went to the vampire's house. He said you were either a liar or really, really stupid. He said that house has a curse on it."

Anthony propped himself up by his elbows. "You and Stuart are just a couple of dumb little kids. There's no such thing as vampires or curses. I went inside that house and nothing bad happened to me."

"You're lying! You've got no proof!"

For an instant, Anthony considered showing his brother the statuette, but quickly thought better of it. If he did, he knew Calum would immediately run and tell their mum. And the shadow had insisted that he be patient. So he would bide his time. Even though Anthony wanted more than anything to prove them all wrong.

"You'll see," he told Calum. "You'll find out soon enough."

Anthony turned over in bed and feigned sleep. He listened to the TV playing downstairs, the sound of his mum opening the fridge to pour herself a glass of wine. Before too much longer, he heard Calum doze off and start to snore. If anything, his brother was even more annoying when he was asleep. The sound of his snoring reminded Anthony of someone incessantly rustling a packet of crisps.

Eventually, his mum turned off the TV and came upstairs to bed. Anthony knew it never took her long to fall asleep, but stayed in bed for another fifteen minutes or so, just to make certain. Then, once he was satisfied that everyone was sleeping soundly, he eased himself out of bed.

After gathering up his clothes, Anthony tiptoed downstairs and quietly got dressed. Slipping out of the cottage, he set off towards the revenant's house.

As he'd expected, the front door to the house was open. Standing on the doorstep, Anthony angled his torch beam into the darkened hallway. The thick murk inside seemed almost impenetrable, so solid you could reach out and touch it. His torch did very little to hold back the darkness, but if nothing else, its light at least provided a modicum of comfort.

When he arrived in the study, the first thing Anthony noticed was the oil painting hanging above the desk. He recalled it clearly from the day before: the setting sun, the lush green foliage of the trees. But inexplicably, the painting had changed. While the contours of the landscape looked identical to the picture he remembered, the sun had now sunk almost entirely beneath the horizon, transforming the painted sky into a swirling wash of reds, oranges, and pinks. And the trees were no longer green. Somehow, autumn had begun to creep into the painting, withering the leaves and draining them of their colour. All that remained was a muddy patchwork of oranges and browns.

As Anthony stood there gaping in disbelief, he saw the shadow creeping into the pool of light cast by his torch beam.

I didn't think you were coming, it said reproachfully.

"I...I had to s-sneak out," Anthony stammered, still nonplussed by the changes in the painting. "I got in trouble for leaving my brother alone yesterday."

The shadow considered this. *Families can be a heavy burden,* it said.

Finally tearing his eyes away from the picture, Anthony turned and sank down into the armchair. "Sometimes, yeah."

A strong man must forge his own path in life, Anthony. Unswayed by the needs of others.

"Yeah, but they're my family," Anthony insisted. "I love them. Most of the time, anyway."

Of course you do, the shadow agreed. *But letting go of the things we love is a necessary part of life, is it not?*

Anthony felt a faint prickle of unease. He desperately wanted to be strong, but surely you held onto the things you loved. Wasn't that the whole point? "I don't know what you mean," he said.

I wonder whether you might not be much happier away from your family, the shadow suggested. *Away from that dingy little peasant's cottage. Freed from your mother's expectations and your brother's constant prattle, so like a chittering little monkey.*

"But how? Where would I go?"

The shadow gestured with its long thin arms. *You could live here. This house has a great many rooms. All this living space is useless to me now. After all, a shadow can exist anywhere, go anywhere.*

Anthony gazed around in silent wonder. Could this really all be his? A whole house of his very own?

The shadow seemed to know exactly what he was thinking. *And no one would ever bother you here,* it added.

After giving it a moment's consideration, Anthony sighed and reluctantly shook his head. "I couldn't live here all on my own," he muttered. "I'd have to bring my family with me."

He glanced worriedly up at the shadow. It didn't move or make a sound, but he could sense its mounting impatience.

We discussed the importance of invitations, did we not? it said at last.

Anthony's heart sank. "Are you saying they're not allowed to come?"

That isn't quite what I meant. The shadow paused thoughtfully. *But you can hardly expect me to invite your family to stay when I haven't even met them, can you?*

When Anthony returned home a couple of hours later, he was confident he'd managed to sneak all the way upstairs without waking anyone. But he hadn't even finished taking off his jeans when Calum opened his eyes and sat up in bed.

"I'm telling Mum," his brother said.

Anthony sat down on the mattress, his face defiant. "Fine, tell her if you want," he replied. "But if you do, you'll ruin everything, and then we'll all be stuck in this crappy cottage forever."

Calum eyed him suspiciously. "What do you mean?"

"Do you want your own bedroom again?"

"Course I do. But Mum said..."

"Mum doesn't know anything about this yet. It's my secret." Anthony paused and watched Calum fidget for a second. "But it can be yours too, if you promise not to tell."

"What's the secret?" his brother said loudly. "Tell me!"

Anthony shushed him, then got down on his hands and knees and fished under the bed. Retrieving the rucksack, he reached inside and produced the snake statuette. Relishing the look of disbelief on Calum's face, he handed his brother the antique. Caught unawares by its weight, Calum nearly dropped it.

"Be careful!" Anthony hissed. "It's solid gold."

Calum goggled. "No way!" he exclaimed. "How much is it worth? Where'd you get it?" Anthony saw his face darken suddenly. "Did you *steal* it?"

Anthony shook his head firmly. "I wouldn't do that. It was a present."

His brother's eyes dropped to the snake again, filled with wordless awe. "Who from?"

"That's the secret."

Calum looked incensed. "You said you'd *tell* me the secret!"

Anthony reached out and grabbed the statuette back. "It's easier if I just show you."

"When?"

"Tomorrow, after school. But you can't tell anyone. Not your mate Stuart, and definitely not Mum. Otherwise, we won't get what's been promised."

"What's that?"

Anthony gave a studiedly casual shrug. "A nice big house to live in. All the money we'll ever need."

But instead of excitement, he once again saw a guarded look creeping across his brother's face. "Mum would say that all sounds too good to be true," Calum said.

Annoyed, Anthony tucked the snake back into its hiding place. Pulling off the rest of his clothes, he climbed into bed. "What do you know?" he snapped. "You're just a kid."

"I might be a kid, but I'm not stupid!" Calum shot back. "I know that you should never take presents off a stranger!"

"This person's my friend, idiot!" Anthony retorted. "God, why would a complete stranger give me a priceless antique?" He paused. "And now they want to meet you. So maybe you'll get a present too."

Pouting, Calum tugged the bedclothes around his shoulders. "I dunno."

Anthony shifted around to plump up his pillows. "Fine, do whatever you like," he said. "But if you don't come and introduce yourself, you won't be allowed to move to the new house with me and Mum."

"You wouldn't just leave me!" his brother squealed.

"Oh, you wait and see what I might do," Anthony murmured, settling down to sleep. "You just wait and see."

Calum didn't say anything else after that.

The instant Calum laid eyes on the old house, Anthony saw him flinch and shake his head. "I don't wanna go in there," he insisted.

"It's just a house," his brother said impatiently. "Nothing's going to happen."

"Stuart said—"

Anthony shoved him. "Stuart's just trying to scare you. He's never been inside. But I have."

Unconvinced, Calum took a wary step backwards. Anthony scowled. "Well, *I'm* going inside," he said. "You can wait out here on your own if you want. Or just go home. I don't care."

He set off down the garden path, then glanced back at Calum. He noticed his brother peering worriedly over his shoulder, his eyes studying the wooded trail that led back to the entrance gate. It was always dark beneath those trees, even at 4 o'clock on a sunny June afternoon.

His decision made, Calum broke into a trot and scurried up the path behind Anthony. "Just for a few minutes," he mumbled. "Just until you show me the secret."

He reached up and took his big brother's hand, his sweaty little fingers curled tightly around Anthony's own. He allowed Anthony to lead him the rest of the way up the path, and then, with some trepidation, across the threshold and into the house's gloomy interior. Calum gazed around at the deserted hallway, a combination of nervousness and excitement mingling on his face.

But as Anthony led him over to the study entrance, Calum began to drag his feet. "What's in there?" he whispered, abruptly relinquishing his grasp on his brother's hand.

"It's where I found the snake," Anthony whispered back. "There's all kinds of cool stuff inside."

He elbowed the study door aside, holding it open for Calum. After a moment's hesitation, the little boy reluctantly followed his brother into the room.

Anthony's eyes immediately sought out the painting above the desk. He was not particularly surprised to see that the image had changed once again. The dying sun had now vanished completely, blanketing the heavens with icy blue-black night. The trees in the forest below were denuded of all their leaves, resembling a swathe of scorched bones erupting crookedly from the earth. It looked exactly like the sort of place that a young child might wander into and never be seen again.

As Anthony gazed over at the painting, he felt an unearthly cold seeping into the marrow of his bones. Shivering, he hurriedly glanced away. But not before his younger brother had noticed the look of unease on his face.

"What's the matter?" Calum asked, his own features growing ever more anxious in turn.

"Nothing," Anthony insisted. "Look at all the cool stuff in here."

His brother turned to scan the contents of the room, resolutely unimpressed. "It's just a bunch of old books," Calum said. He leaned in towards one of the bookshelves and pulled a disgusted face. "They're all *foreign*."

"Check this out." Stepping closer to the desk, Anthony snatched up a silver letter opener, its hilt sculpted into the shape of a grinning clown's head. "I'll bet it's valuable too."

"Huh." Calum's nervousness was already starting to give way to boredom. "So where's this big secret?"

The little boy had his back turned to the far wall, so could not see what Anthony now saw: the shadow, soundlessly materialising behind him.

"It's coming," Anthony said softly, replacing the letter opener on the desk. "If you turn around, you'll see."

Calum glanced around expectantly. The instant he glimpsed the shadow looming up on the wall before him, his face turned pale. He was not yet old enough to scoff at stories of ghosts and the supernatural, and so accepted the dreadful truth of what he was seeing without so much as a moment's hesitation.

Letting out a wail of terror, the little boy turned and stumbled towards the study exit. But no sooner had he taken his first step than Anthony heard the shadow commanding him to intervene. Lashing out with his foot, he violently tripped Calum to the rug. Ignoring his brother's screams, he reached down and grabbed him by the scruff of the neck.

Come closer, the shadow instructed.

Anthony dragged Calum over towards the desk. When the little boy tried to break free, he stopped and punched him twice in the side of the head. Dazed, Calum ceased struggling.

His older brother glanced up at the shadow, seeking its approval. "I brought him here, just like you said."

Yes. I accept your offering to me.

Anthony felt the freezing cold throbbing inside his bones all over again. "What?"

The shadow gestured towards the letter opener. *Now, take the blade.*

"No!" Anthony shrieked. "That isn't what we agreed!"

This is the bargain you made, whether you understood it or not.

"I won't! You can't make me!"

But even as he said it, Anthony could see his hand reaching out to pick up the letter opener. He tried desperately to make it stop, but his limb seemed to have a mind all of its own.

Anthony watched his fingers close around the handle, the clown grinning its eager encouragement. Raising the blade, he pressed it to his brother's throat. He saw Calum open his mouth and knew that he was screaming, but all he could hear was the shadow's voice murmuring inside his skull. It sounded like the voice of the forest in the oil painting, a thousand dead trees whispering in unison.

You invited me in, Anthony. I do not go where I am not wanted...

Even as Anthony plunged the blade into Calum's windpipe, he couldn't be certain whether the shadow was forcing him to do it, or if he was killing his brother of his own free will.

When the boys' mother arrived home from work that evening and discovered that her youngest son was missing, she immediately contacted the police. When questioned, Anthony was adamant that Calum must've sneaked out while his back was turned. Initially, his mother was far too distraught to reprimand him for failing to keep a proper eye on his brother. Then, as the minutes turned into hours, and the hours into days, and her missing son was still not found, she eventually stopped saying very much at all.

Weeks passed. The authorities continued to fruitlessly hunt for Calum. Anthony made sure to pay close attention to any media reports of the ongoing search, fully expecting that the police would eventually inspect the old house at the top of the hill. But they never did.

Not that he could be certain what they'd find if they did ever search the place. The last thing Anthony remembered before fleeing the house was seeing Calum's blood slowly draining into the floor. As though the building itself was sucking it right out of him. So who could say how much of his brother's body would be left by now?

Even if he'd been able to summon the courage to go back and check for himself, he couldn't. After the light faded from his mum's eyes and she stopped speaking to anyone, his dad had taken Anthony back home with him. So in a funny sort of way, he supposed he'd got exactly what he wanted, just like the shadow promised. Anthony had his own bedroom again, and was back at his old school with all his old friends. But the strange thing was, nothing was quite the same. He hadn't really been away very long at all, but everyone treated him as though he'd changed somehow. Like his face didn't really belong to him anymore.

Eventually, all his friends drifted away, leaving Anthony alone. He would find a quiet place to spend his lunch hour, and sit and think about the revenant. Anthony wondered if it had ever truly wanted to be his friend, or whether it was just tricking him to get at Calum. Lying to him, just like his parents had.

The revenant told him that it was lonely, that it missed having someone to talk to. But the more Anthony thought about it, the more he doubted whether the revenant was alone anymore. Increasingly, he has come to understand that he left a part of himself behind in the house. When he sees his old friends looking at him oddly, Anthony now realises that some nameless part of him might truly be missing.

He'd first noticed it shortly after Calum disappeared. Unable to bear his mother's incessant weeping any longer, Anthony retreated upstairs to bed. Switching the bedside light on, he was about to start undressing when he glanced over at the wall and the whole world suddenly turned upside down.

It wasn't so much as what Anthony saw there as what he *didn't* see there.

His shadow.

By all rights, he should've been able to see his own silhouette on the bedroom wall, but there was nothing there. Even when Anthony leaned in close and waggled his fingers right in front of the bedside light, all he could see was an empty white space where his shadow should be.

All he can think is that his shadow is still back there in the revenant's house. He can't decide whether it's being held prisoner, or if it simply wanted to stay behind and be rid of him. Anthony only knows that it doesn't belong to him anymore. A vital part of him has been ripped away, perhaps forever.

These days, whenever he closes his eyes to sleep. Anthony dreams about returning to the house. And each and every time, the front door is wide open, as though he is expected. But standing paralysed on the doorstep, Anthony quickly realises he's far too scared to set foot inside.

Anything could be lurking in there. By now, his absent shadow might have been transformed into something else completely. Something malign and cunning. Something that understands exactly what kind of whispered lies an unhappy teenager desires to hear.

And he can't be certain how much of his brother might yet linger inside the house and whether whatever is left will be pleased to see him or not. Anthony imagines Calum crouching there in the darkness, his bloodless flesh spoiled and cold, waiting patiently for his big brother to return.

And then, once the two siblings are finally reunited, he'll whisper to Anthony all the dreadful secrets he's been saving up to tell him, then drag him shrieking down into the wormy darkness where all dead things go, where Calum will talk and talk and never stop talking.

Anthony always wakes up screaming from the dream. When he awakens, the bedclothes are tangled wet and stinking around him, and then his dad runs into the room to try and calm him down and gives Anthony a pill, but it's no use because he knows he won't sleep again tonight. On the verge of tears, he begs his father to leave the bedside light on when he leaves.

And yet, that might be the very worst thing of all.

Afterwards, Anthony lies there and looks at the vacant space on the bedroom wall, the space where his stolen shadow used to be, and before he knows it, his mind is once again transported back to the house.

Because there can never be any escape for him, no more than a trapped fly can escape from the jaws of a carnivorous plant.

Because one day, whether it's in a week or a month or in fifty years' time, Anthony understands that he will once again find himself walking through that rusted iron gate, underneath those hungry, clutching trees, and along the garden path towards that old stone house.

And he knows that the next time he sets foot inside it, he will never, ever leave.

Sean Hogan is a writer and filmmaker based in the UK. He has published several books of cinema metafiction, including England's Screaming *and its sequel* Twilight's Last Screaming *(each named as one of the five best genre novels of their year by* The Financial Times*)*, That Fatal Shore, Three Mothers, One Father *and* The Corpse Road. *His feature film credits include* The Devil's Business, The Borderlands, *the documentary* Future Shock! The Story of 2000AD, *and most recently, the critically acclaimed folk horror* To Fire You Come at Last. *He is currently in post-production on his next film,* Scenes From A Young Girl's Disappearance.

A CANDLE IN THE DARK

by **Simon Bestwick**

IT WAS CLOSING TIME AT THE STATION HOTEL, AND APART FROM ME AND SADIE—WHO HAD TO BE THERE, AS WE WERE RUNNING THE BAR—THERE WERE ONLY TWO PEOPLE LEFT. VICTOR JEPPS, THE DOORMAN FROM DAHLIA'S, I WASN'T WORRIED ABOUT; he was a big hard-faced man, frightening enough to look at and more than capable of wreaking havoc, but, ex-Para or not, he was a light drinker—he'd only had a couple of Tia Maria and Cokes all evening—and more importantly, he was a peaceable and easy-going sort in reality. It took a lot to make him turn nasty, which thankfully I'd only witnessed once.

No, if there was a problem, I knew it was going to come from Droopy Sykes, even though the only act of violence he'd ever committed was the one that had landed him here on Bone Street in the first place. Droopy was even more thunderously drunk than usual tonight and had sort of sagged into himself, like an enormous collapsed pudding. He gazed, oyster-eyed, at nothing in particular, and his jowls looked as if they might slip off his face entirely. Moreover, he seemed to have developed selective deafness, not reacting to any calls to leave.

Normally the modus operandi here would have been to gently help the customer to his or her feet and usher, drag, or carry them out of the front door (and if necessary all the way home,) but Droopy Sykes tipped the scales at around thirty stone—around four hundred and twenty pounds, or a hundred and ninety kilos if you use the metric system—most of it, well, rather loose and flabby. Good luck moving that without his cooperation.

Vic chuckled. "Rather you than me," he muttered. I wondered how many Tia Maria and Cokes it would take to enlist his help, assuming he'd be persuadable at all.

Luckily, Sadie stepped in. I don't quite know what it is with her, but she's basically the Drunk Whisperer; she has a well-nigh unique ability to calm, charm, reach, and persuade the inebriated, no matter how aggressive, unruly, or near-comatose they might be. "Droopy," she said, shaking him gently by the shoulder. "Droopy. Wakey-wakey, mate."

Droopy remained unmoving and didn't

even blink at first, which made me worry he'd died. Aside from the problem of getting the body out of the bar, everyone on Bone Street is here because they caused a life to end—whether by murder, self-defence, or sheerest accident—and it's our only sanctuary from the Closers that would otherwise have claimed us. But if you cause another death, that sanctuary is forfeit, so anything that might potentially leave you responsible for one, in any way, shape, or form, is always a concern. Thankfully, he blinked, then grunted and focused, blearily, on Sadie.

"Miss Harrower," he rumbled. Droopy Sykes' voice, slurred though it might be, was deep and rich and plummy; back in his barrister days, it must have been impressive to hear. "A pleasure to behold your charming countenance, my dear."

"Give over," she said, "or you'll have me leaving Tim and running away with you." She grinned at me, just in case I hadn't worked out she was joking.

Droopy sighed miserably. "Ah," he said. "The love of a good woman is something to have."

Sadie looked a little worried for a moment, then squeezed his shoulder. "Come on, Droopy, on your feet. Some of us have homes to go to."

"Of course, Miss Harrower, of course." Droopy levitated, swaying, from the bar stool; Sadie hesitated again, looking as though she couldn't decide whether she should try steadying him or run like hell to avoid being crushed if he toppled. As it turned out, it was neither. "Only one true law—*The* Law—pertains here, the same law Moses carried down from Mount Sinai in times of yore: thou shalt not kill. But nonetheless, there are still rules we must all obey."

He wobbled unsteadily from the snug; Sadie kept pace with him to the front door. "Thank you, my dear," he rumbled as he went out, fumbling in a pocket on his overstrained waistcoat, as if there was something he wanted to show her. "Your Mr. Van Geldern is a lucky man indeed. The love of a good woman is a thing to be grateful for, as I have said, and I should know. I once had the love of the best one of all."

There was silence; Sadie knew better than to encourage a punter who was that drunk. The last thing you wanted was them turning maudlin and breaking down. They could be a nightmare to get shot of when that happened.

But instead, there was only a long, boozy sigh, and a single word: "Marilyn," said Droopy Sykes.

"Marilyn?" Sadie asked. I winced, and she told me later that she had too, as soon as she'd said it, but despite herself she was curious. It was the first time either of us had heard any hint of a romantic entanglement in Droopy's past.

"Marilyn Monroe, of course," Droopy said. "The one and only. Whatever I may be now, nothing can take that away from me."

And then the front door closed, and he was gone.

Sadie came back through, chuckling, but I could see she was exhausted; her face was even paler than usual, dark rings around her eyes. "I need my bed," she said, before I could say anything. "Can you finish up here?"

"Course I can, love."

"G'night, chuck," said Vic. He and Sadie knew each other from when she'd worked at Dahlia's, and, as she did with most people, she brought out his protective side.

"Night, Vic," she said, and I heard her footsteps ascend the stairs. Vic took a swig of his drink.

"Marilyn Monroe, eh?" I said. "Heard it all now."

"Well, it's true," said Vic. "Sort of, anyway," he added, with a grin, once he'd had time to relish my gobsmacked expression.

"Marilyn Monroe?" I said. "What's the joke?"

His smile faded. "Well, it's not a joke. Not really."

"So?"

"Funny story," he said. "Funny peculiar, not funny ha-ha. Interesting one, though, if you want to hear it."

I took the hint, decanted a double Tia Maria into a highball glass and squirted some cola into it before setting it before him. "On the house," I said.

Vic grinned, and knocked back the last of his old drink before reaching for the new.

"Thank you kindly," he said. "Well, you know Droopy wasn't always like that." He jerked a thumb over his shoulder in the direction the older man had gone. "He always liked the sauce, but not like now. He was reasonably together when he got here. and apparently not bad-looking, as blokes go. Looked like he wouldn't actually have to pay for it, you know? And like he'd actually be able to perform. I wasn't there myself. I got all this from Justin Adewayo—he worked the door at Dahlia's before me, showed me the ropes a bit. Anyway, he used to pass the time by telling me people's backstories."

There was a stool behind the bar and I pulled it up; my feet were killing me after the long shift. I leant on the counter, arms folded, and waited for more.

"So, the night Droopy came out from under the viaduct, he wasn't alone. There was a woman with him. Thirtyish. Blond hair, all up around her head and wavy. And American—sounded it, anyway. And she said she was Marilyn Monroe."

"First celebrity we'd have had here," I said. "Never mind being a dead one."

"Just repeating what I was told," said Vic. "But Justin always said that if she wasn't Marilyn, she was the spitting image of her. And he'd have known. He was a big fan of films from back then—fifties, sixties. Seen pretty much everything she'd done." He sipped his drink. "Even sounded the same—the voice and everything. Used to sing 'Happy Birthday, Mr. President' in the bar here, back then. I dunno. Maybe she was a working girl, earned a few quid dressing up as her. You get some punters like them to dress up as this or that, don't they?" He grimaced. "Marilyn Monroe'd be bloody mild compared to some of the stuff we've had over at Dahlia's, I can tell you."

"So what about her and Droopy?" I said.

"Well, they took up together. Might have been an item before they got here, all I know, though doesn't seem to fit with what we know about Droopy. He never talks about her—well, never did, till just now. It's the most I've ever heard him say about her. Anyway, if they weren't together before they got here, they were very soon. Where Droopy lives now, that little maisonette on Bone Square? That's where they used to live. There was an old piano there, back then—Justin said they used to have dinner parties. She'd sing, and Droopy'd play the tunes on it. Before my time, like I say, but I remember the piano. Droopy pawned it to Paul Manktelow for booze money."

He broke off for a moment, suddenly awkward, at the mention of Paul Manktelow; a good man, and one we both missed. I grabbed a tumbler, fired a shot of Bushmills into it, and we clinked our glasses together. "To Paul," we mumbled, and each took a sip before Vic went on.

"All I know, apart from that, is that there was a big party one night," he said. "Biggest of the lot. Justin wasn't at that one because he had to work. And no one who went there wanted to talk about it afterwards. But the next day? She was gone. Poof. Vanished. And Droopy? He was never the same. Didn't speak for over a month after that, except to ask for a refill." Vic waggled his glass. "By the time I got here, he was the way he is now."

I waited, but that seemed to be it. "Not much of a story," I said. "Lot of holes."

"Like I said, it's just what I heard. Can't tell you what I don't know." He grinned. "Got a Tia and coke out of it, anyway."

"Uh-huh," I said. "And on that note..."

"All right, all right, I can take a hint." Vic drained his glass. "Laters, mate."

I locked the door behind him, cleaned up in the bar, then went upstairs. I expected to find Sadie fast asleep, but she was sitting up in bed reading a book. She gets a second wind like that sometimes.

"You took your sweet time," she said as I undressed.

"Sorry, love."

"What was so interesting?"

I relayed the tale I'd been told, climbing into bed beside her. "So, it's all still a bit of a mystery," I concluded.

"Maybe not for long." Sadie reached over to the nightstand. "See this?"

It was a silver charm bracelet; it clinked softly in my hand. "What about it?"

"Droopy dropped it on his way out."

I remembered him rooting in his waistcoat pocket as he left. I studied the bracelet; it was built for quite a narrow wrist. An adult's, I thought, not a child's, but still one a good deal slimmer than that of Droopy Sykes.

"I'll take it back to him tomorrow," she said. "Might ask him if it's Marilyn's. Want to come with?"

"Nosey, aren't you?" I said, grinning.

"Just curious," she said, and grinned back. "I know it's hard to believe, but I never said I was perfect."

I thought about what curiosity did to cats, but kept my mouth shut.

THE NEXT MORNING, a couple of hours before the Station Hotel was due to open, we trudged across Bone Square, towards the row of Georgian houses at the back. We went past the statue in the middle of the square and, as always, I paused to study the ragged stone where the face had been, and the empty patch where the name-plaque had been torn away. I'm not the only one to have looked for a clue as to who the hell the statue was supposed to represent, and no one's ever found any clue to its identity, but there's something about it, somehow, that demands you try.

Sadie tugged my arm, and we carried on across the square. The door to the house was ajar, but that was no cause for alarm; it had been broken for years, and there wasn't much thieving on Bone Street. That could all too easily go wrong and escalate into the kind of thing that left someone dead, and if that happened you were done. Even if no one knew you'd done it, the Closers would.

A staircase led up to the first floor and the door to Droopy's maisonette. Sadie tapped on the door, but there was no answer. I banged on it hard, then after a short pause, did so again, harder still.

"All right!" bellowed a voice from within, which sounded as though it came from the disturbed and somewhat annoyed occupant of an ancient tomb. "I'm awake!"

I wasn't sure if that sounded more like an announcement or a threat, particularly when the floor began to vibrate. *Droopy in motion,* I thought, and was suddenly convinced he was going to answer the door in the nude. Not a prospect I relished.

But when the door swung open, he was wearing his usual badly rumpled three-piece suit. An odour of stale sweat, whisky, and tobacco washed out to greet us, along with an odour of unemptied bins.

He glowered at us for a moment, then blinked. "Mr. Van Geldern?" he said. "Miss Harrower?"

"Hi Droopy," she said, and waved.

He'd started to look worried—maybe wondering if he'd managed to get himself barred from the Station Hotel by dint of some outrageous behaviour that was still shrouded in the mists of his hangover—but that seemed to set him a little more at ease. "Miss Harrower," he said again. "And to what do I owe this unexpected pleasure?"

"You left something in the bar last night," she said, holding out the charm bracelet. "Thought you might want it back."

Droopy's normal expression was one of bleary confusion, except when he tried to recapture the oratorial spirit of his long-gone courtroom days, but for the first time I saw him overwhelmed with a surge of real emotion. He put a hand to his mouth; he looked for a moment as though he was going to cry. Then he rallied, reached out and took the bracelet from Sadie with one swollen, thick-fingered hand, handling it with surprising delicacy. "Thank you, Miss Harrower," he said at last, in little more than a whisper.

"Was it Marilyn's?" she asked.

He looked as though she'd slapped him; there was raw hurt on his face, then anger, but then it cleared and there was only a deep, resigned sadness. "It was," he said. "I suppose you want to hear about her."

"Only if you want to—"

But he was already turning away, leaving the door open. "You may as well come in, then."

The flat was in an appalling mess, every inch of floor strewn with books and papers, empty Carlsberg Special Brew cans and whisky bottles, overflowing ashtrays, and the remains of meals from Ahmed's Kebab House of Death that looked as though new and previously unheard-of life forms were about to evolve from them. The kitchen door was open; most of the floor there was crowded by bulging rubbish sacks. I was just glad the bathroom was on the floor above; wild horses wouldn't have dragged me near *that*.

Droopy collapsed into a battered and long-suffering armchair that somehow survived the experience, despite creaking alarmingly. "Sit, sit," he said. There was a chaise-longue nearby, the only thing in the room with a clear surface, and we perched there.

He reached over to the small table beside him, toying with the bottles and decanters on it. "A small libation?"

"No, thanks," I said.

"I'm okay," said Sadie.

"You won't mind if I partake? I'm sure the sun is above the yardarm somewhere," he said, not that I'd ever known such considerations trouble him before. Perhaps some vestige of decorum still lingered.

Droopy filled a glass and rooted among several cigarette packets until he found one, lighting it and puffing away in silence. I looked around the room. It was big and well-decorated, or had been once. It must have been quite grand in its heyday, and impressive even some time afterwards. Vic had said Droopy and Marilyn had held parties here. It was hard to imagine now, but I almost managed; it was like seeing a troop of ghosts nearly shimmer into existence, then change their minds and dissolve again.

Sadie stood up, suddenly, and crossed the room; I didn't understand why till I saw there was one small corner of it which remained bizarrely neat and tidy. Above a little sideboard, on the wall, was mounted a poster of—who else?—Marilyn Monroe, the famous one of her from *The Seven-Year Itch*, holding down the skirts of her white cocktail dress against the breeze blowing up from the subway grating. There were other, smaller pictures too, and bits and pieces of memorabilia of one kind or another; I saw Sadie stoop to examine one in particular.

I went to join her, and saw this picture, unlike the others, was a Polaroid. It showed a man who—if you looked very closely and carefully—was just about recognisable as a younger, slimmer version of Droopy Sykes. Before everyone started calling him Droopy, maybe. It occurred to me, with something of a pang of guilt, that I didn't know his first name.

But Droopy wasn't alone in the picture. Beside him, wearing that same famous white dress as in the big poster, was a blonde-haired woman.

Was she Marilyn? I don't understand how she could have been, but Bone Street is a strange place. The flotsam and refugees it collects come from all times and places; the idea that there might be some other timeline in which Marilyn Monroe had come to a different ending than the one I knew about didn't seem as far-fetched here as it might have somewhere else. All I can do, really, is echo what Vic Jepps had said: if it wasn't her, it was her living double.

"Is this her?" said Sadie, one finger reaching out to touch the Polaroid.

"Please don't touch," said Droopy, more softly than I'd ever heard him speak. "But yes."

I touched Sadie's arm gently, and we left the little shrine, heading back to the chaise-longue. The three of us sat in silence for nearly a minute, before Sadie finally asked the big question. "Was she really...?"

"I honestly cannot say," said Droopy. "Or even, for certain, whether she believed herself to be. I only know that if it *was* a pretence on her part, it was an absolutely perfect one. And if she didn't believe herself to be Marilyn Monroe, I never saw, in all the time we spent together, even the slightest hint of it."

Droopy had come here the same way everyone does. He'd felt the Closers on his tail—that feeling of inescapable dread that somehow compels you to run, and run, till the familiar streets disappear and you find yourself in the long dark tunnel of brick and stone that finally opens out under the viaduct at the bottom of Bone Street.

It was an old and grubby story—a junior partner at his law firm had caught him with his hand in the till, and in drunken panic (he'd liked his whisky even then) Droopy had hit the boy, who'd then struck his head on a table corner in the office as he fell. Clunk. Lights out. And Droopy Sykes had become a murderer.

He'd stuffed his pockets with all the cash he could lay hands on and run to his car, meaning to drive to Dover and flee to France. But the car had suddenly broken down, and the terror of the Closers had been upon him. So he'd scrambled out and run, and the rest was history.

But he very nearly hadn't made it. We often speculated how many of those marked by the Closers made it here—how many never found the viaduct, or were caught before they reached it, or otherwise failed. In Droopy's case, he admitted, he'd found his way into the tunnel and begun staggering along it, but the dread had grown and grown until it proved overwhelming. The tunnel had seemed dark and hopeless and without end, unknown terror all around him, and his desperate onward flight had given way to paralysis. He'd fallen to his knees on the wet and filthy cobbles and curled up on himself, shaking and waiting for the inevitable.

"And then someone grabbed me," he said. "I remember a voice, a woman's voice, shouting in my ear, telling me to get up. I couldn't budge at first. I was sure she'd give up. Leave me. But she didn't. She kept screaming at me and dragging at me, even though...even though I could feel them. So close. On top of us by then, almost.

"She got me to my feet," Droopy went on, "and we staggered along. And then, I remember—she screamed. A terrible scream. For an instant she stopped, froze, and of course, so did I, along with her. And I thought, that's it, we're finished. But then we were moving again. I don't know which of us started moving, but thankfully one of us did, and then...she was still screaming, even as we staggered out from under the viaduct. I'm not sure, but I think she may have glanced back." His face tightened, then seemed to ripple, like a half-set jelly. "And saw...something."

"You mean a Closer?" said Sadie. "I thought no one saw them and lived."

"As a general rule," Droopy pointed out, "if you're close enough to see one, you're about to become its lunch. In which case you're unlikely to live to tell the tale. Perhaps the occasional soul catches the merest, briefest glimpse and is lucky enough to escape with their life, but is forever after called mad. There are some passages through which no one can travel and remain unchanged."

He bent and I saw that by the foot of his chair was an ornate metal crematory urn, overflowing with ashes and cigarette butts. Grunting with effort, he bashed his cigarette out, then reached for his glass again.

"Whatever the truth of it, the two of us staggered out from under the viaduct, still feeling the Closer, or Closers, on our tail. There was a shop, an abandoned building—the first one we came to as we stumbled up the street. We clawed at the door, and it flew open. We scrambled inside, slammed it closed, hurled ourselves against it to pin it shut—and sank down, exhausted, still clinging to one another as the storm raged outside..."

Droopy blinked at his glass, looking genuinely surprised to find it empty. He refilled it quickly, almost to the brim. "When I woke—when we woke—it was daylight. That was when I saw her, properly, for the first time, and when we introduced ourselves. And she insisted, from that moment until the last, that she had been born Norma Jean Mortenson, later Norma Jean Baker, later Marilyn Monroe. It was soon clear she became distressed—violently so—if anyone contradicted her, so I learned to humour her, and so did everyone else. After all, this new existence we'd found ourselves entering into seemed the very stuff of madness as it was—was it really any stranger to take her at her word? And the resemblance truly was uncanny, as you've both seen." He motioned towards the shrine on the wall. "Perhaps she'd made her living as an impersonator, before. Whether she believed herself to be Marilyn before passing through the viaduct is impossible to say. Perhaps, if she did see a Closer, it was her refuge, the only way she was able to bear what she'd seen. A retreat into fantasy. People do such things, don't they? And for far less reason."

Droopy shrugged. "Well, I was still a young man back then, or at any rate young enough. Old enough, yes, to make a fool of myself over money and end a life over it, although there's no lower age limit on that last, but still young enough to fall in love at the drop of a hat. Perhaps I was as just as deluded as her. Telling myself I couldn't truly be a wicked person if I was in love."

"And you were," said Sadie, very gently. "Weren't you?"

"Of course I was," said Droopy. "How could I not be? She was beautiful and talented and charismatic, and she'd saved my life. She was intelligent, too, and kind, but I was far too young and callow to realise those were more valuable qualities by far. But above all, she needed to be loved. No, not loved. If it had been only that. She needed to be *adored*, Miss Harrower. To be worshipped. Not just to be a star, but the very centre of the universe. Looking back, she was unmoored, I think, and terrified where she might be swept away to. I think she thought that worship would keep her safe. That if she was the most important thing in the world to enough people, that would make it true, and nothing could happen to her. That she'd be safe. That didn't do the real Marilyn any good, of course. But it was what she needed, or seemed to need, and so I gave it to her. All I could, and more. But of course, it wasn't enough. I wasn't enough."

It had begun to rain outside; little spots of water dotted the dirty glass of the window beside the shrine. Droopy's wet eyes shifted to the dull grey square of sky visible beyond it, then traversed the room.

"I know it's hard to believe now," he said, "Miss Harrower, Mr. Van Geldern, but this was once quite the place. We had such parties here. She used to sing in the bar of the Station Hotel—before your time, of course—but that wasn't enough. She needed to be the centre. She needed not to be alone. Quite unlike the real Marilyn, in that, who valued having time alone, to simply be herself. But of course, I say 'the real Marilyn,' but can't be certain it wasn't her. If it was, something had changed her. What she saw in the viaduct, perhaps..."

He shook his head. "In any case, our parties were fairly glamorous affairs, at least for Bone Street. Not that this is saying much, I am aware. But there were canapés and hors d'oeuvres, even champagne. She pawned her jewellery—the money I'd taken with me soon ran dry. I knew it couldn't last. It became very clear, soon enough, that there was a hole in her, a void. And it couldn't be filled, no matter how we both tried. The parties, I suppose, helped a little. Staved off the inevitable for a short spell, but for less and less time on each occasion. And sooner or later, there'd be no more money, and then no more parties. And then...well, I just kept hoping that *this* time it would be enough, or at least that *this* time the void would be filled long enough for my love for her to heal it. I was still young, as I say. Young enough, at least, not only to fall in love easily, but to believe it could conquer anything."

He sipped, very lightly, at his whisky, seeming to actually taste it for once. "Where was I? Ah, yes. The parties. And then The Party. Capital T, capital P. The biggest, grandest soirée we ever held. Here." He motioned around that squalid, ruined room, letting his gaze drift, once more, to the shrine on the wall. "Not everyone came. Even by then, interest was waning. They'd been exciting at first—you don't need me to tell you that any break in the routine is always welcome here—but I think Marilyn's desperation had begun to come through more and more strongly. People didn't want to see it. But still, we drew a crowd. And at first, it didn't go badly."

The rain outside had risen to a steady downpour.

"She sang," said Droopy, "and I played. The audience applauded. And The Party carried on. But then she insisted on performing again. And then again. And again. On and on. Refusing to let the party end. The guests were growing exhausted—I remember all the faces, drained and sagging, shadowed eyes—but on and on it went, on and on she sang, on and on I played. I knew she was heading toward disaster, but I had no idea what to do. I loved her. I wanted her to have what she wanted. And so on I played until my fingers ached. I think there was even blood on the piano keys, although that may simply be my overactive imagination, working in hindsight." He chuckled; a grim, cynical sound. Then the smile faded, and his face—all of him—seemed to sag in the chair. "And then..." he said. "And then..."

Thunder growled outside. The light in the room was very dull now; everything had crumbled into shades of grey.

"That was when she got up for the last time. She was exhausted, too, but still standing, still determined to persevere. Her eyes were bright. As if she had a fever. She started introducing the next song. She began with an anecdote about President Kennedy, about singing 'Happy Birthday' to him on that famous occasion. I could hear the sighs from the audience, the weary, weary sighs and the mutterings, and I knew nobody believed. But did she hear them? I think she did her best not to. Clinging on, as if by her fingernails. But then... then, someone laughed."

Droopy shook his head.

"There was no missing it. The sound rang clear and bright—and so very, very cruel. I saw it on her face. It was as though a knife had been slid into her. A light went out. I never found out who laughed. Had I done so, I think I would have killed them." He grunted. "Which is probably why nobody would tell me who it was. Perhaps for the best. I'd have died myself, after all. Although..." a heavy sigh, as though he was deflating, and he gulped down the rest of his whisky in a single swallow. "I suppose some would say I did."

He refilled his glass. "She rallied superbly. A professional to the end, a trouper. She gathered herself, sang one final song, and it truly was glorious. 'Somewhere Over The Rainbow,' she sang, and my God, I don't think I'll ever be able to describe the intensity of the yearning she communicated. I freely admit I wept as I played, and it wasn't any matter of cheap drunken sentiment, I assure you. I think everyone there was affected in the same way. I may delude myself, Miss Harrower, but I think even that anonymous heckler would have taken back that cruel laughter of theirs if they'd been able to. But of course, that can't be done.

"And then the performance was at an end. She smiled and she curtseyed, and with perfect charm and grace she thanked the guests for coming, for being a wonderful audience, and bid them good night, telling me to see them out. And then she went upstairs..."

Wind blew hard, outside, and we both jumped as the rain slashed against the glass like gravel. Droopy didn't seem to hear it.

"I did as I was told," he said, "because that's what I always did, where she was concerned. But I rushed through the job, hurrying people out, and when I'd slammed the door behind them I fairly raced up the stairs. In those days I was considerably fitter, Miss Harrower." He gave Sadie a grim, lopsided smile. "I was certain—terrified—I'd find her in the bath with her wrists cut, or more likely nude on the bed with an empty bottle of pills, as she'd died in real life. Whatever *that* may be. But no. She was already in bed, in her negligee. She'd been crying, of course—her eyes were red, her cheeks tear-stained—but she was, once more, composed. I asked if she was all right, of course—a ridiculous question, in retrospect—but she assured me she was. And so I undressed and climbed into bed with her, took her in my arms, and we slept."

The rain had risen now to a thunderous, unrelenting drumming, battering on the roof and sills and windows. The room had grown very dark; I couldn't see Droopy's expression, just hear the low, wet painful sigh he released.

"And then I woke up," he said, "and she was gone."

None of us spoke; the only sound was the roar of the rain. I wondered if that was the end.

"I went after her, of course," he said. "It was still night. Raining, in fact, as it is now. I threw on my clothes and ran outside—I knew, already, where she must be going. I'd missed her only by a matter of minutes, because I crossed the square just in time to see her disappear under the viaduct.

"She stood out, you see. She was wearing that dress," and he motioned to the famous poster on the wall. "Although it was already plastered to her by the rain, and her hair too. Drenched. But anyway, she was there. Only for a moment, and then gone."

He gulped at his whisky.

"I followed her under," he said. "Didn't hesitate. I give myself that much credit, at least. The tunnel was very black, but I could make her out, just. I suspect I went farther back under the viaduct, that night, than any man or woman has done and lived to tell the tale. I'm not sure how far we went, or how far I'd have followed before my nerve failed. I suppose I had some great romantic idea of saving her once again. Or an equally romantic, and equally foolish, idea of dying with her. All for love, et cetera. In any event, she soon stopped running. Slowed down, and then...collapsed.

"I caught her up quickly enough. She'd fallen to her knees and was rocking to and fro, holding herself. She'd been crying again, but not any longer. She stopped rocking, too, as I reached her. Just huddled there, gazing into the darkness.

"I remember," he went on, "hearing the rain outside the tunnel, out on Bone Street. Soft and distant, another world. And the drip, drip, drip of water, inside the tunnel itself. It should have been pitch black but I could glimpse details—little hollow stalactites, hanging from the ceiling, where limestone from the mortar had been washed out. Funny, really—funny peculiar, I mean—the details one remembers from such moments."

Funny peculiar; Victor Jepps had used that phrase only the night before. It jolted me back to the maisonette, the grime and stench of it, and I realised that for a moment I'd been in the tunnel with Droopy and Marilyn.

"I knelt beside her and talked to her," he said slowly. "I promised, I comforted, I cajoled. I pleaded, begged—I might even have threatened, I'm not entirely sure. Anything I could think of that might make her move, but none of it worked, nothing at all. 'No,' she said. 'I've had enough. Enough. I can't do it anymore, Bernard. I'm too tired.'"

So that was what he'd been called, before he'd become Droopy Sykes. Before he'd become this.

"I couldn't budge her," he said. "Not verbally, not by persuasion. So I resorted to force. I grabbed her up, tried to carry her out of there. Then she came to life. Screamed. fought. Clawed at me. I had to let her go.

"I told her I wasn't leaving. I wasn't going to go. I was going to stay with her, come what may. Romantic fool that I was, I might even have thought I meant it. If she was going to kill herself, she'd have to take me with her. But she didn't seem to hear. She was rocking back and forth again, on her knees, looking into the darkness...

"And then, I felt it. Just as I'd felt it before, the night I killed young Spalding. That slow, terrible dread. You know what I'm talking about, Miss Harrower, and you, Mr. Van Geldern. All of us here on Bone Street know it well. No dread quite like it, is there? Can't put a name to it as such, can't articulate what it is you're so frightened of, but at the same time you're certain of its existence, and that it is coming. Relentlessly, inexorably, mercilessly, you know that it's coming—and coming for you."

The rain had begun to slacken; the room was quieter, which was all to the good, as Droopy's voice was little more than a whisper now.

"The Closers," he said. "The Closers had come. She wasn't rocking any longer. The tears were running down her cheeks. She was shaking. But she didn't move, except when I made a last attempt to pull her to her feet. She threw up an arm to ward me off. She wasn't fighting me, not that time. It was a command. Imperious. And then she folded her arms and drew herself up straight, her chin raised, to face what was coming. And..."

His face crumpled in on itself, screwing up in an expression of helpless misery. His mouth yawned open; he let out a faint, breathy moan. Then his face went slack again, almost blank, as if nothing really mattered anymore. "I ran," he said simply. "All my fine words and promises. I ran. The dread—the terror of them—it was just too much, and—I broke. I broke that night." A long sigh. "And have remained broken ever since. I didn't look back."

He shuddered violently as he said that; gripped the glass in his hand so tightly it seemed sure to crack. When it didn't, he refilled it once more from the whisky bottle and gulped greedily at it. "I *didn't* look back," he said again. "I didn't."

I don't think he was trying to convince either of us. *There are some passages,* he'd said, *through which no one can travel and remain unchanged.*

He drank off the whisky and poured another. He sipped this one with a little more restraint. "I just remember this scream," he said. "This terrible, terrible scream. And then, behind me—something. But by then I was out of the tunnel and charging back along the street. I drew level with the shop—the same empty shop we'd taken shelter in that first night. I wrenched the door open, dived inside and threw myself against it to hold it shut. While outside—outside, raging..."

The worst of the deluge had tapered off; the rain still fell against the window glass, but it was a gentle pattering now, and the room lightened again, drawing Droopy's puffy features out of the shadows, and the tears on his cheeks.

"I left her there," he whispered. "I left her there."

Sadie went to him then, and put her arms around him, but Droopy remained unresponsive, like stone. Some things are beyond comfort. After a moment, he raised a swollen hand and very gently patted her shoulder, but also very gently pushed her away. "Look after her," he told me, then returned his attention to Sadie. "And thank you," he said to her, holding up the bracelet. "For this, at least." He shook his head. "I was still clutching it...afterwards. I must have pulled it off while struggling with her for the last time..."

There was a long, uncomfortable silence. Sadie drifted back to my side but hovered above the chaise-longue, unsure whether or not she should sit back down. Droopy gazed down at the bracelet, the gleam of the silver links reflecting in his wet, glassy eyes. "If there's nothing else...?" he said at last.

I got up, touching Sadie's arm, and we moved awkwardly towards the door. "See you later?" I said, as we went.

"Oh, yes," he said, not looking up. "I'll be around."

Sadie cried as we made our way back across the square through the rain, and back at the Station Hotel we held each other very tightly for a long time. Saying nothing, because sometimes there's nothing to say. But I resolved that the next time Droopy Sykes came by, he'd get a triple whisky, on the house. After that story, I figured, it was the least I could do for him.

And the most.

Described as "Brilliant" by The Guardian, *"among the most important writers of contemporary British horror" by Ramsey Campbell, and "completely lacking in common sense" by his mother, Simon Bestwick is the author of ten previous novels, seven under his own byline and three as "Daniel Church," along with five novellas and four full-length short story collections. His short fiction has appeared in* Phantasmagoria, ParSec Magazine, *and* The Joining, *and been reprinted in* The Best Horror of the Year. *His "Daniel Church" novels* The Hollows *and* The Ravening *were both short-listed for the August Derleth Award, and the third,* The Sound of the Dark, *is out now. He continues to live on the Wirral with fellow author Cate Gardner, and his addictions to tea, Pepsi Max, and semicolons continue unabated.*

Photo credit: Marilyn Monroe in *The Seven Year Itch* (1954, 20th Century Fox); still shot by Sam Shaw.

THE TAXI STOPPED IN FRONT OF A BUILDING OF IMPRESSIVE SIZE, BUT IT APPEARED TO BE UNDER CONSTRUCTION. The exterior brick was marred by a variety of cracks, boarded up windows, and dangling steel. Scaffolding hid a sizable portion, with extensive gaps covered in black plastic. Several stories up, on the blank wall remaining, someone had graffitied NO ONE MAKES IT OUT OF HERE ALIVE. Alan wondered how someone climbed that high. The "here" was ambiguous. Did they mean this building, or life in general?

His daughter Jane read it aloud and snorted. It had been an unpleasant plane ride north into Canada. They weren't in the air more than half an hour before she asked to change seats. She didn't ask Alan first; she just signaled the stewardess. He had no right to object—she was eighteen.

He'd been an absent father. Her mother raised her. He had a lot to make up for. He was paying her way through college in a foreign country, even though the cost was breaking him. When Alan arrived back in the U.S., he might not even have a job. His ex warned him if he kept failing their daughter, he'd lose her forever. As with most things in their relationship, she'd been correct. But he still had to try.

"Are you sure this is the right place?"

The driver gestured toward the temporary wooden sign by the double doors.

OPEN DURING REMODELING
THE CANADIAN ARMS HOTEL
PARDON OUR DUST

"Didn't you check this place out before you booked?" Jane avoided eye contact. Alan's stomach dropped. He didn't see how, but he'd made a terrible mistake. He remembered the hotel website and all the impressive pictures.

The interior was more consistent with the hotel's advertising. The foyer was at least three stories high and layered in brass, crystal, and polished wood. The ambient light, however, had a yellowish tinge. At certain angles, he could see all the floating particles. Smoke? Or was it the dust they'd already apologized for? He felt Jane pressing against him. She was just being impatient, but for an instant he imagined her as this shy little girl again, needing Daddy to take the lead. He headed toward the fortress-like front desk, fumbling with his passport and registration information. The desk clerk watched impassively as he sorted through his papers and presented them. "I have a reservation."

The clerk started punching keys. "Business or pleasure?" Alan had no idea how to answer. Might someone have both? And in his case, this was certainly the business of parenting, and it should be pleasurable, but so far it hadn't been. The clerk frowned.

"I'm so sorry, but your room isn't ready yet. We expected you tomorrow." He had a vague accent Alan couldn't place.

"I'm sure I made the reservation for today." He wondered how badly he was embarrassing Jane, but she was busy playing with her phone and might not have heard.

"No worries," the desk clerk said, suddenly animated. "We'll find you a room, although we may have to move you tomorrow. Have a nice dinner. We'll put your luggage in storage until this evening."

The clerk continued to press keys, muttering to himself in some unfamiliar language. Could it have been French? Alan was terrible with languages but didn't believe it was French. The clerk's lip movements appeared asynchronous with his words, as if in a badly dubbed film.

"Alan, I've already made plans. Some of us are going for pizza. Do you think Canadian pizza is different from the American kind?" He so wanted her to call him Dad. She'd tried the word out a few times over the years, but it never stuck.

"We just got here. You don't know anyone. How could you have plans?"

"*Text messages*, Alan. I've been texting my future classmates for months. There's an internet group for freshmen. I've got *friends* already." She put special emphasis on *friends*. Perhaps her mother told her about his difficulty making them.

"Well, I thought on this first night we could have a nice dinner together."

"Alan, they're on their way. We can grab a meal later. Is that okay?"

"Of course. You're eighteen. Can I wait with you?"

"If you want."

It wasn't okay, but what could he do? His major guideline with his daughter was to avoid conflict at all costs. He was on thin ice with her. One wrong move and he might never see her again. On their way out the door, the clerk called out. "And sir? Please pardon our dust."

In a few minutes, a car full of laughing teenagers pulled up to the curb, and Jane climbed in. "I'll be staying at Marnie's house tonight. I'll catch you up in the morning." She handed him a slip of paper. "Here's Marnie's phone number and the address of a breakfast place near the college. I'm told everybody goes there. Meet me there at 8 AM. We'll eat, then you can help me move into the dorm. Then you can fly home. I know you must be anxious to get back." Before Alan could object, the car was gone. Should he have tried to stop her? He thought about calling her mother but decided that would make things worse. He'd promised to make sure he got Jane settled. There was still time for that.

He went back into the lobby and sat down. He felt ill and couldn't imagine eating anything. This trip had taken its toll.

After an hour, a short man in a red uniform approached. "Your room is ready, sir. I'll take you right up. We wouldn't want you to get lost. With all the construction, the upper floors are a bit confusing."

The bellhop stuffed Alan's two bags awkwardly under his arms and led him into the elevator. He pressed number 4 on the panel, but when they got out, the number tacked by the elevator doors was a six, the numeral cracked with part of the loop missing. "All this remodeling, so stressful. Frankly, I wish they'd settle on a plan and stick to it. Stay close and follow me. And sir, please pardon our dust."

The walls were heavily scuffed, the wallpaper ripped, and the wood trim battered. Alan tasted the dust, but he could not see it. Most of the ceiling lights were off or missing.

The cluster of rooms immediately outside the elevator had their numbers scraped off. Bits of the numerals lay scattered across the partially stripped carpet. Alan followed the bellhop out of the first hall and into an enormous ballroom featuring giant crystalline chandeliers and towering wall tapestries. The designs on these hangings were too dingy to see clearly, but they appeared to depict a fox hunt on one side of the room and some sort of medieval fair on the other. A cold breeze forced Alan to slip on his coat. The distant chandeliers swayed dramatically, sounding like breaking glass. The bellhop picked up the pace.

Alan struggled to keep up. He kept stumbling on the wrinkled carpet. They weren't half-way across the ballroom. The floor appeared warped, the remaining carpet rippling ahead of him. His footing unsure, he was afraid of falling.

The bellhop paused and glanced back at him. "Not much further. This is the old First Ballroom. We've got one more to go before we reach the next section of guest rooms. That's where they've put you. I hope you like privacy. I don't believe there's anyone else assigned to this floor." The isolation didn't feel like a bonus. The man's small mouth was disconcerting to watch, his lip movements progressively removed from his words. Perhaps an effect of Alan's jet lag. He concentrated on the bellhop's eyes instead: large, and watery, and surprisingly kind.

"Excuse me, but isn't this floor warped? Is there something wrong with the beams, maybe?"

The bellhop laughed. "Canadian architecture of the period. We're justly proud of our architects. The theory being the rise and fall of the floorboards provide additional muscular interest, reducing fatigue. Canadian ergonomics—have you never heard of the principle?"

"I can't say I have."

"The Canadian Arms is a prime exemplar of the theory. We care about our guests' welfare here in the North. It's quite different in the States, I imagine." The bellhop turned and increased his pace again.

Alan was impressed. He knew how heavy his luggage was. He'd crammed his bags as full as possible. "Don't know." he wheezed. "Never thought about it, I guess."

"I don't mean to insult your country," the bellhop's voice suddenly amazingly loud, echoing over their heads. "I wanted to take the family on vacation in the States. But the danger always put me off."

Now they were in a second, larger ballroom, although the extent of it was obscured by dim lighting. Alan could only make out pieces of a wall and some corners where small yellow ceiling lights glowed like distant stars. The draft was even stronger in this room. Alan heard screeching and banging overhead. A scattering of folding chairs barred the way. The bellhop casually knocked them aside without slowing.

Alan was distressed by the state of the place but didn't feel he should complain. He was a guest in this country, wasn't he? And no one forced him to make the reservation. He didn't want to be the ugly American. "You should still visit America someday. I believe the dangers are exaggerated."

"All the crime. All the shootings. I couldn't expose my children to that."

"I understand, but the news focuses on the negative, don't you think? I've never felt... you have crime here too, don't you?"

"Very little. We mind our manners, we Canadians."

"The famous...Canadian politeness. But surely..."

"Surely, yes. Believe me. You're much safer here than you were at home in your cozy American bed."

But this hotel did not make Alan feel safe, and certainly not cozy. The more he experienced the interior of the Canadian Arms, the less it felt like luxurious accommodations.

They exited the last ballroom into a jumbled maze of hallways and rooms. Alan could make little sense of the layout. Given their spacing, he figured many of these rooms were tiny as their doors practically butted against each other, and others enormous given the amount of wall space between them. Many of the room numbers—where there were numbers—were out of sequence, hung crookedly, or temporarily taped to their doors. "Four thirty-two, that's the one!" the bellhop exclaimed and swiped a key card. The door popped open as if the room exhaled.

Most of this room was gone, vanished into the Canadian night. Alan stared into the gaping cavity. He could see a series of overlapping towers and office buildings beyond the bit of missing wall, dark clouds hovering over a distant horizon of orange haze.

"My apologies, sir. I must have gotten the room number wrong."

"Why haven't they covered that hole? What if it rains?"

"Canadian weather forecasting, mate. Best in the world. But I'll leave a note with the manager. Best keep on this side of the threshold. Safety regulations, you understand." When the bellhop stopped speaking, his lips continued to move, but no sound came out. Alan felt increasingly ill. He wanted nothing more than to fall into bed, assuming they could find a room with a bed.

The bellhop's voice came back again. "I'll let you in on a little secret. I don't think they've decided yet what this remodel is finally going to look like. Design by committee, you know? It's amazing how versatile the hotel's bones are. It has a solid skeleton beneath all this, I promise you that. No chance of an imminent collapse. It's not like the hotels you have in your country."

Alan wondered where the bellhop was getting his information, but it seemed pointless to inquire. Alan knew little about Canada, so why should the bellhop know all about the United States?

The bellhop continued down the hall, referring to a slip of paper decorated with a tangle of notes. "Let's give four sixty-one a try." He slid the card in. There was a click, and the door sprang open. Alan was relieved to see solid walls and a bed. The bellhop brought his bags inside. "If you need anything, call the front desk. Ask for Brunin." He touched the shiny brass nameplate on his red uniform. He left and did not wait for a tip. Only then did Alan notice there was no phone in the room, so how was he supposed to call the desk?

Alan couldn't remember ever being so tired. He opened the curtains. The view was blocked by scaffolding. A few distant lights blinked through the gaps in the paint-streaked steel and wood frame, but there wasn't enough visibility to give any sense of the skyline. He closed the curtains and sat on the edge of the bed. He checked his cell phone. It wasn't working here. Did he have to do something special to make it work in Canada? Jane's phone appeared to work fine, but she was young and good with technology. Alan had always struggled with such things. So no messages from Jane.

As tired as he was, Alan hesitated to undress. He expected the bellhop to return at any moment, apologizing for another mistake and making him move again. He kicked his shoes off and stretched out on the bed. He heard muffled voices coming through the walls, although he didn't think they were from the rooms on either side. Hadn't the bellhop said he was the only guest on this floor? There was an echo of music, and a faint blend of other sounds suggesting that construction was still going on in distant parts of the hotel: staccato hammering, and a drilling that although soft seemed to vibrate sympathetically with his dental work.

Alan felt profoundly uncomfortable here, but he frankly couldn't remember the last time he'd felt comfortable anywhere. The realization began to settle in that this trip might have been a mistake. His ex tried to warn him. Jane was never going to forgive him. Not that he blamed her.

He closed his eyes and took a few deep breaths trying to relax. He could feel the dust filling his throat and then his lungs. It was like trying to breathe soup.

Alan was hurrying to the hotel exit—he'd overslept and was about to be late for breakfast with Jane—when a man in a dark suit stopped him. The man wore a bright red maple leaf lapel pin, ridiculously oversized.

"Mr. Blake? I need to speak with you." The man's voice was firm and full of trouble. Alan considered running, but that would have been foolish.

"I'm meeting my daughter. I'm afraid I haven't the time."

"I'm sorry, but you can't leave the hotel. And I'll need your passport."

Alan stared at the man. "I've done nothing wrong."

"If it's a mistake, we'll have it corrected soon. But I need your passport, please."

"But I must meet my daughter. She'll be worried." He wasn't sure whether that was true or not.

"You can call her. Your passport, please, sir."

"I'm an American citizen. I've done nothing wrong. You Canadians are supposed to be friendly."

"So sorry, there's nothing I can do." The man nudged Alan in the chest with his open palm.

Alan imagined slapping the man's face. The impulse shocked him. He handed over his passport.

Brunin, the bellhop, appeared at his side. "I'll take you somewhere quiet where you can phone her." He guided Alan into a small room with a padded bench and a phone by a window. He punched in Jane's friend Marnie's number. After some confusion—he heard someone say *Who's Jane?*—she came on the line. He tried to explain the situation, but it made no sense to him. "He said he was sorry, but there was nothing he could do. I'm sorry too, sweetheart. There's nothing I can do either. It's the government."

There was a long pause, then she said, "You always do this."

"What do you mean? When has this situation ever come up?" But she'd already hung up on him.

Brunin was outside the room waiting. "What about a nice long lunch? You shouldn't let this ruin your whole day."

"I don't have much money, and I can't stay in this country long."

"There are funds available for such situations—you would be surprised how often this occurs. We want you to have the best possible stay under the circumstances. I know it won't take long. It rarely does. The Canadian government is quite efficient about these things."

He led him upstairs and to a small table at the edge of yet another grand ballroom. Musicians played in an empty area near the center of the floor, surrounded by dancing couples, while other well-dressed people dined at tables nearby. The tables were copiously decorated with flowers and figurines conveying a celebratory impression. Due to the room's great size, all this was happening some distance away, the music rising and dissipating into the ornate wooden rafters.

The bellhop stood a few feet away, gesturing animatedly to a fellow in a crisp white uniform. The bellhop trotted over breathlessly. "It's all set. Order anything you like from this." He handed Alan a hastily scribbled list.

"What's happening here?" Alan gestured at the small celebration.

Brunin studied the crowd. "They're older, I believe. A retirement party, or a wake. We host them all the time."

The food was bland, but warm. Fish and potatoes and green beans. Alan thought he might be losing his sense of taste and texture. Everything felt like soggy cardboard in his mouth.

The moment he finished eating, Brunin reappeared, offering to escort him back to his room. They moved quickly through the crowd. At several of the tables, people were slumped over, unmoving. One man looked covered in dust, but perhaps it was simply the lighting. Whatever it was, the sight made Alan ill. As soon as he was back in the room, he needed to purge. He kneeled slumped over the toilet bowl for over an hour before he could stand up again.

Alan wasn't aware of when he fell asleep, but it must have been quite early. He didn't remember lying down. He was awakened by a voice out in the hall. "Elizabeth? Elizabeth?" He opened the door and stood there in his pajamas. When had he put them on? Had Brunin undressed him? The notion seemed absurd.

A man in a tattered bathrobe walked up and down the hall, murmuring, "Elizabeth," tear tracks gleaming on his cheeks. He stopped in front of Alan and said, "I have lost my Elizabeth."

"You should go back to your room. It's the middle of the night."

"My room? They took my room, and now I can't find my Elizabeth."

ALAN WAS AT the front desk first thing the next morning. "Can I have my passport back, please? I really need to visit my daughter. She's starting college. Today is her first day, or maybe it's tomorrow." Alan realized he and Jane hadn't discussed schedule.

The clerk thumbed through some papers. Out of the corner of his eye, Alan saw the slow approach of a security guard. "I'm sorry, sir. They're still conducting their investigation into your discrepancies."

"My discrepancies? What are my discrepancies?"

"The ones they are investigating, sir. Do you have others?"

Alan stared at the clerk. "I need to see my daughter. Why am I being punished?"

The security guard put his hand on Alan's forearm. "She can visit you here. Step away from the desk, please, sir. I'm asking you not to impede commerce."

"Impede commerce?" Alan looked around. No one else was waiting.

"Sir!"

Alan backed away. He found the little room again and punched in the number for Jane's cell phone. A stranger answered, some giggling girl. "Jane's phone," she said.

"I need to speak to Jane. This is her father. Why...why do you have her phone?"

"Your daughter is very generous, sir." She laughed. "Jane says to tell you everything's fine. Her things arrived yesterday, and we all helped her move into the dorm."

"Could I speak to her, please?"

There was more giggling in the background. "I'm afraid she can't come to the phone. She'll call you later."

"I need to talk to her. I'm her *father.*"

There was a pause. "So sorry, nothing to be done."

"Wait. *Who* are you?"

"I have to go! We've got classes. We're *busy*!" She laughed again and hung up. Alan tried calling back several times with no answer. He tried to call his ex-wife to explain things but received a message that the call could not be completed. Maybe because it was out of country, but no explanation was given.

He was being punished. Of course, he knew why. Choices have consequences. He'd been a neglectful father, and now it was catching up to him. He needed to make this right.

Alan spent most of the day checking in with the desk, trying Jane and his ex-wife again with no luck, taking advantage of the free coffee and pastries. Eventually Brunin came and found him.

"Congratulations! The government has agreed to subsidize your stay for the entire length of the investigation."

"How long will that be?"

"As long as it takes, I suppose. They're upgrading your room. Well, not exactly upgrading, to be honest. Construction has spread to that part of the hotel. I *must* move you."

Brunin led him upstairs again. This time it was even more of a race, with the bellhop far ahead and Alan struggling to keep up. Brunin opened the door to Alan's hotel room and barged ahead. Alan stood in the doorway, staring at the dust and debris scattered over the rug, the bed, the clothes he'd left out yesterday on top of the dresser. There were new cracks in the wall around the window and several holes in the ceiling.

"I'll take your dirty clothes to the laundry service for you. No charge, of course. If there is any permanent damage, please let us know. We will be happy to reimburse you. It's our national policy."

"But what happened? I was just here."

"Canadian construction. The fastest, most efficient in the world!" Brunin ran out of the room, bits of clothing hanging out of the two suitcases, dragging on the floor. "Hurry along," he shouted. "We don't want the work to catch up with us!"

They went down the hall, up a short flight of stairs, past piles of construction wreckage, and then to a door in a dark corner with no ceiling fixture. The bellhop fumbled nervously with the keycard, then the door eased open. A mattress partially blocked the passage. "Give me a moment, please." The bellhop squeezed inside and shut the door. After several minutes and much noise he opened it again.

This room proved slightly larger than the other, but oddly shaped, so the result was less usable space. It was a warped triangle. Two curved walls met at an acute angle in the corner. A triangular-shaped chair was wedged there. Alan couldn't imagine trying to sit in it, but that corner had the only window, a narrow strip of glass no wider than a foot. No curtain. The bed was on the straight wall by the exit door. There was no closet.

A narrow passage on the other side of the bed led to the hidden bathroom. Alan needed a good washing, so he went there first. The bar of yellow soap by the sink looked old. Was it used? He dropped it into the trash. The water pressure was quite low, but at least it ran. The shower didn't work at all. The toilet, wedged into another sharp corner, managed to be both tiny and forbidding. When he sat on it his knees rubbed against the walls. Alan splashed water on his face and washed his hands as best he could with no soap.

Again, he could find no phone to call the front desk with his complaints or entreaties. He lay down on the bed—hard as concrete—and stared at the tiny gray TV screen on a small nightstand by the bed. His hand found the remote beneath his pillow.

The TV had two channels. Channel 4 displayed a rotating view of the hotel's public areas, with the occasional glimpse of a private room, and a guest in bed sleeping. He couldn't make out the face. He hoped it wasn't he. Of course he wasn't sleeping, but the video might have been from last night. The image of the sleeping head outside the covers was fuzzy, but it certainly could have been him. Channel 6 had a documentary about Canadian wildlife. Footage mostly of beavers and a moose named Abe.

He tried to go to sleep. He kept the TV on—he found the scenes of beavers and the moose living together in harmony—was that the message or had he misunderstood?—somehow comforting.

He woke up sometime later, hearing other residents milling around in the hallway, but when he came out of his room, he saw the hall had become a maze of scaffolding. A solitary worker was up on a ladder replacing ceiling tiles.

When he went back inside, he saw that the TV was smoking. He yanked the power cord out of the wall, giving himself a shock. Did they have 110 volts here, or 120? Either way, a shock was still a shock.

IT REQUIRED considerable time the next morning to maneuver through all the scaffolding, the passage through the hall having narrowed to a foot in places. In the elevator, he pushed the button for the lobby. It descended for a few seconds, the lights blinked on and off, and the car shuddered and stopped. Alan wasn't sure where, maybe between floors? The lights slowly came on again, and he noticed mildew around the bottom edges of the fake wooden veneer covering the walls. The car smelled faintly of decay.

The elevator started up again but ascended and let him out back where he started, on his original floor. He wasn't enthusiastic about using the stairwell, but he wasn't going back into that car again.

Dust and cobwebs layered the stairs along with what seemed to be a huge amount of crumbling concrete and bits of rusted, twisted iron. He worried about an imminent collapse. But at least the stairs were passable. He arrived at ground level and opened the door. Brunin stood nearby and rushed over. He grabbed Alan by the arm. "We need to hide you somewhere."

"Wait! What?" Before Alan could stop him, the bellhop pulled him into the elevator, and they were going up, albeit shakily. He noticed that several of the floor numbers were now covered with black tape. When did that happen? He'd been in this car only minutes before.

"The government sent two agents. They're looking for you. They want to take you in for questioning."

"But I haven't *done* anything wrong!" Which wasn't completely true—he'd been a bad, or at least an indifferent parent—but nothing that should have concerned the Canadian legal authorities.

"I'm sure you haven't. But we Canadians, we believe in caution. Boldness is overrated, don't you think? I have a place where you can stay until things blow over. I'm confident they'll discover their mistake and apologize. Here in the North, we believe in apologizing. In fact, I'd like to personally apologize to you for all the dust and inconvenience."

Brunin led him to a floor with no number, then through an out-of-the-way door at the far end of an unlit corridor, obscured by a square post which took up half the width of the hall. They arrived at another door with no number labeled STORAGE. Brunin knocked three times, and a small girl answered. Her eyes lit up, and she wrapped her arms around the bellhop's legs. "Papa!" she squealed.

These were small quarters for this family of six, but everything appeared neat and in its place. They'd cleared out a large closet and put in a bedroll for Alan and a small TV. If nothing else, it was at least a place where Alan could expire in peace. He had an ugly rash all over his arms and legs. A pronounced twitch plagued both thumbs. He didn't know what was wrong with him, but he strongly suspected it was terminal.

RESTRICTED AREA!
DANGER! CONSTRUCTION ZONE!

During the years which followed, these signs appeared everywhere, even in places where no apparent construction was taking place. Alan grew comfortable sleeping in the Brunin family closet, eating meals with them, watching TV as a group, and playing games. The smaller children called him Uncle American. In fact, he was more than comfortable—he hadn't felt this welcome in years. He couldn't imagine living anywhere else.

His health continued to decline, albeit slowly. Most of his hair fell out. Brunin offered to take him to see a doctor. "Canada has the finest healthcare system in the world!" But Alan was afraid of what might happen if he revealed himself. Besides, he'd become somewhat used to the pain and discomfort. He wouldn't know who he was absent the pain. Maybe this was what old age was supposed to be like.

There'd been a huge turnover in hotel staff, and as far as he could determine no one was actively looking for him anymore. He moved freely about the massive and complicated structure, but he remained cautious.

Periodically the hotel posted a chart in the lobby laying out the timeline and stages of construction. Alan tried to follow along, but the information lacked logic and consistency. Several floors were rebuilt multiple times, while others remained unimproved or in a state of ruin. Designs were often inconsistent from room to room. Some floors became a smorgasbord of styles. Furniture went missing, and getting the right replacements proved problematic. There were rumors of widespread theft, theoretically due to the staff's low wages. Brunin said black market racketeers were working from inside the building. Alan didn't know about any of that, nor did he want to.

Now and then Alan ate in the ground-floor restaurant where he had a view of the surrounding architecture, endless vistas mirrored in the windows: towers disintegrating and plazas plowed under, massive structures disappeared or moved overnight. The Canadian weather was increasingly severe—violent windstorms tearing through dark boiling clouds. Flooding was a constant threat, causing periodic closings of the hotel.

Alan had more regrets than he could keep track of. Jane was unreachable, no doubt graduated and off living a life of her own. Perhaps he had grandchildren by now. Brunin offered to find her on the internet, but Alan declined. What would he say to her after all these years? Alan himself had no interest in the internet, or much of anything outside the walls of this hotel. Brunin would ask him if he wanted to know the latest news, and he always refused. He wrote Jane letters but never mailed them. He had no address. Brunin offered to help him find one, but Alan was reluctant. "If she didn't write back I'd be devastated."

One month a virus swept through the building and several people died, including Brunin's youngest child. The family, including Alan, was inconsolable. Alan couldn't understand why he wasn't the one taken—he'd been in poor health for years.

As time passed large sections of the hotel were closed for more extensive renovations. There wasn't a day without construction barriers, throngs of workmen, and high-decibel noise. Several floors were briefly converted into flat rentals. Stores popped up overnight on the ground floor only to be gone after a week or so.

Walls and halls shifted location, and Alan became inured to the many changes. Nothing surprised him anymore. Fractures appeared in the staff. Some employees were in active rebellion against management. Petitions were passed around, meetings were held, followed by the occasional strike or riot.

Alan lost weight and eventually was able to fit into Brunin's uniforms. He helped around the hotel, cleaning, working in the kitchen, carrying people's bags. He received no salary and shared his tips with Brunin's children. He had no use for money.

Squatters moved into many of the rooms. No one knew what to do about them. He and Brunin regularly had to clean out the hoarded-out spaces. Some rooms were relegated to repositories for trash. The best solution seemed to be to keep those doors closed.

Graffiti art experienced a resurgence. They didn't have the supplies or the staff to remove it anyway. Some walls became a confusion of signatures and abstract designs. Multiple cries of desperation, pleas from the heart, were overwritten so many times the language in those messages became an incomprehensible ornamentation.

A few days before Brunin's death they had lunch together in the old ground-floor restaurant. The menu had been reduced. One could order an unnamed meat accompanied by an unnamed vegetable. Water was the only beverage available to wash it down.

Brunin appeared to have lost his characteristic enthusiasm. "So, the children are all grown, moved away. My wife and I, now we're empty nesters."

"But you still have me," Alan replied. His body hurt so much he was having difficulty focusing on the conversation. He hoped this wasn't an overture to Brunin kicking him out.

"And we appreciate your company. For once the three of us have enough room. But I miss them. I miss those days when we were raising small children."

"You stay connected, though. It's not like with Jane and me. You haven't lost them completely."

"No, I haven't. I worry, and they are gently impatient with me for being worried. They're secretive about their private lives. My wife and I aren't really part of the conversation anymore. That's what happens in most families. They make you less involved as they assert their independence."

"At least you still have your wife. You still have me."

"And I'm grateful. Events lose their importance if you have no one to share them with."

A FEW WEEKS AFTER Brunin's death Alan returned to an empty flat. Brunin's wife rarely spoke to him after the funeral, held in the now much less impressive lobby of this grand hotel. Now she was gone.

It was an opportunity for Alan to find another place to live, start a new chapter in his life. But he could not imagine it. This small, oddly-shaped space in an out of the way corner of the hotel was home. It had endured despite all the massive reconfigurations of the Canadian Arms. He continued to sleep in the closet, even though the rest of the flat was empty. Once you discover a comfortable way of sleeping you are reluctant to abandon it.

That flat was the sole still point within a maelstrom of change. Hallways grew longer every time he turned around. The hotel's long-standing difficulty with floor and room numbers continued. Staircases were chaotic, some leading to doors which opened out onto empty air. (Alan put up hand-written warning signs wherever management had forgotten them.) Frequently the ceilings of adjoining corridors were at different heights.

Periodically he learned of walls and stairs collapsing, although he never witnessed such things. He just saw the rubble afterwards.

Although Alan failed to make any more friends in the hotel, he had acquaintances aplenty. Longtime employees, guests who never bothered to leave, expatriate Americans in similar circumstances to his own. Most were talkers, gossipers, complainers. All had a different theory as to what was going on in the hotel.

Floors and entire sections of the hotel were evacuated on a regular basis, yet no one explained why. Sometimes in his bed at night, he heard explosive noises suggestive of some portion of the hotel collapsing into ruin.

He heard that one part of the hotel had been on fire for weeks. Why weren't they evacuated? Hotel services had declined to a deplorable degree.

IN THE CORRIDOR OUTSIDE Alan's flat someone spray painted IT IS THE END OF ALL THINGS in huge red letters. In parentheses below, using much smaller lettering, someone else had written (PARDON OUR DUST.)

He'd felt the vibrations all night. He didn't get much sleep. His skeleton felt ready to evacuate from his skin.

When the sirens and the calls to leave began, he didn't pay them much attention.

There'd always been calls to evacuate, but they never amounted to anything.

But then the building began to shake more vigorously, and the sirens died in a prolonged screech, and Alan headed for the stairs.

On the way down he found more than a few steps missing, necessitating the occasional risky leap. Most of the landings were cracked and falling apart. But people still poured into the stairwells from the evacuating floors, and Alan saw some people he hadn't seen in years and probably would not see again.

He waited with the others across the street from the hotel, then out of caution they were moved further back. Just before the building came down hundreds more people poured from the exits like rats leaving a sinking ship.

Moments later he lay broken on the concrete, leveled by the impact. Some people were crying, but most had nothing to say.

Someone was moving through the bodies with a can of spray paint, tagging each one Alive or Dead. He wondered which designation would get him out of Canada at last.

Steve Rasnic Tem's writing career spans over 45 years, including more than 500 published short stories, 17 collections, 8 novels, miscellaneous poetry and plays. His collaborative novella with his late wife Melanie, The Man on the Ceiling, *won the World Fantasy, Bram Stoker, and International Horror Guild awards in 2001. He has also won the Bram Stoker, International Horror Guild, and British Fantasy Awards for his solo work, including* Blood Kin, *winner of 2014's Bram Stoker for novel. In 2025, he received the Horror Writers Association Lifetime Achievement Award. Visit his website at:* www.stevetem.com

---

www.ingramcontent.com/pod-product-compliance
Lightning Source LLC
LaVergne TN
LVHW081319110826
845149LV00006B/1544

* 9 7 9 8 9 9 2 7 0 9 2 3 0 *